BILL THE

P.G. Wodehouse was born in Guildford, Surrey, in 1881 and educated at Dulwich College. After working for the Hong Kong and Shanghai Bank for two years, he left to earn his living as a journalist and storywriter.

During his lifetime he wrote over ninety books, and his work has won worldwide acclaim. He was hailed by *The Times* as 'a comic genius recognized in his lifetime as a classic and an old master of farce'. P.G. Wodehouse said: 'I believe there are two ways of writing novels. One is mine, making a sort of musical comedy without music and ignoring real life altogether; the other is going right deep down into life and not caring a damn'.

In 1975 he was created a Knight of the British Empire and he died on St.Valentine's Day in the same year at the age of ninety-three.

BY P.G. WODEHOUSE
ALSO AVAILABLE IN VINTAGE

Aunts Aren't Gentlemen
Carry On Jeeves
The Code Of The Woosters
A Few Quick Ones
The Inimitable Jeeves
Jeeves And The Feudal Spirit
Jeeves In The Offing
Jeeves Takes Charge
Joy In The Morning
The Mating Season
Much Obliged, Jeeves
Nothing Serious
Right Ho, Jeeves
Stiff Upper Lip, Jeeves
Thank You, Jeeves
Very Good, Jeeves
The Clicking Of Cuthbert
Frozen Assets
Jill The Reckless
Meet Mr. Mulliner
Mr. Mulliner Speaking
Mulliner Nights
The Old Reliable
Something Fishy
The Heart Of The Goof
Plum Pie
Vintage Wodehouse
Ice In The Bedroom
The Coming Of Bill
The Girl In The Boat
Louder And Funnier
Bill The Conqueror
Barmy In Wonderland

P.G. Wodehouse

BILL THE CONQUEROR

His Invasion of England in the Springtime

VINTAGE

Published by Vintage 1996

2 4 6 8 10 9 7 5 3 1

First published in Great Britain by
Methuen & Co Ltd, 1924

Vintage
Random House, 20 Vauxhall Bridge Road, London SW1V 2SA

Random House Australia (Pty) Limited
20 Alfred Street, Milsons Point, Sydney
New South Wales 2061, Australia

Random House New Zealand Limited
18 Poland Road, Glenfield,
Auckland 10, New Zealand

Random House South Africa (Pty) Limited
Endulini, 5A Jubilee Road, Parktown 2193, South Africa

Random House UK Limited Reg. No. 954009

A CIP catalogue record for this book
is available from the British Library

ISBN 0 09 910201 3

Papers used by Random House UK Ltd are natural, recy-
clable products made from wood grown in sustainable
forests. The manufacturing processes conform to the
environmental regulations of the country of origin

Printed and bound in Great Britain by
The Guernsey Press Co. Ltd., Guernsey, Channel Islands

TO

MY FATHER AND MOTHER

CONTENTS

BILL THE CONQUEROR

CHAPTER ONE

A MARRIAGE HAS BEEN ARRANGED

§ 1

WITH a sudden sharp snort which, violent though it was, expressed only feebly the disgust and indignation seething within him, Sir George Pyke laid down the current number of *Society Spice* and took up the desk-telephone.

' Give me *Spice* office,' he said curtly.

There was a brief interval.

' Roderick ? '

' He has not yet returned from lunch, Sir George,' said an obsequious voice.

' Ah, is that you, Pilbeam ? ' Sir George's expression softened. Pilbeam was one of his favourites. A youth with a future. A man he had his eye on. ' Kindly tell Mr. Roderick when he comes in that I wish to see him.'

' Very good, Sir George.'

The founder and proprietor of the Mammoth Publishing Company, that vast concern which supplies half—the more fat-headed half—of England with its reading-matter, hung up the receiver : and after a few moments of frowning thought seized a pencil and began to write. The occupation effected in his appearance a striking change for the better. His brow grew smooth : his eyes ceased to glitter : something resembling a smile relaxed the drawn tensity of his lips. He bent over his pad, absorbed.

One of the things that makes the lot of the reader

of a story such as this so enjoyable is the fact that, in addition to being uplifted, entertained and instructed, he possesses all the advantages of a disembodied spirit. He can go anywhere and see everything. Any ordinary man, for instance, who wished to enter the presence of Sir George Pyke would be obliged to go down Fleet Street, turn to the right along Tilbury Street till he came to Tilbury House, interview a discouraging official in the vestibule, fill up a form stating name and business and hand this to a small boy in buttons. And in the end, after waiting for anything from ten to forty minutes, he would probably get no further than a brief word with one of Sir George's secretaries. For the man behind the Mammoth does not see every one. His time is valuable, his sense of his own importance keen, and he is hedged about by a crowd of willing helpers whose chief duty it is to ensure the respecting by casual callers of that motto of all great men—Keep Out! This Means YOU! An army with banners would be halted on the threshold, and not even Cabinet Ministers may crash the gate.

The reader, however, being both noiseless and invisible, can walk right up to the office on the fourth floor and go in without knocking. He will find Sir George still writing.

The discovery of a man in Sir George Pyke's position engaged in such an occupation is surely stirring enough to thrill the most blasé. For who can say what literary task it is that occupies him? It may be anything from a snappy column article for *Pyke's Weekly* on Should Engaged Couples Kiss? to an editorial for the *Daily Record*, a page of helpful thoughts for the *Sabbath Hour*, or even a bedtime story for *Tiny Tots*. But, as a matter of fact, it is none of these things. What Sir George is so busily jotting down on that large pad is a list of names.

He has already written

Ilfracombe
Forshore
Waynscote
Barraclough

> Wensleydale
> Creeby
> Woodshott
> Marlinghue

and now, as we look, he adds to the collection the word
Michelhever

This one seems to please him particularly, for he
places against it a couple of crosses. Then, inspiration
apparently leaving him for the moment, he pushes back
his chair and, rising, begins to pace the floor.

It is the custom nowadays to describe all successful
men who are stumpy and about twenty pounds over-
weight as Napoleonic. But, hackneyed though the adjective is, it must be admitted that there was indeed something suggestive of Napoleon in the port of Sir George
Pyke as he strode up and down his office. His generously
filled waistcoat and the habit he dropped into in moments
of meditation of thrusting the fingers of his right hand
in between its first and second buttons gave at any rate
a superficial resemblance to the great Corsican—and this
resemblance was accentuated by the gravity of his plump,
determined face. He looked like a man fond of having
his own way : nor in the last twenty years of his life
had he often failed to get it.

The desk-telephone emitted a discreet buzzing sound,
as if it shrank from raising its voice in the presence of
such a man.

' Mrs. Hammond to see you, Sir George.'

' Send her in, send her in. Good heavens, Francie,'
exclaimed the proprietor of the Mammoth Publishing
Co. as the door opened, ' I've been 'phoning your house
half the morning, trying to get hold of you.'

' How fortunate that I happened to look in,' said Mrs.
Hammond, settling herself in a chair. ' What is it ? '

Frances Hammond, *née* Pyke, was a feminine replica
of her eminent brother. She lacked his second chin,
but had the same bright and compelling eyes, the same
over-jutting brows which lent those eyes such keenness,
the same high colouring and breadth of forehead. Sir

George was conscious once again as he looked at her of that little thrill of admiration which she always awoke in him.

'What did you want to see me about?' asked Mrs. Hammond.

Sir George drew a deep breath. He had tremendous news to impart, and an instinct for drama urged him not to spoil this moment by blurting the secret out too abruptly. But ecstasy was too strong for his sense of the dramatic.

'Francie, old girl,' he cried, 'what do you think? They've offered me a peerage!'

It was not easy to shake Frances Hammond's poise, but these words accomplished that miracle. For a full ten seconds she sat there staring open-mouthed, while Sir George, blushing, and on the very verge of giggles, pulled self-consciously at his scarlet knitted-wool waistcoat, the famous Pyke waistcoat which was one of the sights of London.

'A peerage!'

'Letter's over there on that desk. Came this morning.'

'Georgie!'

Mrs. Hammond scrambled out of her chair and kissed her brother fondly. There were tears in her commanding eyes.

'I thought it would please you!'

'I *am* proud of you, Georgie dear. What a culmination for your splendid career!'

'And who helped me build that career? Hey?'

'I have always done what I could,' said Mrs. Hammond modestly. 'But of course it was you——'

Sir George thumped the desk: and, happening to strike the sharp edge of a wire paper-basket, wished that he had expressed his emotion a little less muscularly. He sucked his hand for a moment before speaking.

'You have been the making of the business,' he said vehemently when the agony had somewhat abated. 'I couldn't have got anywhere without you. Who suggested the How Many Pins Does The Prime Minister's Hat Hold competition in *Pyke's Weekly* when it was touch and go if it could turn the corner? From that moment *Pyke's Weekly* never looked back. And on *Pyke's* my whole present fortune is founded. The fact is, from the very start we have worked as a team. If I had the ginger, you had the judgement. I don't suppose there's a person in the world whose judgement I respect as highly as I do yours, Francie.'

Mrs. Hammond beamed.

'Well, Georgie, I'm sure I'm only too glad if my efforts to play Egeria have been successful.'

'Play what?' said Sir George, looking a trifle blank.

'Egeria was a goddess who helped and inspired the Roman king Numa Pompilius. At least, so Sinclair tells me.'

She referred to Mr. Sinclair Hammond, the well-known archæologist, who enjoyed the additional distinction of being her husband.

'Now, there's a fellow', said Sir George, 'who, if he had a little drive and initiative, would go far. Plenty of brains.'

Mrs. Hammond forbore to discuss her husband. She had grown used to his dreamy lack of ambition, his undynamic acceptance of his niche in the world. There had been a time when she had chafed at these things, but recently she had come to accept it as her cross in this life that she never seemed to marry any one with ginger and pep. Her first husband, acquired in the days before prosperity had dawned on the family, had been a Mr. Herbert Shale, courteous and popular assistant in the Hose and Underwear department of Harrod's Stores, and him not even her powerful driving force had been able to shove higher up the social ladder than the rank of shop-walker. Whatever his shortcomings, Sinclair was better than Herbert.

'What title did you think of adopting, Georgie?' she asked, changing the subject.

Sir George, whose massive mind never wholly relaxed even in its social moments, was speaking into the dicta-phone.

'Editor, *Pyke's Weekly*, attention,' he was saying.

'Article next week on Famous Women Who Have
Inspired Famous Men. You know—Egeria and so forth.'
He turned away apologetically. ' I beg your pardon ? '
'I said, have you thought of a title yet ? '
'Just jotted down a few suggestions, that's all.' He
picked up the pad. 'How do you like Lord Barraclough ?
Or Wensleydale ? Or Marlinghue ? The one that pleased
me most was Michelhever. There's a swing about Michel-
hever.'

Mrs. Hammond shook her head.

'Too florid. They're all too florid.'

'Well, you know, a title ought to have a bit of a ring.
Look at some of the ones there are already—Beaver-
brook—Stratheden—Leverhulme. Plenty of zip to them.'

'I know, but——'

'And, mark you,' urged Sir George, ' it's deuced hard
to pick something good that hasn't already been taken.
The fellows who got in first skimmed the cream.'

'I know. But none of these you have mentioned
sound just right to me. There is nothing actually wrong
with them, and a man with your personality could carry
them off : but they are all just the least bit ornate.
You must not forget that eventually Roderick will have
to succeed to whatever title you choose. We must not
select anything which would seem ridiculous in connection
with Roderick. His actual name is bad enough, as it is.
Roderick ! ' Mrs. Hammond winced. This was a painful subject with her. ' How often I pleaded with poor
Lucy to call him Thomas ! '

The frown which had been so long absent from Sir
George's happy face returned, blacker than ever. He
had the air of one into whose cup of joy an unfriendly
hand has dropped a dead mouse.

'I'd forgotten all about Roderick,' he said moodily.

§ 2

There was a pause. The future Lord Michelhever (or
possibly Wensleydale or Marlinghue) drummed irritably
on the desk with his finger-tips.

'How the deuce I came to have a son like that ', he

complained, as many a stout father had done before him and many would do when he was dead and gone, ' beats me ! '

' He takes after poor Lucy,' said Mrs. Hammond. ' She was just the same timid, feeble creature.'

Sir George nodded. The mention of his long-departed wife stirred no sentimental chord in him. The days when he was plain George Pyke, humble clerk in a solicitor's office, and used to thrill at the soft voice of Lucy Maynard as she took the order for his frugal lunch at the Holborn Viaduct Cabin, had long since faded from his memory. That quite unsatisfactory woman had now definitely become ' poor Lucy '—a thing to be spoken of in much the same tone as would be accorded to measles or any other mild ailment which had attacked a great man in his infancy.

' Reminds me ', said Sir George, reaching for the telephone, ' that I want to have a word with Roderick. I'll do it now,' he said, unconsciously quoting the motto which, by his instructions, had been placed in a wooden frame on every editorial desk in the building. ' I rang up the *Spice* office just before you came, but he was still out at lunch.'

' Wait one moment, Georgie. There is something I want to speak to you about before you send for Roderick.' Sir George, always docile when it was she who commanded, put down the telephone. ' What has he been doing that you want to see him ? '

Sir George snorted.

' I'll tell you ! ' The agony of a disappointed father rang in his voice. ' I gave that boy his head far too much while he was up at Oxford. I let him have a large allowance, and what did he do with it ? Published a book he had written on the Prose of Walter Pater ! At his own expense, in limp purple leather ! And on top of that had the effrontery to suggest that the Mammoth should take over the *Poetry Quarterly*, a beastly thing that doesn't sell a dozen copies a year, and let him run it as editor.'

' I know all that,' said Mrs. Hammond a shade impa-

tiently. If Georgie had a fault, it was this tendency of
his towards the twice-told tale. 'And you made him
editor of *Society Spice*. How is he getting on ? '

'That's just what I'm coming to. I started to break
him into the business by making him editor of *Spice*,
never dreaming that even he could make a mess of that.
Why, the position is a sinecure. Young Pilbeam, a
thoroughly able young fellow, really runs the paper. All
I asked of Roderick, all I wanted him to do, was to show
some signs of Grip and generally find his feet before
going on to something bigger. And what happens ? I
would like you', said the stricken father, ' just to glance
through this week's issue.'

Mrs. Hammond took the paper. There was a silence,
broken only by the rustling of leaves and Sir George's
deep, overwrought breathing.

'Lacks Vigour,' announced Egeria at length.

'Lacks Grip,' said Numa Pompilius.

' Mild.'

' Tame.'

' Wants Pep.'

' Needs Ginger. I made inquiries,' proceeded Numa
Pompilius bitterly, hurling the offending journal into a
corner, ' and what do you think ? Young Pilbeam tells
me that Roderick deliberately vetoes and excludes from
the paper all the best items he submits. That's his idea
of earning his salary and being loyal to the firm that
employs him ! '

Mrs. Hammond clicked her tongue concernedly.

' It seems incredible.'

' It's quite true.'

' But what possible motive could he have ? '

' Motive ? A boy like that doesn't have to have
motives. He's just a plain imbecile. I wish to heaven ',
cried this tortured parent, ' that he would get married.
A wife might make something of him.'

Mrs. Hammond started.

' What an extraordinary thing that you should say
that ! It was the very thing I wanted to speak to you
about. I suppose you realize, George, that, now you

are going to receive this peerage, Roderick's marriage becomes a matter of vital importance? I mean, it is even more essential than before that he should marry somebody in a suitable social position.'

'Let me catch him', said Sir George grimly, 'trying to marry anybody that isn't!'

'Well, you know, there was that girl you told me about—the one that worked as a stenographer in the *Pyke's Weekly* office.'

'Sacked,' said Sir George briefly. 'Shot her out five minutes after I discovered that they were having a flirtation.'

'Has he been seeing her since?'

'Wouldn't have the nerve to.'

'No, that is true. Deliberate defiance of your wishes would be out of keeping with Roderick's character. Has he shown any signs of being attracted by any other girl? Any girl in his own class, I mean?'

'Not that I know of.'

'George,' said Mrs. Hammond, leaning forward, 'I have been thinking of this for some time. Why should not Roderick marry Felicia?'

§ 3

Sir George quivered from head to foot. He gazed at his sister with that stunned reverence which comes over men whose darkness has suddenly been lightened by the beacon-flash of pure genius. This, he felt, was Francie at her best. This was the latest and greatest of that stream of epoch-making ideas which had begun with the How Many Pins Does The Prime Minister's Hat Hold competition. It was inspirations such as this that gave the lie to the theory that the female brain is smaller than the male.

'Could you work it?' he quavered huskily.

'Work it?' Mrs. Hammond's eyebrows rose the fraction of an inch. 'I don't understand you.'

'Well, I—er——' The rebuke to his coarse directness abashed Sir George. 'What I mean is, Felicia's an uncommonly attractive girl, and Roderick—well, Roderick——'

'Roddy is not at all unattractive, if you do not object to the rather weak type of young man. He inherits poor Lucy's pretty eyes and hair. I can easily imagine any girl admiring him.'

At this statement Sir George's mouth opened. He shut it again. The remark he had intended to make concerning the mental condition of a girl who could admire Roderick was suppressed at its source. In the circumstances, he felt, it would be injudicious.

'And, of course, he is a very good match. He will have your money some day, and the title. I should call him an excellent match. Then, again, I know Felicia is not in love with anybody else. And I have a great deal of influence with her.'

This last sentence removed Sir George's lingering doubts. Translated into less feminine English, its meaning was clear. He had a complete faith in Francie's ability to make any one do anything she wished. It was, in his opinion, asking a lot of a girl, to require her to accept as husband a young man who deliberately excluded Grip and Ginger from the columns of *Society Spice*: but if Francie undertook to put such a transaction through it was all over but cutting the wedding-cake.

'If you can persuade Roddy to propose,' said Mrs. Hammond, 'I think I can answer for Felicia.'

'Persuade him! Roderick will do anything I tell him to. My goodness, Francie,' he exclaimed, 'the thought of that boy safely married to a girl who has been trained by you is—well, I can't tell you what I think of the idea. I only hope Felicia's had the sense to pattern herself on you. Ah, there you are, Roderick.'

A timid knock had sounded on the door while he was speaking, and into the room there now came sidling a young man. He was a tall young man, thin, and of an intellectual cast of countenance. The eyes and hair to which Mrs. Hammond had alluded, those legacies from 'poor Lucy', formed the best part of his make-up. The eyes were large and brown, the hair which swept flowingly over his forehead a deep chestnut. The rather large and straggling bow-tie which he wore was also admired in certain circles, but not by Sir George.

'How do you do, Aunt Frances ? ' said Roderick.   His manner was nervous, and suggested that of men who visit dentists, or small boys who go by request into the studies of head-masters.   'Pilbeam says you want to see me, father.'

'I do,' said Sir George coldly.   'Sit down.'

Mrs. Hammond rose with her customary tact.

'I think I will be running away,' she said.   'I have some shopping to do.'

Roderick watched her go with something of the emotions of a shipwrecked sailor on a raft who sees a sail vanishing over the horizon.   He was not particularly fond of his aunt Frances, but almost any one who made a third at interviews between himself and his father was welcome to him.   He sat down and fingered his tie uncomfortably.

'Don't fidget ! ' snapped Sir George.   He glowered at the tie.   'What the deuce do you wear that thing for ? It makes me sick.'

A more spirited youth might have retorted that a man who habitually appeared in public in a waistcoat of scarlet wool could hardly lay claim to be considered *arbiter elegantiarum* in the matter of dress.   Roderick, unequal to this shattering come-back, merely smiled weakly.

'I want to talk to you about *Society Spice*,' said Sir George severely, dismissing the minor subject of costume. He retrieved the copy of the paper from the corner into which his just indignation had caused him to fling it, and began to turn its pages with knitted brow, Roderick eyeing him the while with all the care-free *insouciance* of a man watching a ticking bomb.

'Ha ! ' barked Sir George suddenly, lifting his son and heir a clear two inches off the seat of his chair. 'Just as I thought !   It isn't there.'

'What, father ? '

'The fourth instalment of that series on Bookmakers' Swindling Methods.   It has been discontinued.   Why ? '

'Well, you see, father——'

'Pilbeam told me it was a great success. He said there had been a number of letters about it.'

Roderick shuddered. He had seen some of those letters—the ones which Pilbeam, a jovial enthusiast, had described as the fruitiest of the bunch.

'Well, you see, father,' he bleated, 'it was so frightfully personal.'

'Personal!' Sir George's frown seemed to darken the room. 'It was meant to be personal. *Society Spice* is a personal paper. Good heavens, you don't suppose these bookmakers can afford to bring libel actions, do you?'

'But, father——'

'All the better if they did. It would be an excellent advertisement, and no jury would award them more than a farthing's damages.'

Roderick shuffled unhappily.

'It isn't so much libel actions.'

'What do you mean?'

'Well, father, it's like this. I happened to be down at Kempton Park last Saturday, and I met a man who told me that Ike Bullett was going about uttering the most awful threats.'

'Ike Bullett? Who's Ike Bullett?'

'He's one of the bookies. The articles have been particularly outspoken about him, you know. And he was threatening that if I didn't stop them he would put the Lads on to me and they would come and butter me over the pavement.'

Sensational as this announcement was, it seemed to leave Sir George completely unimpressed. He did not actually snap his fingers, but he made an odd contemptuous noise at the back of his throat which amounted to a finger-snap. Having done this, he proceeded to speak his mind.

It was a manly, sturdy attitude that he adopted. He defied Ike Bullett and all his kind. Ike Bullett, he seemed to suggest, might put all the Lads in the world on to Roderick, but he couldn't intimidate him, Sir

George. He faced with a fine, fearless unconcern the prospect of people buttering Roderick over the pavement. Not since the days of Lucius Junius Brutus had there been a father so ruggedly careless of the comfort of his son.

' The series ', said the proprietor of the Mammoth Publishing Company tensely at the end of a striking passage in which he had voiced some of the resentment he felt at the mean trick which Providence had played upon him in making him Roderick's father, ' will be resumed. At once. Understand that ! '

' Yes, father.'

' And if ', said Sir George valiantly, ' this Ike Bullett of yours doesn't like it he can lump it ! '

' Very well, father,' said Roderick hopelessly. Through his mind there had flashed again a recollection of those letters. Crude, almost illiterate documents they had been, written under the stress of strong emotion by rough and uncultured men, yet not even Walter Pater in all the glory of limp purple leather had ever expressed his meaning with a more exact precision.

He turned to go, but the painful interview was not, it seemed, yet concluded.

' Wait,' said Sir George, ' I have something else to say to you.'

Roderick poured himself into his chair once more.

§ 4

Mr. Sinclair Hammond, easy-going consort of the Egeria of the Mammoth Publishing Company, basked in the sunshine in the garden of Holly House, his residence on Wimbledon Common. There was a note-book on his knee, and he was scribbling industriously with a stubby pencil.

Mr. Hammond was fond of his garden. It was—for a suburb—quite an Eden. Several acres in dimension and shut off from the outer world by high brick walls, it contained almost more than its fair share of trees : and later on, when summer came, it would, he knew, blaze very nobly with many-coloured flowers. There were smooth lawns, hedges of lavender, and a decent-sized stone pool with goldfish. Not a bad place at all, felt Mr. Hammond as he put down his pencil, removed his glasses and leaned back in his deck-chair ; by no means a bad place for a man of quiet tastes who asked little more from life than to be left alone to do his writing.

His tranquillity now was largely due to the fact that he was alone. It had been quite an hour since any one had bothered him. This was almost a record, and he had an uneasy feeling that it was too good to last. He was on the point of replacing his glasses and resuming his work when he saw that his forebodings had been well grounded. A female figure had come out through the French windows of the drawing-room and was making for him across the lawn.

Mr. Hammond sighed. Fond though he was of his wife, the Pyke blood in her made her occasionally a companion too restless and uncomfortable for a man who liked to sit and dream. Francie's life was a series of small wars in which cooks, housemaids, parlourmaids, chauffeurs and tradesmen followed one another in the rôle of enemy, and she was apt to combine in herself the parts of fighter and war-correspondent. If this was Francie coming now, it probably meant that he was in for half an hour's military gossip. With the cook, if he recollected rightly, an armistice had been concluded yesterday, but he seemed to remember hearing something said at breakfast about an ultimatum to the grocer, the stringiness of whose bacon had recently been causing alarm and despondency in the Hammond household.

With a little moan he put on his glasses, and was relieved to see that it was not his wife who was approaching, but his niece Felicia. This altered the situation entirely. He had no objection whatever to abandoning work in favour of a chat with Flick. They were firm friends and allies. Moreover, Flick shared his ability to see humour in the little things of life—a valuable gift in woman and one of the few great qualities which his admirable wife lacked.

He looked at her, as she drew near, with the same

mild wonder which he always felt when he saw her nowadays. Seven years ago, when she had been dumped on him like a parcel on the death of his sister and her husband Jack Sheridan in a railway accident, she had been a leggy, scraggy, tousle-haired, freckled thing, with nose and eyelids pink from much weeping, a curious object giving as little promise of beauty as a week-old baby. And now the sight of her suggested to him, given as he was to drawing his images from the Classics, a Hamadryad or some shepherdess strayed out of an Idyll of Theocritus. Just when the astounding change had taken place, it would have been beyond him to say. It had come so gradually and imperceptibly, first one feature then another ceasing to offend the eye—here a leg shortening to a decently human length, there a mop of amber hair miraculously tidying itself. He supposed vaguely that it was always this way with girls.

'Hullo, Uncle Sinclair,' said Flick. She held out the overcoat which she was carrying. 'Get up!'

'I will not get up,' said Mr. Hammond. 'I refuse to get up for any one.'

'Aunt Frances says it's getting chilly and she wants you to put on your light overcoat.'

Mr. Hammond put on the coat. He knew that the sleeves would brush against the paper when he resumed his writing, thus distracting his thoughts and leading to intemperate language, but the alternative, throwing the beastly thing into the goldfish pond, was impossible. If he continued to sit out here as he was and after a lapse of two months caught a cold, that cold would, he was aware, be put down to his reckless refusal to take the elementary precaution of wearing the light overcoat.

'You know, of course, that you are an abominable nuisance, child?' he observed, reseating himself.

Flick glanced up. She was looking, Mr. Hammond thought, unusually pensive. Her mouth was a little drooped and white teeth showed below her lip. Her blue eyes, that always reminded him of a rain-washed sky, were clouded. This surprised Mr. Hammond, for as a rule she took life lightly.

'Are you really busy, Uncle?'

'Of course not. Something on the mind, Flickie?'

Flick pulled at the grass thoughtfully.

'Uncle Sinclair, I know you always say you never give advice to anybody, but I wish you would give me some.'

'Oh, you're different. I'll give you all you want. State your case.'

'Roderick has asked me to marry him. What do you think I ought to do?'

Mr. Hammond was appalled. Ironic, he reflected, to think that when he had found that it was Flick who was coming to disturb his privacy he had been relieved. But who would have supposed that she intended flinging frightful problems like this at his head? He was fifty-three years old and had grown to regard life as a spectacle, content to watch it without rushing in and grabbing hold of the steering-wheel. He shrank aghast from advising this girl about a thing like marriage. Besides, what business had a child like her to dream of marrying any one? And then Mr. Hammond realized that time had not been standing still. Flick was twenty-one.

'What does your aunt think?' he asked feebly, fighting for time.

'She thinks I ought to. But—I don't know——'

A pang of pity for her innocence shot through Mr. Hammond. Francie had given her decision, and here the poor child was treating the matter as if it still lay open for debate.

'Your aunt knows best,' he said, and blushed hotly at the words. They sounded to him like something out of one of the novels of his boyhood.

'Yes, but this is something I've got to think out for myself, isn't it?'

Mr. Hammond felt uneasy. He liked peace in the home, and this speech of Flick's seemed to suggest that conditions might conceivably arise to render peace a memory of the past. He, personally, never opposed Francie. It suited him to have a power outside himself directing his life for him. But the Younger Generation, he was aware, might look on the matter with different eyes. Flick's chin was round and soft, but it was a strong chin. You could not dragoon a girl like Flick.

'Of course, I like Roddy,' said Flick meditatively.

'Splendid fellow,' agreed Mr. Hammond heartily, growing more cheerful. He knew, as a fact, little or nothing of Roderick, for he was a man who avoided the society of his juniors : but if Francie endorsed him that settled it.

Flick ran her fingers over the short grass.

'He isn't very—exciting,' she said.

'You don't want a jumpy husband, surely ? Not a fellow like the chap in the Bab Ballads who " couldn't walk into a room without ejaculating ' Boom ! ' which startled ladies greatly ". Is that what you're yearning after ? '

'I don't think I've got quite the right word. I meant —oh well, this is what I mean, though it sounds horribly silly when one says it. I suppose every girl is sort of half in love with a kind of Fairy Prince. A sort of ideal, you know. Doesn't it sound idiotic ! Still, there it is, you know. And Roderick isn't a fairy prince, is he ? '

Her rain-washed eyes were more cloudy and serious than ever, but Mr. Hammond stuck doggedly to light persiflage. The conversation seemed to be displaying a perilous tendency to plunge into the depths, and he disliked depths.

'I know exactly what you mean,' he said. 'We all have one big romance in our lives which is apt to make everything else seem commonplace and dull—a beautiful, opalescent dream, very pleasant to dig up every now and then and brood over. In my case it was the passion I conceived at the age of fourteen for a lady who played in comic opera at Terry's Theatre. Heavens, how I loved that woman ! Well, now, tell me your romance. From the way you were speaking, I'm sure you've had one. Some fatal, fascinating boy with a jammy face and a Lord Fauntleroy suit whom you met at a birthday party, eh ? '

Flick smiled indulgently.

'It isn't quite so long ago as that.'

Bob, the Sealyham terrier, had wandered up. Flick rolled him over on his back and pulled his ears absently for a moment without speaking.

'I wonder', she said, 'if you remember taking me to stay with a Mr. Paradene when we were over in America. The time you did the lecture tour, you know. About five years ago, just before you married Aunt Francie.'

'Certainly. Do you suppose I'm as senile as all that? I can remember back much further. Cooley Paradene is one of my best friends.'

'It was then that it happened.'

'What happened?'

'All the beautiful-opalescent-dream stuff.'

Mr. Hammond regarded his niece with grave concern.

'Don't tell me you are nurturing a secret passion for old Cooley? A little elderly for you, my child. Besides, you aren't interested in old books. You wouldn't appeal to him.'

'Don't be silly. It was Bill.'

'What was Bill?'

'Bill West. Mr. Paradene's nephew. He's my great love, as you would call it.'

Mr. Hammond frowned thoughtfully.

'Bill? Bill? I must be getting senile after all. This William absolutely eludes my memory.'

'Oh, you must remember Bill. Mr. Paradene's nephew at Harvard.'

'Bill? Bill?' Mr. Hammond's face cleared. 'Of course! A pimply youth with outstanding ears.'

'He wasn't!' cried Flick, revolted.

'Ears', insisted Mr. Hammond firmly, 'which he used to hang his hat on when the rack in the hall was full.'

'Nothing of the kind. He was frightfully handsome and wonderful in every way.'

'Name one way in which he was wonderful,' said the sceptical Mr. Hammond.

'Well, I'll tell you something wonderful that he did. He saved my life.'

'Saved your life?' Mr. Hammond was interested. 'How did that happen?'

'We were bathing in Mr. Paradene's lake, and I went out too far. As a matter of fact, we had finished bathing and I was supposed to be in my hut, dressing. But I couldn't resist one last swim. It very nearly was my last, too. Bill had dressed, but he came out just in time and saw me struggling, and he dived in with all his clothes on——'

'Ass! Ought to have taken off his coat.'

'Well, perhaps he did take off his coat, and I wish you wouldn't interrupt and spoil the story. He dived in and swam out to where I was kicking and screaming and brought me in safe and sound. I should have been done for in another half-minute. I had swallowed most of the lake.'

'And why is this the first I have heard of it?'

'We kept it dark. Bill, I suppose, was modest. At any rate, he begged me not to say anything about it, and I didn't say anything because I jolly well knew I should be stopped bathing again if I did. He left next day to join some friends near Boston, and I've never seen him since.'

Her voice shook a little. Mr. Hammond lit his pipe thoughtfully. Though sympathetic, for he understood Flick, he decided to continue in the light vein.

'I shouldn't worry about him, Flickie,' he said. 'A fellow like that is sure to have been snapped up by now. Concentrate on the sternly practical side of things, my dear. Fix your mind on Roderick. Here's a young fellow whom you admit you like—good-looking, amiable, and the heir to a title and more money than you'll be able to spend in half a dozen lifetimes even if you start collecting old books. Upon my word, I think you could do worse. You can have a lot of fun in this world with a title and a million pounds, you know. Besides, think how jolly it will be marrying into the Mammoth Publishing Company and being able to read all the articles in *Pyke's Weekly* days before they appear in print.'

Flick was silent. She was wishing in a vague and formless way that life had not arranged itself quite like this : and yet she could not have said exactly what was her objection to the existing state of affairs. After all, she did like Roddy. And she had known him a long time. Not like being asked to marry a stranger.

And again—though everybody was very kind and pleasant and never so much as hinted it to her—there was no getting away from the fact that she was a penniless orphan, hardly in a position to take nebulous and fanciful objections to the quite attractive sons of millionaires.

' Yes, I think I'd better marry him,' she said.

A chill little wind blew across the garden, and she shivered. Mr. Hammond was glad now that he had been made to put on the light overcoat. Francie, he reflected, was always right.

CHAPTER TWO

BILL UNDERTAKES A MISSION

§ 1

WILLIAM PARADENE WEST sat in the middle of the road at that busy spot where Forty-Second Street joins Fifth Avenue. Always crowded, this centre of New York appeared now to be even more congested than usual. On every side, as far as the eye could reach, vast hordes of people with peculiar faces passed and re-passed ; and as they went jeered at Bill unfeelingly. A policeman, chewing gum, surveyed him with quiet dislike—offended, doubtless, for policemen are prudish in these matters, by the fact that he was bare-footed and clad only in a suit of mesh-knit underwear. Somewhere close at hand a steam-rivetter was at work, making a noise singularly afflicting to the nerves.

How Bill had come to be in this conspicuous and embarrassing position he was not precisely clear. He could recall in a vague way riding a motor-bicycle across a wide prairie and subsequently being chased by leopards through a forest, but after that there occurred a gap in his memory. Still, here he was, and it now became apparent to him that the disadvantages attached to his predicament were even more marked than he had at first supposed. On top of his head somebody had placed one of those iron spikes which road-menders use in breaking up asphalte, and two men with large hammers were hitting this with a rhythmical vigour, each blow causing a jarring pain to run through his entire body. The steam-rivetter, which had stopped for a moment, began its hideous din once more.

Bill felt ill-used and miserable. It was not so much

the pain that distressed him, acute though this was ;
nor the fact that the men with the hammers were respec-
tively his Uncle Cooley, on whose bounty he had been
subsisting for years, and Judson Coker, his best friend,
hand in hand with whom he had passed through both
school and college.　All this he could have endured with
fortitude as part of the ordinary give-and-take of life.
The thing that cut him to the quick was the discovery
that the extraordinarily beautiful girl who held the spike
in position—and did it, what is more, with a radiant
smile as if she thoroughly enjoyed it—was Judson Coker's
sister Alice.

That really was bitter.　That hurt.　He worshipped
that girl with a love not only volcanic but steadfast.
Since their first meeting, nearly a year ago, he had been
circling coyly about her, trying to muster up courage
enough to lay at her feet a strong man's honest devotion.
He had given her flowers, chocolates, and on her birthday a beaded bag.　And here she was jabbing spikes
into his head.　Women are like that.

The noise of the rivetter rose to a demoniacal crescendo.
So insistent did it become that Bill, after stirring uneasily
on his pillow, finally opened his eyes ; and, having blinked
at the sunlight pouring in through the window, became
aware that another day had begun and that the telephone at his bedside was ringing.　At the same moment
the door opened, and Ridgway, his capable man-servant,
entered.

'I think I heard the telephone, sir,' said Ridgway.

'So did I,' said Bill wanly.

The mists of sleep had rolled away, and returning
consciousness was revealing the fact that he felt extremely
unwell.　His head had swollen unwholesomely to about
twice its normal size and shooting pains shuddered through
it.　His mouth was full of some unpleasant flannel sub-
stance, which proved on investigation to be his tongue.
Memory awoke.　It all came back to him now.　Last
night Judson Coker had given a party——

Ridgway had removed the receiver.

'Are you there ?—Yes——' His voice was a well-

modulated coo. The young master's return home at a
little after four in the morning had not passed unnoticed
by Ridgway, and he knew instinctively that soft speech
would be appreciated. 'Yes, I will give Mr. West your
message.' He turned to Bill and cooed anew like a
cushat dove calling to its mate in spring. 'Roberts,
Mr. Cooley Paradene's butler, on the telephone, sir. He
requests me to inform you that Mr. Paradene returned
from his travels yesterday and is very urgent that you
should visit him this afternoon.'

Bill was in but poor shape for paying calls. However,
Uncle Cooley's invitations had the quality of royal com-
mands. You cannot accept a large quarterly allowance
from a man and decline to see him when desired.

'Down at Westbury?' he asked.

'At Westbury, sir, yes.'

'Tell him I'll be there.'

'Very good, sir.' Ridgway relayed this information
to the waiting Roberts and replaced the receiver. 'Shall
I prepare your breakfast, sir?'

Bill considered the point.

'I suppose so,' he said at length, without enthusiasm.
Breakfast was never a popular meal with those who
had enjoyed overnight the hospitality of Judson Coker.
'Something pretty light.'

'Exactly, sir,' said Ridgway understandingly, and slid
from the presence.

Bill lay on his back, staring at the ceiling. His head
seemed more grossly enlarged than ever. He wished he
had told Ridgway to go out and stop those birds singing
in the trees of Central Park across the road. Voluble,
insufferably hearty English sparrows they were, the sort
of birds that in a properly run city would be put down
by law. But it was too much effort to do anything
about it now. Everything was too much effort except
just to lie here very quietly with one's eyes on the ceiling.

He fell to meditation, and was still meditating when
a voice spoke in his ear. It was a nasty rasping voice,
not soft and gentle like Ridgway's, and he recognized

it immediately as that of Conscience. They had had
arguments before.

' Well ? ' said Conscience.

' Well ? ' said Bill defensively.

' Up a bit late last night, eh ? '

' A little.'

' I thought as much.'

' I was at a party at Judson Coker's,' said Bill. ' I
had promised to go, so I had to. A man must keep his
word.'

' A man need not lower himself to the level of the
beasts of the field,' said Conscience coldly. ' It begins
to look to me as if you were something of a young waster.'

It was an offensive remark, but in his melancholy
morning mood Bill found himself unable to combat it.
He was in the frame of mind when men search their
hearts and plunge into sudden reformations.

' I should think you'd have more self-respect and a
rudimentary sense of decency,' proceeded Conscience.
' You love Alice Coker, don't you ? Very well, then.
A man who loves that noble girl ought to consider himself almost in the light of a priest or something. But
do you ? Not by a jugful. Lost to all sense of shame
is the way I'd put it.'

This also struck Bill as true.

' I've had my eye on you, young man, for a long
time, and I've about got you sized up. What's the
matter with you, among other things, is that you're a
worm, a loafer, a sponger, and a shiftless, backboneless
disgrace to civilization. You wasted your time at Harvard. Yes, I am perfectly aware that you were in the
football team. I'm not saying you're not a healthy and
muscular young animal—what I'm complaining about is
your soul. You're simply not among those present when
it comes to soul, and the soul is what brings home the
bacon. As I was saying, you didn't do a stroke of work
at Harvard, and ever since you came out of college
you've been hanging around New York, absolutely idle,
living on your Uncle Cooley. It's no good to say that
he can give you this allowance of yours without feeling

it. That's not the point. I know perfectly well that
he owns the Paradene Pulp and Paper Company and is
a millionaire. What I am driving at is that you're
degrading yourself by sponging on him. You're not a
bit better than your Uncle Jasper.'

' Here, I say ! ' protested Bill. He had been prepared
for a good deal, but this was overdoing it.

' Not one bit better than your Uncle Jasper and your
cousin Evelyn and all the rest of the family leeches,'
insisted Conscience firmly. ' Bloodsuckers, all of you.
Uncle Cooley is the man with the money, and the
entire family, you included, has been bleeding him for
years.'

Bill's spirit was broken.

' What shall I do about it ? ' he asked humbly.

' Do ? Why, bustle about and earn a living for yourself. Get up, you wastrel, and show there's something
in you. Go to your uncle and tell him you want to
work. You're twenty-six and haven't started yet. Do
you intend to loaf through the whole of your life like
this ? '

Bill blinked at the ceiling. Conscience's exordium had
wrought powerfully upon him. That stuff about trying
to be worthy of Alice Coker—that touched the spot.
But what really stung was the suggestion that he was
on a par with Uncle Jasper and Cousin Evelyn. That
was a wicked punch. That most certainly wanted looking into. In all the world the persons he most despised
were these relatives of his who loafed around living on
Uncle Cooley. Incredible, he would have said, that he,
the winning and debonair Bill West, could actually be
classed with these ghastly excrescences. And yet——

The position of affairs in the Paradene family was
one that is frequently met with in this world. Cooley
Paradene, by means of a toilsome youth and a strenuous
middle age, had amassed a large amount of money, and
now all his poor relations had gathered round to help
him spend it. His brother Otis had a real-estate business that required frequent subsidies : his brother-in-
law, Jasper Daly, was an inventor whose only successful

2

inventions were the varied methods he discovered of borrowing money : his niece Evelyn had married a man who was always starting new literary reviews. They were not people who agreed together on many subjects, but on this one point of electing Cooley to the post of family paymaster they had been unanimous.

For some years now Uncle Cooley had been showing in the matter of parting with money a pleasingly docile spirit for a man whose quickness of temper had at one time been a family byword. Something had happened to Mr. Paradene recently, purging the old Adam out of him : and his relatives were inclined to think that what had brought about the change was the hobby of collecting old books which had gripped him in his sixtieth year. Until he had started book-collecting Cooley Paradene had been a little too formidable and uncertain for comfort. He had chafed at the constant calls made on his purse. Once he had thrown a small chair at Jasper Daly, though unfortunately with a poor aim. But now everything was splendid. He just mooned about his library at Westbury and signed cheques in that delightful absent-minded way which we like to see in our rich relatives.

This was the man who had supported Bill West through college days and up to the moment when he lay in bed this morning, tortured by conscience. Yes, Bill decided, Conscience had been right. Of course, he was not really as bad as Uncle Jasper and Cousin Evelyn, but he could see now that he had allowed himself to drift into an ambiguous position, and one that might easily lead people who did not know what a fine fellow he was to form mistaken judgements. Most assuredly he must go to Uncle Cooley and announce his readiness to accept a job of work. He had never felt anything of an urge towards the pulping of paper, but in this new mood engendered by remorse he rather fancied that there must be more pleasure to be derived from it than the casual spectator would imagine. He had no notion how one pulped paper, nor what one did with it when pulped —but these were small technical details which he would doubtless master during the first week. The main thing was to get started.

Filled with resolution, Bill heaved himself up with a groan and made for the bathroom.

There is magic in a cold shower. In combination with Youth few ills of the flesh can stand against it. Drying his glowing body five minutes later, Bill, though still tender about the head and apt to leap at sudden noises, felt on the whole a new man. He thrilled with courage and determination. As he towelled his back, he reviewed the programme before him. He would be content with something quite modest at first, of course ; something that would just enable him to look round and get a grasp on things. This achieved, he would begin to make his presence felt. Toiling with the banked-up energy of one who had never done a hand's-turn in his life, he would soar higher and higher until eventually he got control of the entire outfit.

It was about time that Uncle Cooley had a real live-wire looking after the Pulp and Paper Company's affairs. The old boy had been a hustler in his day, but for the last few years he had allowed a taste for travel and the fascination of his library to take up too much of his time. What the Paradene Pulp and Paper Company wanted was new blood, and he, Bill, was the man to supply it.

He dressed and went in to his light breakfast. So exalted was he by now that his dreams of the future began definitely to include a life-long union with Alice Coker. He brushed aside obstacles grandly. He felt alert and conquering. As he picked up his morning paper he had got his plans so perfectly elaborated that he half expected to find on the front page the headlines :—

SOCIETY ROMANCE.
YOUNG PULP-PAPER KING WEDS BEAUTIFUL
GIRL.
INTERVIEW WITH MR. WEST.

Instead, all that met his eye was the customary

SOCIETY DIVORCE.
EX-WIFE'S HEART-BALM LOVE-TANGLE.

' Ugh ! ' said Bill, disgusted, and attacked his grape-fruit.

' Mr. Judson Coker on the telephone, sir,' said Ridgway, oozing softly in like some soundless liquid.

Bill walked to the telephone in a cold, hard, censorious mood. It was impossible for him, in his reformed condition, to think of his friend and host of last night without a puritanical shudder. Odd, he reflected, how often the noblest girls had these deplorable brothers. Bill's standard in the matter of brothers for the goddess of his heart was perhaps a trifle high, and it is to be doubted whether a composite of Sir Galahad, Good King Wenceslas and St. Francis of Assisi would quite have made the grade. Judson failed altogether to qualify. Why, last night, he recalled, Judson had behaved for all the world like a Licentious Clubman in a super-film being the life and soul of one of those parties out of which the Censor cuts three thousand feet the moment he sees it. Gaiety of spirit is all very well, but there are limits —especially for those closely related to the sweetest of her sex. And these limits Judson Coker had exceeded by several parasangs.

' Hallo ? ' said Bill. He spoke crisply and in a manner to discourage badinage. Not that Judson, after last night's celebrations, was likely to indulge in airy quips. Bill was a little surprised, indeed, that the other should be able at so early an hour as this to speak at all.

A voice sounded over the wire. It was the husky voice of one who has wandered far and long across the hot sands, the voice of a man delicately endeavouring to keep the top of his head from coming off.

' That you, Bill o' man ? '

' Yes.'

' So you got home all right ? ' said the Voice in tones of surprised congratulation.

Bill resented this reminder of a past now discarded for ever.

' Yes,' he said frigidly.   ' What do you want ? '

An unseen throat cleared itself feebly.

' Just remembered, Bill o' man.   Most important thing.
I invited half a dozen of the Follies girls to come on a
picnic this afternoon.'

' Well ?   What about it ? '

' I'm relying on you to rally round.'

Bill frowned.   Such a frown as St. Anthony might
have permitted himself.

' You are, are you ? ' he said sternly.   ' Then listen
to me, you poor fish.   Let me tell you that I'm a changed
man and wouldn't be seen dead in a ditch with a Follies
girl.   And if you'll take my advice you'll pull up and
try to realize that life is stern and earnest and meant
for something better than——'

An awed gasp interrupted his harangue.

' Gosh, Bill,' quavered the Voice, ' I noticed you buzzing around pretty energetically last night, but I'd no
notion you would be quite so bad this morning.   You
must have got the head of a lifetime.   Absolutely of a
lifetime ! '   The Voice sank to an earnest whisper.
' What you want to do, Bill o' man, is to take a couple
of Never-Say-Dies.   That's what I'm going to do.   You
remember the recipe ?   One raw egg in half a wine-
glassful of Worcester Sauce, sprinkle liberally with red
pepper, add four aspirins, and stir.   Put you right in
no time.'

And this man was Her brother !   Bill shuddered.

' I am feeling perfectly well, thank you,' he said
austerely.

' Fine !   Then you will come to the picnic after all ? '

' I will not.   I wouldn't have dreamed of doing so
in any case, but as it happens I have a previous
engagement.   I've got to go to my uncle's place at
Westbury.   He got home yesterday, and 'phoned me
this morning.'

' My dear chap !   Say no more ! '   The Voice was
cordial and sympathetic.   ' I quite understand.   You
mean the uncle who unbelts the allowance on the first
of every quarter ?   Of course you must go and see him.

I suppose you'll grab the chance of touching him for a
bit extra? It must mean you're pretty strong with
him if he's so crazy to see you the moment he gets
home.'

'If you want to know just what I'm going to do when
I see Uncle Cooley,' said Bill coldly, 'I'll tell you. I'm
going to ask him for a job.'

There was an exclamation of annoyance at the other
end of the wire.

'This darned 'phone is out of order,' complained the
Voice. 'You can't hear a thing. It sounded just as
if you said something about asking your uncle for a
job,' said the Voice amusedly, tickled by the quaint
conceit.

'That is exactly what I did say.'

Silence.

'A job?'

'Yes.'

'Do you mean *work*?'

'Work.'

The Voice became almost tearful in its agitation.

'Don't do it, Bill! Don't do it, o' man. You don't
know what you're talking about. You aren't yourself.
It's just having this head that's giving you ideas like
that. Do take the advice of an old pal and mix up a
Never-Say-Die. It never fails. Guaranteed to make a
week-old corpse spring from its bier and enter for the
Six-Day Bicycle Race. Write the recipe down on a
piece of paper, so that you won't forget it. One raw
egg——'

Bill hung up the receiver, revolted. He was returning
to his breakfast when the telephone bell rang again.
Indignant at this pertinacity on the part of his despicable
friend, he strode back and spoke with wrathful brusque-
ness.

'Well! What do you want *now*?'

'Oh, Mr. West, is that you?'

It was not Judson at all. The voice was a female
one: and, hearing it, Bill tottered with indescribable
emotion. All female voices sound very much alike over

the telephone, but this was one which his heart would
never allow him to mistake. It was She! And he—
criminal fool, misguided blackguard that he was—had
spoken angrily! Ye gods! That even in error he should
have addressed her so! That 'Well!' That emphasis
on the 'now'. It was vile, brutal, fiendish. Words
poured from him in an apologetic flood.

'Miss Coker I'm terribly sorry I don't know how to
apologize I thought it was somebody else I didn't mean
I wouldn't have I hope you aren't I hope I haven't I
hope you won't——'

'Mr. West,' said his audience, taking advantage of
a lull, 'I wonder if you would do me a great favour?'

Bill's knees gave at the joints. He swayed deliriously.

'Do *you* a favour!' he breathed fervently. 'You bet
I will!'

'It's very important.—Can you come and see me?'

'You bet I can!'

'Would you be able to manage it this morning?'

'You bet I would!'

'Thank you so much.'

Bill stood for a moment breathing hard. There was
a mist before his eyes. She wanted him to do her a
favour! It was to him that she turned, not to Toddy
van Riter or Eustace Bailey or any other of those who
formed the court of which she was the undisputed queen.
Could he come and see her? Yes, a thousand times
yes, even if the road to her father's house were lined
with fire-breathing dragons.

He returned to the sitting-room and, going to the
mantelpiece, inspected very carefully and reverently all
the photographs of Miss Coker which it contained—
eleven in all, painfully and laboriously acquired by the
slow process of sneaking them one by one out of Judson's
rooms. Alice was a much-photographed girl, and being
devoted to her unworthy brother kept him well supplied
with her pictures. The horror of the moment when he
had found that lost soul using the latest specimen to
cut the pages of a detective novel had never quite left
Bill.

§ 2

To the sensitive visitor, alert at noticing atmospheric phenomena, there would have seemed on this April morning something not altogether right about the residence of Mr. J. Birdsey Coker on East Sixty-First Street. The dwelling-place of the father of Alice and Judson was tastefully, even luxuriously, furnished and exhibited outwardly all the ear-marks of a refined and wealthy home : but over it there seemed to brood a curious awed hush, as if a cyclone had recently passed that way or some great sorrow come upon the inmates. If Bill had not been so immersed in thoughts of Alice, he might have observed a scared expression in the eyes of the maid who admitted him shortly after half-past twelve. But, being so immersed, it was not until he reached the drawing-room and found himself looking into the lovelier eyes of the mistress of the house that he suspected any calamity.

' Good heavens ! ' he exclaimed. ' What's the matter ? '

Alice Coker was an amazingly handsome girl. She was modelled on rather queenly lines, unlike her brother Judson, who favoured his father's side of the family and looked like an Airedale terrier. Her features were perfect, her teeth were perfect, her hair was perfect. The effect she gave at a first encounter was of flawless beauty. But at the moment, what any one presented to her would have noticed was not that she was beautiful but that she was worried. Those who make the nation's songs (so much more admirable than its laws) advise us to look for the silver lining, to seek the Blue Bird, to put all our troubles in a great big box and sit on the lid and grin. Alice Coker had been unable to follow this counsel. Old Man Trouble, that foe of the songwriters, had plainly conquered her proud spirit.

' Sit down, Mr. West,' she said, formal even in her agitation.

For many months now this tendency to a cool formality on her part had irked Bill. With the sisters of

most of his other friends he was on terms of easy com-
radeship. But then he had been brought up with them
from a child : and, though he had known Judson so
long, Alice had only entered his life a year ago. He
did not know all the facts, but he gathered that the
peace of the Coker home had been marred by a good
deal of that ex-wife's heart-balm love-tangle stuff. At
any rate, until last March Alice had lived in Europe
with her mother, and only on that lady's death had come
to New York to keep house for her father and disturb the
peace of mind of the male members of the younger set.

Bill sat down, registering devotion, sympathy, and
willingness to do all that a red-blooded man may for
Beauty in distress.

' It was very good of you to come,' said Alice.

' No, no. Oh, no. No, no. No, no,' said Bill.

' It's about Judson.'

' Judson ? '

' Yes. Father is simply furious. Not ', proceeded the
fair-minded Miss Coker, ' that you can really blame him.
Juddy did behave very badly.'

Bill found himself in something of a dilemma. He
wished to agree with every word she spoke, but horrified
condemnation of Judson at this point might, he felt,
be resented. Besides, he was handicapped in the capacity
of censor of morals by not knowing what his convivial
friend had been doing to excite the parental wrath to
such an extent. He contented himself with making a
low, honking noise like a respectful wild duck.

' Apparently Judson gave a party last night,' said
Miss Coker. She sniffed disdainfully. ' A very rowdy
party to a lot of impossible girls from the theatres.
What pleasure he gets from mixing with such people ',
she went on severely, ' I cannot see.'

' No,' said Bill virtuously. ' No. You're quite right.
No.'

' The trouble with Juddy is that he is weak and his
friends lead him astray.'

' Exactly,' said Bill, trying to look like one of the
friends who didn't.

'Well, what happened was this,' resumed Miss Coker. 'We all went to bed at the usual time, and were sound asleep when, about four in the morning, there was a violent knocking on the front door. Poor father went down in his slippers and dressing-gown—rather cross, for he had had a very hard day at the office and was tired—and there was Judson.'

She paused, and a look of pain came into her fine eyes.

'Judson', she went on in a toneless voice, 'seemed glad to see father. When I looked over the banisters, he was patting him on the back. Father asked him what he wanted, and Judson said that he had lost his Lucky Pig and thought he might have left it on the piano in the drawing-room the last time he was in the house. He came in and hunted about and then returned to his apartment. About half an hour later he was on the doorstep again, banging the knocker, and when father got out of bed and went down Judson said he had only come to apologize for disturbing us. He said he wouldn't have done it, but he had particularly wanted to show the pig to a girl who was at the party. He said this girl was one of those domestic girls, a little home-body, and might be leaving the party any moment now. He came in and had another search, then he went away again. And at half-past five he called up on the tele-phone—it's in father's room—and begged father to have a look round and see if the pig wasn't in the study.'

She paused again. Bill made shocked noises.

'Naturally, father was very much annoyed.'

Bill nodded sympathetically. He quite saw how this might be.

'You ought to have seen him when he left for the office this morning.'

Bill, as he listened to his adored one's word-picture of the passing of her parent from the bosom of his family, was glad he had not seen him. The impression Miss Coker conveyed to his excited fancy was of something resembling one of those peculiar Beasts in the Book of Revelations on one of its bad mornings. J. Birdsey

Coker, he gathered, not infrequently displayed a little tetchiness round about breakfast-time, but the oldest inhabitant could recall nothing to approach these latest manifestations. The description of how he had behaved when the maid, unnerved by his demeanour, had dropped the eggs and bacon was alone sufficient to chill the stoutest.

'And the result is', concluded Alice, 'that he says he has had enough. He says he is going to stop Judson's allowance and send him to grandmamma's farm in Vermont and keep him there till he gets some sense. And what I wanted to ask you, Mr. West, is this. Could you fit it in with your plans to take Juddy away on a month's fishing-trip ? '

'But you said he was going to Vermont.'

'Yes. But I believe that when father has had time to cool down a little he will agree to letting him go on a fishing-trip instead, provided it is with some one who will look after him and see that he gets nothing to drink. It doesn't so much matter where he goes, you see, so long as he gets away from New York and all these people who cluster round him and lead him astray. Juddy ', said Miss Coker, a break in her voice, ' is such a dear boy that everybody is attracted to him, and that makes it difficult for him to be strong and resist temptation.'

Bill hesitated no longer. He had been doubtful for a time as to Judson's exact standing with his sister ; but now that it became manifest that not all the dark deeds which the reprobate had performed on the front doorstep in the small hours could shake her divine affection, he saw his way clear. He embarked forthwith on an eulogy of his late playmate, the eloquence of which surprised even himself. It was the sort of pæan of praise which would have been considered a bit fulsome even by an Oriental monarch from the lips of the court poet ; but its effect on Miss Coker was remarkable. Her proud aloofness thawed. She melted visibly. And presently, as Bill concluded a stirring passage in which he stressed Judson' essential spirituality and came out uncompromisingly as considering him too rare and tender a soul for the rough hurly-burly of modern life as lived in New York City, she beamed upon him like the rising sun.

' I knew you were a great friend of his,' she said with such cordiality that Bill twisted his legs round each other and gasped for air. ' That's why I asked you to come here. You don't know what it would be like for the poor boy at grandmamma's. He would have to get up at seven every morning, and there would be family prayers twice a day.'

In solemn silence they peered into this Inferno from which she had removed the lid.

' Prayers ? ' faltered Bill.

' And hymns on Sundays,' said Miss Coker, tight-lipped. ' It would drive the poor darling off his head. And as far as his health is concerned a fishing-trip would do him just as much good. And he would enjoy it. I know how fond he is of you. I'm sure father will consent, because he likes and trusts you and could rely on you to keep poor Juddy out of trouble. I don't know how to thank you, Mr. West. But I knew you would not fail me. I am tremendously grateful.'

There is a tide in the affairs of men which, taken at the flood, leads on to fortune. It seemed to Bill that the moment of his own flood-tide had arrived. At no time in the past year had so favourable an opportunity for proposing presented itself, and it might be many a long month before such a chance occurred again. For Bill was not one of your glib fellows who can tap the romantic vein at will and under any conditions. He required something in the nature of a push behind before he could dive. Though painfully conscious of that sick, empty feeling about the diaphragm which had attacked him on the occasion when he had stepped out with the rest of the Harvard football team into the Yale Bowl four years ago, he braced himself to play the man.

' Miss Coker—I—that is to say—or putting it another way—I wonder—do you think——'

He paused. He was not sure if he was making his meaning quite clear. He tried again.

' I know—It isn't as if—I quite see—It might happen
—If you would——'

Still not as lucid as he could have wished. He swallowed twice and approached the subject from a new angle.

' Look here,' he said, ' will you marry me ? '

Miss Coker exhibited an unruffled composure. It is
to be assumed that this sort of thing had happened to
her before.

' Really,' she said, ' I wasn't expecting this.'

Nor was Bill. He was still stupefied by the sound of
those reckless words and wondered dazedly how he could
ever have had the nerve to allow them to pass his lips.
Still, they were out now and the subject definitely placed
before the meeting for consideration. He gazed at her
dumbly but hopefully.

' I can't give you a definite answer now.'

' No, no, of course not.'

' Suppose you ask me again when you have brought
Juddy back quite well and strong ? '

The assumption that Judson was an invalid in the
last stages of egg-shell fragility did not quite square
with Bill's recollection of his friend leading the revels
on the previous night, but he let it go. It was unimpor-
tant. The thing that really mattered was that she had
not scornfully rejected his suit and rung the bell for
menials to come and throw him into the street.

' We'll leave it like that, shall we ? '

' Yes,' said Bill humbly.

' And when do you think you will be able to start
on this fishing-trip ? ' asked Miss Coker, who inherited
from her father the gift of being able to shelve sentiment in favour of business. ' At once ? '

' To-morrow, if you like,' said the infatuated Bill.

He perceived dimly that this new arrangement was
going to make it difficult for him to jump right in and
assume control of his uncle's pulp-paper business, but
that seemed of slight importance now. He basked for
a moment in the warmth of the smile which she bestowed
upon him, and was reminded by that smile of a request
which he wished to make. For the smile was the same

smile which rendered the third photograph from the left
on his mantelpiece so rarely beautiful.

' I wonder,' he stammered. ' I mean—Would you—
Do you think—What I want to say is, you haven't by
any chance a photograph of yourself you could give a
fellow ? '

' Why, of course,' said Alice amiably.

' I've been wanting one of you for a long time,' said
Bill.

§ 3

The library of Mr. Cooley Paradene at his house at
Westbury, Long Island, was a room which caused biblio-
philes on entering it to run round in ecstatic circles,
prying and sniffing and uttering short excited whining
noises like dogs suddenly plunged into the middle of a
hundred entrancing smells. Its fame, one might say,
was international, for articles describing it had appeared
in such widely separated periodicals as the *Atlantic
Monthly*, the *Quarterly Review* and the *Mercure de France*.
On each wall were shelves, and on each shelf volume
after volume of oddly ill-assorted sizes—here a massive
tome, there next to it a squat dwarf of a book ; yonder
a thing that looked like a book but was really a box
containing a book. The mere sight of these affected
those who appreciated that sort of thing like some powerful drug.

Bill, not being a bibliophile, bore the spectacle with
more calm. On being shown into the library by Roberts,
who informed him on his arrival at three o'clock that
afternoon that Mr. Paradene would be disengaged shortly
and desired him to wait, he made immediately for the
curtained bow-window, from which, as his previous visits
to the house had told him, there was a view almost
ideally arranged for the contemplation of one in his
emotional state. Beneath the window hung masses of
laburnum, through which the observer might note and
drink in the beauty of noble trees, a silver lake, and a
broad expanse of shady lawn. Just what a man in love
wanted, held Bill.

There was but one flaw. The broad expanse of shady
lawn was, he disgustedly perceived, marred at the moment
by the presence of humanity, for which in his exalted
condition he was in no mood. What he wanted was to
contemplate Nature, and, contemplating, to muse dreamily
upon Alice Coker. He resented the intrusion of an old
man with a white beard and a small boy in knicker-
bockers. These two blots on the landscape were strolling
up and down the middle of the nearest lawn, and they
killed the whole beauty of the scene for Bill. However,
at this moment they started to move towards the house
and presently the laburnum hid them and he was at
peace again. He gave himself up once more to thoughts
of Alice.

His reflections induced a sort of yeasty exhilaration,
akin to—and yet how infinitely purer than—that which
he had felt after the third of the powerful cocktails so
jovially blended yestreen by host Judson at his deplorable party. Of all the amazing things that could have
happened, that he should actually have cast off the
diffidence of months and asked her to marry him was
surely the most amazing. No, not quite the most amazing. That dizzy niche was undoubtedly reserved for the
astounding miracle that she should have received his
proposal in so kindly a spirit. True, she had not actually
committed herself to an engagement, but what of that ?
She had as good as said that, like some knight of old,
he had merely to perform his allotted task and she
would be his. What could be fairer than that ? Oh,
love ! Oh, fire !

His meditations were interrupted by the opening of
the door.

'Mr. Jasper Daly,' said the voice of Roberts.

From his post behind the curtains Bill heard a testy
snort.

'What's the sense of announcing me, my good man ?
There's nobody here.'

'Mr. West was here a moment ago, sir.'

'Eh ? What's he doing here ? '

Bill came out from his nook.

'Hallo, Uncle Jasper,' he said, and strove in vain to make his voice cordial. After what had passed between conscience and himself that morning the spectacle of Mr. Daly was an affliction. The thought that it was even remotely possible that he in any way resembled this wizened, greedy-looking little person, cut like a knife.

'Oh, there you are,' said Uncle Jasper grumpily, looking round with a pale reptilian eye.

'Mr. Paradene is engaged for the moment, sir,' said Roberts. 'He will be with you shortly. Shall I bring you a cocktail, sir?'

'No,' said Uncle Jasper. 'Never drink 'em.' He turned to Bill. 'What you doing here?'

'Roberts called up this morning to say that Uncle Cooley wanted to see me.'

'Eh? That's queer. I had a telegram yesterday myself saying the same thing.'

'Yes?' said Bill distantly. He turned to look at the bookshelves. He was a broadminded man and hoped that he could make allowance for the lowest of God's creatures, but really it was almost indecent that one who had only recently left the golden presence of Alice Coker should have to endure the society of this old crumb.

A moment later he had a fresh burden to bear.

'Mrs. Paradene-Kirby,' proclaimed Roberts in the doorway.

The arrival of his Cousin Evelyn deepened Bill's gloom. Even at the best of times she was hard to bear. A stout and voluminous woman in the early forties with eyes like blue poached eggs, she had never had the sense to discard the baby-talk which had so entertained the young men in her débutante days.

'Ooh, what a lot of g'ate big booful books!' said Cousin Evelyn, addressing, apparently, the small fluffy dog which she bore in her arms. 'Ickle Willie-dog must be a good boy and not bite the books, and maybe Uncle Cooley will give him a lovely cakie.'

'Mr. Otis Paradene and Master Cooley Paradene,' announced Roberts.

Bill now felt drearily resigned. To a man compelled

to be in the same room with Uncle Jasper and Cousin
Evelyn the additional discomfort of Otis and little Cooley
was negligible. Merely registering in his mind the opinion
that Uncle Otis was fatter than ever and that little
Cooley, a glistening child who had the appearance of
having recently been boiled, looked like something that
had come out of an egg, he turned to the bookshelves
again.

'Good God!' cried Uncle Jasper, staring at the new
arrivals. 'Is this Old Home Week? What you all doing
here?'

'Cooley and I were specially telegraphed for,' replied
Otis with dignity.

'Why, how puffickly 'straordinary!' said Cousin
Evelyn. 'So was I.'

'And he', said Uncle Jasper, plainly bewildered, jerking a thumb at Bill, 'had a 'phone-call this morning.
What's the idea, I wonder?'

Cooley, a silent child, said nothing. He stood picking
at the leather of an arm-chair with the nib of a pen,
agitated at regular intervals by a hiccough which sounded
like a diffident man starting to give three cheers for
something and losing his confidence after the first 'hip'.
The rest of the family went into debate on the problem.

'How strange Uncle Cooley asking us all to come here
together like this,' said Cousin Evelyn.

Uncle Otis glanced about him cautiously and lowered
his voice.

'If you ask me,' he said, 'there's something in the
wind. My idea is that Cooley probably realizes that he's
getting pretty old, so he's going to make settlements on
us all.'

'Oh, do you really, really fink so?' exclaimed Cousin
Evelyn rapturously. 'Of course, he *is* old, isn't he?
I always say that when a man has passed sixty he's
simply waiting for the end.'

'I was sixty-two last birthday,' said Uncle Otis coldly.

'Settlements?' said Uncle Jasper thoughtfully. He
scratched his chin. 'H'm. Not a bad idea. Save us a
lot of money on the inheritance-tax.'

Bill could endure no more. Admitting that he was a bloodsucker—and Conscience had made this fact uncomfortably clear—he had at any rate always been grateful for blood received. These ghouls seemed to have no decent human affections whatever.

'You people make me sick,' he snapped, wheeling round. 'You ought to be put in a lethal chamber or something. Always plotting and scheming after poor old Uncle Cooley's money——'

This unexpected assault from the rear created a certain consternation.

'The idea!' cried Cousin Evelyn.

'Impudent boy!' snarled Uncle Jasper.

Uncle Otis tapped the satirical vein.

'You've never had a penny from him, have you? Oh dear no!' said Uncle Otis.

Bill shot a proud withering glance in his direction.

'You know perfectly well that he gives me an allowance. And I'm ashamed now that I ever let him do it. When I see you gathering round him like a lot of vultures——'

'Vultures!' Cousin Evelyn drew herself up haughtily. 'I have never been so insulted in my life.'

'I withdraw the expression,' said Bill.

'Oh well,' said Cousin Evelyn, mollified.

'I should have said leeches.'

The Paradenes were never a really united family, but they united now in their attack upon this critic. The library echoed with indignant voices, all speaking at once. It was only when another voice added itself to the din that quiet was restored. It spoke, or rather shouted, from the doorway, and its effect on the brawlers was like that of a police-whistle on battlers in a public street.

'Shut up!' bellowed this voice.

It was a voice out of all proportion to the size of its owner. The man standing in the doorway was small and slight. He had a red clean-shaven face, a noble crop of stiff white hair, and he glared at the gathering through rimless pince-nez.

' A typical scene of Paradene family-life ! ' he observed
sardonically.

His appearance was the signal for another united movement on the part of the uncles and cousins. After a
moment of startled pause they surged joyfully towards
him.

' 'lo, Cooley. Glad to see you.' (Uncle Jasper.)

' Welcome home, Cooley.' (Uncle Otis.)

' You dear man, how well you look ! ' (Cousin Evelyn.)
Silence. (Little Cooley.)

More silence. (Bill.)

The little man in the doorway seemed unappreciative
of this deluge of affection. Now that he was no longer
speaking his mouth had set itself in a grim line, and the
gaze which he directed at the effusive throng through
his rimless glasses might have damped more observant
persons. The relatives resumed their exuberant greetings.

' I got your telegram, Cooley,' said Uncle Jasper.

' So did I,' said Cousin Evelyn. ' And darling ickle
Willie-dog and me both thought it so sweet of you to
invite us.'

' Hope you had a good time, Cooley,' said Uncle Otis.
' Lot of ground you've covered, eh ? '

' How did you like Japan ? ' asked Cousin Evelyn.
' I always say the Japanese are so cute.'

' We've missed you, Cooley,' said Uncle Jasper.

The taciturnity of his offspring in this time of geniality
and rejoicing seemed to jar upon Otis. He dragged little
Cooley away from the chair on which he was operating.

' Greet your dear uncle, boy.'

Little Cooley subjected that dispenser of largesse to the
stolid unwinking stare of boyhood.

' 'Ullo ! ' he said in a loud, deep voice, and relapsed
into a hiccough-punctuated silence again.

Uncle Jasper took the floor once more.

' Could you give me five minutes in private later on,
Cooley ? ' he said. ' I've a little matter to discuss.'

' I, too,' said Otis, ' have a small favour to ask on little
Cooley's behalf.'

Cousin Evelyn thrust herself forward.

'Give g'ate big Uncle Cooley a nice kiss, darling,' she cried, extending the fluffy dog with two plump arms in the general direction of the benefactor's face.

Mr. Paradene's reserve was not proof against this assault.

'Take him away!' he cried, backing hastily. 'So', he said, 'you aren't satisfied with sponging on me for yourselves, started hunting me with dogs, eh?'

Cousin Evelyn's face expressed astonishment and pain.

'Sponging, Uncle Cooley!'

Mr. Paradene snorted. His glasses fell off in his emotion and he replaced them irritably.

'Yes, sponging! I don't know if you've taught that damned dog of yours any tricks, Evelyn, but if he can sit up on his hind legs and beg he's qualified for full and honourable standing in this family. That's all any of you know how to do. I get back here after two months' travelling, and the first thing you all do is hound me for money.'

Sensation. Uncle Jasper scowled. Uncle Otis blinked. Cousin Evelyn drew herself up with the same hauteur which she had employed a short time before upon Bill.

'I am sure', she said, hurt, 'horrid old money is the last thing I ever think of.'

Mr. Paradene uttered an unpleasant laugh. Plainly he had come back from his travels in no mood of goodwill to all. This was a return to what might be called his early manner, that uncomfortable irritability which had made business negotiations with him so trying to the family in the days before he had been softened and mellowed by the collecting of old books.

'Yes,' he said bitterly, 'the last thing at night and the first thing in the morning. I tell you I'm sick of you all. Sick and tired. You're just a lot of—of——'

'Vultures,' prompted Bill helpfully.

'Vultures,' said Mr. Paradene. 'All so friendly and all so broke. For years and years you've done nothing but hang on to me like a crowd of——'

'Leeches,' murmured Bill. 'Leeches.'

'Leeches,' said Mr. Paradene. 'Ever since I can

remember I have been handing out money to you—
money, money, money. And you've absorbed it like so
many——'

'Pieces of blotting-paper,' said Bill.

Mr. Paradene glared at him.

'Shut up!' he thundered.

'All right, Uncle. Only trying to help.'

'And now', resumed Mr. Paradene, having disposed of
Bill, 'I want to tell you I've had enough of it. I'm
through. Done. Finished.' He eyed Bill dangerously
for a moment, as if waiting to see if he had any synonyms
to offer. 'I called you together to-day to make an
announcement. I have a little surprise for you all. You
are about to acquire a new relative.'

The family looked at each other with a wild surmise.

'A new relative!' echoed Otis pallidly.

'Don't tell me', whispered Uncle Jasper in a bedside
voice, 'that you are going to get married!'

'No,' said Mr. Paradene, 'I am not. The relative
I refer to is my adopted son. Horace! Come here,
Horace.'

Through the doorway there shuffled a small, knicker-
bockered figure.

'Horace,' said Mr. Paradene, 'let me present you to
the family!'

The boy stared for a moment in silence. He was a
sturdy, square-faced, freckled boy, with short sandy hair
and sardonic eyes. His gaze wandered from Uncle
Jasper to Uncle Otis, from little Cooley to Cousin Evelyn,
drinking them in.

'Is this the family?' he asked.

'This is the family.'

'Gee whistikers, what a bunch of prunes!' said the
boy with deep feeling.

§ 4

In the silence which followed this frank statement of
opinion, another figure added itself to the group. This
was a large and benevolent-looking man in a senatorial
frock-coat, whom Bill recognized by his white beard as

the boy Horace's companion on the lawn. Even from a
distance this person had seemed venerable : seen at close
range he achieved almost the impressiveness of a minor
prophet.　He was smiling a grandfatherly smile—the only
smile of any description, it may be mentioned, on view
in the room at that particular time : for a more joyless
gathering it would have been hard to find at any spot
in America where a funeral was not actually in progress.
Uncle Jasper had sagged like a drooping lily, Uncle Otis'
eyes were bulging, Cousin Evelyn gave the impression of
being about to burst. As for the boy Horace, the
realization of the sort of family he had allowed himself
to be adopted into seemed to have taken all the sunshine
out of his life.

He was the first to speak, and his words revealed what
was weighing upon his mind.

'Do I have to kiss them all ? ' he asked.

'You are certainly not going to kiss me,' said Uncle
Jasper definitely, waking from his stupor.　He rounded
on Mr. Paradene, puffing like a seal.　'What is the
meaning of this, Cooley ? ' he demanded.

Mr. Paradene waved a hand in the direction of the
new-comer.

'Professor Appleby will explain.'

The minor prophet bowed.　If he felt any embarrassment he did not show it.　His smile, as he spoke, was as
gentle and insinuating as ever.

'The announcement which my good friend Paradene——'

'How do you mean, your good friend Paradene ? '
inquired Uncle Jasper heatedly.　'How long have you
known him, I should like to know.'

'I met Professor Appleby on the train coming from San
Francisco,' said Mr. Paradene.　'It was he——'

'It was I ', said Professor Appleby, breaking gently in,
'who persuaded Mr. Paradene to adopt this little lad
here.'　He patted the boy's head and regarded his fermenting audience kindly.　'My name', he proceeded,
anticipating Uncle Jasper, who seemed about to speak,
'is possibly not familiar to you, but in certain circles, I

think I may assert with all modesty, my views on Eugenics are considered worthy of attention. Mr. Paradene, I am glad to say, has allowed himself to be enrolled among my disciples. I am a strong supporter of Mr. Bernard Shaw's views on the necessity of starting a new race, building it with the most perfect specimens of the old. Horace here is a boy of splendid physique, great intelligence, sterling character, and wonderful disposition. I hold—and I am glad to say that he agrees with me—that it is better for Mr. Paradene to devote his money to the rearing and training of such a boy than to spend it on relatives who —may I say—have little future and from whom he can expect—pardon me—but small returns. Mr. Paradene intends to found a family that looks forward instead of back. A family of—er—comers instead of a family of has-beens.'

The relatives gave tongue. All through this harangue they had been trying to speak, but Professor Appleby was not an easy man to interrupt. Now that he had paused they broke out, Cousin Evelyn in the lead, Uncles Jasper and Otis following close behind.

'I never heard of such a thing in my life!'

'The fellow's a dangerous crank!'

'Is it really possible that you intend to make this— this uncouth boy your heir rather than your own flesh and blood?'

Professor Appleby intervened gently.

'One must admit', he acknowledged, 'that Horace is at present a trifle unpolished. I quite see that. But what of it? A good tutor will remedy so small a defect in a few months. The main thing is that the little lad is superbly healthy and extremely intelligent.'

The little lad made no acknowledgement of these stately tributes. He was still wrestling with the matter nearest his heart.

'I will *not* kiss 'em,' he now announced firmly. 'No, sir! Not unless somebody makes me a bet about it. I once kissed a goat on a bet.'

Cousin Evelyn threw up her hands, causing Willie-dog to fall squashily to the floor.

'What an impossible little creature!'

'I think, my dear Paradene,' said Professor Appleby mildly, 'that, as the conversation seems to be becoming a little acrimonious, it would be best if I took Horace for a stroll in the grounds. It is not good for his growing mind to have to listen to these wranglings.'

Cousin Evelyn stiffened militantly.

'Pray do not let us disturb Horace in his *home*.' She attached a lead to Willie-dog's collar, and made for the door. 'Good-bye, Uncle Cooley,' she said, turning. 'I consider I have been grossly and heartlessly insulted.'

'Hey!' exclaimed Horace, pointing. 'You've dropped your knitting, and it's dragging.'

With one long, silent look of repulsion Cousin Evelyn gathered Willie-dog into her arms and passed out. Uncle Jasper stumped to the door.

'Good-bye, Jasper,' said Mr. Paradene.

'Good-bye. I shall immediately take steps to have a lunacy commission appointed to prevent you carrying out this mad scheme.'

'And I,' said Uncle Otis, 'I have only to say, Cooley, that the journey here has left me out of pocket to the extent of three dollars and seventy-nine cents. You shall hear from my lawyer.' He took little Cooley by the hand. 'Come, *John*,' he said bitterly. 'In future you will be known by your middle name.'

Horace observed this exodus with a sardonic eye.

'Say, I seem to be about as popular as a cold welsh rabbit!' he remarked.

Bill came forward amiably.

'I've got nothing against you, buddy,' he said. 'As far as I'm concerned, welcome to the family!'

'If that's the family,' said Horace, 'you're welcome to 'em yourself.'

And, placing his little hand in Professor Appleby's, he left the room. Mr. Paradene eyed Bill grimly.

'Well, William?'

'Well, Uncle Cooley?'

'I take it that you have gathered the fact that I do not intend to continue your allowance?'

' Yes, I gathered that.'

His young relative's calm seemed to embarrass Mr.
Paradene a little. He spoke almost defensively.

' Worst thing in the world for a boy your age to have
all the money he wants without earning it.'

' Exactly what I feel,' said Bill enthusiastically. ' What
I need is work. It's disgraceful ', he said warmly, ' that
a fellow of my ability and intelligence should not be
making a living for himself. Disgraceful ! '

Mr. Paradene's sanguine countenance took on a deeper
red.

' Very humorous ! ' he growled. ' Very humorous and
whimsical. But what you expect to gain by——'

' Humorous ! You don't imagine I was being funny,
do you ? '

' I thought you were trying to be.'

' Good Lord, no ! Why, I came here this afternoon
fully resolved to ask you for work.'

' You've taken your time getting round to it.'

' I didn't get a chance to mention it before.'

' And what sort of work do you suppose I can give
you ? '

' A job in the firm.'

' What as ? '

Bill's extremely slight knowledge of the ramifications
of the pulp and paper business made this a difficult
question to answer.

' Oh, anything,' he replied with valiant spaciousness.

' I could employ you at addressing envelopes at ten
dollars a week.'

' Fine ! ' said Bill. ' When do I start ? '

Mr. Paradene peered at him suspiciously through his
glasses.

' Are you serious ? '

' I should say so ! '

' Well, I'm bound to say ', observed Mr. Paradene after
a pause, seeming a trifle disconcerted, ' your attitude has
taken me a good deal by surprise.' Bill thought of
murmuring that his uncle did not realize the hidden
depths in his character, but decided not to. ' It's an odd

thing, William, but the only member of my family for whom I still retain some faint glimmer of affection is you.'

Bill smiled his gratification.

'And you', boomed Mr. Paradene, 'are an idle, worthless good-for-nothing. Still, I'll think it over. You're not going back to the city at once?'

'Not if you want me.'

'I may want you. Stay here for another hour or so.

'I'll go and stroll by the lake.'

Mr. Paradene scrutinized him keenly.

'I can't understand it,' he muttered. 'Wanting to work! I don't know what's come over you. I believe you're in love or something.'

§ 5

For about a quarter of an hour after the parting of uncle and nephew perfect peace brooded upon Mr. Cooley Paradene's house and grounds. At the end of that period Roberts, the butler, agreeably relaxed in his pantry over a cigar and a tale of desert love, was startled out of his tranquillity by the sound of a loud metallic crash, appearing to proceed from the drive immediately in front of the house. Laying down cigar and book, he bounded out to investigate.

It was not remarkable that there had been a certain amount of noise. Hard by one of the Colonial pillars which the architect had tacked on to Mr. Paradene's residence to make it more interesting lay the wreckage of a red two-seater car, and from the ruins of this there was now extricating itself a long figure in a dust-coat, revealed a moment later as a young man of homely appearance with a prominent, arched nose and plaintive green eyes.

'Hallo,' said this young man, spitting out gravel.

Roberts gazed at him in speechless astonishment. The wreck of the two-seater was such a very comprehensive wreck that it seemed hardly possible that any recent occupant of it could still be in one piece.

'Had a bit of a smash,' said the young man.

' An accident, sir ? ' gasped Roberts.

' If you think I did it on purpose,' said the young man, 'prove it! ' He surveyed the ruins interestedly. ' That car ', he said sagely after a prolonged scrutiny, ' will want a bit of fixing.'

' However did it happen, sir ? '

' Just one of those things that do happen. Coming up the drive at a pretty good lick when a bird settled in the middle of the fairway. Tried to avoid running over the beastly creature, and must have pulled the wheel too far round. Because all of a sudden I skidded a couple of yards, burst a tire, and hit the side of the house.'

' Good heavens, sir ! '

' It's all right,' said the young man reassuringly, ' I was coming here anyway.'

He discovered a deposit of gravel on his left eyebrow and removed it with a blue silk handkerchief.

' This is Mr. Paradene's house, isn't it ? ' he asked.

' Yes, sir.'

' Good. Is Mr. West here ? '

' Yes, sir.'

' That's fine. I wish you would tell him I want to see him. Coker's the name. Mr. Judson Coker.'

' Very good, sir.'

Something in the butler's manner, a certain placidity and lack of emotion, appeared to displease the young man. He frowned slightly.

' Judson Coker,' he repeated.

' Yes, sir.'

Judson looked at him expectantly.

' Name's familiar, eh ? '

' No, sir.'

' You don't mean to say you've never heard it before ? '

' Not to my knowledge, sir.'

' Good God ! ' said Judson.

He reached out a long arm and detained the receding Roberts by the simple process of seizing the tail of his coat. Even in his moods of normalcy there was never anything aloof and reticent about Judson Coker : he was always ready to chat anywhere at any time with any one :

and now his accident had brought about in him a still greater urge towards loquacity. Shocks affect different people in different ways. Judson's had left him bubblingly confidential.

'Do you mean to tell me honestly, as man to man,' he demanded incredulously, 'that you have never heard the name Judson Coker before?'

'No, sir.'

'Don't you ever read *Broadway Badinage*?'

'No, sir.'

'Nor *Town Gossip*?'

'No, sir.'

'Good God!'

The failure of this literacy test seemed to discourage Judson. He released the butler's coat-tail and relapsed into a moody silence.

'Shall I bring you a whisky-and-soda, sir?' asked Roberts. It had come home to him by this time that the young visitor was not wholly himself, and remorse swept over him. Long ere this, he told himself, he should have been playing the part of a kindly physician.

The question restored Judson's cheerfulness immediately. It was the sort of question that never failed to touch a chord in him.

'My dear old chap, you certainly may,' he responded with enthusiasm. 'I've been wondering when you were going to lead the conversation round to serious subjects. Mix it pretty strong, will you? Not too much water and about the amount of whisky that would make a rabbit bite a bulldog.'

'Yes, sir. Will you step inside the house?'

'No, thanks. Sit right here if it's all the same to you.'

The butler retired, to return a few moments later with the healing fluid. He found his young friend staring pensively at the sky.

'I say,' said Judson, breathing a satisfied sigh as he lowered his half-empty glass, 'coming back to that, you were kidding just now, weren't you, when you said you didn't know my name?'

'No, sir, I assure you.'

'Well, this is the most extraordinary thing I ever heard. You seem to know about as much of what's going on in the world as a hen does of tooth-powder. Didn't you ever hear of the Silks?'

'Silks, sir?'

'Yes. The Fifth Avenue Silks.'

'No, sir.'

'Good God! Very famous walking-club, you know. Used to assemble on Sunday mornings and parade up Fifth Avenue in silk pyjamas, silk socks, silk hats, and silk umbrellas in case it rained. You really never heard of them?'

'No, sir.'

'Well, I'm darned! Doesn't that just show you what Fame is! I shouldn't have thought there was an educated man in the country who hadn't heard of the Silks. We got a whole page in the Sunday magazine section of the *American* the week the police stopped us.'

'Indeed, sir?'

'We certainly did. With a picture of me. I founded the Silks, you know.'

'Yes, sir?'

'Oh yes. I've done a good deal of that sort of thing. I went up in an aeroplane once, scattering dollar-bills over the city. I'm surprised you've not heard of me.'

'We live very much out of the great world down here, sir.'

'I suppose you do,' said Judson, cheered by this solution. 'Yes, I guess that must be it. Quite likely you might not have heard of me if that's so. But you can take it from me that I've done a lot of things in my time. Clever things, you know, that made people talk. If it hadn't been for me I don't suppose the custom of wearing the handkerchief up the sleeve would ever have been known in America.'

'Indeed, sir?'

'I assure you.'

To some men these reminiscences might have proved enthralling, but not to one who, like Roberts, was in the middle of chapter eleven of *Sand and Passion* and wanted

to get back to it. He removed the decanter gently from
the reach of Judson's clutching hand, and tactfully
endeavoured to end the conversation.

'I made inquiries, sir, and was informed that Mr.
West was last seen walking in the direction of the lake.
Perhaps if you would care to look for him there—— ? '

Judson rose.

'You're perfectly right,' he said earnestly. 'Absolutely
right. I've got to see old Bill immediately. Came here
specially to see him. No time to lose. Which way is
this lake ? '

'Over yonder, sir. . . . Ah, but here is Mr. West,
coming up the drive.'

'Eh ? '

'Mr. West, sir. Coming up the drive.'

And, having indicated Bill's approaching figure to the
visitor, who was peering vaguely in every direction but
the right one, Roberts withdrew into the house. He
paused in the hall to telephone to the occupants of the
local garage that there was man's work for them to do
in Mr. Paradene's front garden, then returned to the
pantry and resumed his reading.

It was the unwelcome arrival on its grassy shores of
Professor Appleby and the boy Horace that had driven
Bill from the lake. He was in no mood for conversation,
for it had suddenly become plain to him that he had
got to do some very tense thinking. Events since his
coming to Mr. Paradene's house had marched so rapidly
that he had not had leisure until this moment to appreciate the problems and complexities with which life had
filled itself. Brooding now upon these, he could see that
Fate had manœuvred him into a position where he was
faced with the disagreeable necessity of being in two
places at one and the same time. Obviously, if his newly
displayed enthusiasm for toil was to carry weight, he
must enter Uncle Cooley's office immediately. Obviously,
also, if he entered Uncle Cooley's office immediately, he
could not take Judson off for a fishing-trip. If he went
off now upon a fishing-trip, what would Uncle Cooley

think of him ? And, conversely, if he cancelled the
fishing-trip, what would Alice Coker feel but that he had
failed her in her hour of need after buoying her up with
airy promises ? Bill staggered beneath the burden of the
problem, and was so preoccupied that Judson had to call
him twice before he heard him.

'Why, hallo, Judson ! What on earth are you doing
here ? '

He wrung the hand of the founder of the Fifth Avenue
Silks with considerable animation. Since their somewhat
distant talk on the telephone that morning his mental
attitude towards Judson had changed a good deal. In
his capacity of practically accepted suitor of sister Alice,
Bill had taken on a sort of large benevolence towards her
entire family. He found himself glowing with brotherly
affection for Judson and even conscious of a certain timid
desire to fraternize with the redoubtable J. Birdsey.

He massaged Judson's shoulder lovingly. Quite suddenly it had come to him that the problem which had
been weighing him down was no problem at all. He
had been mistaken in supposing that two alternatives
of action presented themselves. Now that the sudden
spectacle of Judson had, so to speak, stressed the Coker
motif in the rhythm of life, he saw clearly that there was
only one course for him to pursue. At whatever cost to
himself and his financial future he must keep faith with
Alice. The fishing-trip was on, the spectacular entry into
the pulp and paper business off.

'Hallo, Bill o' man,' said Judson. ' Just the fellow I
want to see. As a matter of fact, I came out here specially
to see you. Had a bit of a smash,' he added, indicating
the debris.

'Good heavens ! ' Bill quivered with a cold dismay at
the thought of Her brother having motor-smashes. ' You
aren't hurt ? '

'No. Just joggled a bit. Say, listen, Bill, Alice has
been tipping me off about what's happened at home.
There's no mistake about this fishing-trip, is there ?
Because if there is I'm sunk. A week at the old lady's
would finish me.'

'That's all right.' Bill patted his shoulder. 'I promised Alice, and that's enough. The thing's settled.' Bill hesitated blushfully for a moment. 'Judson, old man,' he went on, his voice trembling, 'I asked her to be my wife.'

'Breakfast every morning at seven-thirty, if you can believe it,' said Judson. 'And working on the farm all day.'

'To be my wife,' repeated Bill in a slightly louder tone.

'And if there's one thing that gives me the pip,' said Judson, 'it's messing about with a bunch of pigs and chickens.'

'I asked Alice to marry me.'

'And then family prayers, you know, and hymns and things. I couldn't stand it, o' man, simply couldn't stand it.'

'She wouldn't give me a definite answer.'

'Who wouldn't ? '

'Alice.'

'What about ? '

Bill's attitude of general benevolence towards the Coker family began to undergo a slight modification. Some of its members, he felt, could be a little trying at times.

'I asked your sister Alice to marry me,' he said coldly. 'But she wouldn't actually promise.'

'Well, that's fine,' said Judson. 'I mean, you can get out of it all right, what ? '

Revolted as Bill was—and he gazed at his friend with a chilly loathing which might have wounded a more sensitive man—his determination was not weakened. Judson might have rather less soul than a particularly unspiritual wart-hog, but he still remained Alice's brother.

'Wait here,' he said stiffly. 'I must go and see my uncle.'

'Why ? '

'To tell him about this fishing-trip.'

'Does he want to come, too ? ' asked Judson, perplexed.

'He wants me to go to work in his office at once. And I must tell him that it will have to be postponed.'

Mr. Paradene had left the study when Bill got there,

but familiarity with his habits told Bill where to look.
He found him in the library, perilously perched upon
a long ladder, browsing on a volume which he had
extracted from an upper shelf.

'Uncle Cooley.'

Mr. Paradene gazed down from the heights. He
replaced the book and descended.

'I wanted to see you, William,' he said. 'Sit down.
I was just going to ring for Roberts to tell you to come
here.' He lowered himself into the deep chair which had
been the object of little Cooley's recent attentions. 'I
have a suggestion to make.'

'What I wanted to say——'

'Shut up!' said Mr. Paradene.

Bill subsided. His uncle scrutinized him closely.
There was something appraising in his glance.

'I wonder if you have any sense at all,' he said.

'I——'

'Shut up!' said Mr. Paradene.

He sniffed menacingly. Bill began to wish that he
had some better news for this fiery little man than the
information that he proposed to abandon the idea of
work and go fishing.

'You've always been bone-idle,' resumed Mr. Paradene,
'like all the rest of the family. But there's no knowing
whether you might not show some action if you were put
to it. How would you like me to continue your allowance
for another three months or so?'

'Very much,' said Bill.

'Mind you, you'd have to do something to earn it.'

'Certainly,' agreed Bill. 'After I come back from this
fishing——'

'I can't go myself,' said Mr. Paradene meditatively,
'and I ought to send some one. There's something wrong
somewhere.'

'You see——'

'Shut up! Don't interrupt! This is the position.
The returns of my London branch aren't at all satisfactory.
Haven't been for a long time. Can't make out why—
my manager there struck me as a very shrewd fellow.

Still, there's no getting away from it, the profits have been falling off badly. I'm going to send you to London, William, to look into things.'

' London ? ' said Bill blankly.

' Exactly.'

' When do you want me to go ? '

' At once.'

' But——'

' You're wondering ', said Mr. Paradene, placing an erroneous construction on his nephew's hesitation, ' just exactly what I expect you to do when you get to London. Well, frankly, I don't know myself, and I don't quite know why I'm sending you. I suppose it's just with the faint hope of discovering whether you have any intelligence at all. I certainly don't expect you to solve a mystery which has been puzzling a man like Slingsby for two years——'

' Slingsby ? '

' Wilfrid Slingsby, my London manager. Very capable man. I say I don't expect you to go straight over there and put your finger on the solution of a problem that has baffled a man like Slingsby. All I feel is that, if you keep your eyes open and try to learn something about the business and take an interest in its management, you may happen by luck to blunder on some suggestion which, however foolish in itself, might possibly give Slingsby an idea which would put him on the right track.'

' I see,' said Bill. The estimate of his potentialities as factor in solving the firm's little difficulties was not a flattering one, but he had to admit that it was probably more or less correct.

' It'll be good training for you. You can go and see Slingsby and he can tell you something about the business. That will all help ', said Mr. Paradene with a chuckle, ' when you come back here and start addressing envelopes.'

Bill hesitated.

' I'd like to go, Uncle Cooley——

' There's a boat on Saturday.'

'I wonder if I could have half an hour to think it over?'

'Think it over!' Mr. Paradene swelled ominously. 'What do you mean, think it over? Do you understand that I am offering you——'

'Oh yes, I quite see that—it's only—— Look here, let me just pop downstairs and speak to a fellow.'

'What are you talking about?' demanded Mr. Paradene warmly. 'Why downstairs? What fellow? You're gibbering.'

He would have spoken further, but Bill was already at the door. With a deprecating smile in his uncle's direction, intended to convey the message that all would come right in the future, he edged out of the room.

'Judson,' he said, reaching the hall and looking about him.

He perceived that his friend was engaged at the telephone.

'Half a minute,' said Judson into the receiver. 'Here's Bill West. Just talking to Alice,' he explained over his shoulder. 'Father's come home and he says it's all right about that trip.'

'Ask her to ask him if it will be as good if I take you over to London instead,' said Bill hurriedly. 'My uncle wants me to go over there at once.'

'London?' Judson shook his head mournfully. 'Not a chance! My dear old chap, you're missing the whole point of this business. The idea is to dump me somewhere where I can't——'

'Tell her to tell him', urged Bill feverishly, 'that I will pledge my solemn word that you shan't have a cent of money or a drop of drink from the time you start to the day you get back. Say you'll be just as safe in London with me as——'

Judson did not permit him to finish the sentence.

'Genius!' murmured Judson, a smile of infinite joy irradiating his face. 'Absolute genius! I should never have had the gall to think up anything like that.' His face clouded again. 'I doubt if it'll work, though. Father's not a chump, you know. Still, I'll try it.'

There was a telephonic interval, at the end of which Judson relaxed and reported progress.

'She's gone to ask him. But I doubt, I very much doubt—— Hallo?' He turned to the telephone again and listened for a space. He handed the instrument to Bill. 'She wants to speak to you.'

Bill took the telephone with trembling hands.

'Yes?' he said devoutly. Impossible to say anything as coarsely abrupt as 'Hallo?'

The musical voice of Alice Coker trilled at the other end of the wire.

'Who is that?'

'It's me. Er—Bill.'

'Oh, Mr. West,' said Alice, 'I've been speaking to father about Judson going to London with you.'

'Yes?'

'He was very much against it at first, but when I explained to him that you would take such great care of Juddy——'

'Oh, I will! I will!'

'You really will see that he has no money at all?'

'Not a cent.'

'And nothing to drink?'

'Not a drop.'

'Very well, then, he may go. Thank you so much, Mr. West.'

Bill was beginning to try to put into neat phrases the joy he felt at the thought of doing the least service for her, but a distant click told him that his eloquence would be wasted. He hung up the receiver emotionally.

'Well?' said Judson anxiously.

'It's all right.'

Judson uttered a brief whoop of ecstasy.

'Bill, you're a marvel. The way you pulled that stuff about not letting me have any money! As solemn as a what-d'you-call-it! That was what turned the scale. As quick a bit of thinking as I ever struck,' said Judson with honest admiration. 'Gosh, what a time we'll have in London! There's a place I've always wanted to see. All those historic spots you read about in the English

novels, you know—Romano's, the Savoy bar and all that.
Bill o' man, we'll paint that good old city bright scarlet
from end to end.'

It became apparent to the horrified Bill that young
Mr. Coker had got an entirely wrong angle on the situation. Only too plainly, it was shown by his remarks,
the divine Alice's deplorable brother had mistaken his
recent promises for mere persiflage, evidently holding
them to be nothing but part of a justifiable ruse to assist a
pal. He choked.

'Do you really think', he said slowly, struggling with
his feelings, 'that I would deceive that sweet girl?'

'You betcher!' said Judson sunnily.

For a long moment Bill eyed him in cold silence. Then,
still without speaking, he strode off up the stairs to
inform Mr. Paradene that his services were at his disposal.

§ 6

Down on the lawn that ran beside the lake Professor
Appleby paced to and fro with the boy Horace. His
white head was bent, and one viewing them from afar
would have said that the venerable old man was whispering sage counsel into his young friend's ears—words of
wisdom designed to shape and guide his future life. And
so he was.

'Now listen to me, kid,' he was saying, 'and get this
into your nut. I've got you in good and solid in this
house, and now it's up to you. You don't want to hang
around here picking daisies. A nice quick clean-up,
that's what we want from you, young man.'

The boy nodded briefly. The minor prophet continued.

'It's got to be an inside job, of course, but I'll have
Joe the Dip get in touch with you and stand by in case
you need him. Not that the party's likely to get rough
if you only do your end of the thing without bungling it.
Still, it's as well to have Joe handy. So keep an eye out
for him.'

'Sure.'

'And don't go getting lazy just because you're in soft
in a swell home where you'll probably have lots of good

things to eat. That's the trouble with you—you think too much of your stomach. If you were left to yourself you'd lie back in a chair stuffing yourself for ever, without giving a thought to the rest of the gang. You can't run a business that way. Just remember that we're waiting outside and that what we want is quick action.'

'It's no good rushing me,' protested Horace. 'I mayn't be able to do anything for weeks. Got to fix up a house-party, haven't I, so there'll be lots of women around with joolry ? '

Professor Appleby clutched his white beard in anguish.

'Gosh darn it ! ' he moaned. 'Are you really so bone-headed or are you just pretending ? Haven't I told you a dozen times that we aren't after jewels this time ? You don't suppose a hermit like old Paradene gives house-parties to women, do you ? Didn't I tell you till I was hoarse that what we want is those books of his ? '

'I thought you were kidding,' pleaded Horace. 'What's the use of a bunch of books ? '

'If you'll just do as you're told and not try to start thinking for yourself', said Professor Appleby severely, 'we may get somewhere. Those books may not look good to a little runt like you who doesn't think of anything outside of what's for dinner, but let me tell you that there isn't one of them that isn't worth four figures, and lots of them are worth five.'

'That so ? ' said Horace, impressed.

'It certainly is. And what you've got to do is to snoop around and find out just where the best of them are kept and then get away with them. See ? '

'Sure.'

'It oughtn't to be hard,' said Professor Appleby. 'You've got the run of the place. Everything's certainly working nice and smooth. The old man swallowed those references of yours, hook, line and sinker.'

'Well, why wouldn't he ? Gee ! ' said Horace with feeling. 'When I think of all the Sunday Schools I've had to go to to get 'em ! '

Professor Appleby frowned. The boy's tone offended him.

'Horace,' he said chidingly, 'you must not speak in that way. If you're going to say a single word against your Sunday School I just won't listen! Do you get me, you little shrimp, or have I got to clump you one on the side of the bean?'

'I get you,' said Horace.

CHAPTER THREE

FLICK PAYS A CALL

§ I

THERE is something about the manner in which
Spring comes to England which reminds one of
the overtures of a diffident puppy trying to make friends.
It takes a deprecating step forward, scuttles away in a
panic, steals timorously back and finally, gaining confidence, makes a tumultuous and joyful rush. The pleasant
afternoon which had lured Mr. Sinclair Hammond out to
sit in his garden had been followed by a series of those
discouraging April days when the sun shines feebly and
spasmodically, easily discouraged by any blustering cloud
that swaggers across its path, and chilly showers lie in
wait for those who venture out without an umbrella.
But now, two weeks later, a morning had arrived which
might have belonged to June. A warm breeze blew lan-
guidly from the west and the sun shone royally on a
grateful world; so that even Wimbledon Common,
though still retaining something of that brooding air
which never completely leaves large spaces of public
ground on which the proletariat may at any moment
scatter paper bags, achieved quite a cheerful aspect :
and the garden of Holly House, across the road from
the Common, was practically a Paradise.

So, at least, it seemed to Flick, strolling on the lawn.
The trees that fringed the wall were a green mist of
young leaves : a snow of appleblossom covered the turf
of the little orchard : daffodils nodded their golden heads
on every side. There was a heartening smell of new-
turned earth, and the air was filled with mingled noises,
ranging from the silver bubbling of a thrush in the shrub-

bery to the distant contralto of Mrs. Frances Hammond
taking a conscientious singing-lesson in the drawing-room.
And such was the magic of the day that not even this
last manifestation of Spring fever could quell Flick's
mood of ecstasy.

She was trying now to analyse her feelings. Why was
every nerve in her body vibrating with a sort of raptur-
ous excitement ? Certainly not because at four-thirty
that afternoon she was to call at Roderick's office in
Tilbury House and be taken by him to tea at Claridge's.
She was fond of Roderick, but, whatever his merits, the
thought of seeing him was not enough to intoxicate any
girl, even though she and he might be engaged to be
married. No, what was thrilling her, she decided, was
just that vague feeling of something nice about to happen
which comes to the young at this season of the year.
We grey-beards, who have been deceived so often by the
whisper of Spring, are proof against the wheedlings of an
April morning. We know that there is nothing wonderful lurking round the corner and consequently decline to
be lured into false anticipations of joy. But at twenty-
one it is different, and Flick Sheridan had that feeling.

She paused in her walk to watch the goldfish in their
cement-bottomed pool. The breeze was stronger now,
and it ruffled the surface of the water, so that the goldfish had for the moment a sort of syncopated appearance.
The breeze became stronger still and shifted from west
to east : and, as if Spring had repented of its effusive-
ness, the air grew chilly. The white clouds which had
been flitting across the face of the sun began to bank
themselves. Flick turned towards the house to get a
wrap : and as she did so there came through the open
window of Mr. Hammond's study on the ground floor a
cry suggestive of dismay and wrath, followed instantly
by the appearance of papers, which took to themselves
wings and fluttered sportively about Flick's head. Mr.
Hammond came into sight, framed in the window, his
hair ruffled and a splash of ink on his forehead.

' Ass of a maid opened the door and started a draught.
Pick 'em up, there's a good girl.'

Flick collected the papers. She handed them in through the window. Mr. Hammond vanished, and simultaneously the weather did another of its lightning changes. The wind dropped, the sun shone out stronger than ever, and Flick, abandoning all ideas of wraps, returned to her stroll. She had just reached the lawn again when she became aware of a derelict piece of paper, overlooked in her recent gleaning. It was gambolling over the turf in the direction of the pool, hotly pursued by Bob, the Sealyham terrier, who was obviously under the impression that he had before him one of the birds which he spent his life in chasing.

The paper dodged and doubled like a live thing. It paused till Bob was almost on it, then playfully skipped away. Finally, finding that Bob stuck to the chase, it took the only way out and dived into the pool. Bob, hovering uncertainly on the brink, decided to let the matter rest. He turned and trotted off into the bushes. A last puff of wind from the expiring breeze attached the paper to a lily-pad, and Flick, angling with a rake, was enabled to retrieve it. She was just reaching down to lift it ashore when her eyes fell on the opening words :

> *Sir.*
>
> *If you would save a human life—*

Flick, who had nice views about the sanctity of other people's letters, read no further. But her heart was beating quickly as she raced across the lawn towards Mr. Hammond's study.

' Uncle Sinclair ! '

There was an exclamation of patient anguish on the other side of the window. Mr. Hammond was having a little difficulty with his article for the *Fortnightly* on ' Crawshaw and Francis Thompson, a Comparison and a Contrast ' ; and this was the third time he had been interrupted since breakfast.

' Well ? ' The window framed him once more, and his severity diminished. ' Oh, it's you, Flick ? Will you kindly get right out of here, young woman, and give a man a chance to work. Go and make daisy-chains.'

' But, Uncle Sinclair, it's frightfully important.' She

held up the letter. ' I couldn't help reading the first line. It says something about saving a human life. I thought you ought to have it at once.'

Mr. Hammond reached behind him cautiously. The next moment a flannel pen-wiper sailed through the air and hit Flick between her earnest eyes.

' Good shot ! ' crowed Mr. Hammond exultantly. ' That'll teach you to come interrupting me about begging-letters in the middle of my work.'

' But . . .'

' I remember the letter. I get dozens of them. They all say that the bed will be sold from under some poor dying woman unless one pound seven shillings and three-pence is sent by return of post, and they are all written by nasty grubby men who need a shave. Incidentally, if you ever set up in the begging-letter business, Flick, never ask for any round sum like five pounds. Nobody ever gives five pounds, but the world is full of asses who will tumble over themselves to send one pound seven and three or two pounds eleven and fivepence.'

' But, Uncle Sinclair, how do you know ? ' persisted Flick with the resolute perseverance of her sex.

' Because I've looked into the thing. When I have leisure I will give you some statistics from the Charity Organization. They prove that nine-tenths of the beg-ing-letters which go out are written by professionals, who make an excellent living at it. Now leave me, child, first restoring to me that pen-wiper. If I hear from you again before lunch, I will brain you with the poker.'

' But this may be one of the really genuine. . . .'

' It isn't.'

' How do you know ? '

' Instinct. Away with you to your childish pastimes.'

' Do you mind if I read it ? '

' Frame it if you like. And don't forget what I said about that poker. I am a desperate man.'

Flick returned to the lawn. She read the letter as she walked, and the sun, though it was doing its honest best now to pretend that midsummer had arrived, seemed to fade out of the sky. A chill desolation stalked through the pleasant garden.   It was all very well for Uncle Sinclair to talk like that, but how could he *know*?   This was the first begging-letter which had ever come Flick's way, and she drank it in with that agonized sinking of the heart which begging-letter-writers hope for so earnestly in their clients and so rarely bring out.   To Flick every word of it rang true, and she shivered with sheer misery at the thought that such things could be on a planet which ten minutes before had seemed filled to overflowing with pure happiness.

The letter was not that of a stylist, but it told a story. Written by a Mrs. Matilda Pawle, of Number 9, Marmont Mansions, Battersea, it raised the curtain on a world of whose very existence Flick had until now been but dimly aware—a world of sickness and despair, of rent overdue, of wolves and landlords howling about the door.   Flick, as she read it, sickened with sympathetic horror, and the gong for lunch, which reached her as she paced the lawn in agony of spirit, seemed like the cry of a mocking fiend. Lunch !   Hot, well-cooked meats . . . toothsome salads . . . fruit . . . potatoes . . . all the bread you wanted . . . and Mrs. Matilda Pawle, of 9, Marmont Mansions, Battersea, so reduced by Fate that only three pounds sixteen and fourpence, sent promptly, could save her from the abyss !

Suddenly, as if a voice—that of Mrs. Pawle, possibly— had spoken in her ear, Flick remembered that in her bedroom upstairs she had certain gew-gaws—rings, necklaces, a brooch . . .

She walked to the house, and half-way there espied the corduroy trouser-seat of John, the gardener.   He was bending over a flower-bed, a worthy and amiable fellow with whom she had become almost chummy in February in connection with a matter of bulbs.

'Them tulips', observed John, not without a certain paternal pride, hoisting himself up at the sound of her approach, ''ll be out now before you know where you are, miss.'

An hour ago Flick would have plunged light-heartedly into chatter about tulips.   But not now.   Tulips, once

of absorbing interest to her, had ceased to grip. Mrs.
Pawle's pneumonia had put them where they belonged,
among the lesser things of life.

' John,' said Flick, ' have you ever pawned anything ? '

John's manner took on a certain wariness. His story
about that missing pair of shears back in July had been
well received and he had assumed that the matter was
closed. But you never knew in this world, for the world
is full of scandal-mongers who spread tales about honest
men. To gain time he hitched up his corduroys and
gazed woodenly at an aeroplane which purred in the blue
like a distant cat. He was about to secure a further
respite by stating that there had been none of them things
when he was a boy, but Flick spared him the necessity.

' I was reading in a book about somebody pawning
something, and I wondered how they did it.'

John was relieved. Now that he was assured that the
subject was purely academic, he could approach it with
an expert's ease. He proceeded to do so, and a few
minutes later Flick was able to go in to lunch a mistress
of the procedure of what gardener John described as
' putting up the spout ' or, more briefly, ' popping '.

The lunch was just as well cooked and appetizing as
Flick had supposed it would be. But it did not turn to
ashes in her mouth. She had found a way.

§ 2

Something of the effervescing happiness which, until
the intrusion of Mrs. Matilda Pawle, had animated Flick
in her garden at Wimbledon, was making life a thing of
joy and hope for Bill West at the hour of one that same
afternoon as he strode buoyantly along Piccadilly—for
who would ride in cabs or buses on such a day ?—to keep
a tryst at Mario's Restaurant with Mr. Wilfrid Slingsby,
the London manager of the Paradene Pulp-Paper Company of New York. It was not only the weather that
seemed to Bill to have lost its bleakness, but life itself.
This morning, for the first time since their departure
from America two weeks ago, Judson Coker had emerged
from his black cloud of gloom and shown a disposition to

amiability. And in a small furnished flat it is amazing what a difference a touch of cheerfulness can make in the atmosphere.

Judson, there is no disguising, had taken Bill's disciplinary measures hardly. From a point coinciding with the passing of the three-mile limit by the steamship *Aquitania* he had run through the gamut of the emotions, from blank incredulity to stunned despair. The negativing of his suggestion—made almost before the *Aquitania* had got her stern across that vital spot in the ocean— that Bill and he should adjourn to the smoking-room for a small one, had struck him at first as rich comedy. Bill, he had felt, was ever a kidder. Whimsical of him to keep up with a perfectly straight face that farce of not letting a fellow have money or liquid nourishment. But towards the middle of the afternoon Judson's view began to be that, while a joke was a joke and he as fond of a laugh as any one, there was such a thing as overdoing a jest, running it to death : and when Bill firmly declined to collaborate with him in that ante-dinner cocktail without which, as everybody knows, food can hardly be taken into the system, Tragedy definitely reared its ugly head. From that moment shades of the prison-house began to close about the growing boy, so to speak, and our gentle pen must decline to pursue the subject in detail. It is enough to say that Judson Coker arrived in London a soured man, and it had required many a glance at Alice's photographs to console Bill for having to pass the days in the sufferer's society. Apart from anything else, Judson's piteous appeals for even the smallest sum of money would have wrung the toughest heart ; and life had been but a dreary affair in the flat which Bill, after two days' experience of expensive hotels, had rented furnished for three months.

But to-day things seemed different. Whether it was the influence of Spring, or whether Judson's abused liver had at last begun to pick up a bit, Bill could not say : but the fact remained that the teetotaller appeared noticeably more cheery. Twice Bill had caught him smiling to himself, and at breakfast that morning, for the first time in thirteen days, he had actually laughed. A short, sad, rasping laugh, to evoke which it had been necessary for the maid-of-all-work to trip over the carpet and spill a pint of coffee down Bill's legs—but still a laugh. This, thought Bill, was encouraging. Things, he felt, were looking up.

This lunch with Mr. Slingsby was the outcome of one visit to the office and two telephone conversations. Mr. Slingsby may have been letting the profits of the business fall off, but he certainly appeared to be no loafer. Time was money with him, and it was only now, five days after Bill had presented himself and announced his identity, that he had been able to find leisure for a sustained conversation.

Even in their brief acquaintance Mr. Slingsby had rather overpowered Bill. In the few moments which the manager had been able to give over to casual chat his personality had made a deep impression on the young man. Wilfrid Slingsby was one of those shiny, breezy, forceful, nattily tailored men of any age from forty to fifty, who always look as if they had just had a shave and would be needing another in the next few hours. A dark jowl was Mr. Slingsby's, perfectly setting off his flashing smile.

His smile flashed out as Bill entered the lobby of the restaurant. He came forward with outstretched hand, radiating efficiency and goodwill, and once more Bill had the feeling that this man's personality was something out of the common. He felt in his presence like a child, and what is more, like a child with flat feet and one lobe of its brain missing.

Mr. Slingsby led the way into the restaurant, sat down at his reserved table, urged Bill into another chair, straightened his tie and called for the waiter. And it then became apparent that he was one of those dominant men who have a short way with waiters. He addressed the waiter in a strong, carrying voice. He heckled the waiter. He bullied the waiter. Until finally another waiter suddenly appeared, and the first one flickered

away and was seen no more. Next morning, one felt,
a body in dress-clothes with a spot on the shirt-front
would be taken out of the Thames. Banished from Mr.
Slingsby's presence, the man had seemed to feel his disgrace acutely.

'Yessir?' said the second waiter briskly. He had a
pencil and a note-book, which the other had lacked. In
fact, the more one thinks the thing over, the more convinced one becomes that the first waiter was—in the
truer and deeper meaning of the word—no waiter at all,
but merely one of those underlings whose bolt is shot
when they have breathed down your neck and put a
plate of rolls on the table. This new arrival was made of
sterner stuff altogether, and Mr. Slingsby, seeming to
recognize a kindred spirit, became more cordial. He even
deigned to ask the new-comer's advice. In short, by the
time the ordering was concluded and the *hors d'œuvres*
on the table, a delightful spirit of *camaraderie* prevailed,
and Mr. Slingsby had so far relaxed from his early austerity
as to tell a funny story about an Irishman. This com-
pleted and the fish having arrived, he embarked on genial
conversation.

'So you're the old man's nephew, eh?' said Mr.
Slingsby. 'Great old boy. And what have you been
doing with yourself since you arrived?'

Bill related the simple annals of his first week in London,
touched on Judson, mentioned two theatrical performances
of a musical nature which he had attended.

'Oh, so you've seen The Girl In Pink Pyjamas?' said
Mr. Slingsby, interested. 'How did you like it? Think
it would go in New York? I own part of that show,
you know.'

Bill's feeling of belonging to a lesser order of creation
became more marked. He had not Judson's airy
familiarity with the theatrical world, and men who owned
parts of shows were personages to him.

'Really?' he said.

'Oh yes,' said Mr. Slingsby carelessly. 'I do quite a
lot of that sort of thing.' He nodded in friendly fashion
at a passing exquisite. 'Renfrew,' he explained. 'He's

starring in It Pays to Flirt, at the Regent. You ought
to go and see that. Good show. I'm sorry I didn't
take a part of it when they offered it to me. But somehow or other the script didn't seem to read right. One
misses these chances.'

Bill was perplexed. For a manager of the London
branch of one of the largest firms in America, pulp-paper
seemed to mean very little in Mr. Slingsby's life. He
began to think that the solution of the mystery of the
fallen-off profits might be simpler than Uncle Cooley had
supposed. Something akin to dislike of this splendid
person crept over him. Mr. Slingsby made him feel
inferior, and Bill was not fond of feeling inferior. And
what right, Bill asked himself with some warmth, had
fellows to make fellows feel inferior when fellows—the
first fellows—couldn't handle an excellent business in such
a manner as to make it show a decent profit ? He looked
critically across the table at Mr. Slingsby. Yes, he disliked the man. And if the bounder continued trying to
impress him with his beastly theatrical ventures and his
rotten theatrical friends he ran a grave risk of being told
precisely where he got off.

In fact, decided Bill—no time like the present—he
would give him this information now. True, he was the
man's guest and full of his *hors d'œuvres* and meat, but
as these doubtless would be charged up to the office no
nice scruples need restrain him.

'Uncle Cooley,' he said, changing the subject with an
abruptness perhaps a trifle brusque, for Mr. Slingsby had
just been commenting—apropos of a spectacular young
lady who had recently passed the table—on chorus-girls,
their morals, and the opportunities a man financially
interested in the theatre had of enjoying their stimulating
society, 'Uncle Cooley ', said Bill coldly, now thoroughly
convinced that his dislike amounted to positive loathing,
'asked me while I was over here to try and find out why
the profits on the London end of the business had fallen
off so badly. He's very worried about it.'

There was a pause. The introduction of the cold business
note seemed to have stunned Mr. Slingsby. He looked

surprised, hurt, astonished, wounded, pained, amazed and cut to the quick.

'What!' he cried, and his demeanour was that of one who has been stabbed in the back by a trusted friend. For half an hour he had been honouring Bill with his cordial geniality, and now this had happened. You could see that Wilfrid Slingsby was shaken. But he pulled himself together. He laughed. He laughed nastily.

'Profits fallen off?' he said, regarding Bill unfavourably. He did not try to conceal his opinion that Bill, a brief while before the companion of his revels, now ranked in his esteem about on a level with the first waiter. 'If you ask me, I should say your uncle ought to be glad there are any profits at all. Let me tell you that there aren't many men in my position who could show such a good balance-sheet. Not many, believe me.' He glowered darkly at Bill. 'You understand the pulp and paper business thoroughly, of course?'

'No,' said Bill shortly. It was just the sort of question this sort of man would ask. Bitter regret for a mis-spent youth surged through him. If only he had employed those wasted hours in learning all about pulp-paper—and what more entertaining subject could a young man in the springtime of life find for his attention?—he would now be in a position to cope with this Slingsby. As it was, he feared that Slingsby was going to trample on him.

His surmise was correct. Mr. Slingsby trampled all over him.

'Ah,' said that gentleman with odious superiority. 'In that case it is hardly worth while for me to go into the matter. Still, I will try to put it in the simplest nursery language.'

Mr. Slingsby's idea of putting it in simple nursery language was to pour over Bill a flood of verbiage about labour conditions, rates of exchange, and economic practicabilities which had his young friend gasping like a fish before he had spoken ten words. No wood, entering Mr. Paradene's paper-factory, had ever been more well and truly reduced to pulp than was Bill at the end of fifteen

minutes. And when, after taking a quick breath at the
conclusion of this period, his host showed signs of beginning chapter two, he could endure no more. He realized
that he was retiring in disorder and leaving the field to
the enemy, but that could not be helped. Glancing at
his watch, he muttered an apology and rose. Mr. Slingsby,
restored to his old cheery self by this triumph, became
instantly cordial once more.

' Got to go ? ' he said. ' Perhaps I ought to be moving
myself.'

He called for the bill, signed it in a bold hand, hurled
silver on the plate, nodded like a monarch in acknowledgement of the waiter's charmed gratitude, and led the
way out.

' Coming my way ? '

' I think I'll be getting back to my flat. I have some
letters to write.'

' Why not go to your club ? '

' I don't belong to any clubs in London.'

' Hope you're comfortable in this flat of yours. If you
feel like moving, mention my name at the Regal and they'll
treat you right.'

' I have taken the flat for three months,' said Bill,
resolved that nothing would ever induce him to mention
this man's name anywhere.

' Where are you living ? '

' Battersea. Marmont Mansions.'

Mr. Slingsby raised his black eyebrows.

' Battersea ? Why on earth do you want to go and
bury yourself in a hole like Battersea ? '

' Because it's cheap,' said Bill between set teeth.

' Taxi ! ' said Mr. Slingsby, scorning to plunge any
deeper into the degrading subject. And bowled swiftly
away like a Roman emperor going somewhere in his
chariot.

So strangely is human nature constituted that it was
this unconcealed contempt on the other's part for his
little nook that definitely set the seal on Bill's dislike.
The captain-of-industry manner, the theatrical swank, the

lecture on pulp-paper—all these things he might have for-
given. It would not have been easy, but he might have
done it. But this was unpardonable. Be it never so
merely rented furnished, a man's little home is his little
home, and if he is a man of spirit, he resents fellows with
blue chins sneering at it. By the time Bill put his latchkey in the door of Number 9, Marmont Mansions, he was
in a state of such nervous hostility to Mr. Slingsby as
only tobacco and the ungirt loin could soothe. He
removed his coat, his collar, his tie and his shoes ; lit a
pipe ; and settled down on the sofa in the sitting-room.
He brooded sullenly.

' Darned gasbag ! '

He brooded further.

' Pulling all that stuff ! '

He brooded yet again.

' I believe the man's a crook. And I'm going to keep
an eye on him ! '

He was still chewing on this stern resolve when the
door-bell rang. He got up reluctantly. He assumed the
ringer to be Judson, who had a habit of forgetting his
latchkey. He went along the passage and opened the
door.

It was not Judson. It was a girl.

§ 3

There was a pause. It is always disconcerting for a
young man of orthodox views on costume to discover,
after going to the door to admit a male friend and not
having bothered to put on his coat, collar, or shoes for
the task, that he is face to face with a strange girl. And
this was a distinctly attractive girl. Bill, as we know,
was in love with Alice Coker ; nevertheless, his eyesight
remained good and he was consequently quite able to see
how distinctly attractive this girl was. Girls, of course,
fell into two classes—Alice Coker and others : but there
was no disguising the fact that his visitor came very high
up in the ranks of the others. She was a slim, fair-haired
girl with a trim figure delightfully arrayed in a dress of
some brown material. (It was not really brown, it was

beige, but Bill had not an eye for these niceties.) He
was particularly aware of her eyes. They were very blue
and seemed unusually large. She was staring at him—
and to his embarrassed thinking staring with a sort of
incredulous horror, as if he hurt her in some sensitive
spot.

Bill blushed pinkly, and endeavoured to wriggle his
feet under the mat. In the shop in the Burlington Arcade
where he had purchased them those socks had looked
extremely pleasing, but now he would fain have hidden
their gleaming pinks and greens from sight : and he
reflected moodily how rash a young man is who in this
world of sudden and unexpected crises takes off his shoes
in the daytime. So that, taking one thing with another,
Bill in that first instant contributed nothing towards the
task of making this interview go off with a swing.

The girl was the first to speak.

' Good gracious ! ' she said.

Bill felt that this was getting worse and worse.

' Surely ', she went on, blinking those large blue eyes,
' it's Mr. West ? '

To his other discomforts Bill now became aware that
a species of cold perspiration had added itself. It was
bad enough to encounter this distinctly attractive girl
in a shoeless, coatless, collarless and, as he now perceived,
a hole-in-the-sockful condition : but to make it worse
she seemed to remember meeting him before and he
couldn't even begin to place her. It was not one of
those cases of a mere name slipping from the mind, pre-
venting the sufferer from applying a label to a remembered
face. She was a complete stranger.

' You've forgotten me ! '

' Forgotten you ! ' responded Bill stoutly, feeling the
while as if some muscular person were stirring up his
interior organs with a pole. ' I should say not. Forgotten you ! ' He laughed metallically. ' What an
idea ! It—it's just—the fact is, I'm bad at names.'

' Felicia Sheridan.'

Bill felt that his face must be turning grey.

' Felicia *Sheridan*,' he said. ' Sheridan. Of course.'

'Well, considering that you once saved my life,' said
Flick, ' I should have been hurt if you had forgotten me
altogether.'

One of the advantages of being sparing in one's acts of
heroism is that it makes them easy to remember. Bill
was in the happy position of having saved only one life
in his whole career. A wave of the most poignant relief
flooded over him.

' Good heavens, yes ! ' he ejaculated. He stared at her
with an intensity that rivalled her own of a few moments
back.

' But you've altered so,' he said.

' Have I ? '

' Have you ! ' babbled Bill. ' Why, when I saw you
last you were a skinny kid, all legs and freckles . . . I
mean . . .' He gave it up. ' Won't you come in ? '
he said.

They went into the sitting-room. Bill hastily thrust
his feet into the shoes which lay brazenly near the sofa,
and feverishly started to don his collar. All this took
time, thereby enabling Flick, who had looked delicately
away during the operation, to inspect the room. Inspecting the room, she could hardly fail to observe the photographs of Miss Alice Coker. If she had missed half a
dozen of them she was bound to see the other six. She
observed them.

Something like a shadow seemed to fall upon Flick.
She endeavoured to be reasonable. It was hardly to be
expected that a splendid fellow like Bill would have
remained uncaught after five years. Besides, he had
only met her about ten times when she was, as he had
justly remarked, a skinny kid, all legs and freckles.
Furthermore, she was engaged to be married to an
estimable young man of whom, she told herself, she was
very, very fond. Nevertheless, a shadow did fall upon
her.

Bill, meanwhile, shod and no longer in the semi-nude,
had leisure to speculate on the mystery of her visit. It
puzzled him completely.

' I expect ', said Flick at this moment, ' you are wonder-

ng how on earth I come to be here. The fact is, I must
have called at the wrong address. The policeman at the
corner told me this was Marmont Mansions.'

' It is.'

' Marmont Mansions, Battersea ? '

' Marmont Mansions, Battersea.'

' Number nine ? '

' Number nine.'

' Then who ', demanded Flick, ' is Mrs. Matilda Pawle ? '
Bill could make nothing of the question.

' Mrs. Who ? '

' Pawle. Mrs. Matilda Pawle.'

Bill shook his head.

' I never heard of her.'

' But she lives here.'

The implied slur on the bachelor respectability of his
little home drew from Bill a shocked denial.

' Well, that's the address she gave in her letter,' said
Flick, fumbling in her bag. ' Look. This letter came
for my uncle—you remember my uncle—it came this
morning.'

Bill's face as he took the letter expressed only bewilderment. This bewilderment, as he started to read, seemed
to Flick to deepen. And then suddenly there came a
startling change. All his features appeared to dissolve
in one enormous grin, and the next moment he had tottered to the sofa and was holding on to its friendly support,
laughing helplessly.

' It's Judson,' he moaned, meeting Flick's astonished
eyes and reading in them a demand for some clue to this
strange behaviour.

' Judson ? '

Bill's hand swept round in a spacious wave of indi-
cation at the photographs.

' Man who lives with me. Judson Coker. Brother of
the girl I'm engaged to.'

' Oh ! ' said Flick.

She spoke dully. Women are inexplicable. There
was no reason why she should have spoken dully. She
was engaged herself to an estimable young man of whom

she was very, very fond, and she was even now on her
way to pick him up at his office and be taken by him to
tea at Claridge's. What could it matter to her if a com-
parative stranger like Bill West was engaged too ? Nevertheless, she spoke dully.

Bill was wiping his eyes.

' I brought Judson over from America with me. He
had been cutting up a bit too freely, and I'm acting as a
sort of nursemaid to him. He isn't allowed to have any
money at all, and this is the way he's trying to get it !
I thought he looked more cheerful the last day or two.
Can you beat it ! I could expect almost anything of old
Jud., but writing begging-letters is a new one.'

Flick joined in his laughter, but a little wryly. No
high-spirited girl likes to realize that she has been wrong
and her elders right.

' Well, I wish I had known that before,' she said. ' I
pawned my brooch to get money for this Mrs. Pawle.'

Bill was touched. He had still quite a lot of unex-
pended laughter left inside him, but he decided that it
would be best to keep it in.

' That was awfully kind of you. Don't leave it here
for Judson ! '

' I won't ! And if you feel like hitting your friend
Judson with something hard and heavy when he comes
in,' said Flick forcefully, ' don't stop yourself because
you think I may not approve. I'd like to be here to see
you do it.'

' Why not ? He'll be back soon. Stay on.'

' I can't, thanks. I've got to be in Fleet Street in
half an hour. Good-bye, Mr. West. How strange our
meeting again like this. How is your uncle ? '

' Oh, very fit. And yours ? '

' Very well, thanks.'

Reassured as to the health of their respective uncles,
they seemed to find difficulty in selecting a topic of
conversation. Flick moved to the door.

' I'll come down and put you into a cab,' said Bill.

' No, don't bother,' said Flick. ' It's such a lovely
day, I think I'll walk as far as Sloane Square.'

Here, Bill perceived, was an opening for him to offer to accompany her. But a boat was sailing to-morrow, and he had not yet written his bi-weekly letter to Alice. Alice's claims were paramount.

'Well, good-bye,' she said. 'We shall meet again soon, I hope?'

'I hope so. Good-bye.'

Bill, as the front door closed, suddenly realized that he had omitted to ascertain where she lived. For a moment he thought of running after her and inquiring. . . . No. . . . He really must get on with that letter to Alice. He returned to the sitting-room.

Flick, as she walked out into the sunshine, had an odd feeling that life, promising as it had seemed this morning, was in reality rather flat. And, strangely—but women are strange—she found herself thinking a little unkindly of Roderick.

§ 4

Bill had finished his letter to Alice—read, re-read, sealed, stamped and addressed it—when a key clicked in the front door and presently there entered to him Judson Coker.

'Any mail for—er—anybody?' inquired Judson.

Physically, enforced abstinence had done Judson good. His face had lost a certain unwholesome pallor which had characterized it a fortnight back and there had begun to steal into his cheeks quite a rosy pinkness. His eyes, moreover, were clear and bright, and he no longer indulged in that little trick of his of blinking and wriggling his neck round the edge of his collar. Against these corporeal gains must be set a gravity of demeanour which was entirely new. Judson's habitual manner was now that of the man who has looked upon life and found it a wash-out.

'You're always asking for mail this last day or two,' said Bill.

'Well, why not?' said Judson defensively. 'Why shouldn't a fellow ask for mail?'

'Anyway, there isn't any,' said Bill. 'You must be

patient, my lad. You can't expect people to answer by return of post.'

Judson started. The recently acquired pink left his face. He licked his lips.

'What do you mean?'

'I think it's a shame,' said Bill vehemently. 'If you've got pneumonia and are behind with the rent and haven't tasted food for three days, why the devil doesn't Mr. Pawle get busy and support you?'

Judson stared hideously. Through a mist he saw that his friend was giving way to unseemly mirth.

'How did you find out?' he choked.

Bill partially recovered himself. He sat back, feeling weak. There had been moments since their departure from America when he had regretted having taken Judson along with him, but the sight of the other's face now more than made up for all the trifling discomforts he had had to undergo.

'There was a girl in here just now', he explained, ' who was so touched by your letter that she had pawned her brooch to get money for you.'

Judson shook with emotion.

'Where is it?' he asked eagerly.

'Where's what?'

'The money the girl brought.' His face assumed a cold expression. 'I need hardly remind you, West,' he said stiffly, ' that that money belongs to me. Legally, I shouldn't wonder. So, if you have pouched it, I'll thank you to hand it over immediately.'

'Good Lord, man, you don't suppose I've got it, do you? Directly we found that it was you who had written the letter I told her to take the money away.'

Judson gave him one withering look.

'And you call yourself a friend!' he said.

Bill, undaunted by his attitude, followed him as he swung off and strode down the passage. He wanted to clear up further points that had perplexed him.

'How did you come to think of this stunt?' he asked, as Judson opened the front door. 'It was the smoothest trick I ever heard of.'

'Father was always getting begging-letters,' said Judson coldly. 'I saw no reason why it shouldn't work.'

'But how did you happen to pick on Miss Sheridan?'

'I never sent any letter to any Miss Sheridan. She must have an uncle or something whose name begins with an H. I wrote to all the H's in Who's Who.'

'Why the H's?'

'Why not? That's where the book happened to open.'

He withdrew his coat sleeve aloofly from Bill's grasp and proceeded down the stairs. Bill leaned over the banisters, still curious. Another aspect of the matter had occurred to him.

'Half a second,' he called. 'Where did you get the money to pay for the stamps?'

'I pawned a gold pencil.'

'You haven't got a gold pencil.'

'You had,' said Judson, and clattered out into the great open spaces.

CHAPTER FOUR

ACTIVITIES OF JUDSON COKER

§ 1

RAPIDITY of movement had never been congenial
to Judson Coker. He disliked having to hurry.
Finding, therefore, on reaching the end of the Prince of
Wales Road that he was not being pursued, he slowed
down. At a leisurely walk he turned the corner into
Queen's Road and presently found himself on Chelsea
Bridge. Here he decided to halt. For Judson had man's
work before him. He intended to count his money.

He took it out and arranged it in three little heaps on
the palm of his left hand. Yes, there it was, just as it
had been this morning, last night and the night before
—thirteen shillings, two sixpences and five pennies. The
view from Chelsea Bridge is one of the most stimulating
in London, but Judson had no eyes for it. However
picturesque, it could not hope to compete with the view
afforded by the palm of his left hand. Thirteen shillings,
two sixpences and five pennies—a noble sum. His
business correspondence had entailed an expenditure
which had eaten sadly into the original proceeds from
the sale of Bill's pencil, but he had no regrets. If you
don't speculate, Judson was well aware, you can't accu-
mulate. He gloated for a few minutes longer, then
salted the treasure away in his pocket, and resumed his
walk.

Students of character who have been examining Judson
Coker since his appearance in these pages may seem to
detect at this point a flaw in the historian's record—
finding themselves unable to reconcile the fact that he
had had the sum of fourteen shillings and fivepence in

his possession two nights before with the statement that
he had in his possession fourteen shillings and fivepence
now. They are too hasty. They do not probe deeply
enough. Judson was not one of your shallow fellows
who will fritter away here a sixpence and there a penny
until they wake up to find their capital gone and nothing
to show for it. It was his intention, difficult though it
might be, to hold off until he had the chance of shooting
the entire works in one majestic orgie—a binge which
he could look back to and live again in the lean days to
come.

He walked on, luxuriating in the pleasurable anguish
of a thirst that grew with every stride. He left Chelsea
Barracks behind him and the cosy little dolls'-houses in
Lower Sloane Street where the respectable live in self-
contained flats. The rattle of busy traffic greeted his
ears. It was like some grand, sweet anthem, for it meant
that he had arrived at that haven where he fain would
be, the King's Road, full from end to end of the finest
public-houses, practically one per inhabitant.

An admirable specimen of this type of building chancing
to rear its hospitable façade almost in front of him, he
made for it like a homing rabbit : and it was only when
he reached its doors that he discovered that there lay
between them and himself a securely padlocked iron gate.

As he stood there pawing in a feeble, bewildered fashion
at this astonishing and unforeseen barrier, a passer-by
stopped to gaze at him, a fellow of Bohemian aspect clad
in a frock-coat, flannel trousers and a pink cricket-cap
and wearing upon his feet cloth bedroom slippers, out of
one of which peeped coyly a sockless toe. To him Judson
appealed for an explanation of the ghastly state of things
which he had come upon. The man seemed like one who
would know all that there was to be known about public-
houses.

' I can't get in,' moaned Judson.

The other cleared his throat huskily.

' They don't open till ar-par-six,' he replied. Amazed
that in the heart of London, that hub of civilization,
there could be walking the public streets a man ignorant

of this cardinal fact of life, he groped for light. ' Stranger round these parts, ain't yer ? ' he hazarded.

Judson acknowledged that this was so.

' Foreigner, ain't yer ? '

' Yes.'

' From Orsetrylier, ain't yer ? '

' America.'

' R ! ' said the Bohemian, nodding. He spat sagely. ' I 'ear you can't get a drop of no description or kind whatsoever in America.'

Judson was about to refute this monstrous slur on the land he loved by giving a list of the places in New York (a) where anybody could get the stuff and (b) the more select, where you could get it by mentioning his name, when his companion moved on, leaving him alone in the desert.

A hideous gloom came over Judson. He was now enduring the extremes of drought. Six-thirty seemed æons ahead, like some dim, distant date lost in the mists of the future. The thought of passing the time till then weighed on his soul like a London fog. Eventually, deciding that, if the time had to be passed, it would be perhaps a little less dreary living it through up in the West End, he made for the Underground station at Sloane Square, bought a ticket for Charing Cross and descended to the platform.

A train was just leaving as he came down the stairs. He shuffled dully to the book-stall to see if there was anything there worth reading. The bright cover of *Society Spice* caught his eye. He knew little of the weekly papers of London, but its title seemed promising. He yielded up two of his pennies. A train came in. He sat down and began to turn the pages.

The twopence which Judson had spent on *Society Spice* proved an excellent investment. The *Church Times* or the *Spectator* he would not have enjoyed, but *Society Spice* might have been compiled for his especial benefit. It gripped him from the first page. Even though the issue in his hands was one of those on which Roderick had tried so hard to exercise a depressing influence, that craven's co-worker, young Pilbeam, had by no means failed in his efforts after zip. The Vice In The Pulpit article, for instance, was full of body ; nor was there any lack of fruitiness in the one on Night-Clubs Which Are Living Hells. Judson began to feel happier.

And then, like an electric shock, a shudder ran through his entire frame. It was as if somebody had beaten him over the head with a sand-bag. His heart seemed to stop, his scalp bristled, and there escaped from his twisted lips so sharp a yelp that it drew all eyes upon him. But Judson did not notice the eyes. His own were glued upon an article on page six.

It was not an article of which young Pilbeam had been particularly proud. He had had to dig it out of the archives in a hurry when Roderick's veto of the Bookmaker series had caused a gap in the make-up on the eve of press-day. It was headed ' Profligate Youth ', and it dealt with the behaviour and habits of the idle offspring of American plutocrats. The passage which had so stunned Judson ran as follows :—

' *Another instance which may be cited is that of the notorious Fifth Avenue Silks, as they were called, a club whose habit it was to parade up Fifth Avenue on Sunday mornings in silk hats, silk socks, silk pyjamas, and silk umbrellas. This was founded and led by the well-known " Toddy " van Riter, the recognized chief and guiding spirit of these young sparks.*'

Judson shook as with an ague. Not even on the morning after seeing in a New Year had he ever felt so thoroughly unstrung. Of all his great exploits the one of which he was proudest, the one on which he relied most confidently to hand his name down to posterity, was the founding of the Fifth Avenue Silks : and to see that masterpiece of ingenious fancy attributed to another— and to Toddy van Riter at that, his humble follower and henchman—was more, he felt, than a man should be called upon to bear. It seemed to steep the soul in abysmal blackness.

'The well-known Toddy van Riter' (Ha !) . . . 'The recognized chief and guiding spirit' (Oh, ha ha !) . . . It was monstrous, monstrous. These papers simply didn't care what they said.

The train rattled on, bearing a raging Judson eastward. Something tremendous, he felt, must be done, and done without delay. A sweeping and consummate vengeance for the outrage alone could satisfy him. But what to do ? What to do ?

He toyed with the idea of a libel action. But he had no funds for one. Then how ensure that Justice be done and the righteous given their due ? There was only one way—he must see the editor and demand that a full apology and retractation appear in the earliest possible issue.

He searched the paper, but could find no editor's name. All he learned was that the lying sheet was published by the Mammoth Company of Tilbury House, Tilbury Street, E.C. Well, that was enough to work on.

The train had stopped, and he got out, steely cold and filled with a great purpose. And the authorities of the Underground Railway increased his generous wrath by their pin-pricking policy of demanding from him another penny for having allowed his reverie to carry him on a couple of stations farther than the scope of his ticket. Having given them this with an awful look, he went up into the street and inquired the nearest way to Tilbury House.

§ 2

In alighting at Blackfriars instead of at Charing Cross, Judson had done better than he knew, for the policeman in the middle of the road outside the station informed him that to Tilbury House from where he stood was but a step. He strode off and was presently standing in a dingy alley-way before a large, gaunt building of discoloured brick. That this was the object of his quest was hinted by the rumble of presses within and confirmed by the scent of printer's ink and paper gallantly endeavouring to compete with that curious smell of boiling cabbage which always pervades any mean street in London. Nevertheless, Judson decided to make quite certain by verbal inquiry of the commissionaire in the doorway.

' Is this Tilbury House ? ' asked Judson.

' Ur,' said the commissionaire. He was a soured, moody-looking fellow with a ragged moustache, a man who seemed to have a secret sorrow which the spectacle of Judson did nothing to allay. He gazed at him with a bilious eye.

' Is this where *Society Spice* is published ? '

' Ur.'

' I want to see the editor.'

The commissionaire wrestled for a moment with his sorrow.

' D'you mean Mr. Pyke ? '

' I don't know his name.'

' Mr. Pyke's the editor of *Society Spice*. If you want to see him you'll 'ave to fill up your name and business.'

These formalities irked Judson. He resented this check. The spirit of Tilbury House had descended upon him and he wanted to Do It Now. He wrote his name on the form handed to him, fuming. A buttoned boy appeared from nowhere and regarded him with what seemed to Judson's inflamed senses silent mockery. He did not like the boy. The boy looked as if he might be in this plot to exalt Toddy van Riter at the expense of better men.

' Take this ', he said haughtily, ' to Mr. Pyke.'

' Gem' wants to see Mr. Pyke,' added the commissionaire, with the air of one interpreting the ravings of a foreigner.

The boy glanced disparagingly at the document. He had the trying manner of a schoolmaster examining a pupil's exercise.

' You ain't filled up your business,' he said superciliously.

Judson was in no mood for literary criticism from boys in buttons. He spoke no word, but he cut at the stripling viciously with his stick. The boy, dodging expertly,

uttered a derisive cry and disappeared. The commissionaire picked up his evening paper.

'You'll 'ave to wait,' he said.

He turned to the Racing page and began to read.

Up on the third floor in the office of *Society Spice*,
Roderick, a prey to a gloom which almost rivalled that
of the commissionaire, was lugubriously watching young
Pilbeam ginger up the next issue. There seemed to
Roderick something utterly gruesome in the fellow's
cheerful industry. His emotions were not unlike those
of a man shut up in a small room with a lunatic who has
started juggling with sticks of dynamite. Sustained by
the Verdict of the court of appeal, the sub-editor of *Society
Spice* was giving the freest play to his ideas of what a
paper that provided weekly scandal should be : and some
of the choice items which he had read out from time to
time had chilled Roderick to the marrow. To Roderick
it seemed utterly inconceivable that even the mildest of
these paragraphs should not bring about an immediate
visit from indignant citizens with shot-guns. And, when
he remembered Mr. Isaac Bullett's brief but pregnant
remarks concerning the Lads, his heart turned to water
within him.

A fairly frequent attendant at race-meetings in the
neighbourhood of London, Roderick knew all about the
Lads. They ranged the world in gangs, armed with
hammers. Sand-bags and knuckle-dusters were to them
mere ordinary details of what the well-dressed man should
wear. They lay in wait for those at whose actions they
had taken offence and kicked them with heavy boots.
In short, if there was one little group of thinkers in existence whose prejudices ought to be respected by a man
with any consideration for the pocket of his Life Insurance
Company, it was these same Lads. And here was Pilbeam
going out of his way to jar their sensibilities.

Roderick groaned in spirit, and turned absently to take
the form which was being held out to him by the boy in
buttons who had just entered.

'What's this ? ' he asked, his eyes still on young

Pilbeam, who was hammering away at a typewriter in the corner.   Pilbeam had just emitted a low chuckle of child-like pleasure at some happy phrase.   To Roderick it had sounded ghoulish.   He was torn between the desire to know what his young assistant had written and a strong presentiment that it was better not to know.

' Gem' waiting to see you, sir.'

Roderick wrenched his mind away from the essayist in the corner and inspected the card.   His attention was immediately enchained by the same omission which the boy had detected.

' He doesn't say what his business is.'

' Wouldn't fill up his business, sir,' said the boy eagerly. A sensationalist at heart, this fact now appealed to him as pleasingly sinister.

It appealed in precisely the same way to Roderick.

' Why not ? ' he said uneasily.

' Dunno, sir. Just wouldn't do it. I says to him, " You ain't filled up your business," I says, and all he done was take a crack at me with his stick.'

' Crack at you with his stick ! ' echoed Roderick pallidly.

' Crack at me with his stick,' repeated the child with relish.   ' Dunno what's the matter with 'im, but he seemed in a fair old rage, sir.   Boilin' over 'e seemed to be.'

Roderick blenched.

' Tell him I'm busy.'

' Busy, sir ? Yessir. All right, sir.'

The boy disappeared.   Roderick sat down at his desk and gazed before him with unseeing eyes.   The clatter of young Pilbeam's typewriter still rang through the room, but he did not hear it.   At last, he felt, the blow had fallen and the Avenger had arrived.   Just which of the paragraphs printed during his editorship had brought this on him he could not say, but he was strongly of the opinion that almost any one of them might have done so. His nightmare had come true.

Roderick Pyke, as has perhaps been sufficiently indi-cated by the remarks of his Aunt Frances, was not of the stuff of which heroes are made.   He was, as she had justly observed in her conversation with Sir George, a timid, feeble creature. There was once an editor of an organ of opinion catering to the literary wants of a Western mining-camp who, sitting in his office one day, noticed a bullet crash through the glass of the window and flatten itself against the wall behind his head. Upon which a relieved and happy smile played over his face. 'There!' he exclaimed. 'Didn't I say so? I knew that Personal column would be a success.' Roderick Pyke was the exact antithesis of this stout-hearted man. He liked peace and quiet, and shrank from all turbulent forms of Life. Where a sturdier fellow would have welcomed with joy the prospect of an interview with a boiling stranger who cracked at people with his stick, Roderick quailed. He sat huddled in his chair in a sort of catalepsy of panic.

This cataleptic condition had not passed when Flick arrived to be taken out to tea.

§ 3

Marked as Roderick's air of gloom was, Flick did not observe it. She was feeling oddly preoccupied. Something strange seemed to have happened to her since she had parted from Bill, expressing itself in a vague and general discontent combined with a curious dreaminess. She greeted Roderick mechanically, and mechanically allowed herself to be introduced to young Pilbeam, who, ever a warm admirer of the sex, had ceased his writing and risen gallantly at her entrance. There was not much that went on in Tilbury House that Pilbeam did not get abreast of, and the news of Roderick's engagement had long since reached him. So this was the boss's niece. A delectable girl, much too good for Roderick. He bowed genteelly, smiled, spoke a courteous word or two, opened the door. The young couple passed out. Pilbeam heaved a not unmanly sigh and returned to his writing. Much too good for Roderick, he was now certain. He held no high opinion of his superior officer.

Roderick escorted Flick downstairs. He led her by secret ways, for it was not his purpose to use the main stairway which ended in the vestibule guarded by the commissionaire. The information that he was busy had, he hoped, brought about the departure of the stick-cracking visitor, but he was taking no chances. He emerged with Flick from a small and insignificant door farther down the street ; and, looking apprehensively about him, saw with relief that no danger was in sight. Except for the usual fauna of localities in which printing-houses are situated, shirt-sleeved men with blackened faces and the like, Tilbury Street was empty. Somewhat calmed, Roderick proceeded on his way.

Unfortunately it chanced that at this precise moment the commissionaire, who had finished the racing news, elected to step out for a brief breath of air ; and still more unfortunately Judson, tired of waiting and realizing that the fortress was carefully guarded and that he was merely wasting time remaining in the vestibule, decided to get up and go home. The two came out almost simultaneously, and Judson was only a yard or so in the commissionaire's rear when the latter, sighting Roderick and wishing to show zeal and possibly acquire a small tip, touched his hat and uttered these fateful words :

' Shall I call you a cab, Mr. Pyke ? '

Judson, hearing the name, froze in his tracks.

' No, let's walk along the Embankment,' said Flick, ' and go to the Savoy instead of Claridge's. It's such a lovely day.'

The commissionaire, disappointed but apparently feeling that in a world of sorrow this sort of thing was only to be expected, withdrew. Flick and Roderick turned down the street towards the Embankment. And Judson, recovering from his momentary trance, had just started off in hot pursuit, when he was delayed by the sudden arrival of a large truck, which drew up across his path and began to unload rolls of paper. By the time he had rounded this obstacle his quarry was out of sight.

But Judson had caught the word ' Embankment '. He needed no further clue. He hurried in the direction of the river, and there sure enough, halted opposite a taxi-cab which had drawn up at the pavement, was the man he sought. He seemed to be trying to persuade the girl to ride, while the latter appeared to favour walking. Judson dashed feverishly up.

'Are you the editor of *Society Spice*?' he thundered.

Roderick spun round. The voice sounded to him like the voice of Doom. He had had his back turned and so had been unaware of Judson's approach until the latter spoke : and one may perhaps be permitted charitably to assume that it was the suddenness and unexpectedness of the onslaught that undid him. Some excuse, some theory in extenuation of his behaviour, is, one cannot deny, urgently needed. For at the sound of these words Roderick disintegrated. His fatal timorousness, that disastrous legacy from ' poor Lucy ' was too strong for him. He cast at Judson a single quick, horrified look ; then, jettisoning in one mad craving for self-preservation all thoughts of manhood and chivalry, he sprang from Flick's side, leaped into the cab, hissed in the driver's ear, and was off, wafted away like some Homeric warrior snatched from the thick of battle in a cloud.

His departure not unnaturally created in both Flick and Judson a certain astonishment. Judson was the first to recover. With an anguished cry he started to race after the receding taxi, leaving Flick standing on the pavement.

For some moments Flick stood there motionless, her gaze on the flying Judson. A dull flush had stolen into her cheeks, and an ominous steely light was turning the blue of her eyes to glazed stone. Then she beckoned to another taxi that was ambling up from the east and got in.

§ 4

Had Flick waited a minute longer before taking her cab, she would have perceived Judson returning baffled from the chase. Even in his Harvard days, when he was young and lissom, athletic feats had never been in Judson's line ; and nowadays a twenty-yard dash was about the limit of his sprinting capacity. This being in the nature of a special occasion, he had extended himself to a matter of fifty yards before admitting defeat, but at that point his legs and lungs had united in a formal protest too vigorous to be overruled.

But, though checked, Judson was not checkmated. Even as he paused, doubled up and gasping with his back against the friendly railings of the Embankment Gardens, an idea had come to him. When—or if—he got his breath back again, he would return to Tilbury House and there acquire certain information. He was now on his way to put this scheme into action.

The commissionaire was still out having his breath of air when he reached the familiar vestibule. In his seat there sat a boy in buttons—not the one with whom Judson had had the little unpleasantness, but another and more likeable-looking lad. To him Judson addressed himself.

' Say, listen ! ' said Judson.

' Sir ? ' said the infant courteously.

Judson bent nearer and lowered his voice.

' I want to know Mr. Pyke's private address.'

The boy shook his head, and into his manner there crept the dawning of a new austerity.

' Ain't allowed to give private addresses.'

Judson had hoped not to be compelled to call up his last line of reserves, but it seemed unavoidable. From the slender store in his trouser-pocket he produced a shilling and a sixpence. He held them up in silence.

The boy wavered.

' It's against the rules,' he said wistfully.

Judson spake no word, but he clinked the coins meditatively in his hand. The little fellow's agitation visibly increased.

' What d'you want to know it for ? ' he quavered.

Judson, with masterly strategy, dropped the shilling, allowed it to roll in a wide circle, then picked it up and clinked it once more against the sixpence. The boy was but flesh and blood : he stole to the foot of the stairs and listened intently for a moment : then, creeping back, whispered in Judson's ear.

The money changed hands and Judson took his departure.

§ 5

It was nearly half-past seven when Flick returned to Holly House. She had driven in her cab to the Savoy Hotel and there in one of the writing-rooms had remained for a considerable period of time, most of which was spent in chewing a pen and staring straight in front of her. Eventually, seizing a sheet of note-paper, she had dashed down a few lines, and without stopping to re-read them had sealed the envelope and posted it in the lobby. Then, feeling oddly uplifted, she had walked composedly out and taken an Underground train to Wimbledon. She felt defiant but calm. Her heart sang rebel songs as she walked up the drive, songs as old and dangerously intoxicating as the Spring itself.

Mrs. Hammond came out of the drawing-room as she was crossing the hall.

' How late you are, Felicia. Be quick and dress. Your Uncle George and Roderick are coming to dinner at eight.'

This was news to Flick.

' Are they ? ' she said.

' Surely Roderick told you,' said Mrs. Hammond. ' It was settled just after lunch on the telephone. It is the only night your uncle can manage, as he is obliged to go to Paris to-morrow and expects to be away at least a week. The Bagshotts and one or two other people are coming. Very strange Roderick saying nothing about it to you.'

' He left me in rather a hurry,' said Flick. ' I suppose he would have mentioned it if he had not been interrupted.'

' Poor Roderick ! I suppose he is kept very busy,' said Mrs. Hammond. ' How was the dear boy ? '

' Very agile.'

' Agile ? ' Mrs. Hammond stared. ' What do you mean ? '

Flick stopped at the foot of the stairs.

' Aunt Frances,' she said, ' I've something to tell you. I am not going to marry Roderick. I have written to him breaking off the engagement.'

CHAPTER FIVE

NIGHT OPERATIONS AT HOLLY HOUSE

§ 1

WHILE the stirring events just recorded were in progress in and about the head-quarters of the Mammoth Publishing Company at Tilbury House, Bill West had been sitting in markedly gloomy meditation on the little balcony which ran outside the dining-room of his flat in the Prince of Wales Road, Battersea. He had come out here because the silent reproach in the lovely eyes of the twelve photographs of Alice Coker in the sitting-room had proved after a while too much for his sensitive conscience to endure. The disappearance of Judson had left him ill at ease and apprehensive, filling him with a guilty sense of having failed in his duty as a guardian : and the photographs, staring at him like so many accusing angels, deepened this feeling.

' Why ', they seemed to ask, ' were you so remiss ? You were my brother's keeper. Why did you not bean him with a shoe before he could make his getaway ? '

The question was unanswerable. The most rudimentary intelligence should have told him that the course he ought to have pursued was to jump on Judson's neck, even if it involved diving down two flights of stairs, and thus prevent that earnest young inebriate from galloping out into the heart of London with money in his pocket. Now, goodness knew what would happen or when—and in what shape—the heir of the Cokers would return to the fold.

These Prince of Wales Road balconies are pleasant eyries. From their agreeable eminence you can see over the trees into Battersea Park and revel, if you are in the

mood for it, in the delicate green of turf and shooting
leaf. You can also see down the road for quite a distance
both ways. And so it came about that, just as dusk
had begun to fall and the golden lamps shone out in the
street below, Bill was aware of a familiar figure tramping
along the pavement towards the entrance of Marmont
Mansions.

At first he was blankly incredulous. It could not be
Judson. Judson must now be miles away, out where the
West End begins, slaking a two-weeks-old thirst with
cocktails. But the figure came into the light of a lamp,
and it was indeed Judson. He entered Marmont Mansions : and Bill, leaving his balcony and hurrying to the
front door, could hear him wheezily negotiating the stairs.
The flat was on the fifth floor and there was no lift—two
facts of which Judson had frequently and vehemently
complained. He arrived now, puffing painfully, and for
a space was deaf to Bill's reproaches.

' Eh ? ' he said eventually, a little restored.

' I said " So here you are ! " ' observed Bill, selecting
for repetition one of the milder of his recent remarks.

Judson led the way into the sitting-room, where he
sank down on the sofa and, as Bill had done earlier in the
afternoon, removed his shoes.

' Nail or something,' he explained.

' You're a nice chap ! ' said Bill, returning to the attack.

Judson was defiant and unashamed.

' As a matter of fact,' he replied stoutly, ' I haven't
had even one. To start with, I find that in this infernal
country the saloons don't open till midnight or some
ghastly hour. So I couldn't get a drink at first. And
after that I was too busy.'

' Too busy to get a drink ! ' cried Bill.

He followed his friend, bewildered. Judson had risen
from the sofa and proceeded to his bedroom, where he
now began to put on another and more congenial pair of
shoes.

' Too busy to get a drink ? ' repeated Bill.

' Well, too preoccupied,' said Judson. He poured out
a basin of water, washed his travel-stained face and hands,

and, moving to the mirror, brushed his hair. ' I've had a very disturbing afternoon, Bill o' man.'

' How much money have you got on you ? '

' Never mind about money, o' fellow,' said Judson, waving aside the tactless question. ' I want to tell you about my disturbing afternoon.' He lit a cigarette and returned to the sitting-room. ' Can only stop a minute, Bill,' he said. ' Got to go out again in a second.'

Bill laughed a frosty laugh.

' Any old time you go out . . .'

' Must,' said Judson. ' Matter that affects my honour. Got to see a fellow and have justice done me.'

' You don't want justice done you,' said Bill, beginning to doubt his friend's professions of abstinence. There was a wild look in Judson's eye and his manner was peculiar. ' If they started doing justice to you, you'd be in the penitentiary.'

Judson drew pensively at his cigarette. He seemed not to have heard this opprobrious remark.

' Most disturbing afternoon,' he continued. ' You ever read a paper called *Society Spice*, Bill o' man ? '

' No. What about it ? '

' Only this,' responded Judson. ' There's a piece in it this week saying that it was Toddy van Riter who founded the Fifth Avenue Silks. Toddy van Riter ! ' A spine-chilling laugh escaped him. ' You know as well as I do, Bill o' man, that a poor fish like Toddy wouldn't have been able to hit on an idea like that in a million years. I was the little guy that founded those Silks, and I'm not going to have all England thinking I wasn't. Toddy van Riter ! ' sneered Judson. ' I ask you ! Toddy ! ' The cigarette burned his fingers and he threw it into the grate. ' I read that while I was on a train in the Subway, and I went straight to the place where the rotten rag was published and asked to see the editor. Fellow must have a guilty conscience, because he refused to see me. And when I cornered him on the street a bit later he just shot into a cab and streaked off. But I was too smart for him,' said Judson with a hard chuckle. ' It will be a cold day when any pie-faced scandal-sheet buzzard can make a monkey out of me. I got his home-address. I'm going right out now to see him and insist on an apology and retractation in the next issue.'

' You aren't going to do anything of the sort.'

' I am, believe me.'

Bill tried an appeal to his reason.

' But what does it matter if the man did say Toddy founded the Silks ? '

' What does it matter ? ' Judson's eyes grew round. He stared at Bill as if questioning his sanity. ' What does it *matter* ? Do you think I'm going to have the whole of Europe believing a thing like that ? Not while I have my strength. I suppose if you were Marconi, you'd take it lying down if people went about saying you hadn't invented wireless. Well, mustn't waste time sitting here. See you later.'

Six photographs on the mantelpiece gazed at Bill pleadingly. Three on the what-not, two on the console-table and one on a bracket near the door caught his eye and urged him to be firm.

' Where does this *Society Spice* man live ? ' he asked.

' Number Seven, Lidderdale Mansions, Sloane Square,' said Judson promptly. He had no need to consult the back of the envelope in his breast-pocket, for the address was graven upon his heart. ' I'm going there now.'

' You aren't going there or anywhere ', said Bill firmly, ' without me. What do you think '—he choked—' what do you think She would say if I let you run about all over London, getting into trouble ? '

Judson followed his sweeping hand in the direction of the mantelpiece, but showed little emotion. Too few brothers in this world are capable of being melted by a sister's photograph. But, though he appeared unimpressed by the thought of Alice and her possible concern, a certain bias towards prudence did seem to enter his mind.

' Not a bad idea, your coming too,' he admitted. ' Quite likely fellow may turn nasty. Then you could sit on his head while I kicked him in the slats. Only way with these birds. Treat 'em rough.'

Bill was cold to this outline of policy.

' There isn't going to be any rough stuff,' he said firmly.
' And you aren't going to butt in and start anything.
You will leave the whole business to me. This sort of
affair needs a man with a calm, clear mind. I want you
to understand right from the beginning that I am handling this. You stay in the background and leave me to
do the talking. No violence ! '

' Not if he doesn't turn nasty. If he does,' said Judson,
' we will form a wedge and sail in and disembowel the
mutt.'

' He won't turn nasty. Why should he ? He will
probably be only too glad to correct an error in his paper.'

' He'd better be,' said Judson grimly.

§ 2

The descent through the roof of Holly House and sub-
sequent explosion on the drawing-room carpet of a large
bomb would doubtless have caused a certain excitement
and dismay among the inmates of that fair home : but
such consternation could hardly have been more marked
than that which had followed Flick's announcement that
she had broken off her engagement to Roderick Pyke.
Sir George, arriving in a luxurious limousine a few minutes
after the blow had fallen, was in nice time to join the
commission appointed by his sister to inquire into and
examine the tragedy.

' She gives no *reason* ! ' wailed Mrs. Hammond for the
tenth time. For once in her masterly life this great
woman was completely unnerved. Any ordinary disaster
she might have coped with, but this was too shattering.
The ghastly suddenness of it was perhaps its most appalling feature. No warning, no shadow of a warning had
preceded the blow. Shortly after two o'clock Flick had
left the house, thoroughly and completely engaged to
Roderick, and at half-past seven she had come back
with a hard gleam in her blue eyes, freed from all sentimental entanglements. And that was all that Mrs.
Hammond or anybody knew ; for Flick, as she was now
remarking for the eleventh time, gave no reason. In

addition to being terrible, the thing was achingly mysterious : and quite half of Mrs. Hammond's exasperation and fury was due to the fact that she was being excluded from sharing in a secret. She raged impotently : and when Sir George was ushered in by Wace, the butler (demurely grave as only a butler can be when something is 'up' above stairs), she had just snubbed the unfortunate Sinclair rather ferociously for the second time in three minutes.

Upon receipt of this second rebuff, Sinclair Hammond had withdrawn from the discussion. · As a rule, so long as people did not interrupt him when he was writing or attribute to Basius Secundus sentiments which had actually been uttered by Aristides of Smyrna, it was not easy to ruffle Sinclair Hammond. But irritability was in the air to-night, and, having twice been requested for goodness' sake not to talk such nonsense, he retired wounded into a corner and buried himself in a first edition of *Robert Burns' Poems Chiefly In the Scottish Dialect*, printed by John Wilson, Kilmarnock, 1786, uncut in the original blue wrappers. How deeply he had been hurt is shown by the fact that even this did not altogether soothe him.

Sir George, taking his place in the debate, was at first as helplessly concerned as any one. It was he who pointed out the dramatic feature of the affair—to wit, that poor Roderick, who could not possibly have received Flick's letter yet, might be expected to arrive at any moment in complete ignorance of what had occurred. How, Sir George demanded, was the news to be broken to him ?

The question started a train of thought. How also, Mrs. Hammond inquired feverishly, was the scandal to be kept from the half-dozen or so of Wimbledon's elect who had been invited to dine to-night expressly to meet the about-to-be-happy couple ? The Wilkinsons from Heath Prospect were coming. The Byng-Jervoises from The Towers were coming. Pondicherry Lodge was contributing Colonel and Mrs. Bagshott. What possible explanation could be made to these leaders of Society of Felicia's absence ?

' Felicia's absence ? ' Sir George started. ' What do you mean, Felicia's absence ? '

' She refuses to come down to dinner ! '

' Tell them she's got a headache,' said Mr. Hammond, glancing up from his *Burns*.

' Oh, do be quiet, Sinclair ! ' begged his suffering wife.

Mr. Hammond returned to his reading. Sir George, whose face and bearing had taken on that stiff solemnity which always reminded his employees at Tilbury House so strongly of a stuffed frog, puffed vigorously.

' Refuses to come down to dinner ! I never heard of anything so ridiculous. I will speak to her. Send for her at once.'

' It's no good sending for her,' moaned Mrs. Hammond. ' She has locked herself in her bedroom and won't come out.'

' Which is her room ? '

' The second door to the left on the first landing. What are you going to do, George ? '

Sir George turned on the threshold.

' I am going to Speak To Her.' he said.

There was an interval of some three or four minutes. In the drawing-room a tense silence prevailed. Mrs. Hammond sat rigid on her chair. Bob, the Sealyham, slumbered on the rug. Mr. Hammond put down his *Burns* and, rising, walked to the French windows and threw them open. He stood looking out into the gentle night. The garden slept under the stars, and a breeze floated across the lawn. Peace, peace everywhere save in this stricken home. A distant rumble from above proclaimed that Sir George was still Speaking To Her.

Presently the rumble ceased. Footsteps descended the stairs. Sir George entered. His face was red and he was breathing a little heavily.

' The girl's mad,' he announced briefly. ' There is nothing to be done for the present but make some excuse to these people who are coming here to-night. Better tell them she's got a headache.'

' An excellent idea,' said Mrs. Hammond with enthusiasm. ' We will.'

'Colonel and Mrs. Bagshott,' proclaimed Wace, the butler, in the doorway. His slightly prominent eyes swept the little group before him with respectful commiseration. 'Do the best you can,' his glance seemed to say. 'It's beyond me!'

§ 3

A taxi-cab drew up at the door of Lidderdale Mansions, Sloane Square. Bill West alighted, and spoke through the window.

'You wait here,' said Bill. 'I'll go up and see this man.'

Judson appeared doubtful.

'Well, I don't know,' he said. 'It seems to me this is a business that wants handling. Are you sure you're equal to it?'

'If only you keep out of it, I can settle the whole affair in two minutes,' said Bill firmly.

He felt unusually calm and capable as he entered the building. As a rule, it is a nervous task to call upon a perfect stranger and ask favours of him: but Bill felt no diffidence. He looked forward to an amusing chat. It was only when he had gone up a couple of floors in the lift and was interrogated by the attendant as to where he wished to stop, that he remembered that he had omitted to ask Judson the name of the man he had come to interview. A little ruffled by the captious manner of the attendant on being requested to take him down again after a brief indulgence in what the latter evidently looked upon as a joy-ride, he went out to the cab.

'Well?' said Judson eagerly, popping out like a cuckoo out of a clock. 'What did he say?'

'I haven't seen him yet,' Bill explained. 'I forgot to ask you what his name is.'

'Look here,' said Judson in an anxious voice, his faith in his ambassador now plainly at zero, 'are you *sure* you're equal to this? Hadn't I better push up?'

'You stay here, damn you,' said Bill. He had lost that easy calm.

'I have a feeling that you'll bungle it.'

'Don't be a chump. What's his name?'

'Pyke. But . . .'

'Pyke. All right. That's all I wanted to know.'

He re-entered the lift and was shot up to the third floor, only to receive another check. If Bill had been a superstitious man, he would have realized at this point that the omens were bad and that it would be a wise course to abandon the expedition. A man-servant, answering this ring, informed him that Mr. Pyke had gone out.

'Just gone this moment, sir.'

'But I've only just come up,' argued Bill. 'Why didn't I meet him?'

'Perhaps Mr. Pyke walked downstairs, sir.'

It seemed a tenable theory. At any rate, the man was gone. Bill, unwilling to trouble the lift-attendant again, walked downstairs himself and, reaching the cab, found Judson in a state bordering on the febrile. Judson was dancing on the pavement.

'I knew you would bungle it,' he cried. 'The fellow sneaked out half a second ago. Tried to get into my cab!'

'Tried to get into your cab?'

'Yes. Didn't know there was anybody in it. He peered in, saw me, turned deadly pale, and . . .' Judson broke off, pointing. 'Look! Quick! There he is, getting into that taxi over there. Get in! Jump in, you poor fish.'

The affair, which had started out in so orderly and well-planned a manner, was now beginning to take on a hectic aspect which flustered Bill. The jerk with which Judson dragged him into the taxi helped further to disorder his faculties. And when his companion, leaning across him and speaking out of the window, uttered those words familiar to every reader of detective stories, 'Follow that cab wherever it goes!' the enterprise stepped definitely into the ranks of waking nightmares.

To call upon a stranger and ask him civilly to insert in his paper a correction of an inadvertent error is one thing: to hound him about London in cabs quite another.

Bill had a well-regulated man's dislike of scenes, and it
seemed to him that this pursuit could only end in a scene
of the most disagreeable nature. Already Judson had
begun to babble harsh comments on the man whose taxi,
keenly pursued by their own, was moving rapidly down
the street towards Sloane Square. It was Judson's firm
belief that the fellow was in the pay of Toddy van Riter.
If not, why should he jump ten feet sideways every time
they met? Taken by and large, the whole thing looked
like a pretty black business to Judson. He seethed with
generous indignation and even went so far as to state his
intention, should they ever catch up with him, of busting
the fellow one on the snoot.

As the moments went by, it almost seemed as though
these sentiments must have communicated themselves
by some sort of telepathy to the man in the other cab:
for his taxi went on and on and on. The theory that he
was going out to dine somewhere now seemed thin.
Would any diner-out dine so far out as this? Already
they were well into the Fulham Road and he showed no
signs of stopping. They rattled over Putney Bridge.
They climbed Putney Hill. And still the taxi in front
moved forward. It began to appear absurd even to Bill,
reluctant as he was to abandon the common-sense view,
that this Pyke could simply be on his way to dinner. It
seemed more probable that his intention was to go on till
he reached the coast and then jump off the edge.

In attributing these qualms to Roderick, his pursuers
had erred. True, Roderick had had what amounted to
the start of a lifetime when that glance into Judson's taxi
had informed him that the mysterious stranger was still
on his trail, but panic had passed as soon as he had got
into a cab of his own and driven off. It had not occurred
to him that he was to be chased. Arriving at Holly
House, he paid his driver and rang the door-bell without
even a look behind. It was only as he waited on the step
for Wace to answer the bell that the crackling of gravel
in his rear caused him to turn his head. The shock he
received on observing a second cab tearing down the
drive was severe. A faint hope that this might be a

peaceful cab containing blameless dinner-guests of his Aunt Frances vanished as he perceived Judson's inflamed face protruding from the right-hand window. He lunged desperately at the bell again, and waited for Wace as the Duke of Wellington in another crisis had waited for Blücher.

The cab stopped. From one door Judson shot out, from the other Bill. Roderick rang the bell again, staring glassily over his shoulder.

Oddly enough, it was the sight of Bill that set the seal on his horror. And yet, had he but known, Bill was here in the purest spirit of pacifism. What had caused Bill to project himself so vigorously out of the cab was the kindly desire to be on the scene of action in time to keep Judson from committing the mayhem of which he had spoken so feelingly at practically every stage of the journey. Bill was the wise, cool, clear-headed man who was there to stop any violence. But to Roderick he seemed the most dreadful thing that had come along in the whole course of this dreadful day.

Judson, so held Roderick, was bad enough. He was pretty scared of Judson. But about Judson there was this consoling feature, that he had a certain weediness, a lack of thews and sinews. With Judson, a fellow, if driven into a corner, might possibly cope. But Bill was quite another matter. A man cannot fulfil the exacting duties of left-tackle on a Harvard football team without having a fairly impressive physique. No mere amiability or charm of manner will fit him for the post : he must be equipped with india-rubber legs, a chest like an ice-box and the shoulders of a prize-fighter. These qualifications Bill possessed. He stood five feet eleven in his socks and weighed on the hoof one hundred and ninety-three pounds, and Roderick, watching him bound up the drive, unhesitatingly cast him for the rôle of star in this murder-scene.

The consequence was that, when Bill reached the steps just as Wace opened the door, Roderick, trapped and desperate, saw nothing for it but to sell his life dearly. Whirling his stick madly in the air, he brought it down with a solid whack on Bill's head. Bill, totally unprepared for anything of this kind, tripped and fell : Judson, hurrying up, stumbled over Bill : and Roderick, snatching at the chance thus presented of effecting a masterly retreat, dashed into the house and slammed the door after him.

Of all the things calculated to modify a wise, cool, clear-headed outlook on life, few are more effective than a brisk buffet on the skull from a heavy stick. In this case the blow was rendered all the more powerful by the striker's terror : and Bill's hat having fallen off in his sprint down the straight, there was nothing to break the force of it. He remained for an appreciable space of time sitting dazedly on the gravel : and when eventually he rose his mood had undergone a complete and remarkable change. No trace remained of his recent desire to keep this business free from violence. Violence was what he wanted more than anything on earth. He looked on the world through a crimson mist.

In this new frame of mind the spectacle of Judson hopping about in a futile manner exasperated him intensely. He was in the mood when men usually tolerant of their fellow-creatures conceive a sudden dislike for whoever happens to be nearest. He glowered at Judson.

' Go and sit in the cab,' he commanded with set teeth.

' But look here, Bill o' man. . . .'

' Go on ! I'm going to attend to this business.'

' What are you going to do ? '

Bill's finger was on the bell, and he kept it there without pause. A few short hours before, life had been a thing opening out before him in a prismatic vista of manifold ambitions. He had had all sorts of plans—plans for making a fortune, plans for marrying Alice Coker, plans for scoring off Wilfrid Slingsby. Now all these rainbow visions had passed from his mind, and he had but one object in the world—just one : and that was to get into this house, find the fellow who had sloshed him on the bean and methodically kick the man's spine up through his back hair. He was in the mood which used to send ancient Vikings berserk, which makes modern Malays run amok and prod the citizenry with long knives. Like most big men, Bill West was good-natured. He did not readily take offence. But hit him an absolutely unprovoked wallop on the head with a stick and you started something. He continued to ring the bell.

'I'm going to have a heart-to-heart talk with that fellow,' he said grimly.

Judson's feelings were now those of a child who, sporting idly with a pocket-knife beside a reservoir, finds suddenly that he has bored a hole in the dam. He had unchained passions which overawed him. Frothily though he had talked of inflicting violence on the erring Roderick, Judson had never really intended business. He knew now that he would not have proceeded beyond words. But in Bill's programme words had only too plainly no part at all. To see Bill, that mild and good-humoured young man, standing there with his teeth bare, his eyes glittering, and a thin trickle of blood running down his forehead, appalled Judson. He felt weakly unequal to the situation. With a pale face and limp knees he returned to the cab. And as he did so the door opened.

Wace, the butler, had been annoyed by the strident persistence of the bell. It was with the intention of administering a severe rebuke that he now presented himself. But the words he had framed were never uttered. Something large and solid brushed Wace out of the way ; and, staggering back, he saw a big man without a hat careering along the hall in the direction of the drawing-room.

'Hi!' he said feebly.

The intruder paid no attention. He had stopped for an instant, as if uncertain of his destination ; but now a burst of voices from behind the door put him on the scent. His fingers closed on the handle.

'Hi!' said Wace again. 'Stop!'

Bill did not stop. He plunged on into the drawing-room.

The drawing-room was full of men and women dressed and eager for the feast. Here Mr. Wilkinson of Heath

Prospect chatted about the weather to Mrs. Hammond:
there Mrs. Byng-Jervoise of The Towers spoke to her host
of new plays.   Colonel Bagshott was drinking sherry and
entertaining Mrs. Wilkinson with an account of his most
recent passage of arms with the local Council.   Sir George
and Mr. Byng-Jervoise were talking politics.   Roderick,
a solitary figure attached to no group, stood by the open
window.

Into this refined gathering Bill charged like a ravening
wolf.   And Roderick, turning with the others at the
sound of the opening door and catching sight of his ghastly
face, acted promptly.   This was the fourth time to-day
that he had felt the imperative need of flight from forces
beyond his control, and, nimble though he had shown
himself on each of the previous occasions, his movements then had been leaden-footed compared with the
turn of speed which he exhibited now.   He shot out
into the garden like a cannon-ball, with Bill in close
attendance.

§ 4

The young need careful handling.   Into the life of the
most docile and well-regulated girl, there comes crises
where only tact and sympathy can avert disaster: and,
ever since Flick Sheridan had made her momentous
announcement respecting Roderick, tact and sympathy
had been very notably absent from the attitude of her
immediate circle.   It was perhaps unfortunate that Mrs.
Hammond, always prone to supersede her husband in
the conduct of delicate operations about the home, had
declined with some asperity to allow the amiable Sinclair
to go up and have a chat with his niece: for this elim-
inated from the situation the one person to whom Flick
in her mood of bristling defiance would have listened with
any calmness.   Instead of a gentle talk with Uncle Sinclair, Flick had been plunged into a battle royal with her
Aunt Frances—a contest which had left her, though un-
defeated, badly shaken: and immediately on top of this
had come Sir George's brief address through the locked
door.   At about the time when the cab of Roderick and

that of Bill and Judson were toiling up Putney Hill,
she was seated on her bed, staring into the future.

It was not a very agreeable future for any girl to look
at, certainly not a girl who, like Flick, was of a quick and
gallant spirit and had always held herself to be the captain
of her soul. It was a future filled with wrangling arguments, cold, hurt silences, a never-ending strain. Never-
ending, that is to say, unless she meekly yielded and
consented to marry Roderick. And at the thought of
marrying Roderick, Flick's teeth clicked together and she
blinked rebelliously. Nothing should ever induce her to
marry Roderick. She loved Bill West. Uncle Sinclair
had spoken flippantly about juvenile romances, but that
extraordinary meeting with Bill this afternoon had shown
her that these were not things to jest about. They were
beastly, solid facts that hurt you indescribably.

Oh, she knew how absurd it was of her. She knew that
Bill was in love with some starry-eyed cat of a girl out
in America and wouldn't look at her anyway, but that
made no difference. If she couldn't have Bill, she
wouldn't have any one. Least of all Roderick, who
jumped into cabs and left her standing on the pavement
at the mercy, for all he knew, of men who looked like
Airedale terriers.

She jerked up her head with a sudden unconscious movement of defiance and resolution. She had made her
decision. The next moment she was opening her bag
and feeling in it for the money earmarked earlier in the
day for the relief of the distressed Mrs. Matilda Pawle.
She pulled out the notes and dropped them in a rustling
heap on the bed. They made an encouraging display.
If she had ever thought of weakening and drawing back,
the sight of this money gave her strength. It seemed to
her a vast sum, the sort of sum on which a girl of careful
habits could face the world indefinitely. And, in the
distant future when she had spent all this wealth, there
was all the rest of her jewellery to fall back on. She
hesitated no longer.

She went to cupboards, ransacked drawers. She pulled
a suit-case out from under the bed. After a thoughtful

interval devoted to making a selection of the things she
could not possibly do without, she packed the suit-case.
She scribbled a hasty note in pencil and fastened it to her
pin-cushion. She tore the sheet from the bed and tied
knots in it. She attached the sheet to the rail of the bed,
dragged the bed to the window ; and had just flung the
window open, when from the garden below there came
to her ears a sudden uproar. With a startling abruptness the quiet night had become filled with noise and
shouting.

Flick leaned out, deeply interested. If there is one
spot in the world free as a rule from alarms and excur-
sions, it is the aristocratic quarter of Wimbledon, that
row of large mansions along the edge of the Common
where Wealth and Respectability dream and let the world
go by. In all the five years of her residence at Holly
House Flick could recall no event of any description that
had even bordered on Drama. Yet now, if she could
believe the evidence of her ears, Drama was stalking
abroad in the night as nakedly as in the more vivacious
portions of Moscow. Dark figures were racing on the
lawn ; voices shouted hoarsely. She could detect the
deep bay of Colonel Bagshott of Pondicherry Lodge, the
shriller yapping of Mr. Byng-Jervoise of The Towers.
Her Uncle George was bawling to somebody to fetch a
policeman.

Flick forgot her troubles in the thrill of these amazing
goings-on. She leaned farther out of the window,
annoyed by the fact that her vision was much impeded
by the roof of a sort of outhouse immediately below her
window. A few moments before, she had been extremely
grateful to providence for having supplied this outhouse
roof as an aid to her escape : but now she resented its
presence. The spirit of Youth called to her not to miss
a bit of this, for it was good ; and she chafed to think
that she was missing practically all of it.

The shouts increased in volume. The flying figures
continued to fly. Then suddenly there echoed through
the night a tremendous splash. Even an onlooker whose
view was cut off by an outhouse roof could interpret the

inner meaning of this, and Flick understood it instantly. Somebody had fallen into the pond.

She hoped it was her Uncle George.

§ 5

It was her Uncle George. And he made his own personal needs so manifest in a vigorous speech from the depths that the pursuit ceased on the instant and all present rallied round to lend him aid and comfort.

All except Bill. Bill was otherwise occupied. Retired altogether now from the maelstrom of activity on the lawn, he was crouching in the shadow of a large bush, reviewing his position.

The first fine frenzy that had carried Bill through the front door into the drawing-room and through the French windows of the drawing-room, out into the garden in pursuit of Roderick, had kept him going nicely for perhaps two minutes. At the end of that time the folly of chasing people about strange gardens in the dark was brought home to him in no uncertain manner by a wheel-barrow, left by gardener John in the shadows at the edge of the lawn. It was a low, underslung wheel-barrow, quite invisible in the gloom, and he had dived over it with a shattering bump which gave him a momentary impression that Wimbledon and neighbourhood had been convulsed by an earthquake. A young man less accustomed to falls on the football field might have lain there indefinitely, but Bill staggered dizzily to his feet, and it was at this point that he discovered that the fever of the chase had completely left him.

As he stood there, dazedly wishing himself elsewhere, he perceived that the whole aspect of the world had undergone another change. A moment before it had been a roomy place with nobody in it but Roderick and himself, but now there appeared to be people everywhere. Large though the garden was, it seemed uncomfortably crowded : and the chase, which had started out as a straight issue between himself and Roderick, had become quite a public affair. The thing had developed into a sort of Walpurgis Night. Phantoms whizzed to and fro.

Demon voices bellowed advice and threats. An unseen dog was barking its head off.

Bill was appalled by his position. That is the worst of Berserk moods—they lure you into stupendous acts of imbecility and then coolly abandon you to extricate yourself as best you can. A chilly remorse flooded over him. He saw now where his initial mistake had lain. He ought to have taken from the start an attitude altogether more dignified and formal. Instead of charging into the house of a complete stranger, breathing fire through his nostrils and seeking whom he might devour, he should have gone quietly away and on the morrow approached some good lawyer with a view to bringing suit against the man Pyke for assault and battery. Not having taken this prudent course, he was, he ruefully admitted, in a distinctly unpleasant hole.

The descent of Sir George into the goldfish pond had given him a respite, but it was plain that it was not to last long. A nasty spirit of vindictiveness prevailed in the enemy camp, and voices were urging once more that the police be summoned. He must get out of this infernal garden, and that right speedily before they started to make a systematic search. Unfortunately, it was only too clear that to leave the garden now he would have to fight his way out, for already people were shouting to other people to guard the exits. The task that lay immediately before him was to find some nook, some haven, some retired spot where he might hope to avoid discovery.

The night, as mysteriously happens when we stay out in it for any length of time, had now become appreciably lighter. Objects previously hidden began to reveal themselves. And among them was a sort of outhouse place that stood against the wall of the building some six feet from the bush in which he was lurking. Only a fraction of a second passed between the sighting of this outhouse by Bill and his realization that here, if anywhere, safety lay. The entire strength of the company appeared to have their attention concentrated at the moment on the goldfish pond, from which proceeded squashy sounds as of some solid body being gaffed and hauled ashore. Bill seized his opportunity with the promptitude of a strategist. Sliding softly out of his bush, he heaved himself in one scrabbling leap on to the outhouse roof and lay there motionless.

Nobody appeared to have observed him. A detachment of the enemy forces moved across the lawn and passed beneath him, Sir George walking squelchily in their sympathetic midst. The others, calling to one another at intervals, were prowling about, beating the bushes. But nobody thought of examining roofs. And after a lapse of time which might have been ten minutes or ten hours, the pursuit finally sagged away to nothingness. First one, then another of the prowlers gave the thing up and drifted back into the house, until at long last the garden was its silent sleeping self again.

But Bill remained where he was. At times of tense emotion we tend to extremes, and the vanishing of the Berserk mood had been followed by one of the utmost wariness. He had the night before him, and he meant to allow himself a generous margin of safety. The longer he waited, the better his chances of slipping away without any uncongenial brawling. He had had all the brawling he wanted for one night.

At length, however, when he had begun to feel that he had been lying on the roof since early childhood, he decided that it was safe to make a move. He slithered cautiously into a sitting position and rubbed his cramped limbs. And then, as he was about to rise and lower himself to the ground, every nerve in his body leaped simultaneously and twisted itself at the ends. Something had fallen with a thud not two feet from where he stood. Spinning round defensively, he discovered that it was a suit-case. Why people were throwing suit-cases out of windows at such an hour he could not imagine.

His speculations on this problem were interrupted by the sight of something even more remarkable—a dark figure apparently crawling down the side of the house.

§ 6

A man with all the world—or at any rate, part of Wimbledon—against him inclines naturally to see enemies everywhere : and Bill's reactions on becoming aware of this figure descending on to what he had grown to regard as his own private roof were at first purely militant.   He retired a few steps and braced himself for combat.   It was too dark to get a clear view, but the person who was crawling down the wall appeared to be of a slender physique, and he looked forward to the coming encounter with a bright confidence.   For while he was not afraid of the bulkiest foe, it is always pleasanter if you are going to have a rough-and-tumble, to have it with somebody a trifle undersized.   He could eat this midget, and unless the midget behaved itself he proposed to do so.

The figure alighted.   And at the same moment Bill made his spring.   It was only when a startled squeak rang out in the darkness that he was embarrassed to discover that he was grappling with a girl.   At which point the militant mood vanished abruptly, to be succeeded by one of amazed consternation.   The man who lays a hand upon a woman, save in the way of kindness, is justly looked askance at by society.   What then can be said for the man who tackles her as if she were trying to get past him on the football field ?   Bill was bathed in a prickly shame.

' I beg your pardon ! ' he cried.

Flick did not reply.   It had never occurred to her when she began her descent of the knotted sheet that violent giants were going to bound out at her from the night, and the shock had almost caused her to faint.   She stood there panting.

' I'm awfully sorry,' said Bill contritely.   ' I thought . . . I didn't know . . . I had an idea . . .'

' I've dropped my purse,' said Flick dizzily.

' Allow me ! ' said Bill.

A match sputtered.   Its light shone on Bill's face as he groped about the roof on all fours.

' Mr. West ! ' cried Flick, amazed.

Bill, who had just found the purse, sprang upright. Of all the bizarre events of the night this was the most astonishing.

'I'm Felicia Sheridan,' said Flick.

Such was Bill's perturbation that for a moment the name conveyed nothing to him. Then he remembered.

'Good heavens!' he exclaimed. 'What are you doing here?'

'I live here.'

'But what are you doing crawling down walls, I mean?'

'I'm running away.'

'Running away!'

'From home.'

'You're running away from home!' said Bill, mystified. 'I don't understand.'

'Don't speak so loud,' whispered Flick. 'They may hear.'

The good sense of this warning appealed to Bill. He lowered his voice.

'Why are you running away from home?' he asked.

'What are you doing on this roof?' asked Flick.

'What's the idea?' inquired Bill.

'What has been happening out in the garden?' countered Flick. 'I heard all sorts of noise and shouting.

Bill felt it would be a beginning in the direction of clearing up the situation if he answered her questions before putting his. Otherwise they might stay here all night, conducting an endless duologue. It was not a brief task, explaining the motives which had brought him to this house, but, this done, the rest of his story was simple and straightforward. He related it crisply.

'The man biffed me over the head with a stick,' he concluded, 'and after that nothing in the world seemed to matter except getting in here after him. It was a crazy thing to do, of course. I see that now. But it seemed a darned good idea at the time.'

'Biffed you over the head with a stick!' said Flick, marvelling. 'Who hit you with a stick?'

'This fellow. Pyke his name is.'

' Roderick ! '

' No, Pyke.'

' His name ', said Flick, ' is Roderick Pyke. That's why I'm running away.'

This struck Bill as a *non sequitur*. Women do eccentric things, but surely the most temperamental girl would hardly leave her home simply because a man's name was Roderick Pyke.

' They wanted me to marry him.

Bill's mystification vanished. He shuddered with sympathetic horror. A moment before he had been conscious of a certain disapproval of Flick's scheme of running away from home, and had intended, when the opportunity presented itself, to try to dissuade her. But this piece of news altered the whole aspect of the matter. Naturally she was running away. Anybody would. No lengths to which a girl could go to avoid marrying the bounder who had biffed him with a stick appeared extreme to Bill. There and then he executed a complete change of attitude and was now whole-heartedly in favour of the project, and resolved to do all that in him lay to push it along.

' Marry that blighter ! ' he exclaimed incredulously.

' Of course, in some ways he's quite nice.'

' He is *not* ! ' said Bill vehemently, and passed a gingerly hand over his corrugated skull. To his sensitive imagination the lump under his hair seemed to stick up like a mountain peak.

' Well, I'm not going to marry him, anyway,' said Flick. ' So the only thing to do is to run away. The trouble is,' she said ruefully, ' I don't in the least know where to go.'

' Your best plan is to come back with me to Marmont Mansions,' said Bill. ' We can talk it over quietly there, and decide on something.'

' I suppose that is best ? '

' We certainly can't stay on this roof. Any moment somebody may come along and find us.'

Flick betrayed some agitation.

' I wonder if it's safe to try to get away ? '

'There seems to be nobody in the garden.'

'I can't hear anybody. I suppose they've all gone in to dinner. There was a dinner-party on to-night, and I know Colonel Bagshott, for one, wouldn't want to wait too long for his food, whatever had been happening. What do you suppose the time is?'

'I haven't an idea. It must be long past eight. It was nearly that when I got here.'

'I tell you what,' said Flick. 'You jump down and creep round the house till you get to the front door. If the windows next to it are lighted and you can hear voices, it will mean they're in at dinner.'

'Good idea. If everything's all right I'll whistle.'

Flick stood in the darkness, waiting. The tremulous excitement which had filled her as she started to climb down the sheet had given way to a calmer and more agreeable mood. Bill, it seemed to her, had been sent from heaven to assist her in her hour of need. She had had only the vaguest idea of what she intended to do when she had escaped from Holly House, but now there was some one she could lean on. Bill was so big and comforting. A rock of strength. Slightly overestimating his mental capacity in her enthusiasm, she considered that there was no problem in existence too big for Bill to tackle.

A low whistle cut through the little night-sounds of the garden. She leaned over the edge of the roof.

'All right,' said Bill's voice in a cautious whisper. 'Drop me down your suit-case.'

Flick dropped the suit-case. He caught it skilfully. She lowered herself over the roof and was seized by a strong pair of hands and deposited gently on the ground.

'They're all in at dinner,' said Bill. 'Shall we get out by the front, or do you know a better way?'

'There's a door in the wall across the lawn. It'll be safer using that.'

They crept cautiously across the lawn. Something small and white snuffled in the darkness. Flick stooped with a little cry.

'Bob!' She rose with a dog in her arms. For the first time a sense of bereavement swept over her. 'Oh, I can't leave Bob.'

'Bring him along,' said Bill.

Flick's heart swelled with adoration for this god-like man who made no difficulties, raised no chilling obstacles or objections. She choked. Bob, who had had a great night so far and approved of the way things were shaping, licked her face frantically as they passed through the door.

The latch, closing behind her, clicked a brief farewell. Holly House was a thing of the past. Flick stood in the road with the world before her.

'All right?' said Bill understandingly.

'Quite all right, thanks,' said Flick, but in a voice that shook a little.

§ 7

Bill stood with his back against the mantelpiece of his sitting-room and smoked a thoughtful pipe. He was glad to be safe once more in the castle-like seclusion of Marmont Mansions. Apart from the spiritual relief of being several miles away from the house from which he had—probably quite illegally—helped a young girl to escape, there was the bodily comfort of being warm again. Almost immediately after the exodus from Holly House the mellowness of the night had changed to a raw chill, aided and abetted by a penetrating wind that sprang up from the east : and they had had to walk a shivering mile before they found a cab. Now they were home, the fire was blazing, and everything was jolly.

He looked down at Flick. She was lying back in an arm-chair with her eyes closed, Bob the Sealyham slumbering on her lap. The sight of her did something to diminish Bill's sense of well-being. And yet, mysteriously, at the same time it seemed to make it deeper. It was as if two conflicting voices spoke simultaneously in Bill's subconsciousness—one saying 'You poor impulsive ass, what have you let yourself in for ? ' the other ' It makes the old home look very cosy, does it not, a girl sitting in an arm-chair with her hat off and a dog on her lap ? '

He weighed the contending claims of these two voices. Most certainly there was much in what the first voice said. Not legally, perhaps not even morally, but beyond a doubt romantically he was responsible for this girl. The gods of high adventure do not permit a young man in the springtime to smuggle a girl away from her home by night, and then bid her a civil good-bye and think no more of her. Bill, as has been repeatedly stated before, was pledged for all eternity to Alice Coker (whose twelve photographs stared down from the mantelpiece and what-not—one might have said a little austerely) : but he felt very keenly a bond between himself and Flick. The details of the thing could be thought out later, but about the broad outline there was no argument possible. Here she was, under his charge, and somehow or other he had got to look after her and see that she came to no harm. He managed after a while to quiet the first voice by advancing the suggestion that a girl would not run away from home without some sort of a plan in her mind ; and moreover, living in a house of that magnificence she prob-ably had a large private income. She would be all right, he urged. He then had leisure to listen to the second Voice.

There was no denying the truth of what the second Voice was saying. The presence of Flick did make the place look cosy. She was not Alice Coker, of course ; but somehow at the moment the fact did not seem to matter so much. Bill found himself oddly soothed by the mere act of looking at Flick. To attempt to pretend, simply because his whole soul was wrapped up in Alice Coker, that Flick had not a decorative effect on his sitting-room would have been merely foolish. He ad-mitted freely that she had. Indeed—without the slightest disloyalty, of course—he was obliged to own that in such a position her flower-like prettiness had certain advan-tages over Alice's queenly and, to a diffident man, rather overpowering beauty. The thing turned on a matter of personality. Flick, if one might put it that way, blended gently and harmoniously into the atmosphere of a fellow's sitting-room ; whereas there was that about Alice's

stupendous loveliness that always seemed to make her
hit any place which she entered like a shell bursting in
the midst of a fanfare of trumpets.

Before Bill could penetrate any further into the depths
of analysis, Flick gave a little sigh and sat up.   She stared
for a moment at her surroundings as if bewildered.

' I couldn't think where I was,' she said.   ' Have I
been asleep ? '

' You did dose off for a minute or two.'

' How rude of me.'

' Not at all,' Bill assured her.   ' How are you feeling
now ? '

' Hungry,' said Flick.   ' Starving.   I haven't had a
bite to eat since lunch.'

' Good Lord ! '

' And I had a very light lunch because it seemed wicked
to be stuffing oneself with food when people like Mrs.
Matilda Pawle hadn't tasted a thing for three days.   That
reminds me—didn't you say that your friend lived here
with you ?   Where is he ? '

Bill lowered his pipe in sudden consternation.

' I'd clean forgotten about Judson,' he exclaimed
blankly.   ' Good heavens !   He may be running all over
London.'

' When did you see him last ? '

' When the man Pyke whacked me over the head I told
him to go and sit in the cab.   You don't think he's still
sitting there ? '

' It'll be awfully expensive if he is.   I suppose the clock
was ticking up threepences all the time ? '

' No.   He must have left, of course.   Then goodness
knows ', said Bill dejectedly, ' where he is now.'

Flick was a healthy girl and had a healthy appetite.
The question of Judson's whereabouts competed but
feebly for her interest with the thought of food.

' You haven't such a thing as a biscuit or anything,
have you ? ' she asked wistfully.   ' Or a leg of mutton or
a tongue or a round of beef or a piece of cheese or anything
like that ? '

' I'm awfully sorry,' said Bill, aroused to a realization

of his position as host. 'I should have got you something long ago. I'll forage in the larder.'

He left the room hurriedly and returned some minutes
later with a laden tray ; which he nearly dropped on
the threshold in his dismay at the sound of a muffled
sob. He did drop a knife and two forks, and the clatter
caused Flick to start and turn a tear-stained face in his
direction.

'It's nothing,' she assured him.

Bill put the tray down on the table.

'What's the matter ? ' he asked, agitated. Like most
men, he was conscious of a grisly discomfort in the presence of a crying woman. 'Can I do anything ? '

'It's nothing,' said Flick again. She dabbed at her
eyes and smiled a faint smile. 'Do cut me some of that
ham. I'm simply famished.'

'But look here. . . .'

Flick attacked her meal composedly. She appeared
to have woman's gift of rapid change from mood to
mood.

'Is that coffee ? ' she said. 'How splendid ! ' She
drank a mouthful. 'It warms one, doesn't it,' she said.
'Makes one feel braver. I was only crying because I
was a little scared. And—well, yes—because I suddenly
happened to think of Uncle Sinclair.'

'Uncle Sinclair ? '

'Do you remember him ? He was staying with your
uncle the time you saved my life. He hadn't married
Aunt Francie then, and he and I were together all the
time.' She choked. 'This coffee *is* hot,' she said in a
small voice.

'I remember him,' said Bill. 'Good Lord, isn't it
funny how things come back to one. I liked him.'

'I love him,' said Flick simply.

There was a silence.

'Some more ham ? ' said Bill.

'No, thanks.'

Flick stared into the fire.

'It's horrible to think of leaving him,' she said. 'But
what was I to do ? '

Bill nodded sagely.

'I had to run away.'

Bill coughed. He wished to approach as delicately as possible the question of future plans.

'Talking of running away,' he said, 'I was rather wondering . . . I mean, had you any particular idea in your mind?'

'Only to get away.'

'I see.'

'You mean,' said Flick, 'had I decided what to do afterwards?'

'It did cross my mind,' admitted Bill.

Flick pondered.

'Do you know,' she said, 'at the time I don't think I had the slightest notion. But I'm beginning to see now. I think I had better write a letter, don't you? I did leave a sort of note pinned to my pin-cushion, but that just said I was going away because I wouldn't marry Roderick.'

'You mustn't on any account marry that chap,' said Bill decidedly. He still had a slight headache.

'Oh no, I'm quite determined about that. But I think I'd better write and say that I'll come back if they promise that I needn't marry him.'

'What made you suddenly find you couldn't go through with it?' asked Bill.

'It was something that happened this afternoon. A man came rushing up to him when he was with me on the Embankment, and Roderick was so frightened that he leaped into a cab and flew for his life, leaving me on the pavement.'

'Good Lord!' said Bill. 'That must have been Judson.' He poured her out another cup of coffee. 'I'll tell you exactly what to do,' he said. 'Write this letter and tell them that if they want you to come back on your conditions to advertise in the Personal column of the *Daily Mail*. Have you got any money?'

'Oh yes. Plenty, thanks.'

'Then all you have to do is just to stick it out. They'll probably quit in under a week.'

' I don't know,' said Flick doubtfully. ' Uncle George and Aunt Francie are frightfully determined people. Uncle George is one of those little square-jawed men who never give way an inch. He was the one who fell into the pond,' she said, bubbling reminiscently.

' No, really ? ' said Bill, amused. ' He made a pretty good splash, didn't he ! '

' I've never heard anybody fall into a pond before. I only wish it had been daylight, so that I could have seen it.'

' If it had been daylight ', Bill pointed out, ' he wouldn't have gone in.'

' No, there's always something, isn't there,' Flick agreed. She got up. ' Well, I certainly feel ever so much better,' she said. ' I needed that food. I suppose I ought to be going now. Though I do hate leaving that fire. Have you ever noticed how cosy a room looks just when you have to leave it ? '

' Going ? ' said Bill. ' What do you mean ? '

' Well, I've got to find a room, haven't I ? Somewhere to sleep to-night.' She looked ruefully at the Sealyham, who was on the rug gnawing the remains of a chop. ' I'm afraid Bob's going to be rather a burden. Do you think a landlady would make a fuss about my having him ? They usually own cats, and Bob gets so temperamental when he sees a cat.'

Bill spoke decidedly.

' It's absolutely impossible for you to go about trying to find a room at this time of night. Quite out of the question. You must stop here, of course. I'll clear out and intercept Judson when he gets back and take him off somewhere.'

' But where ? '

' Oh, I know dozens of places where we can go.'

' It's awfully kind of you,' said Flick, hesitating.

' Not a bit of it. We've got an old woman who comes in by the day and does the cooking and so on. When you hear her in the morning, pop your head out and shout at her to bring you breakfast.'

' It will probably scare her into a fit.

' Oh no, she's a hardy old soul. Well, I'll be saying good night.'

' Good night, Mr. West.'

Bill hesitated.

' I wish you wouldn't call me " Mr. West," ' he said. ' Surely when you were staying at my uncle's you used to call me Bill ? '

' I believe I did.' She stooped and patted Bob, who rolled an eye up at her but did not discontinue his meal. ' And you called me Flick.'

' Flick ! ' exclaimed Bill. ' So I did. Isn't it funny how one forgets things ! '

' I'm rather good at remembering things,' said Flick.

' Well, good night, Flick.'

' Good night, Bill.'

' I'll be round in the morning some time, and then we can discuss what you're going to do.' He paused at the door. ' By the way,' he added, ' you've—er—got . . . ? '

He looked at her suit-case and decided that she probably had.

' Good night,' he said. ' See you to-morrow.'

' Good night, Bill, and thank you a million times for being so wonderful.'

' Not at all,' said Bill modestly.

Bill went downstairs and out into Prince of Wales Road. He began to regret the necessity of having to wait here to intercept Judson. It was a very open question whether Judson, having money in his pocket, would revisit the home many minutes in advance of the morning milk : and meanwhile it was infernally cold. To keep himself warm Bill began presently to pace up and down the pavement outside the block of flats : and he was still doing this when there slouched through the pool of light cast by a street-lamp near the door a wretched, shambling, travel-stained creature with dusty shoes and the beginnings of a cold in its head. It was a heart-rending sneeze, indeed, that first attracted Bill's attention.

' Judson ! '

The figure stopped and leaned wearily against the railings.

'Hullo, Bill o' man.' A groan blended with another sneeze. 'Oh, gosh, Bill, I've had one rotten time!'

'What happened?'

Judson mopped his forehead with his handkerchief, and spoke for a while of blisters on the soles of his feet.

'When you left me', he said, 'I sat in the cab for ages, wondering what the deuce you were up to. And then the cabby shoved his head in and wanted to know what the game was. I said, "Stick around, George. We've got to wait for the gentleman." Upon which the fellow got very nasty. Insisted on having his fare. And I had to cough up, darn it! Took all the money I had and left me owing him threepence. He said it didn't matter about the threepence and drove off with a cheery good night, and I had to hoof it all the way home. All the way home, Bill o' man! Gosh, I don't suppose I've walked that far before in my life. I'm all in. Besides having blisters . . . Well, thank goodness, I've got here at last. Now I'm going to tumble into my little bed.'

'No, you're not,' said Bill. 'There's a girl in it.'

Judson gaped.

'A girl?'

'I'll explain as we go. You and I are going to sleep at the Jermyn Street Turkish baths to-night.'

'A girl in my bed?' repeated Judson blankly.

'Well, she may be in mine. Anyway, I've given her the flat for the night and we've got to go elsewhere. I'll tell you all about her on the way.'

Judson sighed.

'I might have expected something like this,' he said resignedly. 'Everything's on the fritz nowadays. I haven't had a bit of luck since I lost that Lucky Pig of mine. Never did find that pig. Oh, by the way, Bill.'

'Now what?'

'That cab. It cost me thirteen shillings and something. Call it a pound in round numbers. I'd be glad to have that.'

'I suppose you would.'

' You're surely going to refund it, aren't you ? '

Bill turned, astounded.

' Refund it ? ' he cried incredulously. ' Who, me ?
Why, it was your cab.'

The night closed in upon them.

CHAPTER SIX

HORACE CHANGES HIS MIND

§ 1

MR. COOLEY PARADENE'S pleasant domain at Westbury, Long Island, dozed in the April sunshine. It was the sort of day when any ordinary man would have been out in God's air ; but Mr. Paradene, being a book collector, was spending the afternoon in his library.

In front of him, as he sat at his desk, lay the most recent additions to his collection. The necessity of glancing at, dipping into, blowing spots of dust off and fondling these was interfering very much with the task he had on hand at the moment—to wit, the writing of a letter to his old friend Sinclair Hammond, of Holly House, Wimbledon, England. At the point where we discover him he had, indeed, got no further than the words, ' *My dear Hammond.*'

He now assumed an expression of resolution, and dipping his pen in the inkpot, began to tackle his task squarely :

MY DEAR HAMMOND,—

Thank you for your letter, which reached me a week ago, and many thanks for again inviting me to pay you a visit. I am glad to say that at last I am able to accept your very kind hospitality. Unless anything occurs to alter my plans, I propose to sail for England about the middle of next month. I am looking forward with the greatest eagerness to seeing you again.

I shall have one or two nice little things to show you. At the sale of the Mortimer collection I was lucky enough to secure quite cheap—only eight thousand dollars—

Browning's own copy of *Pauline* (Saunders and Ottley, 1833), also Browning's own copy of *Paracelsus* (E. Wilson, 1835) and of *Strafford* (Longmans, 1837). I am sure, too, you will appreciate another capture of mine, the autograph manuscript of Don Juan, Canto Nine. This is entirely in Byron's handwriting and is the only canto lacking in Pierpont Morgan's collection. I would not take twenty thousand dollars for it. I have also a few other good things which I will show you when we meet.

Since writing to you last I have, you may be interested to hear, adopted a son—a splendid little fellow——

A knock at the door interrupted his writing. Mr. Paradene looked up.

' Come in.'

The English language is so nicely adapted to the expression of delicate shades of meaning that it is perhaps slovenly to be satisfied with describing the noise that had broken in on Mr. Paradene's composition as a knock. The word ' bang ' more nearly fits it. And Mr. Paradene frowned with quick displeasure. He was not accustomed to having his hermit's cell battered upon in this fashion. His surprise when the opening door revealed Roberts, the butler, was extreme.

If there is one class of the community that has reduced knocking on doors to a nice art it is butlers. Roberts' discreet tap had been until this moment a thing that blended with rather than disturbed the thoughts. Only some great emotion, felt Mr. Paradene, could have caused him to slam the panel with such vehement impetuosity ; and the next moment the sunlight, falling on the butler's face as he moved forward, showed that his suspicion had been correct. Roberts was foaming at the mouth.

The expression ' foaming at the mouth ' is so often used to suggest a merely mental condition that it must be stated that in the present instance it is employed perfectly literally. A bubbly yellowish-white froth covered the lower part of the butler's face ; and when he removed this with a vicious dab of his handkerchief other bubbles immediately presented themselves. Had Roberts been a dog Mr. Para-

dene would undoubtedly have been justified in shooting
him on sight.   As he was a man, and a trusted employee
at that, he simply stared dumbly.

'Might I speak to you, sir?' said Roberts thickly.

'What on earth——' began Mr. Paradene.

'I would like to be informed, sir, if Master Horace is to
be a permanency in this household.'

Mr. Paradene, hearing these words, felt like one who
sees looming above the horizon a cloud no bigger than a
man's hand.   They struck him as significant and sinister.
For there was that in the butler's tone that suggested
disapproval of that splendid little fellow, his adopted son.

Mr. Paradene's mouth tightened.   He was an obstinate
man.   Disapproval of Horace affected him personally.
It implied criticism of his action in bringing him into the
home, and he resented criticism of his actions, whether
implied or spoken.

'He most certainly is,' he replied curtly.

'Then', said the butler, blowing bubbles, 'I must ask
you to accept my resignation, sir.'

It speaks well for the benevolence of Mr. Paradene's
domestic rule that this kind of announcement was an
astonishing rarity in his life.   Once in his house, servants
were as a rule only too glad to stay.   He had had only two
cooks in fourteen years ; while as for Roberts, that excellent man had joined up nearly eight summers ago and had
looked until this moment as solid a fixture as the pillars
that upheld the front porch.   To see this devoted retainer
blowing bubbles at him and talking of resigning his position afflicted Mr. Paradene with a horrible sense of being
in the toils of some disordered dream.

'What?' was all he could find to say.

The sadness of this parting after so long and happy a
union seemed to affect the butler too.   His manner became less severe and his voice took on a tone of pathos.

'I regret this, sir, deeply,' he said.   'Nobody could
have been more comfortable in a situation than I have
been in your service, sir.   But remain in the house if
Master Horace is to continue here I cannot and will not.'

The hasty and imperious side of Mr. Paradene's nature

urged him to close this interview at once by withering the man with a few well-chosen words and sending him about his business. But curiosity was too strong for him. If he allowed Roberts to leave him without explaining the bubbles, he would worry himself into a premature grave. The thing would become one of those great historic mysteries which fret the souls of men through the ages.

'What's your objection to Master Horace?' he forced himself to inquire.

Roberts plied his handkerchief daintily for a few moments.

'My objection, sir, is both general and particular.'

'What the devil do you mean by that?' demanded Mr. Paradene, bewildered.

'If I might explain, sir.'

'Go ahead.'

'Downstairs, sir, we do not like Master Horace's manner. One of the lower servants summed it up in a happy phrase not many days ago when he described the young gentleman as too darned fresh. We have so much affection—if I may take the liberty of saying so—for yourself, sir, that we have endeavoured hitherto to bear this without complaint. But now things have gone too far.'

Mr. Paradene leaned forward in his chair. Imperiousness had vanished and curiosity occupied his mind to the exclusion of every other emotion. At last, he felt, Roberts was about to speak freely of the bubbles.

'A few days ago I refused to permit Master Horace to raid the larder for food.'

'Quite right,' agreed Mr. Paradene. 'Makes him fat.'

'He appeared at the time to take this in a mutinous spirit. He called me one or two names which', said Roberts, brooding coldly, 'I have not forgotten. But this afternoon, just before he went out for his walk with Mr. Bastable, he approached me with an apology so amiable and apparently sincere that I had no alternative but to accept it. He then offered me an attractive-looking piece of candy, sir. This I also accepted. I have a sweet tooth. I did not immediately eat it, partly because I had only recently finished a hearty meal and partly because Master

Horace specifically urged me to save it up. But when
I——'

Mr. Paradene was an oldish man, but he had been a boy
once. A dazzling light shone on his darkness.

'Good God!' he exclaimed. 'You don't mean there
was soap in it!'

'Exactly, sir,' foamed the butler.

There was a pregnant silence. For a moment Mr. Paradene was, curiously enough, not so much shocked and horrified as filled with a sort of subtle melancholy, the feeling
which the ancient Romans used to call *desiderium.*

'It must be fifty years', he murmured wistfully, 'since
I played that trick on any one.'

'I', said the butler with austerity, 'have never played
it. Nor had it played on me. It came as a complete surprise.'

'Too bad,' said Mr. Paradene, returning from the past
and overcoming with some difficulty a desire to give way
to a mirth which would obviously be ill-timed. 'Too bad.
Young rascal! I'll have a talk with him. Of course, one
can see the thing from his viewpoint.'

'I fear I am unable to do so, sir,' said Roberts stiffly.

'I mean, boys will be boys.'

The butler expressed his disapproval of this too tolerant
philosophy with a lift of the eyebrow so chilling that Mr.
Paradene continued hastily:

'Don't think I'm excusing him. Nothing of the kind.
Can't have that sort of thing. Certainly not! But, good
gracious, Roberts, you don't want to throw up an excellent
situation simply because——'

'I am leaving with the greatest regret, sir, I assure you.'

'Nonsense, nonsense! You aren't leaving at all. Of
course you aren't! I couldn't get on for a day without
you.'

'It is very kind of you to say so, sir,' said the butler,
beginning to melt.

'I'll see the boy and make him apologize. Apologize
humbly. That will make everything all right, eh?'

'Well, sir——'

'And you'll give up all this nonsense about leaving?'

' Well—if you wish it, sir.'

' Wish it ?　Of course I wish it.　Good heavens, you've been with me eight years !　You go back to the pantry and get yourself a good drink.'

' You're very kind, sir.'

' And listen, Roberts.　It's only fair that I should pay some sort of indemnity.　Like a nation does when one of its subjects starts something in another country, eh ? There'll be an extra ten dollars in the monthly envelope from now on.　Leave me, indeed !　I never heard such nonsense ! '

The butler, who, like the month of March, had come in like a lion, went out like a lamb, leaving his employer chewing his pen.　Mr. Paradene was worried.　He hated to confess it even in the privacy of self-communion, but he was disappointed in Horace.　He had not yet actually adopted the boy with full formality of legal papers, but the fact that he had proclaimed him as his adopted son made it impossible for a man of his obstinacy to draw back ; and it was beginning to come home to him that the whole business had been a blunder.　A magnificent gesture, true, and one that had most satisfactorily stunned brother-in-law Jasper and the rest of those grasping sycophants ; but nevertheless a blunder.　Yes, he feared he had been too impulsive.　Impulsiveness had always been his besetting fault from boyhood up.　He was trying to divert his thoughts from this unpleasant matter by finishing his letter to Sinclair Hammond when they were jerked back to their original channel by the sight through the open window of Horace himself, returning from his afternoon walk with Mr. Sherman Bastable, his tutor.

He watched the couple cross the lawn and disappear round the corner of the house.　Horace, he noted, had a weary and sullen mien, in marked contrast to Mr. Bastable's buoyant freshness.　The tutor was a lean and enthusiastic young man, just down from the university, who preferred brisk walking to any other method of locomotion. Horace, to judge from his expression and his drooping slouch, did not share his views.

It had frequently annoyed Mr. Paradene that his son by

adoption, though of a chunky and athletic build, seemed
to like to spend his time lolling in easy chairs. This, he
felt, was not the spirit that makes supermen, and quick
irritation gripped him once more.

He was still brooding fretfully on the boy's shortcomings
when there was a sudden rushing noise without and Mr.
Bastable burst into the room.

' Mr. Paradene ! ' shouted the tutor in a high im-
passioned tenor.   ' I will not put up with it ! '

Mr. Paradene was dumbfounded.   Hitherto he had
always found Sherman Bastable an exceptionally civil and
soft-spoken young fellow, but now the man was trans-
formed.   His tone was one that would have excited comment in the fo'c'sle if used by the second mate of a tramp
steamer.   His face was flushed and contorted, and as he
spoke he thumped the desk violently.

' I've had enough of it ! ' he bellowed.

Mr. Paradene stared at him ; and staring, became aware
of something which in his first astonishment he had overlooked.   He had felt vaguely right from the start that
there was an oddness about the tutor's appearance, and
now he realized what had given him this impression.
Sherman Bastable, in his employer's private and sacred
library, was wearing his hat !   The spectacle brought Mr.
Paradene, already simmering, to the boiling point.

' It has got to stop ! ' cried the tutor.

' Take off your hat ! ' said Mr. Paradene.

The words, designed to bring the young man to himself
in a rush of shamed embarrassment, had the odd effect of
amusing him.   At least, he laughed.   But it was a hideous, hollow laugh that seemed wrenched from his very
vitals.

' I like that ! ' he cried.   ' That's good !   Take off my
hat !   Yes, that's rich ! '

' You're drunk,' said Mr. Paradene, purpling.

' I'm not ! '

' You must be.   You rush in here with your hat on——'

' Yes,' said Mr. Bastable bitterly, ' I do.   And perhaps
you'd like to know why.   Because I can't get the damned
thing off without skinning my forehead.   That little brute

of a boy has gone and rubbed glue all round the inside
band, and now it's melted.   And I want to tell you, Mr.
Paradene——'

The things Mr. Bastable wanted to—and did—tell his
employer were so numerous and couched in language so
harsh and unguarded that one is forced to omit them.   His
final utterance, spoken a brief instant before he slammed
the door, is the only one that need be recorded.

'I'm through ! ' said Mr. Bastable.   ' You can accept
my resignation.   I wouldn't stay here another day if you
paid me a million dollars.'

The bang of the door died away, leaving a quivering
silence.   Mr. Paradene stood for a moment, plunged in
thought.   Then, going to a closet, he took out a long, slim
cane ; and, having swished this musically through the air
once or twice, strode rapidly from the room.

§ 2

Out in the garden, meanwhile, in the shade of a large
locust tree that stood near a handsome shrubbery of rhododendrons, the cause of all these upheavals in the home was
relaxing after the fatigues of his afternoon walk.   His
young body at ease in a deck-chair and his feet restfully
supported by a small rustic table, the boy Horace lay with
closed eyes, restoring his tissues.   Beside him on the turf
a glass, empty except for a fragment of ice, spoke pleasantly of past lemonade, and a close observer might have
detected cake-crumbs on the lad's waistcoat.   Everything
was jake with Horace.

The warm sunshine invited slumber, and it was not
immediately that the soft whistling from the shrubbery
succeeded in penetrating to his consciousness.   For some
time the boy had attributed the sound to one of the birds
that ranged the garden, but presently it became so persistent as to interfere with sleep.   He opened his eyes and
gazed drowsily in the direction from which it seemed to
proceed.   Having done this he became aware of a face
peering at him out of the rhododendrons.

One uses the word ' face ' in a loose sense.   What met
Horace's eyes was a mere congeries of features apparently

carelessly assembled by an inexpert hand, few of them making any pretence of matching one another.

The nose appeared to have been designed for a far smaller man, whereas the chin, which jutted out like the cowcatcher of a train, would have caught the eye if attached to the body of a giant. The forehead, a narrow strip of territory separating the eyebrows from the fringe, was flanked by enormous ears that stood out at a majestic right angle.

To see this strange facial hash protruding from a rhododendron bush might have startled many people. Horace bore the spectacle with calm, almost with indifference. He yawned.

' Hello, Joe,' he said. ' It's you, is it ? '

' Yes, it's me,' replied the other in a voice of marked surliness. ' I've come to find out what you're doin', and I find you doin' what I might have expected I'd find you doin'—doin' nothing.'

' I'm concentratin',' said Horace casually.

Joe the Dip—for the visitor was none other—looked up and down the quiet garden and, satisfied that it was empty, emerged cautiously from his bush. Now that the whole of him had become visible, his social status was even more obvious than before. A criminal, evidently—and belonging, one would have said, to the executive rather than the organizing branch of his particular gang. If you wanted a man to scheme out some subtle confidence game you would pass over Joe. But if, on the other hand, the task on the programme involved the sand-bagging of somebody down a dark alley, then you would beckon to Joe with an immediate ' Eureka ! ' In build he was a solid man of medium height, with thick and stooping shoulders. His feet were large and flat.

' Concentratin', eh ? ' he observed bitterly. ' Dat's about the best thing you do, ain't it ? See here, kid, I've made a long trip out to this joint to get next to youse, and what I want to know is, how about it ? The boss is gettin' worried.'

' Yeah ? ' said Horace.

' We're all gettin' worried. You've got it soft, ain't

you, sittin' pretty in this swell home, livin' off the fat of
the land ? '

' I don't eat fat.'

' It's about all you don't eat. I know youse. Lazy,
dat's what you are. If I'd been here instead of you I'd
have got action long ago.'

' You would, eh ? '

' Yes, I would. What's keepin' youse ? What's de
snag ? '

Horace settled down more deeply into his deck-chair
and eyed his interrogator calmly.

' I been thinkin',' he said.

' You got no time for that sort of thing,' said Joe the Dip
reprovingly. ' We got to get a move on.'

' Thinkin'', proceeded Horace, ' whether we really want
to rob Mr. Paradene.'

' Wot ? ' gasped Joe. ' Thinkin' wot ? '

' I've been going to the movie house down in the village,
and it seems to me it don't pay to be a crook. No, sir !
Every crook that reforms always turns up in a dress suit
in the last reel.'

Joe licked his lips feverishly. He seemed to be feeling
that a stricter censorship was needed for the motion-
picture industry.

' There was one I saw last night ', continued Horace
dreamily, ' where an ugly bad-tempered crook puts a kid
up to stealing from an old gentleman. Kind of coin-
cidence, wasn't it ? '

' Here——'

' Well, the fellow he's robbin' catches him an' says that
he's a big crook himself an' he wants the kid to go to some
town an' get the reputation of being the honestest young
man in the place and then he'll come and spring somethin'
really big. An' the kid goes and he does, an' the big
crook comes and says, " Now's the time ! " An' the kid
says, " No ! I'm honest an' I like it, because I'm president of the bank an' everythin'." And the big crook says,
" Thank God, I only did the whole thing to try and make
you an honest man ! " What do you think of that ? '

' I think it's terrible,' said Joe with emotion.

He stared at his young friend, breathing heavily.

' Well, if you really want to know,' said Horace, chuckling unfeelingly, ' I was only kidding when I said that was why I didn't want to rob old Paradene.'

Joe heaved a sigh of relief.

' Oh, if you was only kiddin'——'

' The real reason why I'm not going to——'

' Eh ? ' cried Joe, starting violently.

' I say the real reason why I'm not going to is what you said yourself just now. You said I was sittin' pretty, and so I am. Gee ! I should be a fine chump, I should, doin' anything that 'ud make me have to duck out of a swell joint like this. This is my dish ! You've got me adopted by this rich millionaire, and I'm goin' to stay adopted. Why, you poor simp, you've got about as much chance of havin' me sneak those books for you as—well, I don't know what. I'm here and I'm going to stay here. And if you want those books you come and break in and pinch them for yourself. As far as I'm concerned, the thing's cold.'

Joe the Dip, as has been pointed out, was not a man of swift intelligence. The problems created by this appalling treachery on the part of his young ally were altogether too much for him. The situation made him dizzy. He was still wondering how this news was to be broken to the boss and what the boss, a man who disliked having his schemes go wrong, would say about it, when the sight of a figure coming out of the house drove him quickly back into the shelter of the rhododendrons. He crouched there, an unhappy man.

§ 3

The figure that had interrupted Joe the Dip's train of thought was that of Mr. Paradene, with cane complete. The walk down the stairs and out into the garden had served only to intensify the wrath of that injured man. His eyes, as he stalked across the lawn, were gleaming fiercely and his mouth was tightly clamped. Mr. Paradene was on the warpath.

Horace, snuggling contentedly in his deck-chair, watched

his approach without qualms. No sense of coming peril
disturbed his peace. The conscience of youth is not
tender, and Horace's spoke no word of warning now.

' Hello, pop,' he said amiably.

Mr. Paradene was a man of action.

' I'll teach you to feed my butler soap and put glue in
your tutor's hat ! ' he said. And with this brief preamble
embarked forthwith on the lesson. It was not a simple
task to try to inject sweetness and light into a boy of
Horace's hard-boiled temperament, but what one man
armed with a springy whangee could do Mr. Paradene did.
A stranger, passing Cooley Paradene with a casual glance
in the street, might have thought his physique too slight
for any violent muscular effort. Horace, after the first
few moments, could have corrected this impression. But
then he was getting first-hand information.

' There ! ' said Mr. Paradene, at length desisting. It
shows how diametrically opposed two persons' views can
be on any given point that Horace's new father was dis-
satisfied with his work. He chafed at the inroads made
by advancing years on a once wiry frame, and considered
that heaviness of arm and scantness of breath had caused
him to stop much too soon. Horace was not seeing eye
to eye with him in this matter. Whatever his views on
Mr. Paradene's lesson in deportment—and he had many
—he certainly did not think that there had not been
enough of it.

' There ! ' said Mr. Paradene again, breathing heavily.
And, turning on his heel, he stalked back to the house.

Not until he was out of sight did Joe the Dip venture to
leave the shelter of the rhododendrons. But when it was
plain that the intruder had definitely withdrawn, he came
out of his retirement, his face wreathed in unwonted
smiles. His young friend's yelps of anguish had been
music to the ears of Joe the Dip. He had only regretted
that the social *convenances* should have rendered it in-
advisable for him to emerge and lend a hand in the good
work. He surveyed Horace contentedly.

' Laugh that off ! ' observed Joe, with quiet relish.
' Serves you right for bein' a little double-crosser.'

Horace gritted his teeth. He was still somewhat stunned by the dreadful unexpectedness of the recent massacre. Deceived by the benevolent exterior of Mr. Paradene, he had not suspected the existence of these hidden fires beneath the surface.

' Who's a double-crosser ? ' he demanded warmly.

' You are,' said Joe the Dip. ' And, say, listen, if it had of been me behind that stick you wouldn't have got off with a few taps like that. If there's one bozo in this world I got no use for it's a little squirt that double-crosses his pals.'

Horace glared. This censure stung him, for now he felt that it was unjust. In the last few minutes his views on existence in the Paradene home had undergone a striking alteration. He had mistaken it after a too superficial inspection for an earthly paradise ; he now realized that there were attached to it drawbacks of the most pronounced kind.

' Double-cross nothin' ! ' he exclaimed heatedly. ' You can go back and tell the boss that I'll have those books he's so crazy about if I have to dig 'em out with a chisel. Leave it to me ! I'm in this game now to get action ! '

' At-a-boy ! ' cried Joe the Dip enthusiastically. ' 'At's the way I like to hear youse talk ! '

CHAPTER SEVEN

MR. SLINGSBY INVITES SUSPICION

IT is one of the delightful features of the English spring that days occur in it—in fact it is almost entirely composed of days on which, as evening draws in, the temperature is such as to render an open fire agreeable, even necessary. The one that blazed in the grate of the sitting-room of Bill's flat in Marmont Mansions, Battersea, some ten days after Flick's impulsive departure from Holly House, was large and cheerful. It threw warm beams of golden light on the Sealyham, sleeping on the rug ; on Bill, smoking in an arm-chair ; on Flick, snug on the settee, her fair head bent over a pair of Bill's socks, which she was darning. Bill, his pipe drawing nicely, had fallen into a pleasant train of thought.

After that hectic night in the gardens of Holly House life had settled down to a smooth placidity. Flick was comfortably established now in a bed-sitting-room round the corner, having stumbled by good fortune on a house whose landlady, so far from objecting to dogs, had welcomed Bob with a motherly warmth and was now conducting a campaign of systematic overfeeding which had already begun to have grave effects on his figure. This admirable woman could also cook in a manner rare among her kind. So that Flick, though after the magnificence of Holly House she could hardly hope to find a bed-sitting-room luxurious, had no complaints to make. Except for an occasional spasm of remorse brought on by remembrance of her Uncle Sinclair, she was enjoying life hugely. She liked the novel feeling of freedom. She liked the sense of adventure. And she particularly liked these daily visits to the home of Bill and Judson. The only

phenomena in her new world which she did not like were
those twelve photographs of Alice Coker, which seemed to
stare at her with a hostile disdain every time she entered
this room.   She had now come definitely to the conclusion
that she detested Alice Coker.

To Bill, also, the present trend of life seemed wholly
excellent.   In a vague way he realized that things could
not go on like this for ever, but he did not allow the
thought to diminish his happiness.   Being at an age
when one does not look very piercingly into the future,
he was satisfied to enjoy the moment, soothed by the
atmosphere of quiet and spluttering fires and sock-mending.   He could not remember a time when any one had
ever darned socks for him.   In the days of his careless
prosperity he had simply worn the things until the holes
became too vast even for his uncritical tolerance, and
then had thrown them away.   He lay back in his arm-
chair, watching Flick's busy fingers, and told himself
that this was life as it should be lived.

Flick's fingers stopped their rhythmic movement.   She
looked up.

' What has become of Mr. Coker ? ' she asked.

She was fond of Judson.   He had at last got over
his embarrassing habit of gaping at her like a fish, as
if the sight of her in his sitting-room made his senses
reel, and there existed between them a firm and growing
friendship.   Their relations were those of a modified
Desdemona and Othello.   She liked him for the hard-
ships he was undergoing, and he liked her that she did
pity them.   Judson had never met a girl more sweetly
disposed to listen to his troubles.   In a black world
Flick restored his faith in human nature.

' He told me he was going to look up Slingsby,' said
Bill, and felt the faint pricking of conscience which always
came to him when the name of the London manager of
the Paradene Pulp and Paper Company was mentioned.
Recently he had rather permitted the dynamic Mr.
Slingsby to pass out of his life, and the thought sometimes made him uncomfortable.   He had achieved, he
realized, absolutely nothing in the direction of fulfilling

the mission which his Uncle Cooley had entrusted to him ; and more and more this visit of his to London was beginning to take on the aspect of a pleasant vacation. This was all wrong, of course ; but on the other hand, what could he do ? As his uncle had justly remarked, if Wilfrid Slingsby was baffled by the problem of why the profits had fallen off, what chance had a novice like himself to solve it ?

'I didn't know he knew Mr. Slingsby,' said Flick.

'Oh yes ; I took him round to the office the other day and introduced him.'

Flick resumed work on the sock.

'I've been thinking,' she said. 'I don't like what you told me about Mr. Slingsby.'

'Oh, he's all right,' said Bill with the tolerance bred of physical well-being.

'I can't help feeling he may be crooked.'

Bill smiled indulgently. This, he supposed, was what they called feminine intuition. The only trouble with it was that it didn't work. Common sense had long since caused him to abandon the doubts he had once entertained of Mr. Slingsby's honesty.

'Oh, I don't know,' he said. 'I wouldn't say I liked the man, but I don't suspect him of anything like that. It's true he has let the profits fall off——'

'And yet you said he was such a capable man.'

'Yes ; but he explained the whole thing to me the day I lunched with him. I couldn't quite follow all of it, but it seemed straight enough. Business conditions and all that sort of thing, you know.'

'I see,' said Flick, and there was a brief silence. Bill changed the subject.

'I've been thinking too.'

'Yes ?'

'Wondering', said Bill, 'what your people are saying about your running away. It seems odd there hasn't been anything in the papers.'

'Uncle George would never allow anything to get into the papers. He would be much too afraid of the scandal.'

'They never put any reply to your letter in the Per-

sonal column of the *Mail*. It begins to look as if they
intended to stick it out.'

' Yes.'

' What will you do if they don't climb down ? '

Flick looked up with a quick flash of her cornflower
eyes. That sudden, impish way she had of jerking up
her head always fascinated Bill. It reminded him of a
startled kitten.

' I shall get a job somewhere. I'm pretty good at
typing and I can do a sort of shorthand. I used to work
with Uncle Sinclair a lot at one time. At any rate, I'm
not going back to marry Roderick.'

' I should say not ! Anything ', said Bill sententiously,
' is better than marrying some one you don't love. Love
is worth waiting for. One of these days you're bound
to find a man you'll fall in love with.'

' Am I ? '

' Absolutely bound to. It comes over you like a flash,
you know—quite suddenly.'

' Does it ? '

' I remember when I first met Alice——'

' What sort of a girl is Miss Coker ? ' Flick interrupted.

' What sort of a—— ' Bill found himself at something
of a loss for words. It is a tough job describing goddesses.
' Why she's—— But I've told you all about her a lot
of times.'

' So you have,' said Flick demurely, returning to the
sock.

' It's been wonderful having somebody like you to
talk to about Alice,' said Bill. ' Judson isn't much use
in that way. But you're different. You're a real pal.
I can—— '

' Would she mend your socks ? ' asked Flick.

The question seemed to disconcert Bill. He had
recently come to regard sock-mending as one of the
noblest pursuits of woman, and it pained him to discover
anything even remotely resembling a flaw in Miss Coker's
perfection. But the fact had to be faced. Try as he
might to envisage Alice mending socks, he could not
do it.

'She's rather the dashing sort of Society type of girl, you know,' he said, and was aghast to find himself speaking quite apologetically.

'I see.'

There was a silence. From the fire a few glowing fragments of coal dribbled into the grate. The Sealyham on the rug gave a little whine as he chased rats through dreamland.

'Don't you usually write to her on Tuesdays?' said Flick carelessly.

'Good Lord!' Bill dropped his pipe and stared at her with fallen jaw. 'I'd clean forgotten.'

'You'd better go and do it now or you'll miss the mail.'

Bill was conscious of a peculiar sensation. Analysing this, he was horrified to realize that for an instant what he had been feeling was a reluctance to get out of his chair; a strange, evil shrinking from the delightful task of writing a long letter to the girl he loved. For one ghastly moment the thing had seemed a bore. Letters at Number 9, Marmont Mansions, Battersea, had to be written in the dining-room, it happening to contain the only table in the flat that did not sway like a lily if leaned upon. And somehow the thought of leaving this cosy fireside and going into the dining-room depressed Bill.

His better nature asserted itself. He heaved himself up and left the room. Flick, laying down the half-mended sock, sat gazing into the fire. Then, with a little impatient wriggle, she started sewing again.

She had been sewing for some minutes when the door opened and Judson came in.

'Hullo!' said Flick. 'We were wondering where you were. Is anything the matter?'

Judson had flung himself moodily into the chair which Bill had vacated, disillusionment and dejection written plainly on his speaking countenance. He was not proof against this womanly sympathy.

'Look here,' he said. 'I'll tell you all about it. You've got a kind heart. You're not the sort who would simply kid a fellow.'

' I should hope not ! '

' Well, then, look here. You know as well as I do
that there are moments, especially in this beastly country
where the wind always seems to be blowing from the
east, when a fellow just has to have a nip of the right
stuff to keep the cold out. It's a simple matter of health
—medicinal. Ask any doctor. You admit that, don't
you ? '

' If it makes you any happier.'

' Well, with Bill West behaving like a darned policeman, I'm pretty much up against it in this direction.'

' He says he's only doing it for your good.'

' Oh, I've no doubt he has some story to explain his
behaviour,' said Judson coldly.

' Besides, he promised your sister to look after you.'

' There is only one word ', said Judson with asperity,
' to describe Bill's attitude of grovelling servility to my
sister Alice, and that word is " sickening ". It isn't as
if she cared a hang about him.'

' Doesn't she ? '

' Not a whoop.'

' But I thought they were engaged.'

' Perhaps they are. But be that as it may, you can
take it from me that she's just using him. I'm very
fond of her, as a matter of fact, and she has always been
decent to me ; but a girl may be all right as far as her
brother's concerned and still be a rough citizen when it
comes to other men. Much as I like Alice, it's no use
kidding myself that she's not a flirt. Ever since I've
known her she's always had a dozen fellows on a string.
Mark my words, she'll let Bill down. Yes, sir ! One of
those days that boy is slated to get a jar that'll shake
his back teeth out.'

Flick, though she felt she would have liked to hear
more on this theme, reluctantly decided at this point
that she had no business to be encouraging these revelations. With a strong effort, therefore, she changed the
subject.

' That's too bad, isn't it ? ' she said. ' But what were
you going to tell me ? When you came in, you know.

You said I had a kind heart and wouldn't make fun of
you.'

'Oh yes.' The animation with which Judson had been
discussing his sister left him. His moodiness returned.
He spoke in a minor key, as befitted a painful story.
'I was saying that in this beastly raw, windy weather
a fellow has simply got to have a drink now and then
or his health gets undermined. And the trouble, as
far as I'm concerned, is that it's a darned tough proposition to know which way to turn. This afternoon I
thought I would try an outside chance.'

'What did you do?' asked Flick, wondering. She
had visions of Judson counterfeiting spectacular fainting-
fits in the middle of the street in the hope of getting
restored with brandy.

'I went to see if I could touch that man Slingsby.'

'Mr. Slingsby! Whatever made you go to him?'

'Well, he's old Paradene's London manager, and
Bill is old Paradene's nephew, and I'm Bill's best pal.
It isn't as if there wasn't a sort of moral obligation.
Anyway, I called on him at about four this afternoon.
I can see now that I didn't choose a particularly
good time for my visit. The man was in a thoroughly
nasty temper—having, I discovered, just fired his steno-
grapher.'

'Why was that?'

'I didn't find out, though I sat there all ready to be
confided in if he wanted to slip me an earful. He isn't
what you would call a very cordial sort of bird, that
fellow. In fact, the whole atmosphere seemed to get so
strained after I'd been there about an hour and a quarter
that I was in two minds about going away and leaving
him flat. Only I wanted that drink, you understand.
So I stuck around, and eventually he decided to close
the office and put the cat out for the night and call it
a day. It was then getting on for six and he said he
was going home. I said I hadn't anything to do for a
while, so I would come along with him.'

'He must have got very fond of you by this time,'
said Flick.

'Well, I don't know,' said Judson doubtfully. 'He seemed to me a trifle grouchy.'

'That's strange. How do you account for that?'

'It beats me,' said Judson. 'But, mind you, I wasn't worrying a whole lot about it. What I was thinking about was that drink.'

'By the way,' said Flick, 'is this story going to end happily?'

'Eh?'

'I mean, does it end with you getting a drink?'

Judson laughed a gruesome laugh.

'Oh, I got a drink all right.' He scowled darkly at the fire. 'I'm coming to that. We left the office and got into the man's car——'

'Has he a car? What sort?'

'I forget. He did tell me. Winch-something.'

'Winchester-Murphy?'

'That's right. Big grey limousine.'

'Expensive?'

'Looked as if it had cost the earth. And that's what makes it all so infernally despicable. Here's this man rolling in money and I gave him every opportunity to invite me to dinner, but he wouldn't bite. This was after we had got to his house.'

'Oh, he has a house, has he, as well as a big car? Where does he live?'

'Burton Street? No, Bruton Street. It's off that square—what's its name?—by Devonshire House.'

'Berkeley Square?'

'That's it—Berkeley Square. You turn to the right. He lives half-way down in a biggish house on the left side. Well, we got out, and he opened the door with his latchkey and stood there looking at me in a sort of expectant way, so I came in. And after a bit I came straight out with it as a man to man and asked him if I could have a drink. And he said certainly.'

'It's very curious', said Flick meditatively, 'that he should have this expensive car and live in a place like Bruton Street.'

'And when it came, what do you think it was?'

'It costs a lot living anywhere round there.'

'It was cocoa,' said Judson sombrely; 'a cup of cocoa on a tray. And when I looked at it in a sort of stupor, if you understand what I mean, he said that Bill had told him that I was a strict teetotaller. Bill, mind you, who has been my friend for more than fifteen years! I explained to this Slingsby bird that he had got the facts all wrong, and hadn't he a drop of Scotch about the place; and the man with a beastly mocking smile said that cocoa was much better for me than Scotch, as in addition to being warming it contained nourishing fats. And then he said would I excuse him, as he had to dress for dinner.'

'I can't understand it,' said Flick. 'If he lives in Bruton Street and has an expensive car he must be quite rich.'

'Crawling with money. And that's what makes it all the more——'

'But he can't get such a big salary as manager for Mr. Paradene. I wonder how much the London manager of a firm like Mr. Paradene's would get a year.'

Judson was impressed.

'I see what you're driving at,' he said. 'You mean the fellow's a crook. I can well believe it.'

'Of course, he might have private means.'

'That's true,' said Judson, damped.

'But, if he had, he would hardly go on being just manager for some one else. He would be in business on his own account. A man in his position wouldn't be paid much more than a thousand pounds a year.'

'If that.'

'I don't see how he does it. . . . I want to think this out. You see, as far as I can make out from Bill, old Mr. Paradene has not paid very much attention to his business for the last few years. He is wrapped up in his old books and has just left things alone. It would be a splendid opportunity for a man in Mr. Slingsby's position to do something underhand.'

'And he's just the man who would do it.'

'He's so clever, you mean?'

' I wasn't thinking of that so much,' said Judson.
' What I feel is that there must be practically nothing
to which a fellow who would offer another fellow cocoa
on an evening like this wouldn't stoop.   That's the way
I look at it.   And laughing nastily, mind you, while
doing so ! '

CHAPTER EIGHT

A JOB FOR PERCY PILBEAM

FLICK SHERIDAN and Judson Coker were not the only two people in London who were taking an interest in the affairs of Mr. Wilfrid Slingsby. Such are the ramifications of this complex civilization of ours that the movements of the manager of the Paradene Pulp and Paper Company had also come under the observation of no less a person than young Pilbeam, the real power behind that entertaining weekly, *Society Spice*, of which Roderick Pyke was the nominal and unwilling editor.

The morning after the conversation between Flick and Judson recorded in the last chapter, Roderick sat at the editorial desk of *Society Spice* gazing wanly at the galley proof of an article by his impetuous assistant which dealt with the nefarious activities of the race of turf commission agents—an article in the course of which, he pallidly noted, the name of Mr. Isaac Bullett was mentioned no fewer than three times, and not once in a spirit of genial praise. This series on Bookmakers' Swindling Methods, initiated by Pilbeam, discontinued by Roderick, and resumed at the express orders of Sir George, had always reached a fair level of zippiness; but never, its reluctant sponsor felt, had it so outzipped itself as in the present instalment. Young Pilbeam, dealing with the swindling methods of bookmakers, and using as his leading instance the laxness of the commercial code of Ike Bullett, made Juvenal seem like a tactful pacifist.

The pallor on Roderick's brow would seem to have been caused entirely by the perusal of this inflammatory piece of prose, and not at all by anxiety as to the safety

and whereabouts of his vanished bride-to-be. Flick's
departure, though it had acted like an earthquake on
others of the family group, had apparently left Roderick
unperturbed. On his arrival at the office, ten minutes
ago, he had been in a noticeably cheerful frame of mind.
He had even been whistling. But at the sight of the
very first paragraph of Pilbeam's philippic the whistle had
died away and, like Flick, had not been heard of since.

To him, shrinking quivering in his chair, there now
entered young Pilbeam in person, striding into the room
with shining morning face, all pep, ginger, efficiency and
alertness. This youth with a future was about twenty-
three years of age, diminutive in stature and shinily
black of hair. He wore a lively young check suit, and
his upper lip was disfigured by a small fungoid growth
of moustache.

He accosted his chief genially. A tactful man, he had
never shown any disposition to rub his recent victory
into Roderick. Roderick was still technically his superior
officer and he always treated him as such.

' Ah,' said Pilbeam, having passed the time of day,
' I see you're reading that little thing.'

Roderick, coming to himself with a start, dropped the
little thing as if it had been an adder.

' How do you like it ? ' added the second-in-command ;
and without waiting for an answer proceeded, ' I say,
I've had a great stroke of luck. Happened by pure
chance to stumble over something last night that looks
pretty bubbly. We shall just be able to bung it into
this week's issue.'

Roderick licked his lips—not with relish, but because
they felt dry and cracked. The thought of bunging into
this or any other week's issue anything which a critic
of Pilbeam's exacting standards considered pretty bubbly
gave him a dull aching sensation in the pit of the stomach.

' What is it ? ' he asked hollowly.

Young Pilbeam removed his coat, hung it on a peg,
donned a faded blazer bearing the colours of the cricket
club which enjoyed his support on Saturdays, and, wield-
ing a skilful pair of scissors, shaped from the cover of

an old number of *Society Spice* the paper cuffs which it was his prudent habit to wear when in the office.

' I happened to go and have a bit of supper last night at Mario's,' said Pilbeam, ' and there was a man a couple of tables off with a girl in pink. I didn't know the girl, but she looked chorus-girlish. I suppose she came from one of the theatres. The man was a chap I've seen around the place, named Slingsby. Know him ? '

Roderick said he had not had that pleasure.

' Wilfrid Slingsby. Does a good deal of putting up money for shows, and so on,' explained Pilbeam. ' Sort of man you're always seeing at Romano's and that sort of place. Well, that's who he is, and he was sitting there having supper with this girl. And suddenly—— Ever meet a girl named Prudence Stryker ? '

Roderick said he had not had that pleasure either, and endeavoured somewhat austerely to make it clear to Pilbeam that his knowledge of the more roystering strata of London society was not so extensive and peculiar as he seemed to imagine.

' American girl,' said Pilbeam. ' Was in the Follies in New York for a long time, but came over last January to join the chorus at the Alhambra. Big, dark, Spanish-looking girl with black hair and large flashing eyes.'

Roderick shuddered. Miss Stryker appeared to be the exact type of girl he disliked most, and he hoped that the story was not leading up to the information that his young assistant proposed to bring her to the offices with a view to securing her reminiscences.

' Well, Prudence Stryker suddenly came in with a chap, and no sooner did she see this fellow Slingsby having supper with this girl in pink than she gave a yell, rushed across the room, swept all the plates and glasses off the table, and then swung her right and plugged Slingsby a perfect beauty in the eye. How's that, eh ? ' said Pilbeam with the honest enthusiasm of a good scandal-sheet conductor. ' Not so bad, what ? The only trouble is that the poor girl was so instantly chucked out by the management that I didn't get a chance to have a talk with her and find out what it was all about.'

Why Pilbeam should allude to the muscular Miss
Stryker, who had apparently acted so dramatically in
accordance with her second name and with so lamentably
little consideration for her first, as 'the poor girl', Roderick
could not understand.

'So what I thought I would do', said Pilbeam, 'was
to go and interview this fellow Slingsby and bring back
a nice story for this week's issue. I find he's got an
office in St. Mary Axe. I can pop down, get a statement from him and have the article in type by lunch-
time. I'll be off there as soon as I've cleaned up these
proofs.'

Roderick looked at the enthusiast with a growing
horror. It seemed to him as if Fate was going out of
its way to make life difficult. An article such as that
envisaged by Pilbeam must infallibly lead to his incurring
in his editorial capacity the enmity of this Miss Stryker,
who would naturally be sensitive about the matter and
disinclined to see it exposed to the myriad eyes of London
in the staring nudity of print. And last night's drama
showed with a hideous clearness what happened to those
whom Prudence regarded with disfavour. A vision of
himself being plugged a perfect beauty in the eye came
to Roderick as vividly as if he had seen it in a crystal.

'I don't think we want that story,' he said tremulously.
'I can't use it.'

Pilbeam stared at him, aghast.

'But it's a corker,' he urged. 'Everybody who reads
Spice knows Slingsby.'

Roderick in his desperation snatched at the suggestion
offered by this statement.

'If he's as well known as that,' he said, 'he may be
a friend of my father's.'

'No, no ; not a chance of the boss knowing him.'

'There is,' persisted Roderick. 'Why shouldn't there
be ? The man may be his closest friend for all you
know. And you remember how furious he was the time
you put in that story about Sir Claude Molesey and the
Brighton bungalow. I shouldn't run the risk of having
that sort of thing happen again if I were you.'

Pilbeam looked thoughtful. Roderick's words had given him pause. The incident to which he had alluded was the only existing blot on the Pilbeam escutcheon. As nice a little ' Things We Want to Know, Don't You Know ' paragraph as he had ever written, and then it had turned out that the victim at whom it was directed was one of Sir George's most intimate cronies. Most certainly he did not want that sort of thing to happen again. A way out of the difficulty came to him.

' I'll go up and see the boss ', he said, ' and ask him.'

He removed the paper cuffs, changed the blazer for his check coat, and thus suitably attired left the room to seek an interview with the great Chief.

Up in his office on the fourth floor meanwhile Sir George Pyke was in conference with his sister Frances, and had been for the last half-hour. The subject before the meeting was, as usual, the total disappearance of Flick.

' Just think how long it has been since she ran away,' Mrs. Hammond was saying, ' and how little we've done. Why, we're no nearer finding her than we were two weeks ago.'

' I know,' sighed Sir George, ' I know.'

The proprietor of the Mammoth Publishing Company was looking more like a stuffed frog than ever. This matter of Flick's mutiny was weighing hardly upon him.

' You surely do not suggest, I hope,' he said, having taken a couple of Napoleonic turns up and down the room, ' that we should give in to her and insert that advertisement in the *Daily Mail* ? '

The last two words escaped him in a sort of miniature explosion of pent-up disgust. If Flick had only known, the one thing in the whole unfortunate business that had smitten her uncle most sorely was her tactless request that the family capitulation should be announced in the alien *Mail* and not in the home-grown *Daily Record*.

' Certainly not,' said Mrs. Hammond decidedly. ' Of course not. Nothing could be farther from my thoughts. I am only saying that we ought to take some definite step of some kind, and you, George, are our only hope. Sinclair is perfectly useless. Sometimes I am not sure that he does not in his heart of hearts secretly sympathize with the girl. You must do something, George, and at once.'

Sir George frowned thoughtfully.

'I did put the matter into the hands of a private detective, you know.'

'A private detective!'

'Using the utmost discretion, of course,' Sir George assured her. 'I told him that Felicia was the daughter of an old friend of mine. Suggested that she must have been stricken with amnesia, which I thought rather a happy idea. But there have been no results. The fact is, these private detectives are no good—no good whatever. They exist only to take fees in advance and do no work to earn them.'

The telephone buzzed discreetly.

'Mr. Pilbeam would be glad if you could see him for a moment, Sir George.'

Sir George turned from the instrument with the air of one whose troubles have been divinely solved.

'Good gracious!'

'What is it?'

'I never thought of him! What an amazing thing! The one man ideally fitted for—— Young Pilbeam wants to see me,' he explained. 'You remember him? Does all the work on *Spice*. One of the brightest, keenest fellows in the place. A man in a million. The finest young chap for this sort of business in London.'

'Have him in at once!' cried Mrs. Hammond excitedly.

'I will.'

To Frances Hammond's keen vision one glance at the assistant editor of *Society Spice* was enough to justify her brother's eulogy. Percy Pilbeam was not an ornamental young man; æsthetic critics would have found much to cavil at in his check suit, and physiognomists might have clicked their tongues disapprovingly at the sight of his mean little eyes and the unpleasant smile on his badly shaped mouth; but for the task in hand

his qualifications stuck out all over him. He looked
what he was—a born noser-out of other people's coyly
hidden secrets. She bowed amiably as Sir George, with
a brief word, made them officially known to each other.

' You wished to see me, Pilbeam ? '

' Just a trifling matter, Sir George. I am on the track
of rather a good story about a fellow named Slingsby—
Wilfrid Slingsby. I just thought, before going any
farther, that I would make certain that he did not happen
to be a personal friend of yours.'

' Slingsby ? Slingsby ? Never heard of him. Who is
he ? '

' He has some sort of business in the city, and he is
rather well known in theatrical and sporting circles about
town. He has had a finger in backing one or two musical
comedies.'

' Just the sort of man the readers of *Spice* are interested
in.'

' Exactly what I thought, Sir George.'

' What has he been doing ? '

' He was mixed up in a rather spectacular affair at
one of the night clubs last night. I thought it might be
worth following up.'

' Undoubtedly. Most decidedly. By all means follow
it up.'

' Thank you, Sir George.'

' Oh, Pilbeam,' said the Big Chief as that promising
young man turned to go. ' One moment.' He went to
his desk and took out the photograph of Flick which
he had recovered from the Wraxhall Detective Agency,
after dispensing with that organization's disappointing
services. ' I want you just to glance at this.'

Pilbeam took the photograph and studied it defer-
entially.

' That ', said Sir George, thrusting his fingers into the
armholes of the Pyke waistcoat and speaking in the loud,
bluff, honest voice of the man who is about to do some
hard lying, ' is a photograph of a Miss—Miss——'

As is always the way on these occasions, he found
himself utterly unable to think of a single name that

sounded even remotely like the sort of name a girl would have. Mrs. Hammond stepped adroitly into the uncomfortable pause.

' Miss Faraday,' she said brightly.

' Exactly,' said Sir George, relieved. ' Miss Angela Faraday.' The name pleased him and he repeated it. ' I want you, Pilbeam, to find that girl for me. She is the only daughter of a very old friend of mine.'

' She left home recently,' said Mrs. Hammond.

' Just so,' said Sir George. ' Disappeared.'

' In fact,' said Mrs. Hammond frankly, ' ran away. You see, Mr. Pilbeam, the poor child had only just recovered from a severe attack of influenza. You know how it is when you are recovering from influenza.'

' Quite,' murmured Pilbeam ; ' quite.'

' We think ', said Sir George, feeling on solid ground once more, ' that she must have got amnesia.'

' Yes,' said Mrs. Hammond, ' there must be some reason like that to account for her staying away. There was no——'

' —trouble at home,' said Sir George. ' None whatever. Don't imagine that for an instant. The girl was quite happy ; perfectly happy and contented.'

' Quite,' said Pilbeam.

He spoke with unruffled calm, but inwardly he was a tortured man. His memory for faces being excellent, he had recognized the photograph the moment it was handed to him as a very good likeness of Roderick's fiancée, that pretty girl, the boss's niece, who had called for Roderick at the *Spice* office a week or so ago. And the realization that he had stumbled upon the most gorgeous scandal of his whole career and that there was no hope of being allowed to use it in the paper was the bitterest thing that had ever happened to him. Not even on the occasion when, piqued by his persistent questioning as to the motives of his wife in suddenly removing herself to East Uganda, a large husband had kicked him down a full flight of stairs, had Percy Pilbeam felt sadder.

' You are a fellow who goes about a good deal,' said Sir George. ' I know that you have a sharp pair of eyes. Take that photograph, Pilbeam, and see if you can't find that girl. She must be somewhere. I must ask you, of course, to treat the matter as entirely confidential.'

' Quite, quite.'

' That is all then.'

' Very good, Sir George. I will do my best. And in regard to the other matter of which I spoke, I will call on this man Slingsby directly after lunch and see what I can find out.'

' Just so. And touching this business of Miss—er—Faraday, you will, of course, charge to the office any expense in which you may be involved.'

' Oh, quite,' said Pilbeam. ' Quite.'

There was a ring in his voice which told his employer that in that side of the affair at any rate he might rely on him implicitly.

CHAPTER NINE

THE CHASE BEGINS

§ 1

IN the heart of the city of London's bustle and din,
some fifty yards to the east of Leadenhall Market,
there stands a small and dingy place of refreshment
bearing over its door the name of Pirandello. In addition
to alluring the public with a rich smell of mixed foods,
the restaurant keeps permanently in its window a dish
containing a saintly looking pig's head flanked by two
tomatoes and a discouraged lettuce. There are also cakes
of dubious aspect scattered here and there. Through
the glass you can see sad-eyed members of the Borgia
family in stained dress suits busily engaged in keeping
up the ancient traditions of the clan.

In the narrow doorway of this establishment, about
three hours after Pilbeam had left Sir George Pyke's
office in Tilbury House, Bill West was standing with
his young friend Judson Coker. They were looking up
and down the street with an air of expectancy.

' You're sure this is the right place ? ' asked Judson
in a voice of melancholy. The Gioconda smile of that
placid pig had begun to weigh upon his spirits.

' It's what she said in her telegram—Pirandello's in
Leadenhall Street.'

' Very mysterious, the whole thing,' said Judson, frowning at the pig.

' Ah ! ' said Bill, stepping from the doorway. He had
observed Flick threading her way through the traffic
from the other side of the street.

Flick, in marked contrast to Judson, seemed in the
highest spirits. She waved cheerily, as she eluded a

passing van. She sprang on to the pavement with a gay leap.

'So you got my wire? That's splendid. Come in; I'm hungry.'

'You aren't going to lunch here?' said Judson incredulously.

'Certainly. It's a very good place. Henry recommended it strongly. He always lunches here. He said he would have treated me to-day only he's in conference with another man at Blake's Chophouse.'

'Henry?' said Bill, perplexed. 'Who's Henry?'

'The office boy where I work.'

Bill and Judson exchanged a bewildered glance.

'Where you work?' said Judson.

'Where you *work*?' said Bill.

'Yes; that's what I've come to tell you about. That's why I wired to you to meet me here. I've got a job as stenographer at the London branch of the Paradene Pulp and Paper Company.'

'What!'

'I can't explain till I've had something to eat. You idle rich don't realize it, but working gives one an appetite.'

They followed her dazedly into the restaurant. A warm, sweet-scented blast of air smote them as they entered. Flick sniffed.

'Smell the cocoa!' she said to Judson. 'Doesn't it tantalize you?' She sat down at one of the marble-topped tables. 'Mr. Cocoa likes coker,' she said to Bill. 'I mean Mr. Coker likes cocoa.'

Bill, staring in astonishment at Judson, found the latter eyeing Flick with the reproachful look of one who has been disappointed in a friend. The light-hearted girl appeared unaware of his penetrating gaze. She was busy with a waiter, who accepted her order dejectedly and wrote it down on a grubby pad with a non-committal air, as if disclaiming all responsibility.

'There,' said Flick, when the lethal provender was on the table and they were alone once more. 'Now we can talk. I chose this place because nobody's likely to come in here.'

'Not unless they're dippy,' said Judson gloomily, poking cautiously at his plate.

Bill, who was less wrapped up in the matter of food than his fastidious friend, was able to turn his mind to the extraordinary statement which Flick had made a moment back.

'You've got a job with Slingsby?' he said, marvelling. 'What on earth for?'

'Because I suspect that sinister man, and I want to keep an eye on him.'

'What *is* this?' demanded Judson, who had now summoned up courage enough to swallow a mouthful. 'I know it's paraffin, but what have they put in it?'

'I don't understand. When did you get this job?'

'This morning at ten o'clock.'

'But how?'

'I just walked in and said I heard there was a vacancy for a stenographer.'

'How did you know there was?'

'Mr. Coker told me so last night. He spent the afternoon with Mr. Slingsby. There must be something awfully attractive about Mr. Coker, because Mr. Slingsby simply wouldn't let him go. Would he?'

'Eh?' said Judson absently.

'I said Mr. Slingsby just kept you sitting in his office for hours yesterday, didn't he?'

'I'm off that man for life,' said Judson with sombre emphasis. 'I have no use for him.'

'You see,' said Flick. 'Mr. Coker thinks there's something wrong with him too. We had a long talk last night,' she went on, 'after you had gone off to write your letter, and we came to the conclusion that Mr. Slingsby is a thoroughly bad man.'

'What on earth made you think that?'

Flick sipped daintily at the odd muddy liquid which the management laughingly described as chocolate.

'What would you think of a man who's probably got a salary of a thousand pounds a year or so and runs a Winchester-Murphy car and lives in Bruton Street?'

' Why shouldn't he live in Bruton Street ? ' asked Bill, mystified. His knowledge of London was small.

' Bruton Street, Berkeley Square,' said Flick. ' You have to be pretty rich to live there. Anyhow, you want a good deal more than a thousand a year.'

' But Slingsby goes in for theatrical ventures. He told me so. He probably makes a lot out of those.'

' Well, how did he get the money to go in for theatrical ventures ? It's no use arguing. The man is a crook. He must be. Apart from anything else, he had a black eye when I called on him this morning.'

' A man like that ', said Judson in a hard voice, ' is bound to get a black eye sooner or later. I wish I had given it him.'

' A black eye ? What do you mean ? '

' Just what I say. Now, do honest men get black eyes ? Of course they don't. And. besides, anybody could tell that he wasn't straight just by looking at him.'

' That man's a scoundrel of the worst and lowest description,' said Judson.

' How do you know ? ' said Bill.

' Never mind,' said Judson darkly. ' I have my reasons.'

He pushed away his plate, and nibbled in a disheartened way at a roll. Bill turned to Flick again.

' Tell me exactly what happened,' he said.

' All right,' said Flick. ' I lay awake in bed last night for ever so long, thinking over what Mr. Coker had told me. About Bruton Street and the car, you know. And the longer I thought, the fishier it looked. And then I remembered that Mr. Coker had also said that when he called at the office yesterday Mr. Slingsby was in a bad temper because he had just got rid of his stenographer. It occurred to me that if I called early enough in the morning I might get there before he had sent out to some agency for another. And, luckily, I did. I saw Mr. Slingsby and he engaged me at once. Didn't ask for references or anything.'

To Bill, though he had little knowledge of what was

the customary ceremonial that led up to the engaging
of stenographers, this seemed somewhat unusual. Surely,
he felt, the proceedings were not always so rapid as that.
The fact was, Mr. Slingsby had happened to be in a frame
of mind that morning when his ideal of feminine attrac-
tiveness was something differing in every respect from
Miss Prudence Stryker; and Flick's fair slimness, so
opposite to the brunette heftiness of that militant lady, had
soothed him on the instant. She would have had to be
a far less efficient stenographer to fail to secure the post.

' Well, there I was,' said Flick. ' He told me to start
right in, so I started right in. There's a nice old clerk
in the office who has been there for years and years.
He was under three other managers before Mr. Slingsby,
and it wasn't long before he was talking to me about
the terrible state of the business now as compared with
the dear old days. I suppose I encouraged him a little,
but he gave me the impression of being the sort of man
who would have confided in any one who was ready to
listen. I found out all sorts of things.'

She purred triumphantly over her chocolate. Bill, in
spite of his sturdy belief that this was all nonsense and
that the well-meaning girl had started off on the wildest
of wild-goose chases, could not help being interested.
As he sat there thinking, another aspect of the matter
struck him.

' But look here,' he said, ' why are you doing all this?
Going to all this trouble, I mean?'

Flick looked up with that swift kitten-look of hers.
There was something odd in her expression which puzzled
Bill.

' Why shouldn't I go to a little trouble to help you?'
she said. ' We're pals, aren't we?'

There was a silence. For the briefest moment Bill
was conscious of a curious feeling, as if the atmosphere
had become suddenly charged with something electric.
There had been a look in Flick's eyes as they met his
for an instant that perplexed him. He felt that he
hovered on the brink of some strange revelation. Then
the spell was shattered by Judson.

'I want the body', said Judson, who had seemed plunged in a deep coma for the past few minutes, 'to be sent to my people in New York.'

Flick's seriousness vanished as quickly as it had come. She laughed.

'What a fuss you are making!' she said. 'I shan't take you out to lunch again in a hurry. The food's perfectly good. Look how I'm eating mine.'

'Women are extraordinary,' said Judson, refusing to be cheered. 'They must have cast-iron insides.'

'Don't be indelicate, Mr. Coker. Remember, there are gentlemen present.'

'I've seen my sister Alice wolf with obvious relish', said Judson, 'stuff that would kill a strong man. A woman's idea of lunch is ptomaine germs washed down with tea and iced lemonade.'

The mention of the absent Miss Coker had the effect of producing another momentary silence. But almost immediately Flick hurried on.

'I was telling you about this old clerk,' she said. 'He seemed to have the worst opinion of Mr. Slingsby as a business man. I can't remember all he said, but one thing did strike me as curious. He told me that almost all the wood pulp is being sold, at prices which allow only the smallest profit to Mr. Paradene, to a firm named Higgins & Bennett.'

'Well?' said Bill.

'Well,' said Flick, 'doesn't that seem odd to you? Only the smallest profit!'

'But you don't understand. That's just what Slingsby was talking about at lunch that day. Business conditions——'

'Nonsense!' said Flick decidedly. 'It's fishy, and you know it is. Because he told me something else. He said that a letter had come from a firm offering a much higher price than Higgins & Bennett, and that he had particularly noticed that no deal for this had been entered in the contract book. Showing that for some reason or other Mr. Slingsby had refused the offer. What do you think of that?'

'It does sound queer.'

'I'm glad you admit it. It sounds very queer to me, and I'm going to keep my eyes open. . . . And now I think you had better be escorting me back to my office, or I shall be getting dismissed on my first day. Henry tells me three-quarters of an hour is the official time for lunch.'

Bill was thoughtful as they walked towards St. Mary Axe. A simple-minded young man, he found these puzzles uncongenial. And suddenly another disturbing thought struck him.

'Look here,' he said, 'is it safe for you to be round these parts? Aren't you apt to run into somebody you know?'

'Of course not. Uncle George never comes into the City. I'm as safe here as I am in Battersea.'

'Oh well, that's all right. I was only wondering.'

They stopped at the entrance of the building on the third floor of which the Paradene Pulp and Paper Company had its offices. And as they stood there a young man in a vivid check suit came out, a small young man with close-set eyes and the scenario of a moustache. He was walking rapidly and in so preoccupied a condition that he almost cannoned into Flick.

'I beg your pardon,' he said.

Flick smiled forgivingly, and turned to Bill.

'Good-bye,' she said. 'Good-bye, Mr. Coker.'

'Good-bye,' said Judson. 'You'll be coming to dinner to-night?'

'Of course.'

Flick entered the building and started to climb the stairs. The young man in the check suit, who had been tying his shoe-lace, straightened himself and followed her. He moved cautiously, like a leopard.

This stupendous stroke of luck, coming so unexpectedly out of a blue sky, had for a moment almost unmanned Percy Pilbeam. He had recognized Flick the instant he saw her, and that feeling that comes to all of us at times of a mysterious power benevolently guiding our movements flooded over him. If he had terminated his inter-

view with Mr. Wilfrid Slingsby two minutes sooner—
and Mr. Slingsby's attitude and behaviour on being
questioned about last night's affray had given him every
excuse to do so—he would have missed the girl. As it
was, everything was working out with the most perfect
smoothness. Though he had recognized her, Flick, he
was certain, had not recognized him. She was entirely
unaware that she was being trailed. The only thing he
had to do was to ascertain where she was going and if
she intended to stay there long, and then to send word
to Sir George Pyke to come and get her.

Warily he tiptoed after her up the stairs. They
reached the first floor. They reached the second. They
reached the third, and Pilbeam, peering with infinite
caution, saw the girl pass through the door he had so
recently left, the window of which bore the legend
'Paradene Pulp and Paper Company'. It was now
necessary only to wait and see if she was paying a brief
visit or if she intended to remain. Pilbeam camped on
the stairs and the minutes went by.

When a reasonable period of time had passed without
any sign of Flick he hurried downstairs. In the doorway he paused and scribbled a note. This he gave,
with a shilling, to a passing boy. Then he stationed
himself in the doorway to await Sir George's arrival.

§ 2

In assuming so complacently that Flick had not recognized him Percy Pilbeam had made a tactical blunder.
It is true that in the first moment of their meeting he
had seemed a stranger, but suddenly, as she started to
mount the stairs, her subconscious mind, which, after
the helpful habit of subconscious minds, had been working all the time on its own account, sounded an alarm.
Vaguely, in a nebulous, uncertain fashion, she began to
feel that somewhere at some time she had seen this check-
suited young man before.

But where ?

And when ?

She had just reached the second floor when memory

leaped into life as if she had touched a spring. It was
in Roderick's office the day when she had called to take
Roderick out to tea, that ever-to-be-remembered day
when all the trouble had started. This was the man—
Pilbeam? Wasn't that his name?—who assisted
Roderick in the control of *Society Spice.*

It was lucky that this illumination came to Flick with
such a startling abruptness, for this very abruptness had
all the effect of a physical shock. It actually jerked her
head sideways as if it had been a blow. And so it came
about that out of the corner of her eye she was enabled
to see her pursuer just a moment before he made one of
his wary slidings into the shadows on the staircase—an
instant later, and she would have missed him.

She gave a little gasp. Of all the unpleasant sensations that can attack us in this world, one of the least
agreeable is the feeling of being hunted. A brief flurry
of panic shook Flick. Then, pulling herself together,
she went on up the stairs. Peril quickens the wit, and
she had thought of a plan of action. The success of this
plan depended entirely on whether that other door in
Mr. Slingsby's private office—a door whose existence she
had completely forgotten until her subconscious mind,
that admirable assistant, now presented a picture of it
for her inspection—led anywhere. It might, of course,
be merely the entrance to a cupboard, in which case
she was trapped. But hope seemed to whisper that a
man of Wilfrid Slingsby's evil mind, a man who got
black eyes and sold wood pulp cheap to Higgins & Bennett
when he could have disposed of it more advantageously
elsewhere, would be extremely likely to select for his
office a room with a bolt-hole for use in case of emergency.
She entered the office with a high heart.

A loud and angry voice proceeding through the door
had warned her before she turned the handle that a
disturbed atmosphere prevailed within. She found Mr.
Slingsby in a state of effervescing fury, engaged in a
passionate passage with Henry the office boy.

One cannot altogether blame Wilfrid Slingsby for his
lack of self-control. His unfortunate encounter with

Miss Prudence Stryker at Mario's Restaurant overnight had brought him to the office in a mood of extreme edginess, and when a good lunch had to some extent pulled him round he had been plunged into the depths once more by the totally unforeseen intrusion of Mr. Percy Pilbeam. These things upset a man and render an office boy's whistling more than ordinarily disturbing to the nerves. The consequence was that Henry, a dreamy youth who was apt to forget his surroundings when he became absorbed in his work, had scarcely got half-way through the latest song-hit before something that seemed for an instant like a charge of cavalry shot out of the private office ; and the next moment young Master Smith—Henry was one of the Smiths of Somers Town—was being told things about himself which even the companions of his leisure hours—and they were a candid and free-speaking band—had never thought of saying. Mr. Slingsby, roused, had a large vocabulary and Henry was getting nearly all of it.

The instinct of self-preservation rules us all. Flick, though their acquaintance had been so brief, was fond of Henry, and had her own affairs been less pressing might have attempted to create a diversion. As it was, she merely welcomed the fact that Mr. Slingsby was busy outside of his private office and walked into that sanctum without a pause. And there was the second door, beckoning her.

Flick opened this second door and thrilled with exquisite relief. It was not a cupboard. The door led into a passage. The passage in its turn led to a flight of stairs. The stairs led into a small dark courtyard full of boxes and barrels. And the courtyard, after she had threaded her way among these obstacles, proved to lead into a street. Flick reached this street, and hurrying down it without a backward look, left the employment of the Paradene Pulp and Paper Company for ever.

§ 3

A matter of half an hour or so after Flick's departure a cab stopped at the main entrance of the building and

Sir George Pyke sprang out. Pilbeam, leaving his door-way, advanced, gambolling about him like a faithful dog.

' Where is she ? In here ? ' demanded Sir George, a man of few words.

' Quite,' said Pilbeam, a man of fewer.

They entered the building, Pilbeam explaining as they climbed the stairs the events that had led up to this tense situation—events which he had had neither time nor space to record in his brief note.

' You're sure it was the right girl ? '

' Quite.'

' Now what in the world ', mused Sir George, as they halted outside the door, ' could the fool of a girl be doing here ? '

Pilbeam, baffled by the same problem, forbore to specu-late. They went into the office. A meek and chastened Henry took Sir George's card into the inner room, where Mr. Slingsby, outwardly calm once more, but inwardly still a mere volcano, scrutinized it captiously.

' Who's this ? '

' Dunno, sir.'

' What's he want ? '

' Dunno, sir.'

' Well, show him in, blast him,' said Mr. Slingsby forcefully.

We have already seen Wilfrid Slingsby considerably persecuted by Fate, but even in the brief interval which has elapsed since his last appearance another blow had befallen him. On top of all the Prudence Strykers, Percy Pilbeams and whistling Henrys that had recently made life so hard to bear, he had now discovered that his stenographer had mysteriously disappeared at just the time when he needed her assistance most. There were a number of important letters waiting to be dictated ; and, if the plight of a man all dressed up and having no place to go is bad, that of one full of dictation with nobody to dictate it to is hardly less enviable. Small wonder that the world looked black to Wilfrid Slingsby.

The Episode of the Vanishing Stenographer, as Mr.

Slingsby would have called it if he had been a writer of
detective stories, had that quality of utter and insane
inexplicability which makes a man moan feebly and stick
straws in his hair. He had with his own eyes seen her
come in, and now she simply was not. The thing got
right in amongst Wilfrid Slingsby's nerve centres. And,
just as he was feeling that he could stand no more, he
saw sailing in in the wake of Sir George the loathly figure
of young Pilbeam.

It is a curious phenomenon, which can be vouched
for by any one who has ever boiled an egg, that a slight
increase of provocation added to a bubbling fury produces
a condition strangely resembling calm. The water which
has hissed and shrieked in the saucepan seems to subside
almost phlegmatically when it reaches boiling point. It
was so with Mr. Slingsby now. The sight of Pilbeam
seemed to produce in him a kind of frozen inertness.
With his unblacked eye he looked venomously at his
visitors, but he did not spring from his chair and bite
them in the leg. And though his fingers closed for an
instant on the large inkpot on his desk, he released it
again.

Pilbeam did the honours.

' This is Sir George Pyke, of the Mammoth Publishing
Company, Mr. Slingsby ' he said.

' Do you publish *Society Spice* ? ' asked Mr. Slingsby
in a dull voice.

' Among a great number of other papers,' replied Sir
George with a touch of pomposity.

' Ah ! ' said Mr. Slingsby. He toyed with the inkpot
once more, but again relaxed his grasp.

Pilbeam proceeded briskly to business. He had had
a word with the elderly clerk in the outer office while
waiting, and ascertained the reason of Flick's presence
in this place.

' We have just discovered ', he said, ' that your stenographer is the daughter of an old friend of Sir George's,
Mr. Slingsby. She recently left home——'

' Amnesia,' said Sir George.

' Quite,' said Pilbeam.

' Indeed ? ' said Wilfrid Slingsby, still in the grip of
that sinister calm.

Sir George glared impressively. He intended to stand
no nonsense from this man. Mr. Slingsby's black eye
and the knowledge of how it had been acquired had
made an unfavourable impression.

' I have come to take her back to her home.'

' Oh, have you ? '

' The poor girl is in an unfit state to be wandering
about alone.'

' Oh, is she ? '

' And so ', said Sir George imperiously, ' I should be
obliged, Mr. Slingsby, if you would produce her.'

Wilfrid Slingsby, his mind working with cold swiftness
during these exchanges, began now to see his way to
getting a bit—a small bit, but nevertheless a bit—of his
own back. He forced a winning smile into his bleak
face.

' I should be only too glad to produce her, as you
put it ; but she is not here.'

' She came in here.'

' Exactly—and went away again. She said she had a
headache and wanted to go home, so I let her off for
the afternoon.'

' But I've been watching the door and she didn't go
out,' said Pilbeam keenly.

' Yes,' said Sir George, ' how do you account for that ? '

' You are at liberty ', said Mr. Slingsby, ' to search the
premises if you wish. Here are the keys of the safe,
and the drawers of this desk are not locked. The waste-
paper basket, as you see, is empty. I imagine ', he continued, for the solution of the puzzle which had been
vexing him had now presented itself, ' that she went out
by that door there, which leads to another exit. By
now, I expect, she is well on her way home.'

' What is her address ? '

' Seven, Paradise Walk, Earlsfield,' said Mr. Slingsby
promptly.

The locality had not been selected by him at random.
Paradise Walk, Earlsfield, was, he knew, in a particularly

unpleasant part of London and had in addition been quite recently the scene of a rather unusually spectacular murder. Mr. Slingsby was not without a faint hope that the inhabitants, if given to that sort of thing and having nothing better on their hands, might turn their talent for slaughter in the direction of his visitors.

'Thank you,' said Sir George.

'Not at all,' said Mr. Slingsby.

'Much obliged,' said Pilbeam.

'Don't mention it,' said Mr. Slingsby.

The visitors picked up their hats. As the door closed behind them there came into Mr. Slingsby's drawn face something almost resembling a smile of happiness.

CHAPTER TEN

THE CHASE CONTINUES

§ 1

THE callousness of Nature in times of human suffering has been commented on so often by poets and others that it has become a truism. If Nature had possessed a heart, the day following that on which Sir George Pyke and his young assistant had visited the office of Mr. Wilfrid Slingsby would have been one of dark clouds and weeping skies. As it was, it reached a level of bright serenity that had not been equalled in London since the summer of the previous year. Tilbury Street, whose inhabitants still seemed to be boiling cabbage as if their lives depended on it, stewed in the sunshine, so that horses drooped their heads and strong men went gaspingly about their work, counting the minutes till the pubs should open. The pavement in front of Tilbury House was all inlaid with patines of bright gold, and sparrows, revelling in the warmth, chirped merrily as they lunched in the gutters. In a word, all Nature smiled.

Nevertheless, as has been suggested by our opening remarks, there were aching hearts in Tilbury Street, hearts to which the glorious weather brought no balm. Chief among these was that of Percy Pilbeam. He sat in the office of *Society Spice* in that dismal half-hour that precedes luncheon, brooding miserably. Of all sad words of tongue or pen, the saddest are these : It might have been ; and the thought of how narrowly he had missed pulling off the coup of a lifetime gnawed at Pilbeam's vitals like a vulture.

If only Flick had proved less elusive, what a triumph

would have been his ! Sir George would have showered
commendation upon him, and what is more, could hardly
in decency have avoided giving him a handsome rise of
salary. Instead of which——

It is a defect in the characters of Napoleonic men
that they are apt to demand from their subordinates
success and nothing but success. To come within an
ace of triumph advances the subordinates' stock not at
all. Indeed, it rather depreciates it. Pilbeam realized
that he would now be standing considerably higher in
Sir George's esteem if he had never got on Flick's trail
at all. His employer had exhibited a disquieting disposition to blame him for everything that had happened.

Number seven, Paradise Walk, Earlsfield, had proved,
when reached after a long and expensive journey in a
taxi-cab, to be an evil-smelling bird-and-snake shop,
owned by a dirty and cheerful old man with grey whiskers
and a skull-cap, who had proceeded to answer their
inquiries for Flick by urging them to examine his stock
with a view to purchase. Sir George had read into the
man's words a suspicious evasiveness, and it had been
his idea that they should sit down and wait. The memory
of that vigil had seared Pilbeam's soul deeply, and the
recollection of the long green snake which he had suddenly found nestling in his lap was destined to haunt
him for many days.

Eventually the realization that Mr. Slingsby, in his
low fashion, had sent them to a false address had dawned
upon them both at about the same time ; and they had
gone away, pursued to the last by the owner of the shop,
who wanted to do a sacrifice deal on a parrot. The last
they had seen of him before threading their way through
the local murderers and starting back to civilization, he
was standing in the street with the parrot on his shoulder,
doing some spirited price-cutting.

It was just about this point that Sir George had become
peevish. Pilbeam sighed. It was hard that he should
be blamed for what was none of his fault. Sir George's
statement that he ought to have had the sense to know
that a man like Slingsby, with one eye black and the

other gleaming with the light of pure deceit, would naturally send them to a wrong address struck him as unjust. Still, there it was. He had failed, and he was suffering the penalty always meted out to failure in Tilbury House.

He had just begun to busy himself with the revision of an article on ' Plague Spots of the West End '—he was alone in the office to-day, Roderick being absent with a cold in the head—when a boy in buttons entered, bearing a form.

' Gem' to see you, sir.'

Pilbeam took the form listlessly. His sufferings had had the effect of subduing his normal pep and ginger, and for a moment, so greatly did he desire solitude in his hour of travail, he had the churlish intention of telling the boy to say that he was out. Then his eye fell on the name written on the paper in his hand—

Judson Coker.

Something stirred at the back of Pilbeam's mind. Coker ? Why was that name vaguely familiar ? Coker ? Why were those two simple syllables somehow oddly significant ? Coker ? Where had he heard——— ?

He gasped, awed by the sudden suspicion of a terrific possibility. Now he knew where he had heard the name before. ' Good-bye, Mr. Coker.' They were the last words that infernal girl—for so he was now unchivalrously accustomed to think of Flick—had spoken before going into her office building. ' Good-bye, Mr. Coker.' He remembered it distinctly. And then he had asked her if she would be coming to dinner, and she had said ' of course'. What could this mean but that she was in the habit of visiting this Coker so frequently that her presence at his dinner table had become a matter of routine.

' What sort of a looking fellow is he ? ' he cried.

The boy in buttons seemed perplexed. It was not usual for the editorial staff of *Society Spice* to demand word-portraits of visitors.

' A kind of bloke,' he said vaguely.

Pilbeam perceived that to continue examining this unprofitable witness would be wasting time. The thing to do was to have the fellow up and inspect him face to face. Unusual as the name Coker was, he dared not allow himself to hope that this could be the same man. That would be too much like a miracle. Yet, as he waited, nervously pulling at his small moustache, he could not keep himself from hoping. And when the door opened and Judson was ushered in he saw with a pang of excitement which seemed to stop his heart beating that his hope had been fulfilled. The million-to-one chance had come off. This was the fellow he had seen yesterday in St. Mary Axe.

'Come in, come in,' he cried ecstatically. 'Do take a seat, won't you?'

'Thanks,' said Judson, a little surprised at this cordiality, but rendered by it distinctly happier. It began to look to Judson as though his mission was to be plain sailing.

It was the story which Flick had told on visiting Marmont Mansions on the previous evening that had brought Judson Coker to-day to the office of *Society Spice*. Flick's description of Pilbeam's pursuit and how she had eluded it had been spirited and absorbing; but though all of it had interested him, the point that interested him most had been the revelation that Roderick was not the only official in charge of things at the *Spice* office. His knowledge of the inner workings of weekly paper offices was slight, and he had assumed until now that the only person to whom he could apply for a correction of that paragraph about Toddy van Riter and the Silks was the fellow who had batted Bill West over the head with his stick—obviously a man of the worst and one from whom it would be hopeless to seek justice. The discovery that Roderick had a partner altered the whole aspect of the affair.

He had come here, of course, in a spirit of the utmost wariness and caution. Very much on his guard, Judson was. On no account, he realized, must he let fall a word that would establish in the mind of this man a connexion between himself and Flick. Pilbeam, he understood from Flick's narrative, was acting as a sort of amateur bloodhound as far as she was concerned. It caused Judson a faint amusement as he sat down to reflect what a lot this man would give to know that he lived in a flat to which the girl he was hunting came every night for dinner.

'What did you want to see me about ?' asked Pilbeam.

'Well, it's like this,' Judson began. 'You had a piece in your paper a couple of weeks ago——'

Pilbeam looked at his watch.

'I didn't know it was so late,' he said. 'You haven't lunched yet, have you ?'

'No,' said Judson, thrilled from head to foot by a sudden spasm of hope. In his wildest dreams he had never foreseen a bit of luck like this.

'How about coming out and having a bite ? I can see you've got all sorts of interesting things to tell me, and we can talk better at lunch.'

'So we can,' said Judson enthusiastically. 'So we can.'

'You're American, aren't you ?' said Pilbeam.

'Yes.'

'Then we'll go to the Cheshire Cheese. You must see the Cheshire Cheese. You aren't a teetotaller by any chance ?'

'No !' said Judson vehemently.

'I only asked because they have some rather special port——'

'Port !' whispered Judson.

'Tawny port.'

Judson's eyes closed for a moment in a prayerful ecstasy.

'Lead me to it,' he said in a low, reverent voice.

It is strange how the views of different people concerning any given individual can differ. There were men in London, dozens of them, who heartily disliked Percy Pilbeam. If you had asked Wilfrid Slingsby what he thought of the young man behind *Society Spice* it would have taken him ten minutes to reply, and scarcely a word

of his remarks would have been printable. Yet Judson
Coker found him one of the most delightful fellows he
had ever met.

The Cheshire Cheese, that historic tavern, pleased Judson immensely. Its old associations, it is true, made
but small appeal to him, and he was only tepidly interested in Doctor Johnson's chair ; but the lark-steak-
and-kidney pudding, that famous speciality of the house,
went with a bang from start to finish. Washed down
with tankards of old ale, it appealed to all that was best
and deepest in Judson. By the time the tawny port
arrived he was in a mood so mellowed that it was difficult
for him to realize that the man with the slightly blurred
outline sitting opposite him had not been a trusted friend
since the days of boyhood.

Besides, apart altogether from the port and the old
ale, Pilbeam had endeared himself to Judson by his
thoroughly sympathetic and understanding attitude in
the matter of that Silks article. It was unforgivable,
declared Pilbeam warmly, that such a mistake should
have occurred. But a man of the world like Judson
would understand how hard it was to keep a paper like
Society Spice free from these occasional errors. (' Of
course, of course ! ') They would creep in from time
to time. (' Exactly ! ') But it should be corrected in
the very next issue.

' Awfully good of you,' said Judson.

' Not at all, not a-tall,' said Pilbeam.

' Oh, but it is ! '

' No, no.'

' Oh, but it is ! '

' Not a bit.'

' Oh, but it is, but-i-toz, but it is ! ' insisted Judson
with enthusiasm. He drained his glass and gazed with
goggle-eyed affection at this obliging man, whom he
liked, he was now convinced, quite a good deal better
than any one else in the world.

' I'll write an article myself,' said Pilbeam, ' putting
the matter straight. And look here, we don't want any
more mistakes—I'd better send you proofs.'

' How's that ? '

' Proofs.'

' No, sir ! ' Judson waved his hand in a wide and generous gesture. ' Don't want any proofs. Take your word for it.'

' Proofs of the article,' explained Pilbeam gently, ' so that you can see it before it appears.'

' Oh—ah ! '

' Where shall I send it ? '

' Nine, Marmont Mansions, Battersea.'

' Right ! ' said Pilbeam. ' And now,' he went on, for triumph had made him kindly, ' tell me all about the Fifth Avenue Silks. You must have had a great time. I can't think how you ever happened to get the idea.'

It was a flushed and uplifted Pilbeam who parted from Judson outside the Cheshire Cheese at a few minutes after two and made his way with great strides down Fleet Street to Tilbury House. The sight of Sir George's limousine drawn up at the kerb told him that his employer had returned from lunch. He went straight up to the office on the fourth floor.

' Well ? ' said Sir George.

His manner was distant, but Pilbeam had been prepared for a cold reception. He would, he told himself, soon thaw the ice.

' I have great news, Sir George. I have found out where we can make inquiries of Miss——'

There was an uncomfortable pause. Pilbeam had forgotten the name and so had Sir George. The latter, after a moment of swift thinking, decided on candour.

' Perhaps I had better tell you, Pilbeam—I am sure that you will treat the information in the strictest confidence.'

' Quite.'

' The girl is my niece.'

' Is *that* so ! ' said Pilbeam, trying to inject a sharp amazement into his voice.

' My niece,' repeated Sir George with gloomy impressiveness.

'It makes me all the happier that I have found her,' said Pilbeam devoutly.

'Found her!'

'Well,' amended Pilbeam, 'found the place which she seems to be visiting every day.'

He told his story with the crisp expertness of one accustomed to squashing the vice of a great city into a column and a quarter. Sir George listened, rapt.

'Pilbeam,' he said, 'I knew all along that I could rely on you.'

'It is very kind of you to say so, Sir George.'

'I train my young men to be bright, and you are the brightest of them all. You may take this note to the cashier.'

'I will,' said Pilbeam fervently, pocketing the slip of paper. 'Thank you.'

Sir George rose.

'I shall go at once to this Marmont Mansions you speak of. I shall see this man Coker——'

'I don't think he will be in for some time,' said Pilbeam. 'When I left him he was saying something about going and having a nap in the park.'

'Then I will wait for him. And when I see him', said Sir George portentously, 'I shall Stand No Nonsense!'

§ 2

A powerful car was standing outside Marmont Mansions when Sir George Pyke arrived at the storm centre. Beside it, one foot on the running-board, a pleasant-faced young man of impressive physique smoked a cigarette. This young man watched Sir George as he alighted and approached. He had no recollection of ever having seen Sir George before, nor did his appearance seem in any way familiar to the older man. Yet they had met and in dramatic circumstances.

Sir George was peering up at the building. His chauffeur had told him that this was Marmont Mansions, but there was no name over the door to prove it. He decided to seek a further opinion.

' I am looking for Marmont Mansions, Battersea,' he said.

' Right here,' said the young man agreeably.

' Thank you.'

' Not at all. Nice day.'

' Very,' said Sir George.

He passed through the doorway. The young man, who seemed to be expecting some one, resumed his vigil. Presently he smiled and waved his hand. A girl in a floppy and unbecoming sealskin coat was advancing briskly along the pavement. Sir George's chauffeur, sitting stolidly at his wheel a few yards down the street, eyed her with approval. He had a nice taste in female beauty, and not even the sealskin coat could hide the fact that Flick was an unusually pretty girl.

' Here I am,' said Flick. ' Haven't I been quick ? What do you think of the coat ? '

' Fine,' said Bill.

' It isn't. It's awful. But it was the only thing I could get that was warm enough. I borrowed it from my landlady.'

She climbed into the car and settled herself cosily.

The idea of hiring a car and taking Flick for a drive out into the country had come to Bill as a luminous inspiration while they lunched together in the neighbourhood of Shaftesbury Avenue, a locality which seemed well outside the danger zone haunted by Sir George Pyke and his minions. The fineness of the day had not escaped their notice, and they had decided that it would be unwise to waste it. Bill, moreover, being a young man used to the possession of a car of his own, had been experiencing for some days that restless and starved sensation which comes to habitual motorists whose motoring is cut off for any long period. His fingers itched to close themselves over a wheel again, and he had sent Flick off to her lodgings to borrow a warm coat while he negotiated for the hire of a car for the afternoon. He climbed in after her.

' Where would you like to go ? '

' It's lovely out at Hindhead.'

' All right. How do you get there ? '

' And of course anywhere down on the river is wonderful.'

' Well, you choose.'

But they were destined to go that afternoon neither to Hindhead's majestic heights nor to any silvery reach of old Thames. While Flick was still trying to make her choice the decision was taken out of her hands. Bill, leaning back in a restful attitude, was startled by a little squeak of dismay, and looking up, saw that she was staring with round and horrified eyes at something beyond him. Turning his head, he perceived that the stout man who had asked him for Marmont Mansions had returned and was coming out of the doorway.

' Quick ! ' gasped Flick. ' Oh, be quick ! '

Bill was quick. Though not an abnormally intelligent young man, he gathered that this was no time for waiting and asking questions. He started the car without a word and they began to glide off. And as they did so the stout man uttered a sharp bellow and became a thing of leaping activity.

The reappearance of Sir George at this point was due to the fact that he had got tired of ringing the bell of Number Nine. There appeared to be nobody at home, and he had decided that it would be more comfortable to wait—and he intended to wait for hours if necessary —down below in his limousine. The sight of Flick seemed to him, as it had seemed to Percy Pilbeam twenty-four hours earlier, direct evidence that Providence looks after the righteous. It was only when he saw her being borne rapidly away from him that he realized that his position was not so advantageous as he had supposed.

In this crisis Sir George lost his head. He shouted uselessly. He galloped along the pavement. Not until Bill's car was twenty yards away and moving swiftly westward along the Prince of Wales Road did it occur to him that he, too, had a car and that the pursuit could be conducted far more agreeably on wheels than afoot. He waved like a semaphore to his chauffeur.

'Hi!' he shouted. 'Here! Hi! Briggs! Come on, you fool!'

The chauffeur, blandly unemotional, stepped with dignity on his self-starter. He drew up beside his fermenting employer. Sir George sprang in and gesticulated with both hands in the direction of Albert Road, the corner of which Bill and his companion had just turned at a high rate of speed.

'Ur! Ur!' gurgled Sir George.

The chauffeur touched his cap aloofly. He gathered that his employer wished him to pursue the other car, but he was not thrilled. It took more than this sort of thing to excite Augustus Briggs.

§ 3

'That was Uncle George,' said Flick.

Bill had deduced as much. He nodded and glanced over his shoulder.

'It still is,' he replied briefly, and drove his foot down on the accelerator. They whirred over the Albert Bridge.

CHAPTER ELEVEN

THE CHASE ENDS

§ 1

ONCE started in flight, the human instinct is to keep on running. It was not immediately, therefore, that Bill recovered from the first stark desire to be elsewhere as quickly as possible and began to turn on to the situation the searchlight of clear reason. For perhaps ten minutes or a quarter of an hour his faculties were entirely occupied with the desire to shake off pursuit ; and with this end in view he kept his large foot firmly on the accelerator and paid only the most meagre attention to the hurriedly expressed criticisms of the various traffic policemen dotted here and there about the winding route.

If he had a thought outside the bare, primitive craving for speed, it was a feeling of relief that he had taken the trouble to hire from the garage a really good car. It was as if some presentiment had warned him not to accept the quaint old relics which they had offered him at the start of the negotiations, but to hold out firmly and coldly till they produced a real hummer. His motorist's eye had told him after one glance at the engines that this was a car of quality, and events were proving his judgement sound. With a smooth and effortless efficiency, it was eating up the asphalt like a racer.

They snapped across Chelsea Embankment, purred up Oakley Street and, turning to the left at the Fulham Road, began—though Bill was not aware of it—to cover the same ground which he and Judson had gone over that night when they had followed Roderick to Wimbledon Common. In Putney High Street they were enabled

to draw away for a while, for the limousine—to Sir
George's manifest discomposure, though Briggs the chauffeur accepted the blow with wooden calm—got itself
blocked by a brewer's dray just across the bridge ;
whereupon Bill, dexterously imitating the ingenious tactics
of the hunted hare, turned down Lacy Road into Charl-
wood Road, turned again into Felsham Road, and so,
doubling on his tracks, crossed Putney Bridge once more
and bowled along the Fulham Palace Road, to emerge
finally into the bustle of King Street, Hammersmith.
It was a manœuvre which might well have settled the
issue ; but Augustus Briggs, for all his woodenness, was
an astute fellow ; and looking over his shoulder as they
reached Hammersmith station, Bill was annoyed to per-
ceive the limousine swerving lithely round a truck, still
in the game.

It was at this point that he began to examine the
situation.

'What on earth is all this about ? ' he asked.

'It's Uncle George.'

'I know. But what are we running away for ? '

'Because I don't want him to catch us.'

'Why not ? '

The question deprived Flick momentarily of speech.
Bill filled the hiatus in the conversation by dodging
an omnibus and turning sharp to the left up Addison
Road.

'What do you mean ? ' said Flick, astonished.

'Well,' said Bill, skilfully avoiding manslaughter with
a quick twist of the wheel, 'what can he do if he does
catch us ? '

It had begun to irk his haughty spirit, this headlong
flight from a little man with a double chin whom he
could have destroyed with a finger. He would have
guaranteed, if challenged to mortal combat, to clean up
Sir George and Briggs the chauffeur, too, inside a couple
of minutes. In the vivid phrase of Mr. Isaac Bullett,
he could butter the pavement with them both. Yet
here he was fleeing like the wicked man in the Psalms,
permitting himself to be chivvied by these persons all

over London.　The pride of the Wests put up a strong
protest.

'What on earth can he do?' he demanded again.
'He can't tie you up and drag you home against your
will.'

'I know,' said Flick.　'It's just that I can't face him.'

'Why not?' persisted Bill, just contriving to avoid
diminishing the juvenile population of Ladbroke Grove
by one.

'You don't know Uncle George,' said Flick, shaking
her head.　'He's such a compelling sort of man.　So
frightfully sort of hypnotic.'

'Oh, come!' protested Bill.

'Well, you know what I mean.　He glares at you
and tells you to do things and you just do them.　When
he looks at me I always feel like a rabbit and a snake.'

'How do you mean, you feel like a rabbit and a
snake?' said Bill, puzzled.

'Well, you know, sort of hypnotized.　I'm sure if my
door hadn't been locked that night, and he had been able
to come in and glare at me, I should have lost my nerve
altogether and come meekly down to dinner instead of
running away.　If he catches us I know exactly what
will happen.　I shall have to go back with him.'

'Nonsense!　Be a man!'

'Well, that's how I feel.'

Bill was in many ways a simple soul, but he had lived
long enough in this world to know that a woman's whims
have to be respected, however apparently absurd to the
view of the more earthy male.　And in a dim way he
could follow Flick and understand her position.　Until
he had got used to him, he had found Ridgway, his
late man-servant, affecting him in rather the same fashion.
Ridgway had had quiet but decided views on ties and
hats; and many a time, Bill remembered, he had had
his way in these matters, sternly overriding the prefer-
ences of the man who paid him his wages.　One cannot
argue about personality.　Its compelling power has to
be accepted as a fact.　If Flick felt like that about her
Uncle George and shrank so timorously from the prospect

of meeting him, then Uncle George must be shaken off
if it took the last drop of petrol in the tank.

He pulled the wheel round and they shot away in
an easterly direction, and from this point the affair took
on a dreamlike aspect which precluded coherent thought.
Bill had no notion where he was going. Like the heroine
of a melodrama, he was lost in London. His simple
policy was to take any road which looked smooth and
fairly empty and to skim down it till he came to another
road possessing the same desirable qualities. And always
the limousine followed. It was impossible to get away
from it in the traffic, and Bill yearned for the open country.
And suddenly, when he had least expected it, the houses
began to thin and he was thrilled by the discovery that
there really was an end to this sprawling city after all.

So sedulously had Bill twisted, retwisted and kept on
twisting his steering wheel that, though he had started
out along the Portsmouth Road, he was now heading
for Hertfordshire. And presently London, with its tram-
lines and traffic, was left behind and they were out on
the open road.

' Now ', said Bill, teeth grimly set, ' we'll show 'em ! '

Although this car of his was but a hired one, he had
come in the course of this stern chase to love it like a
son. It was a beautiful car, obviously only recently
tuned up by expert hands, and what it needed to give
of its best was just such a broad highway as now lay
before it. Tram-lines and traffic fret and hamper a car
of spirit. What it craves is space. This it had now
got, and the roar of the engines as Bill pressed down
his foot sounded like a joyful cheering. The needle on
the indicator crept up to forty, then swiftly to forty-
five.

' Laugh this off ! ' growled Bill over his shoulder at
the pursuing limousine.

It was as if Augustus Briggs had heard the provocative
words. He did not attempt to laugh it off, for he was
a chauffeur and by the rules of his guild not allowed
anything beyond a faint smile at the corner of his mouth ;
but he did indulge for an instant in this faint smile.

The idea of a Cardinal Six—for such he perceived Bill's car to be—attempting to give the dust to his own peerless Brown-Windsor excited in him an almost jovial contempt ; and so sudden was the bound which the limousine made as he opened the throttle that a hen down the road which had planned to make a leisurely crossing saved its valuable life only by a frenzied leap in the last split second.

And so, going nicely, they passed through New Barnet, Hadley Wood, Potters Bar and South Mimms, and came to the town of Hatfield. And it was outside Hatfield, just before you come to Brocket Hall, that the long, long trail reached its abrupt end.

Bill had not been unaware of the new touch of grimness added to the chase. He had noted the chauffeur's spurt and had answered it by putting his needle up into the fifties. But now a chill feeling of impending defeat had begun to lower his mood of exultation. Something seemed to tell him that the car behind had just that extra turn of speed which was going to make all the difference. Sticking doggedly, however, to his guns, he was endeavouring to urge the Cardinal Six to a gait which its maker had never contemplated, when the disaster occurred which subconsciously he had been anticipating all the time.

There was a sudden loud report. The Cardinal Six swerved madly across the road, nearly jerking the wheel out of his hands. And when he had managed to get it into control, he was made aware by a harsh bumping that the worst had happened. At the very tensest stage of the race he had been put out of the running by a burst tire.

The tragedy had taken place almost immediately opposite the neat little gate of a neat little house standing back from the road behind the shelter of a quickset hedge. Bill brought the car to a stop and looked behind him. The limousine, a couple of hundred yards in the rear, was coming up like a galleon under sail. He grasped Flick's arm. It was a moment for swift action.

' Come on ! ' he cried. And jumping out, they ran
through the gate.

The garden in which they found themselves was one
of those beautifully trim preserves whose every leaf and
petal speaks eloquently of a loving proprietor. Neat
little sticks supported neat little plants. Neat little
gravel paths ran between neat little flower-beds. It was
the sort of garden from which snails, wandering in with
a care-free nonchalance, withdraw abashed, blushing and
walking backwards, realizing that they are on holy
ground. And it should have affected Bill and Flick,
those human intruders, with the same self-conscious awe.

But Bill and Flick were in a hurry, and when we are
in a hurry we forget our better selves. In such a maze
of flower-beds it was obviously impossible to keep to
the paths. Taking Flick's hand, Bill raced diagonally
across country to where a shrubbery seemed to offer at
least a temporary refuge.

From a window on the ground floor an agonized purple
face glared at them with an expression of pure hatred.
Two frenzied hands beat madly on the pane. A pro-
testing wail like that of a tortured demon came to their
ears, muffled but awesome.

They stopped for neither apologies nor explanations.
Hand in hand, they trampled over the beds and were
in the shrubbery. There they halted, panting ; and
presently observed, shooting in at the gate, the projectile-
like form of Sir George.

§ 2

Sir George Pyke had marked with a stern triumph
the accident that had checked the Cardinal Six. It had
seemed to him like retribution overtaking the wicked.
So greatly did it stimulate him that he yielded once
again to that overmastering impetuosity of his, and
instead of waiting to be driven up to the gate banged
imperiously on the glass and bounded from the limousine
while still a good twenty yards down the road. The
long period of physical inaction had told upon his nerves,
and he was impatient to be up and doing. As quickly

as his little legs would carry him, he scuttled along the hedge and bolted in at the gate.

He was half-way across the flower-beds, following the clearly defined track of his quarry in the mould, when a roar so loud and anguished that it compelled attention brought him to a momentary halt:

'Stop! You! What the devil do you think you're doing, you —— ——, —— you?'

He perceived a large, mauve-faced individual in golfing costume gesticulating forcefully from the steps of the house.

'——! ——!! ——!!!' added this person, driving home his point.

So great was Sir George's absorption in the business in hand that it is doubtful whether mere words, however eloquent, would have stopped him for long. The speaker had used two adjectives and a verb which he had never heard before, but it was not the desire to pause and inquire into the meaning of these that caused him to remain. What rooted him to the spot was the sudden appearance from behind some bushes of a second man, in corduroy trousers, and the thing about this second man that so compelled respect was the fact that he carried a large and dangerous-looking pitchfork, and—as if this were not enough—was accompanied by a weedy dog of raffish aspect, which now trotted up and began to sniff in a strong, silent way at Sir George's calves. Sir George looked at the dog, and the dog, using one rolling reddish eye for the purpose, looked at Sir George. He could never, even with his face in repose have been a handsome dog, and now his appearance was made definitely repellent by a slightly updrawn lip, revealing a large white tooth. Pressing as his engagements were, Sir George decided to linger.

The man in the golf suit came up.

'——! ——!' he began, enriching Sir George's vocabulary with a new noun.

The owner of the neat little house and garden, though he looked and behaved like a retired Indian colonel of the old school, was in reality no such thing, but techni-

cally a man of peace. He was, in fact, no other than
Montague Grayson, the well-known writer of sunny and
optimistic novels, and it would have been a distinct
shock to his large public could they have beheld him
in his present frame of mind. And yet, had they known
all the facts, they could hardly have denied that his
wrath was justified.

If there is one thing that wakes the fiend which sleeps
in us all, it is getting stuck in the big chapter of a sunny
and optimistic novel. For nearly three hours Montague
Grayson had been writhing in his study like a lost soul,
trying to inject whimsical humour and gentle pathos
into the pivotal scene of his new book. And when,
looking out of the window for the hundredth time, he
saw Flick and Bill ploughing through his beloved flower-
beds all the hatred which he had been feeling toward
his hero and heroine became instantly diverted to them.
He had not thought it possible to dislike any human
beings so much until, coming out of the house and catching sight of Sir George, he realized that what he had felt
for Flick and Bill had been but a pale imitation of the
real thing. If Montague Grayson had been a Dante he
would have gone straight off and started writing a new
Inferno in which Sir George would have occupied a
position in the middle of the innermost of the seven
Hells. As it was, he contented himself with bounding
out into the garden, his bosom seething with that perilous
stuff that weighs upon the soul.

' —— you, sir ! —— and —— you ! ' bellowed the ex-
sunny and optimistic man, brooding over Sir George
like a thunder cloud. It should be mentioned here in
further extenuation of Mr. Grayson's peevishness that he
had had a bad morning's golf. ' What the —— do you
think you're doing ? '

Sir George drew himself up with what dignity he could
muster, painfully conscious of the dog, which was plainly
waiting only for a word of encouragement from the Man
Up Top before starting to give free play to his worst
nature.

' My niece——' he began.

'You come trespassing in here, trampling on my flower-beds——'

'I am sorry——'

'What's the good of being sorry?'

'I should explain that my niece——'

'I've a good mind to shred you up and sprinkle you under the rose bushes.'

The man with the pitchfork, an enthusiast in any scheme that made for the good of his flowers, nodded silent approval of this plan. The dog breathed asthmatically.

'If you will allow me to explain, sir——'

'Explain! What possible explanation can there be? It's an outrage!'

'I——'

'Look at those beds! Covered with your beastly hoof marks!'

'My niece——'

To Bill and Flick, lurking in the shrubbery, only the author's portion of this dialogue had been audible, but that had been enough to send them creeping onward through the bushes with all the speed that they could command. A respect for other people's property is deep-seated in most of us, and already the heinousness of the crime that they had committed was heavy upon them. There is something about the mere act of treading on somebody else's flower-beds that automatically puts back the clock and makes us children again; and Bill and Flick, as they slunk away, were feeling about ten years old. It was just such behaviour as theirs that led to no jam for tea, and they felt their position deeply. It was not till the shrubbery ended in a small hedge and they found themselves out in a field dotted with sheep that the sense of guilt left them, to be replaced by one of elation. Deplorable though their conduct might have been, it had at any rate had the excellent result of giving them a breathing space. From the way the interview between Sir George and Mr. Grayson was developing, it looked as if their pursuer might be occupied for quite some time.

'Take care!' said Flick suddenly, and dropped on the grass. Bill joined her, flopping as if his legs had been mown from under him.

'What's the matter?' he asked a little querulously, for his nerves were not what they had been at the start of this affair, and he was shaken.

Flick pointed. Above the hedge that rimmed the field rose the silhouette of the limousine. Against the pale sky the profile of Augustus Briggs stood out like something carven. Calm, Augustus seemed, with the calmness of the man who is able to unhitch his brain at will and think of absolutely nothing. Only the smoke rising from the cigarette that appeared to be glued to his lower lip showed that he was alive.

Bill looked at Augustus keenly. He was thinking hard. A superbly strategic plan was beginning to shape itself in his mind. At this point good fortune sent to him precisely the ally he required. Close beside them, looking down on them with youth's frankly inquisitive stare, was standing a small boy.

'Hullo,' said Bill, smiling ingratiatingly.

'Hullo,' said the boy. He spoke reservedly, as if wishing to convey that he committed himself to nothing. He was a grave-looking boy with the pinched face of one on whom the cares of the world press heavily. He seemed worried about the cosmos.

'Do you want to earn half a crown?'

'Where is it?'

'Here.'

'Yes,' said the boy, having examined the coin critically.

Bill pointed.

'See that car?'

'Yes.'

'If I give you this half-crown, will you go to the other side of the road and start throwing stones at it?'

'Stones?'

'Stones.'

'D'yer want me to throw stones at that car?'

'At that car,' said Bill patiently.

'And you'll give me that 'alf-crown?'

' This half-crown.'

An instant before one might have thought that it would have been impossible for this stripling to smile, so strained and careworn had been his face ; but now his head seemed suddenly to split in the middle. A vast grin gleamed like a gash beneath his snub nose. Stunned for a moment by the stupendous reflection that he was going to be paid a huge sum for indulging in his favourite sport, he recovered swiftly. He took the half-crown, bit it, put it in his mouth and retired. At a leisurely pace he crossed the field and for an age-long minute there was silence and peace. The sheep browsed in the grass, birds twittered their evensong in the trees, Augustus Briggs smoked his cigarette in the front seat of the limousine.

Then things began to happen.

Appearances to the contrary, the mind of Augustus Briggs was not wholly a blank as he sat at his wheel placidly savouring his gasper. His was the quietude of deep content. This rest from the chase, with the opportunity it afforded for a couple of whiffs, was just what he needed most. So far from having unhitched his brain, he was thinking quite deeply, the object of his thoughts being the tip he had received that morning from the butler on to-morrow's three-o'clock race at Hurst Park. The butler, a knowledgeable man, had recommended an investment on Soapy Sam, and the more Augustus examined the prospect the better it looked. By this time to-morrow it seemed practically certain that he would be a richer man by a matter of ten shillings.

The reflection soothed Augustus Briggs. He gazed almost with benevolence at the small boy who was crossing the road. He was not fond of small boys as a rule, but in his mellowed mood he did not actively dislike this one. He would not have adopted him ; but on the other hand, he would not have clipped him on the side of the head. He watched him indulgently as he disappeared through the hedge. Then he turned to his thoughts again. Two bob on Soapy Sam at five to one——

Something whizzed across the road and clanged against the bonnet of the car. For an instant Augustus Briggs sat gaping. Then, peering over the side, he saw that what had struck the bonnet was a large jagged flint. And a moment later he observed, bobbing up over the hedge, a grinning face.

'Gor!' exclaimed Augustus, and as he spoke a second flint found its billet.

The chauffeur was not a man of deep sensibility. Towards most of the phenomena of the world through which he moved his attitude was one of superior indifference. A primrose by the river's brim a simple primrose was to him, and it was nothing more. But one thing he did love with a strong and holy passion, and that was his paint. And the impact of those flints on his shiny bonnet caused him an anguish more acute than that which he would have felt had his own head been their target. With one short, sharp wail he leaped from the car, raced across the road and burst into a torrent of eloquence.

The hedge, it grieved him to discover, formed an impenetrable barrier. It was one of those hedges through which boys can glide like eels, but which cannot be negotiated by chauffeurs fearful of tearing their uniforms. He had consequently to be content with mere words. And while he stood there, sketching out a list—necessarily incomplete, for it had been compiled on the spur of the moment, but nevertheless impressive—of the things he proposed to do to the boy if he caught him, Bill and Flick hurried silently out from their ambush.

Augustus, startled by the noise of engines, spun round. The car, with a wholly unauthorized driver at the wheel, was moving rapidly out of sight.

§ 3

It is pleasant to be able to record that Bill's first act on returning to the metropolis was to drive, guided by Flick, to Sir George's house in Manchester Square and leave the limousine outside the front door. He had no desire to add larceny to his other offences against the gentleman. This done, he hailed a cab and took Flick off to a restaurant to dine. He was feeling in need of refreshment after the activities of the afternoon, and it had become evident to both of them that the situation which had arisen was one that called for calm and unhurried discussion.

' How on earth ', he said, as the waiter receded from the table which they had taken in a quiet corner, ' your uncle found out that you were likely to be at Marmont Mansions simply gets past me. I suppose we've got to take it that he did come there looking for you ? '

' I'm afraid so. There doesn't seem any other possible reason why he should be in Battersea at all.'

' In any case, he knows that you are to be found somewhere round these parts, so the question now arises, What's to be done ? '

Flick drew little patterns on the tablecloth with her fork. She looked about her at the gradually filling restaurant. She had lived a cloistered life at Holly House, rarely emerging for meals except to go to recognized resorts of wealth like the Ritz, Claridge's and the Carlton, and this sort of place was strange to her. She was trying to decide whether the people at the other tables were interesting or merely flashy when Bill put his question again :

' What's to be done ? '

' Yes, I'm wondering, too,' said Flick. But she spoke listlessly, for the long ride with all its varied emotions had left her tired. She wanted to postpone serious talk, and to that end turned the conversation to the subject of this restaurant in which she was sitting. ' What did you say the name of this place was ? ' she asked.

' Mario's,' said Bill.

' What made you choose it ? '

' I was trying to think of somewhere where your Uncle George would be least likely to drop in for a bite, and I remembered this place. Slingsby took me here to lunch one day. Why ? Don't you like it ? '

' Yes, I think it's—— Oh ! '

She was looking past him at the door, and he was surprised to see that the colour which had been coming back to her face under the influence of food and drink had suddenly left it again. Her eyes had widened in a startled stare of dismay, and for a moment there flashed into his mind the absurd thought that Sir George might miraculously have appeared as if out of a trap. He swung round in his seat and was relieved to find that no such miracle had occurred. Somebody had just come in at the door and was walking down the room looking for a table, but it was not Sir George. It was a young man in a check suit, black-haired and adorned—if you could call it that—as to the upper lip by a small blob of moustache. Bill had no recollection of ever having set eyes on this young man before, nor did the other's appearance give to his thinking reasonable cause for alarm. He turned round again and looked at Flick inquiringly. She was still pale.

'Did you see?' she whispered.

'See?' said Bill, mystified. 'Do you mean the fellow in the check suit?'

Flick nodded.

'Mr. Pilbeam!'

Bill, who had taken up his knife and fork, laid them down again. He eyed Flick incredulously for a moment, then turned once more and looked down the room; and, looking, saw the check-suited one had congealed into a pillar of amazement and was gaping in their direction with open mouth. If he had been a highly paid motion-picture star he could not have registered surprise more eloquently.

Bill flushed darkly. It took a good deal to ruffle his normally good-humoured outlook on life, but it could be done. Roderick Pyke had done it by hitting him over the head with a stick, and Percy Pilbeam had done it now by the mere act of walking into a restaurant where he was having dinner. A man who has been through the sort of experiences which Bill had been having that afternoon does not look at things in the light of pure reason. Mario's Restaurant was open to the entire popu-

lation of London, and Percy Pilbeam had a perfect right
to go there to dine if he wished ; but to Bill, who had
been chased by the other's employer from the Prince
of Wales Road, Battersea, to within a couple of miles
of Brocket Hall in Hertfordshire, his presence in the
place seemed as much an outrage as that of Sir George
Pyke in his flower-beds had seemed to Montague Grayson, the sunny novelist.

It was persecution. That was what Bill felt. Sheer
persecution, and he pushed his chair back and rose with
protruding jaw.

' Where are you going ? ' asked Flick.

The next moment it had become plain where Bill was
going. He was stalking down the aisle in the direction
of the table at which the intruder had now been induced
by a solicitous waiter to seat himself. He reached the
table and, planting two large hands on the cloth, bent
forward and raked the assistant editor of *Society Spice*
with a lowering gaze that seemed to the latter to sear
his very soul. Not for a long time had Percy Pilbeam
seen at close range any one so big and so obviously
unfriendly as Bill. He shrank into his chair.

' Is your name Pilbeam ? '

Pilbeam gulped dryly.

' Yuk ! '

Bill bent a little closer. To the diners at the neigh-
bouring tables the incident seemed a common one of
restaurant life—the old friend spotting the dear pal across
the room and coming over to pass a chummy word.
Pilbeam would have been amazed if he had known that
anybody could possibly so misinterpret the position of
affairs. He was, indeed, wondering dully why the whole
of the assembled company did not instantly rush to the
spot to avert the murder which seemed to him so sicken-
ingly imminent. In the pursuance of his duties as
scandal gatherer for *Society Spice* he had been in some
unpleasant situations, but compared with this one they
had been roses—roses all the way. For a swift instant
he met Bill's eye, and looked pallidly away, horrified
by its red hostility.

'You notice I'm dining with Miss Sheridan?' said Bill in a quiet, rumbling voice.

Pilbeam tried to say 'Quite', but the word stuck in his throat.

'Good,' said Bill. 'Now, do you know what you're going to do?'

Pilbeam smiled the beginnings of a weak smile, intended to convey that he was open to consider in the most favourable spirit any suggestions which Bill might make.

'You're going to wait right here where you're sitting', cooed Bill, clenching and unclenching a fist that looked to the other's fascinated gaze like a ham, 'until we are through. You will then keep right on sitting while we go out, and you will continue sitting for ten minutes after that. I should advise you to make it a little longer so as to be on the safe side, as I shall be out there keeping an eye on the door. See?'

Pilbeam said that he saw.

'That's understood, then. Now don't', urged Bill earnestly, 'go getting absent-minded and forgetting, will you?'

Pilbeam said he wouldn't, and Bill nodded a brief farewell and returned to his table. Pilbeam, after watching him the whole way, took up a fork and began to pick feebly at a sardine.

'What did he say?' asked Flick eagerly.

Bill considered the question.

'Come to think of it,' he replied, 'he didn't say much. But I gathered that he understood all right.'

'Understood?'

'That he wasn't to stir from the table till we had been gone ten minutes.'

'But he will! He'll sneak out the moment we leave and follow me.'

'I think not,' said Bill. 'I think not. Would you mind changing seats? Then I shall be able to watch him. Not that it's really necessary. Come on,' he said encouragingly. 'Don't let a little thing like that spoil your dinner. Try some of this fish. It looks good.'

With gentle solicitude he forced her to make an

adequate meal, and was pleased to note the steady rise of her spirits as she ate. When the waiter had brought the coffee he felt that the time had come for serious discussion of the situation. The intrusion of Pilbeam, added to the shock of discovering that Sir George had followed the trail that led to the Battersea haven, had disturbed him a good deal, and he had been thinking deeply in the intervals of conversation.

' Now ', he said, ' we must talk this thing over and see where we stand. It seems to me that they're beginning to come over the plate a bit too fast.'

Flick nodded. The metaphor was strange to her, but she gathered its meaning.

' Let's get it clear,' Bill went on. ' Your plan of campaign is to stay away till your people throw in the towel and say that this idea of marrying the man Pyke is off. That's straight, isn't it ? '

' Yes ; but how am I to stay away, with them right after me like this ? They know now where you live and any moment they may find out where I live.'

' Exactly ! Obviously, you can't come dropping in at Marmont Mansions any more.'

' No.'

' Two courses ', proceeded Bill judicially, ' are open. We can change our addresses——'

' But even if I do change my address, I shall be all the time in a state of jumps, wondering if Uncle George isn't going to pop out from somewhere and pounce on me.'

' Just what I was going to say myself. It doesn't seem to me worth it. You can't go on with this hunted-fawn business indefinitely. It would give you the willies in a couple of days. So what I suggest is that you clear out altogether.'

' What ? Where ? '

' New York.'

' New York ! '

' I've thought it all out,' said Bill complacently. ' And between you and me, I think the scheme's a pippin. It'll only take a day getting your passport fixed up.'

' But what am I to do when I get to New York ? '

' I've two ideas about that. You might go to my Uncle Cooley at Westbury—where we first met, you know.'

Flick shook her head.

' It wouldn't be safe. He would be sure to cable Uncle Sinclair that I was there. They're great friends.'

' Yes, that's true. Well, then, here's the other idea : I'll give you a letter to Alice Coker. She will look after you.'

If Bill had not at that moment removed his gaze while he reached for a match he might have observed a queer expression flit over Flick's face. She looked at Bill wonderingly. It passed her comprehension how he could possibly be so dense as to imagine that she would go anywhere near the odious Miss Coker, no matter how great the emergency. True, she had never let fall a word to indicate that Alice Coker was in her opinion of all the superfluous women in the world the most super-fluous, but she felt that he ought to have known it by instinct. She bit her lip and her blue eyes clouded.

' She's a great girl,' continued Bill with tactless enthusi-asm. ' You'll love her.'

' Yes ? ' said Flick thinly.

' I'll tell you what. I'll write the letter now.' He called to the waiter, and presently pen, ink and paper were on the table. ' I think this is a wow, don't you ? ' he said buoyantly.

' A what ? '

' A pip,' explained Bill. ' The scheme of a lifetime. It solves the whole thing.'

Flick watched him as he wrote, clenching her hands under the table. She was conscious of a rush of con-tending emotions. At one moment she wanted to bang this dull-witted young man over the head, and the next she was wishing that she could just bury her face in her hands and cry. It was this latter desire which she found it particularly hard to fight down. She was feeling bitterly hurt. The airy way he had suggested that she should go right out of his life like this, with never a hint that he would miss her for an instant! It was illogical, of course. She realized that. He was only trying to help her. But women cannot always be logical.

In itself, considered merely as a way out of her difficulties, the idea of going to America was, she was forced to admit, a good one. The activities of the enemy had rendered London impossible. She simply could not go on being, as Bill had expressed it, a hunted fawn. In New York she would feel safe, and she had plenty of money.

'There!' said Bill.

Flick took the letter and put it in her bag.

'Thank you,' she said. 'I suppose we might as well be going now, mightn't we? I'm rather tired.'

'All right,' said Bill. 'I'll put you into a cab, and then I'll hang around for a while just in case friend Pilbeam starts any rannygazoo.'

But Pilbeam did not start any rannygazoo. He was ostentatiously busy with the leg of a chicken as they passed down the aisle, nor did he allow his eyes to stray in their direction when they went through the door. Safety First was Pilbeam's motto.

Bill closed the door of the cab.

'Good night,' he said. 'Don't lose that letter.'

'Of course not,' said Flick. 'Good night.'

Bill turned back to the door of the restaurant and stood there solidly, in his eyes the watchful look of one on his guard against rannygazoo. The cab turned the corner into Shaftesbury Avenue. A hand waved at him from the window.

The cab had scarcely reached Coventry Street when the hand once more came out of the window. This time it grasped some fragments of paper. It opened and with a vicious jerk scattered these into the road. Then it disappeared again.

§ 4

The good ship *Homeric* lay in her slip at Southampton, preparing for departure. Her decks and alleyways were crowded with voyagers and those who had come to see those voyagers off. Flick, leaning over the rail, stared down at the sun-speckled water, and Bill, by her side, gazed at the gulls circling overhead. For some minutes now conversation between them had taken on a limping gait, and the atmosphere was charged with a strange embarrassment.

' You'll be off soon,' said Bill, urged by the silence to say something.

' Yes.'

The gulls flashed to and fro against the cobalt sky, mewing like kittens.

' This is supposed to be one of the most comfortable boats in the world,' said Bill.

' Is it ? '

' I think you'll be comfortable.'

' I expect so.'

' They rather pride themselves on making you comfortable.'

' That's nice.'

Bill was not sure whether he was sorry or relieved to hear at this juncture the ' All-for-the-shore ' cry that puts an end to the sometimes trying ordeal of ' seeing off '. Up till a few minutes ago everything had been jolly. Coming down in the train and for the first quarter of an hour on board the boat Flick had been full of chatter, a pleasant and cheery companion. But just recently a cloud seemed to have fallen on her mood, and she had tended to long silences and monosyllables.

' I suppose I ought to be going,' he said.

' I suppose so.'

' I hope you'll have a good time on board.'

' Thanks.'

' It'll seem funny to you being in America again after all these years.'

' Yes.'

' I'll look after Bob.'

' Thanks.'

' Well, I suppose I ought to be going.'

'I suppose so.'

A gull wheeled so close to Bill's head that he ducked involuntarily. He laughed a nervous laugh.

'What a lot of people come to see people off,' he said.

'Yes.'

'Friends, I suppose,' said Bill brightly.

'I shouldn't wonder.'

A steward with a voice like a foghorn in pain was once more urging all whom it might concern to make for the shore.

'I suppose', said Bill, struck with a novel idea, 'I ought to be going.'

'I think you'd better.'

'Well, good-bye.'

'Good-bye.'

'You won't lose that letter?'

'Which letter?'

'Why, the one to Alice,' said Bill, surprised.

'Oh yes,' said Flick.

'She'll give you a great time.'

'Yes?'

They had walked to the gang-plank. It was covered with a moving stream of humanity, bustling like bees going into a hive. There was something so suggestive of finality about the spectacle that a curious dull melancholy swept over Bill. He cast a side glance at Flick. The sight of her sent an odd pang through him. Perhaps it was the hugeness of the vessel that made her seem so small and forlorn.

'Gosh!' he exclaimed with sudden fervour. 'I shall miss you! The flat will seem like a desert without you in the old arm-chair. I shall just sit there with poor old Bob——'

He broke off.

'Good Lord!' he said, dismayed.

'It's nothing,' said Flick. Her face was working. She dabbed impatiently at her eyes.

'But——'

'I—I was just thinking of Bob.' She held out her

hand abruptly. 'Good-bye,' she said, and was gone.

Bill stood for a moment, staring into the crowd which hid her.

'Golly!' he mused. 'She *is* fond of that dog!'

He walked ashore thoughtfully.

CHAPTER TWELVE

A VISITOR FOR MR. PARADENE

§ 1

HOWEVER true it may be that Action is the spice of life, there is no denying that an occasional dose of the soothing syrup of Tranquillity makes a pleasant change. And so, after the scenes—always restless and bordering at times on actual violence—which, in order to keep the records straight, the historian of the fortunes of Bill West has just been compelled to describe, it is agreeable to turn aside and relax for a while in an atmosphere of cloistered and scholastic calm. About a month after the departure of Flick Sheridan from Southampton we find ourselves once more in the home of Mr. Cooley Paradene at Westbury, Long Island, in a small upper room looking out over the sunlit garden. It is the room dedicated to the studies of Mr. Paradene's adopted son, Horace. And at the moment when we enter it the hard-boiled lad is receiving a lesson in the French language from Mr. Sherman Bastable, his tutor.

Yes, still his tutor. It is true that a few weeks ago Mr. Bastable definitely announced that not even so substantial a sum as a million dollars would be sufficient to induce him to continue his duties; but the statements a man makes in the first flush of realization that the inside brim of his hat has been doctored with glue are not always carried out when scissors and warm water have done their work and reason resumed its sway. Scarcely half an hour after the hat had been clipped and scoured off his forehead, Mr. Bastable, who had begun by sneering at a cool million, had reduced his terms so considerably that he actually consented to remain in office for a mere additional fifty per month. We find him, consequently, still doing business at the old stand.

But the Sherman Bastable, who was now endeavouring to teach Horace French, was a very different man from the genial and juicily enthusiastic young fellow of a few weeks back. He was now a soured and suspicious despot who, fortified by instructions from his employer to stand no nonsense, had taken on a cold implacability which was having the gravest effects on the latter's comfort.

Of this change in his disposition he gave proof at this very moment. Seeing that Horace, like the room in which he sat, was looking out over the sunlit garden, he banged the table with a forceful fist.

' Attend, can't you ? ' he cried.   ' You aren't listening to a word I'm saying ! '

' All right, all right,' said Horace plaintively.

These passages were beginning to irk him more and more. A free child of the underworld, he had taken unkindly to discipline ; and it seemed to him sometimes as though Mr. Bastable had developed all the less amiable characteristics of the late Simon Legree. He removed his gaze from the shady lawn and gaped cavernously.

' Don't yawn ! ' thundered Mr. Bastable.

' Oh, all right.'

' And don't say " all right " ! ' boomed the tutor, who had a retentive memory and could never look at his little charge even now without a twinge across the forehead.   ' When I speak to you, say " yes, sir," smartly and respectfully.'

' Yes, sir,' said Horace.

A purist might have criticized the smartness and respectfulness of his delivery, but the actual words were up to sample and the tutor appeared satisfied. At any rate, he returned to the task in hand.

' Indefinite articles,' said Mr. Bastable, resuming.   ' A or An is translated into French by Un before a masculine noun, as, for example, Un homme, a man ; un oiseau, a bird——'

'There's a boid on that tree,' interjected Horace, switching abruptly from foreign languages to nature study.

Mr. Bastable favoured him with a basilisk glare.

'Attend to your work!' he growled. 'And don't say "boid". It's a bird.'

'Well, it's making a noise like a boid,' argued Horace.

'. . . and Une before a feminine noun, such as *dame*,' proceeded the tutor. 'Une dame, a lady; une allumette, a match; une histoire, a story; une plume, a pen. Do you get that?'

'I suppose so.'

'What do you mean, you suppose so?'

'Well,' said Horace candidly, 'it sounds to me a good deal like apple sauce. Seems like there ain't no sense in it.'

The tutor clutched his thinning hair and groaned hollowly. That extra fifty dollars a month had raised his salary to a very respectable figure, but it frequently occurred to him that he was receiving but trivial payment for what he had to endure.

'"Seems like there ain't no sense in it!"' he echoed despairingly. 'Can't you *see* that's not grammar?'

'I don't know about its being grammar,' retorted Horace with spirit. 'It gets across, don't it?'

'Sir,' prompted Mr. Bastable automatically.'

'Sir.'

'And don't say "don't it". Say "doesn't it" or "does it not".' He eyed his pupil wanly. The weather was warm and the strain beginning to tell on his sensitive nerves. 'You're incorrigible. I don't know what's to be done with you. You take absolutely no interest in your work. I should have thought that you would have some sense of your position—your chances and opportunities.'

'Oh, I know,' said Horace wearily. 'One ought to grasp one's opportunities and try to improve oneself—at least oncet!'

'Don't say "oncet".'

'Oh, all right.'

' Yes, sir ! ' emended Mr. Bastable, eyeing him bale-
fully.

' Yes, sir.'

The tutor flung himself back in his chair, which creaked
protestingly.

' Do you realize that yours is a position which thousands
of boys would give their eyes to be in ? '

' Can't you *see* that's not grammar ? ' said Horace.
Much as he disliked these séances, it happened now and
then that bits of them stuck in his mind. ' Oughtn't to
end a sentence with " in ". You put me right, so I
don't mind puttin' you right. Had you that time. Hot
dog ! ' he said with a complacency which made the tutor
feel—not for the first time—that his favourite character
in history was Herod the Great. ' You wised me up
to that yourself.'

Every tutor is a statesman at heart. He has to be.
Mr. Bastable, prudently realizing the danger of his position, instituted a counter-attack by assailing his pupil's
pronunciation.

' I wish you would learn to speak properly,' he said
with hauteur. ' Your accent is abominable. Here ! '
He pulled out a massive book. ' It's no good trying to
teach you French till you can talk English. Read a
page or two of this aloud. And try to do it like a human
being and not '—he searched his mind for an adequate
simile—' and not like a caddie at a third-rate golf course.'

' What's wrong with caddies ? ' demanded Horace, who
was intimate with several and in leisure moments had
occasionally done a bit in that line himself.

' Go on. Don't waste time,' said Mr. Bastable, refusing to be diverted to an argument. ' Begin at the top
of page ninety-eight.'

Horace took the book—it was entitled *Beacon Lights
of History*, Vol. II, The Middle Ages—with a disrelish
which he made no attempt to conceal.

' " It was at this perriod——" ' he began sourly.

' Period.'

' " It was at this period, when the convents of Yurrup——" '

' Europe.'

' I *said* Yurrup,' protested Horace, aggrieved. ' " It was at this period, when the convents of Yurrup rejoiced in ample possessions, and their churches rivalled cath-e-*drals*——" '

' Cath-*e*-drals.'

' " —in size and magnificence, that Saint Bernard ——" ' He broke off, mildly interested for the first time. ' Say, I knew a gink that had a S'n-Bernard. Big, hairy dawg with red eyes . . .'

' Get on,' said Mr. Bastable coldly.

' " Saint Bernard, the greatest and best rep-res-en-tat-ive of Med-i-æ-val mon-as-ti-cism——" ' *Gawd !* ' said Horace under his breath, tenderly massaging his aching jaw. ' " —was born, 1091, at Fontaine, in Boigundy." '

' Burgundy.'

' " Boigundy. He belonged to a noble family. His mother had six sons and a daughter, whom she early con-se-crated to the Lord. Bernard was the third son, a beautiful, delicate, refined young man, tall, with flaxen hair, fair complexion, and blue eyes from which shone a superhuman sim-plic-i-ty and purity." '

He stopped, revolted. He did not know much about saints, but he knew what he liked, and something told him that he was not going to like Saint Bernard.

' Sounds like a cake-eater,' he sniffed.

Mr. Bastable was just drawing himself together for a Legree-like reproof, when there was a gentle tap at the door.

' Pardon me for interrupting, sir,' said Roberts, the butler, hovering delicately on the threshold.

' You haven't made *me* mad, Bobby,' Horace assured him gratefully.

' What is it, Roberts ? '

' Professor Appleby has called to see Master Horace, sir. Mr. Paradene would be glad if you would allow him to step down to the library for a moment.'

His announcement evoked universal enthusiasm. Horace beamed upon him as people must have beamed on the man who brought the good news from Ghent to

Aix. Nor was Mr. Bastable displeased. He was conscientious and had been prepared to continue his task for another hour, but the thought of being relieved of Horace's society gave him the sensations of a reprieved convict.

' Certainly, certainly,' he said.

' I'm not goin' to put up any stiff argument, neither,' declared Horace.

He trotted joyfully out of the prison-chamber. Mr. Bastable, with the air of one from whose shoulders there has been removed an intolerable weight, lit a cigarette and put his feet on the table.

§ 2

The arrival, some ten minutes before, of the venerable Professor Appleby had surprised Mr. Paradene at his customary occupation of fiddling about with the books in his library. He had just scuttled up the ladder to one of the top shelves and dumped on his already congested table a pile of mouldering volumes when Roberts brought the news of the visitor's advent.

For a moment Mr. Paradene felt a little like a dog who has been hauled off a bone, but his native courtesy asserted itself, and it was with a cordial smile that he greeted the professor when he made his entry.

' Nice of you to look in,' he said.

' I chanced to be in the neighbourhood,' said Professor Appleby, ' and I thought I might venture to call and inquire after the little lad. He is busy at his studies, no doubt ? '

' I imagine so.   Won't you take a seat ? '

' Thank you, my dear Paradene, thank you.'

Professor Appleby relaxed in a chair with the contented sigh of a man who is not in the best condition. He tapped his domed brow with a silk handkerchief and combed out his white beard with a delicate forefinger. He was looking more like a benevolent minor prophet than ever.   His mild eyes wandered to the bookshelves, and there came into them a sudden, predatory gleam, which vanished almost instantly, to be replaced by their habitual expression of calm goodwill.

'A warm day,' he observed.

'Very. Do you find it close in here?'

'Not at all,' said Professor Appleby, 'not at all. I enjoy the peculiar and distinctive scent of old books. I never find it stuffy in a library.'

This was so exactly what Mr. Paradene felt himself that his affection for his visitor deepened.

'And how is Horace?' inquired the professor.

'Physically,' said Mr. Paradene, 'he could not be better. But——'

Professor Appleby raised a deprecating hand.

'I know what you are going to say, my dear Paradene. I know just what you are going to say. It was on the tip of your tongue to tell me that the little lad is not taking kindly to his studies.'

'Not very kindly,' admitted Mr. Paradene. 'Mr. Bastable, his tutor, reports that it is difficult to get him to take a real interest.'

'I expected as much. No enthusiasm?'

'None.'

'It will come,' said the professor. 'It will come. We must have patience, Paradene, patience. We must emulate the assiduity of the polyp that builds the coral reef. I had anticipated this. It was on my advice that you adopted a totally untutored lad, a child of the people, and I still maintain that I was right in giving you that advice. How much better, even though progress may at first be slow, to have a boy like this to work upon; a boy whose mind is not a palimpsest that has been scrawled over by other hands. You have nothing to worry about. It would have been perfectly easy, no doubt, for you to have adopted a son from some family of the gentlefolk; but in my opinion—and I know I am right—the results would have been far less satisfactory. Horace is virgin soil. He has not been ploughed by others. Sooner or later you will find that you will reap your reward. Sooner or later—I say it confidently —you will find that by the mere process of living in your home the little lad is beginning to imitate your mental processes, to acquire your own tastes.'

'It's odd that you should say that,' said Mr. Paradene thoughtfully.

'Not odd,' corrected the professor with a gentle smile. 'I based my observation on a knowledge of psychology which has rarely led me astray. But why did it strike you as peculiar? Am I to infer that he has already begun to show signs of this?'

'As a matter of fact, he has. It is a remarkable fact, Appleby, but the only thing outside his meals in which Horace shows the slightest interest is this library of mine.'

The professor coughed a gentle cough and gazed at the ceiling with a far-away look in his eyes.

'Indeed!' he said softly.

'He is always pottering in here and wanting to know which of my books are the rarest and most valuable.'

'The dawning intelligence, the dawning intelligence. The little mind begins to expand, to develop. Like a plant groping out for the sunshine.'

'It makes me feel that there may be hope for him.'

'I', said the professor, 'have great hopes of Horace. I had right from the beginning.'

'Perhaps after he has had a year or two of school in England——'

'What!' cried Professor Appleby.

A moment before, it would have seemed impossible that anything could disturb the calm serenity of this venerable man. But now he was sitting forward on the edge of his chair, staring at his host in the most manifest concern. His lower jaw had fallen and his white beard wabbled agitatedly.

'You are not sending him to school in England!' he gasped.

'Taking him,' corrected Mr. Paradene. 'I am sailing in a few days to pay a long-delayed visit to an old friend of mine—Sinclair Hammond. I intend to take Horace with me and enter him at one of the large English schools —possibly Winchester. Hammond was at Winchester.'

'But is this wise? Is this prudent?'

'Well, I'm going to do it,' said Mr. Paradene with a

touch of that belligerent manner which had so often caused adverse comment in the family.

Professor Appleby pulled at his beard. His discomposure was plain. Mr. Paradene, looking at him, was conscious of a passing wonder as to why he should take the news so hardly.

'But the education a boy gets at these English schools! Surely it has become a commonplace that it is too superficial, too machine-like. Read all these novels of the younger English writers——'

'I never read novels,' said Mr. Paradene with a slight shudder.

'And then again—this visit to England—— Are you not afraid to leave your books here—your priceless books —entirely unguarded?'

Mr. Paradene uttered an amused laugh which sounded to his visitor like a knell.

'You talk as if I had never left the house before. I'm always travelling. I was travelling when I met you. And besides, if you think I leave my books unguarded, try to get through the steel shutters over those windows. Yes, and try to pick your way through that door. I had this room specially constructed. It's like a safe.'

'I see,' said Professor Appleby unhappily.

'In any case, my library is insured, and I'm taking all the most valuable of my books with me to England.'

'Eh?' cried the professor, starting as if the fingers combing his beard had suddenly encountered a snake. 'Taking them with you?'

'Yes; Hammond is a collector too. He will be just as excited over these books as if they belonged to himself.'

'Will he?' said the professor, brightening like a summer sky when the sun comes out from behind a cloud. 'Will he, indeed?'

'Yes; he's that sort of man; one of those rare collectors who have no small jealousies.'

'He sounds delightful.'

'Yes, you would like Hammond.'

'I am sure I should. . . . Of course, when you are

in England you will keep these books at some bank or safe desposit ? '

' No, I see no reason for that. Books are not like jewellery—their value is not obvious to the lay eye. If any burglar invades Hammond's house at Wimbledon he would hardly have the intelligence to take away what to him would be merely a bundle of dilapidated books.'

' True, true.'

' I shall keep them in my bedroom in an ordinary suit-case.'

' An excellent notion. . . . Ah,' said the professor, breaking off, ' here is our young friend. Well, Horace.'

' Hallo,' said that youth.

Professor Appleby glanced at his watch.

' Good gracious ! I had no idea how time had flown. I ought to go immediately. I shall just be able to catch a good train. Perhaps the little lad might be spared from his studies to accompany me to the station ? Thank you. Get your hat then, Horace. We must be hurrying.'

In spite of the statement that he had need for haste, it was at a leisurely pace that Professor Appleby started down the drive. He walked as if troubled with corns, and as he went spoke earnestly to his young companion.

' Kid,' said Professor Appleby, ' it's a lucky thing I happened to look in this afternoon. Do you know what's happened ? That old June-bug back there doesn't seem able to stick in one spot for a coupla days on end. He's taking you over to England right away.'

Horace stopped in his tracks, displaying as great a concern at the news as the professor himself had shown a short while back in the library.

' Takin' me to England ? What for ? '

' To put you to school over there.'

' Who, me ? '

' Yes, you.'

' Well, wouldn't that jar you ! ' cried Horace in deep disgust. ' I might have known there was a catch to this thing of gettin' me adopted. It's bad enough here, with everybody pickin' on me and me havin' to spend all day learnin' French and everythin'; but, gee, I'd

always got my get-away to look forward to. But goin'
to school!' He frowned resolutely. 'Say, listen! I
ain't goin' to no school. See? I ain't goin' to no school,
not in England nor anywheres. I——'

'You talk too much,' said Professor Appleby curtly.
'If you'll give me a chance to get a word in I'll tell you
something. You won't have to go to any school. The
old man's going over to England to visit another book-
collecting nut, and he's taking a stack of his best books
with him. You'll be able to make a quick clean-up and
fade-out. He's going to keep the stuff in his bedroom
in a suit-case.'

'Yes, he is!' said Horace derisively. 'That's likely,
ain't it, when he locks the things up here as if they was
gold dust.'

'He is, I tell you. He told me so himself. He thinks
there's no chance of anybody trying for them when he's
there. And why should they? No ordinary yegg who
happens to blow into a house is going to load himself
up with a bunch of books.'

'Something in that,' agreed Horace.

'I'll have Joe go over the same time you do, and you
and he can get together and fix things.'

'All right,' said Horace. 'Say, that's a pretty girl.'

The object of his commendation, a slim girl with fair
hair and a boyish figure, was walking rather wearily up
the road that led from the station. He eyed her critically
as she passed, and so confirmed in his good opinion was
he by this closer inspection that he stood gazing over
his shoulder at her receding form, and was awarded by
his austere companion a disciplinary thump on the head.

'You've no time for rubbering at girls,' said Professor
Appleby like a minor prophet rebuking the sins of the
people. 'You just listen to me when I'm talking to you.
I want to get this thing straight in your ivory skull.'

'Oh, all right,' said Horace.

§ 3

The girl who had so pleased Horace's critical eye
walked on till she came to the gate of Mr. Paradene's

grounds, then turned in and proceeded down the drive towards the house. This was familiar territory to her. She was surprised to find how clearly she remembered all the various landmarks. There was the funny old shingled roof, there the window of her bedroom, and there through the trees gleamed the lake. Her eyes dimmed and she caught her breath with a little gasp as she saw the lake. The two dressing-sheds were there, also the diving-board—all just the same as they had been centuries ago when she was sixteen, skinny and freckled.

She walked on and rang the bell. And presently Mr. Paradene, once more up his ladder, was aware of Roberts, the butler, on the floor below him.

' Eh ? ' said Mr. Paradene absently.

' A lady wishes to see you, sir.'

Mr. Paradene almost slid down the ladder. It was a rare, almost an unprecedented occurrence for ladies to wish to see him.

' Who is she ? '

' A Miss Sheridan, sir.'

There had been no affecting reunion between Flick and Roberts. To each the other had appeared as a stranger. Flick remembered that on her visit to this place five years ago there had been a butler, but the personality of Roberts had not stamped itself on her mind. As for Roberts, if he recalled the small girl who had stayed at the house in the third year of his butlership, he did not associate her with this attractive young person.

' Did she say what she wanted ? '

' No, sir.'

' Where is she ? '

' I have shown her into the morning-room, sir.'

' I suppose you had better ask her to come up here.'

' Very good, sir.'

The uneasy suspicion which had disturbed Mr. Paradene's mind that his visitor had come to collect funds for some enterprise of the Community church vanished as she entered the room. The Community church, when it made its periodical assaults on his purse, did so through

the medium of females of a maturer vintage. He looked
at her inquiringly, so obviously puzzled that Flick, though
she was far from being in a cheery frame of mind, smiled
faintly.

' You don't remember me, Mr. Paradene ? '

' Why—er—to be frank—— '

' Well, it's quite a long time since we met. I stayed
here five years ago with my uncle, Sinclair Hammond.'

' Good heavens ! ' Mr. Paradene, who had contented
himself so far with a wary bow at long range, sprang
forward and shook her hand warmly. ' I'd never have
known you. Bless my soul, you were quite a child then.
I remember you perfectly now. Bless my soul, yes.
So you're back in America, eh ? Do you live here now ?
Marry an American, eh ? '

' No, I'm not married.'

' Just visiting ? Well, well ! I'm delighted to see
you again, my dear. You caught me just in time.
Oddly enough, I'm on the very eve of sailing for England
to stay with your uncle.'

' I know. That's why I've come here. Uncle Sinclair
wants you to take me back to England with you. You've
had his cable ? '

' Cable ? ' said Mr. Paradene. ' I remember no cable.'
He rang the bell. ' Roberts, has a cable come for me
recently ? '

' Yes, sir. One arrived yesterday. If you remember,
sir, I brought it to you in this room. You were busy
at the bookshelves at the moment, and instructed me
to place it on the table.'

The table was covered with a deep top-dressing of
books and papers. Mr. Paradene rummaged among these
and presently came to the surface bearing triumphantly
a buff envelope. Roberts, vindicated, left the room.

' I really must apologize,' said Mr. Paradene. ' I have
a bad habit of snowing my correspondence under. All
the same, Roberts should have reminded me. Cables
are important things.' He opened the envelope and read
its contents. ' Yes, this is the one. Your uncle says
you will be calling on me and will I bring you over to

England. Of course. Only too delighted. Where are
you staying ? With friends in New York ? '
  ' No, I'm all alone.'
  ' Alone ! ' Mr. Paradene replaced his rimless glasses,
which had fallen off, and stared at her. ' You don't
mean to say your uncle let you come over here all
alone ? '
  ' I ran away,' said Flick simply.
  ' Ran away ! '
  ' From home. And now ', she said with a crooked
smile and a little lift of her shoulders, ' I'm running back
again.'
  Even with the aid of his glasses Mr. Paradene seemed
to find it hard to inspect her as closely as he wished.
He came a step nearer, peering at her, bewildered.
  ' You ran away from home ? But why ? '
  ' They wanted me to marry somebody I found I didn't
want to marry. Uncle Sinclair ', she went on quickly,
' hadn't anything to do with it, poor dear. It was the
others—Aunt Frances and Uncle George.' Mr. Paradene
would have liked footnotes explaining these two new
characters, but he hesitated to interrupt the flow of a
narrative which was gripping him strongly. ' Things ',
continued Flick, ' got rather unpleasant, so I ran away
and came over here. I thought I could get work of some
kind.'
  ' I never heard of such a thing ! '
  ' That's practically what everybody said whom I asked
for work. I never dreamed anybody could be so little
wanted as I was. I had a certain amount of money
when I got to America, and I supposed it would last
ever so long, but it seemed to melt away. And one night
I had my bag stolen, with almost every penny I possessed
in it. That finished me. I stuck it out for another
couple of days, and then I spent my last two dollars
on a cable home.'
  Mr. Paradene, though capable on occasion of behaving
like a volcano, was a soft-hearted and romantic man.
Flick's story touched him.
  ' And then ? '

' I got a cable back telling me to go to you and you
would look after me and bring me back to England.'

' My dear child, of course I will, of course. Your
room shall be got ready at once. The same one you
had five years ago.'

' I'm afraid I'm an awful nuisance.'

' Nothing of the kind,' said Mr. Paradene heatedly.
' How dare you say you're a nuisance ? You're nothing
of the sort. Would you like some tea ? '

' I should, rather, if it's not giving too much trouble.'

The ringing of the bell did Mr. Paradene the service
of helping him cover his embarrassment. There was to
him something poignantly pathetic in this meekness on
the part of a girl who only a short time back had on her
own showing been so abundantly equipped with spirit
as to run away from home and cross the Atlantic to try
her luck in a foreign land. Until the tea arrived he moved
about the room with his back turned, fussing over his
books.

' But if you go home ', he said, when Flick had drunk
a cup of tea and seemed the better for it, ' you will have
to marry this man you dislike.'

He realized that it might be tactless, this harping on
a delicate subject, but curiosity overcame delicacy. He
was feeling like a child being told a story.

' Oh, I don't dislike him,' said Flick tonelessly. ' I'm
very fond of some one else, who isn't fond of me, so I've
decided I might just as well marry Roderick as do anything. Trying to live in New York on nothing has
changed my views of life a good deal. It has made a
comfortable home and lots of money seem more attractive.
One has got to be practical, hasn't one ? ' She got up
and began to walk about the room. ' What a lot of
books you have ! ' she said. ' Ever so many more than
Uncle Sinclair.'

' He has some I would be very glad to own,' said Mr.
Paradene handsomely.

He would have liked to hear more of this man whom
Flick was fond of but who was not fond of her, but he
gathered that she looked upon her narrative as com-

pleted and would resent further questioning. He followed her across the room and touched her shoulder with an awkward little pat of condolence. She looked round at him and he saw that her eyes were misty. There was a momentary pause, tense with embarrassment, and he covered it by picking up the photograph at which she had been looking. It was a full-length snapshot of a burly young man in football costume, staring out of the picture with the doughy stolidity habitual to burly young men in football costume.

'That is my nephew William,' said Mr. Paradene.

Flick nodded.

'I know.'

'Of course, yes,' said Mr. Paradene. 'He was staying here when you and your uncle visited me, wasn't he?'

'He looks very strong,' said Flick. She felt that she must say something.

'He is strong,' said Mr. Paradene. 'And', he added gruffly, 'he is an idle, worthless young waster.'

Flick uttered a sharp exclamation.

'He isn't! Oh, I beg your pardon,' she hurried on. 'What I meant was that I don't think you know how hard he is working now to try to find out what is wrong with your London business.'

'Hallo!' Mr. Paradene put up his glasses. 'How do you know anything about that?'

'I—I met him.'

'Over in London?'

'Yes.'

'That's odd. Where did you run across him?'

'Er—in our garden.'

'There!' said Mr. Paradene. 'What did I say? He spends his time fooling around at garden-parties.'

'It wasn't exactly a garden-party,' said Flick. 'He really is trying his hardest to find out why those profits have fallen off so much.'

'Oh yes!'

'Oh, but he is!' insisted Flick. She refused to allow herself to be intimidated by the old man's gruffness. The fact that he still kept Bill's photograph in his library, that holy of holies, must surely be significant. ' I'll tell you something he's found out already. He discovered that Mr. Slingsby is selling nearly all your wood pulp to a firm named Higgins & Bennett at a very small profit, when he has had much better offers elsewhere.'

' What ? '

' It's quite true. I think—we both think—that Mr. Slingsby isn't very honest.'

' Nonsense ! As straight and able a man as I ever met. And I'm a judge of character.'

' You can't be a very good judge of character if you think Bill is an idle waster,' said Flick warmly.

' Hallo ! You seem very friendly towards him.'

' I am.'

' Why, you hardly know him ! '

' I've known him for years.'

' Yes, I suppose you have if you like to put it that way. This is interesting, what you tell me about those sales. I can't understand it. Did William tell you how he found out ? '

' No. But he's awfully clever.'

' H'm ! *I* never noticed it.'

' Well, he is. And I'm sure that if you would take him into your business and give him a fair start he would do wonders.'

Mr. Paradene chuckled.

' If I ever think of founding a William-boosting Club I shall know where to go for a president.'

' I think he's rather hurt that you haven't sent him a word since he got to England, asking him how he's getting on.'

' I'll bet he hasn't given me a thought since he landed,' said Mr. Paradene callously. ' Still, if you think he's so sensitive, I'll send him a wireless from the boat and arrange a meeting.'

' I wish you would.'

' But I don't even know where he is.'

' Nine, Marmont Mansions, Prince of Wales Road, Battersea Park, London,' said Flick glibly.

' Good gracious ! How do you know that ? '

' He told me.'

Mr. Paradene looked at her curiously.

' I don't know how long you were talking in this garden of yours,' he said, ' but there doesn't seem to have been much that he didn't tell you. I suppose he roasted me, eh ? '

' He said you were a perfect darling,' said Flick, ' who tried to make people believe you were a terror and didn't deceive anybody.'

She stooped and bestowed a swift kiss on the bald spot in the centre of Mr. Paradene's mop of stiff white hair.

' I'm going out into the garden,' she said. ' I want to see if you've been and changed everything since I was last here. If I find you have I'll come back and smack you.'

Mr. Paradene followed her with a round-eyed gaze as she left the room. His thoughts strayed back to the story she told him, and he gave a discontented sniff.

' A man who isn't fond of that girl ', he mused, ' must be a damned fool ! '

He picked up the photograph of Bill and looked at it, a rather wistful smile curving his lips. An idle young hound, William, but not unattractive. By no means unattractive.

He put the photograph down and toddled off to his ladder.

CHAPTER THIRTEEN

BILL MAKES A DISCOVERY

§ 1

HIS long form draped in a flowered dressing-gown, Judson Coker sat breakfasting in the dining-room of Number 9, Marmont Mansions, Battersea. A gentle breeze, floating in through the open window, brought pleasant Spring scents from the park across the road to blend with the robuster aroma of coffee and fried bacon. Propped up against the coffee-pot was a copy of the *New York World*, which had arrived that morning by the American mail. The hour was 10.30.

A strange sense of well-being filled Judson. He took another mouthful of bacon and marvelled, as he had been in the habit of marvelling lately, how extraordinarily fit he felt these days. It seemed to him that this mystery of his glowing health was one that would interest doctors—achieved, as it had been, in spite of the fact that for nearly two months now he had been deprived of that regular stimulus of alcohol so highly recommended —indeed, insisted upon—by the medical profession. He was in tremendous shape. Why, back in New York he would have shied like a startled horse if any one had suggested that he should wrap himself round half a dozen slices of bacon at daybreak like this ; whereas now he was in two minds whether or not to send out to the kitchen for a further supply.

He came to the conclusion that it must be something to do with the London air. It probably possessed curious tonic properties. And having decided definitely that another order of bacon was essential, he went down the passage to the kitchen to put it in commission. When he came back he found Bill West staring moodily at the laden table.

'Hallo, Bill o' man,' said Judson buoyantly. 'Come to join me in a bite? Sit down and draw up a chair —I mean, draw up a chair and sit down. A relief expedition is on its way with more food.'

'I had my breakfast hours ago,' said Bill with gloomy unresponsiveness. 'Haven't you finished yet? I want to use the table to write a letter.'

The champagne-like air of London, which had brought new youth to Judson, seemed to have missed Bill out when distributing joy and elasticity about the metropolis. For the last few weeks Bill had been restless and subject to sudden fits of irritability—a fact which had disturbed Judson not a little. Filled as he was nowadays with an almost maudlin benevolence towards all created things, Judson wanted to have smiling faces around him.

'You've all day before you,' he pointed out. 'Park yourself on a chair and watch me eat. Shan't be long.'

'There's a letter for you in the sitting-room,' said Bill. 'From Alice.'

'Yes?' said Judson, with a brother's indifference. He scanned his paper. 'Listen to this: "Broadcasts His Love; Sweetheart Muffs It. Wellington, Mass. Miss Luella Phipps of this city took her ear from her radiophone at just the wrong time last night, for she failed to hear her sweetheart's voice in Forest Hills, New York, announcing their engagement. James J. Roper, of Forest Hills, New York, is the lucky man, and is a radio expert. It occurred to him to let his fiancée hear his voice tell the world the glad tidings of their approaching nuptials——"'

'Why do they print drivel like that?' said Bill sourly.

'Don't you think it's rather touching?' inquired the Polyanna behind the coffee-pot. In his sunny mood he was prepared to find heart-interest everywhere.

'No!'

'Oh!' Judson returned to his literary research. '"Would Match Miss Bauer Against Men Swimmers,"' he proceeded, having now meandered on to the sporting page.

' Who would ? '

' It just says "would". Her pals, I suppose. During the recent six-day swimming carnival Miss Bauer hung up four new world's standards and two new American marks.'

' What of it ? '

Judson turned the pages.

' Here's a good one,' he said, chuckling. ' Girl tries to get into a taxi. Taxi-man says, " I'm engaged." " That's fine," says the girl. " I hope you'll be very, very happy." '

He gazed wistfully at his companion, but Bill's face remained coldly unresponsive. And Judson, having now tried him with heart-interest, sporting gossip and humour, gave the thing up and looked at him with concern.

' What's the matter, Bill o' man ? '

' Nothing's the matter.'

' Oh, but there is. You've become a regular gloom. All the time these days you're acting like a wet Sunday in Pittsburgh. I believe you're sickening for something.'

' I'm not.'

' How do you know you're not ? ' said Judson earnestly. ' You've got all the symptoms. You're jumpy and restless, and you haven't smiled since six weeks ago last Wednesday. I'll tell you what it is, Bill o' man. I'm becoming more and more convinced that we ought to keep a little brandy or some other healing spirit always in the house in case of sickness.'

' You are, are you ? '

' I've heard of fellows who were saved from the tomb by a tot of brandy administered at just the right moment. Dozens of them. Absolutely snatched from the undertaker's grasp. We could keep it in here,' urged Judson. ' In that closet. It wouldn't take up any room.'

He scanned Bill's forbidding features for a moment with a hope that swiftly ebbed.

' Oh, very well,' he said stiffly. ' I was only suggesting it for your own good.'

The second instalment of bacon had arrived and he attacked it with an offended aloofness. Presently, having finished his meal, he took himself off to the sitting-room, and Bill, clearing a space on the table, sat down to write.

§ 2

Bill's days for writing to Alice Coker were Tuesday and Friday. To-day was Friday, and it was consequently to compose a letter of love that he was now addressing himself. One would have supposed that with such a treat before him his eye would have gleamed with a tender light. But no, it was dull and fishy ; and after he had written half a dozen words he stopped and began to chew his pen drearily.

Literary composition can often be a slow and painful process, but if there is one occasion when a writer should surely find the golden sentences bubbling up without an effort it is when he is inditing a letter to the girl he loves. The fact that for some time it had been getting harder and harder to think of things to fill up the pages on these occasions was beginning to weigh upon Bill's spirits. Impious as it was to entertain even for an instant the supposition that writing letters to Alice could have become a bore, honesty compelled him to admit that his primary motive in routing Judson out of the room at this early hour had been the desire to tackle the task and get it finished and off his mind.

He ran his fingers through his hair. It was no good. Words would not come.

What made it all the more strange was the fact that in the earlier days of his sojourn in London he had handled these bi-weekly prose poems with an absolutely inspired ease. His pen had started racing the moment he sat down. Phrases of the most admirable and pulpy sentiment had leaped into his mind so quickly that he could not keep pace with them, and stuff that you could have bound up in mauve covers and sold a dozen editions of had cost him practically no effort at all. And here he was now without an idea in his head.

He got up and went into the sitting-room. If anything could give him inspiration it would be those twelve photographs of Alice that smiled down with such queenly sweetness from the mantelpiece, the what-not and the console table. He was inspecting the one third from the left on the mantelpiece, dully conscious that it was giving him no kick whatever, when a grave voice addressed him from the depths of the arm-chair.

'Bill o' man.'

Bill turned sharply.

'What's the matter now?' he snapped.

It was wrong, of course, of him to speak so curtly to his faithful friend, but one cannot deny that he had a certain amount of justification. Judson was eyeing him with a peculiar and inscrutable expression on his face, goggling at him in an indescribable sort of sad, leering way that crashed into his nerve centres like a bullet. To a man in his condition of irritable despondency the spectacle of Judson's face even in its normal state was hard enough to bear. With this peculiar expression added, it had become intolerable.

'What are you looking at me like that for?' he demanded.

Judson made no direct reply to the question. Instead, he heaved himself up from his chair, and stalking to Bill, patted him gently on the shoulder. Then he grasped his hand and shook it for a few moments; and finally, having patted him on the shoulder once more, resumed his seat.

'I've got news for you, Bill o' man,' he said in a hushed voice.

'What news?'

'Bill o' man,' said Judson solemnly, 'you were wrong just now. Believe me, you were wrong. In the attitude you took up about my suggestion that we should keep a little brandy in the place, I mean.'

'What is this news of yours?'

'Anybody', said Judson, 'is liable to get ill at any moment. And every house, therefore, should have its supply, however small, of brandy or some other healing

spirit always ready, so that you can get at it at a moment's
notice. I've been reading up about brandy, Bill o' man.
It is employed a great deal medicinally as a food capable
of supplying energy in a particularly labile form to the
body. It is also a very valuable stimulant, carminative
and hypnotic. Well, I mean, that shows you ! '

' Will you stop drivelling about brandy and tell me——'

' There have been thousands of cases where the sudden
breaking of bad news has caused apparently healthy
people to keel over and faint, and if there hadn't happened to be somebody in the offing with a nip of the
right stuff their name would have been mud. If you'll
give me the money, Bill o' man, I'll be only too glad
to pop round the corner to a pub and get a pint or two.'

' What is this news ? '

' I heard my father say once that when he got badly
hammered in the panic of 1907—— No,' said Judson
carefully, ' I'm lying to you, it wasn't my father ; it
was a pal of his. This bimbo was ruined in the panic,
and he went straight home and opened up a bottle and
took a couple of good strong snifters quick, and before
he knew where he was he was feeling like a two-year-
old again. And, what's more, those drinks gave him
an inspiration which enabled him to pull half his fortune
out of the wreck—more than half. . . . It's not far to
the pub. I can get there and back in ten minutes.'

' Look here,' said Bill tensely, ' if you don't tell me
what this news of yours is I'll step on you.'

Judson shook his head sadly. He seemed to be deplor-
ing the headlong impetuosity of Youth.

' All right,' he said. ' If you must have it. Alice has
gone and got engaged to a bird in the steel business
with pots of money. She asked me to break it to you
gently.'

§ 3

Bill stared dumbly. The fateful words sank slowly
into his consciousness.

' Engaged ! '

Judson nodded a death-bed nod.

' That's right.'

' To a fellow in the steel business ? '

' Absolutely in the steel business, o' man.'

There was a long silence, and suddenly Bill became aware with a sort of shock that his only clearly defined and recognizable emotion in this stupendous moment was a feeling of intense relief at the thought that now he would not have to finish that letter. All the morning it had been pressing on him like some heavy weight ; and, try as he would, he could not check a horrible sense of exhilaration.

He realized dully that it was all wrong to be feeling like this. It was shameful that a man in his position, confronted with the wreck of all his hopes and dreams, could find nothing better to do than to stand congratulating himself on having got out of writing a difficult letter. Besides, the letter ought not to have been difficult. All the evidence, in short, appeared to point to one conclusion—that he was utterly lacking in the most rudimentary spirituality.

Presently, as he stood there trying not to feel gay and light-hearted, he perceived that the heir of the Cokers was behaving in an odd manner. Judson had risen once more from his chair, and now, sidling up, he was thrusting into Bill's hand a sheet of paper. As the latter's fingers closed over this he sighed, patted him on the shoulder again and began to steal softly towards the door. Pausing on the threshold, he nodded twice with extraordinary solemnity. Then he slid out. It was only after he had been gone some moments that it dawned upon Bill that this was Judson's idea of handling a delicate situation with gentlemanly tact. There are times, Judson seemed to consider, when the strong man prefers to be left to wrestle with his grief alone.

Left thus alone, Bill endeavoured to carry out his part of the programme. He glanced at the document in his hand. Recognizing Alice's handwriting, he deduced that this must be the letter which had brought the news. Presumably Judson had intended him to read it. But what was the use ? Once a man has grasped the essential fact that the girl to whom he was under the impression that he was betrothed has gone and got engaged to birds in the steel business with pots of money, treatises on the subject are superfluous. He put the letter down on the table, unread.

There now came to him a pleasing theory that seemed to offer an explanation of his strange lack of decent sorrow. Men who are shot frequently feel no immediate discomfort beyond a dull shock. This, he came to the conclusion, must be what had happened in his case. His faculties must have been stunned. Later on, no doubt, the agony would commence.

Feeling considerably relieved by this reflection, he decided to go out and grapple with his tragedy in the open air. Dimly remembered novels whose heroes had received the same sort of blow suggested that this was the correct course for one in his position to pursue. In those novels, he recalled, shepherds, tending their flocks on the wind-swept hills, used to be startled by the swift passing of tall, soldierly men with pale, drawn faces, striding through the storm with mouths set like bars of steel, and eyes glittering like flames, staring sightlessly out from under the peaks of their caps. He put on his shoes and was about to go in search of his hat, when suddenly there presented itself the problem of the photographs.

Those twelve photographs! What to do with them?

In the matter of the faithless one's photographs, two plans of action are open to the jilted swain. He can either lay them up in lavender and live out his lonely life brooding over them as his hair gradually whitens, or he can do the strong, manly thing and destroy them out of hand. It came as a further shock to Bill when, after five minutes' tense thought, he decided on the latter course, to realize how little anguish the prospect caused him. He made his decision without a tremor and did the photographs up in a brown-paper parcel with as little remorse as a grocer wrapping a pound of tea. Undoubtedly his faculties must have been stunned.

It was Bill's intention to get rid of these mementoes of

a dead past somewhere in the great outdoors. For over a week now the weather had been too warm for fires, which prevented one handy way of disposing of the things; and it was obviously impossible for a sensitive man to tear them up and put them in the waste-paper basket where Judson would see them. Bill wanted no jarring comments on his action. He was grateful now for the other's indifferent attitude towards all photographs of his sister. Judson was not an observant young man, and the odds were that the novel bareness of the walls and mantelpiece would entirely escape him.

It is one of the defects of London, from the point of view of a man whose heart has just been broken, that it is practically devoid of wild spots in which to stride with a sightless stare. The nearest thing it seemed to provide to the wind-swept hills was Battersea Park; and thither Bill betook himself with his parcel, stepping lightly down the passage to the front door in order not to be intercepted by Bob the Sealyham, who, if aware that one of the gang contemplated going for a walk, would, he knew, show a disposition to count himself in. And much as Bill respected and liked Bob, he had no wish for his company now. The Bobs of Battersea are not permitted inside the park's exclusive boundaries unless attached to a leash; and it seemed to Bill scarcely decent that on this supreme occasion he should be hampered by a wriggling dog. Any moment now the agony might be beginning, making solitude essential. He tiptoed out and hurried down the stairs.

It was a lovely morning. Comment has already been made in these records on the callousness of Nature in times of man's distress, and it is enough to say that on this occasion Nature more than lived up to her reputation. It was a day when the most prudent would have left his umbrella at home; and Bill, wandering through the green avenues and listening to the merry cries of children sporting in the sunshine, continued to have that peculiar illusion of light-heartedness. If he had not known that such a thing was impossible, he would have said that his spirits were rising higher and higher every moment.

The way he jerked his wrist when, having reached a
spot secluded from human eye, he threw the brown-
paper parcel containing the photographs from him was
positively rollicking. He heard it flop behind him without a pang, and was caracolling gaily on down the path,
when a shrill voice spoke in his ear.

'Hi! Mister!'

So unexpected was this voice that it had for one brief
instant an uncanny effect of being the voice of the brown-
paper parcel. A moment before Bill had been convinced
that there was not a soul within a hundred yards. But it
is a peculiarity of the London parks that no spot in them
is ever really secluded from the human eye ; and now
there had sprung up—apparently through the asphalte—
a small and grubby girl in a print frock. She was trotting towards him, her face beaming with helpfulness and
goodwill. With her left hand she dragged along a small
male relation, who in his turn dragged a still smaller
male relation ; with her right she waved the brown-
paper parcel.

'You dropped this, mister.'

Bill was a kind-hearted young man and he shrank
from wounding the child. He took the parcel with as
much gratitude as he was able to summon up on the
spur of the moment, and with a smile a little too mechani-
cal to be really brilliant handed over sixpence as a reward.
The family melted away.

Bill walked on. The episode had had the effect of
shaking his nerve ; and though he passed several deserted
nooks which might have been constructed by the London
County Council with the sole purpose of acting as dump-
ing grounds for the photographs of girls about to marry
into the steel business, he made no use of them. And
presently, roaming aimlessly, he found himself on the
edge of a large sheet of water. Here, like Alastor on the
long Chorasmian shore, he paused.

The margin of the pool was fringed with children and
dogs, the latter held in leash by nurses or tied to benches.
The nurses exchanged dignified confidences one with
another, the children sailed toy boats, the dogs barked

continuously.   In the trees on a small island in the middle
of the water a colony of rooks cawed in raucous competition with the dogs.   It was a jolly spot ; but to Bill
its chief charm lay in the fact that every individual
present, whether nurse or child or dog or rook, appeared
to be intensely occupied with his own affairs and consequently in no position to observe and comment upon
the strange behaviour of any well-dressed young man
who should stroll up and start throwing brown-paper
parcels into the depths.   It seemed too good a chance
to miss.   With an abstracted eye on the rooks, he sent
the parcel spinning through the air, and was just turning away, humming a careless air, when the splash was
followed by another of such magnitude that he thought
for a moment that the rather stout child who had been
trimming the sails of his yacht close by must have fallen
in.   And it is shameful to have to record that the first
emotion that came to Bill—a man with one life saved
from drowning already to his credit—was a feeling of
regret at the prospect of having to go in after the little
chump.

But he had wronged the stout child.   There he was,
still safely on the water's edge.   The creature that had
caused the splash was an enormous dog with long black
hair and an expression of genial imbecility, and was now
swimming vigorously out to where the brown-paper
parcel floated.   And even as Bill looked he snapped it
up between two rows of sharklike teeth and started for
the shore.   A moment later he had laid it at Bill's feet,
shaken himself like a shower bath and was gazing up
into his playmate's face, his idiot grin urging him as
plainly as if he had made a set speech to keep the fun
going by throwing the thing in again.

Bill picked up the parcel and hurried away.   He was
now in a mood of acute exasperation.   It was not the
fact that he was quite noticeably wet that infuriated
him ; nor was his indignation due to disapproval of the
phenomenon of an unleashed dog where, according to
the park's clearly printed by-laws, no unleashed dog
should have been.   What was gnawing at his vitals was

a dull hatred of this brown-paper parcel and all it stood for. It amazed him now that he could ever have supposed himself in love with Alice Coker. Apart from anything else, apart altogether from her evil habit of going about marrying birds in the steel business, there must be a curse of some sort on a girl whose photographs were so impossible to get rid of. It was with all the depression of a Eugene Aram that he strode from the pond and buried himself in a quiet, leafy by-way.

If anything could have soothed Bill's mood of raging fury, this murmurous lane with its fringe of tall trees in which he now found himself should have done so. Even more than any of the other nooks through which he had passed that morning, it seemed apart from the world of men. Birds sang in the branches to his left, and in the flower-beds to his right bees were buzzing happily. It is proof of the shattered state of Bill's *morale* that the solitude of this sylvan retreat did not encourage him at once to drop his parcel. He was in the grip of a sort of superstitious coma. He had a presentiment that, solitary though the place seemed, he would not be alone for long, and a moment later his presentiment was fulfilled. Round the bend in the walk, concealed until they were almost on him by a large bush, came pacing slowly a young couple, a man and a girl.

The girl was trim and pretty, but it was the man who arrested Bill's attention. He was a tall young man with brown eyes and chestnut hair, of an aspect rendered vaguely artistic by a long and flowing tie of mauve silk. And the thing about him that attracted Bill's notice was his oddly familiar look. Somewhere, he felt, he had met the fellow before.

The man looked up. And as he did so there came into his face an expression which Bill could not interpret. It was recognition—that was clear enough—but it was also something more than recognition. If the idea had not been so absurd he would almost have said it was fear. The brown eyes widened, and a breeze rippling through the chestnut hair—he was carrying his hat in

his hand—gave it a momentary suggestion of standing
on end.

' Hullo ! ' said Bill. He could not place the fellow,
but it was plain from the other's expression that they
must have met.

' Hullo ! ' said the young man huskily.

' Nice day,' said Bill.

The observation seemed to have a reassuring effect on
the other. It was as if he had expected hostility from
Bill and was pleasantly relieved by the cordiality of his
tone. He brightened visibly.

' Beautiful,' he said. ' Beautiful, beautiful, beautiful ! '

Each having shot his conversational bolt, there followed one of those awkward silences. And then Bill,
acting automatically under the influence of a powerful
urge proceeding he knew not whence, extended his
hand.

' Here ! ' he said briefly.

And, thrusting the brown-paper parcel into the other's
grasp, he walked rapidly away. He was conscious, as he
went, of a whirl of mixed emotions ; but the one that
stood out above all the others was a stupendous feeling
of relief. A memory of his boyhood came to him, of the
time when he had first read Stevenson's *Bottle Imp*. It
must have been quite a dozen years ago, but he could
still recall the exquisite exultation he had felt on reaching the passage where the hero gets rid of the fatal bottle
to the drunken sailor. It was exactly so that he was
feeling now. His recent acquaintance might—probably
would—think him mad, but the chances were all against
him running after him to tell him so and to force the
parcel back upon him. If he did it would be necessary
to take firm steps.

Bill stopped. His train of thought had just been jarred
violently off the rails by the sudden discovery of the
reason why the man's face had been familiar. He knew
him now, and he remembered where it was that they
had last seen each other—in the garden of Holly House,
Wimbledon, when he, Bill, had chased him hither, thither
and roundabout through the darkness with the intent to

do violence upon his person. It was the man Roderick Pyke.

Bill smiled grimly. Roderick Pyke! No, there was no likelihood of Roderick Pyke running after him with parcels.

And then his thoughts began to flow in such a rapid stream that he could not keep up with them. The discovery that this man was Roderick Pyke immediately caused him to wonder what on earth he was doing, strolling about Battersea Park with a girl. Why, by all the laws of romance and even decency, he should have been brooding forlornly on his vanished fiancée! It offended Bill to think that a man who had so recently lost Flick should be behaving so callously.

And then his thoughts shot off at another tangent, and this time they were such weighty thoughts that he was obliged to sit down on a handy bench to grapple with them.

Flick! . . . Of course, he had never actually forgotten Flick for an instant ; but it was certainly true that his meeting Roderick had brought her into his mind with a curious vividness that had all the effect of making her seem like something suddenly remembered. Flick! . . . He could see her now, as clearly as if she were standing before him . . . Flick, happy and smiling ; Flick, tired and tearful ; Flick, frightened and looking to him for support . . . a whole gallery of Flicks, each more attractive than the last. And quite suddenly, as if he had known it all along, Bill realized that he loved Flick. . . .

Of course . . . He was a fool not to have guessed it earlier. Judson had accused him of being like a wet Sunday in Pittsburgh. Quite justly. He had been like a wet Sunday in Pittsburgh. And why? Because the withdrawal of Flick from his life had made that life seem so empty and unprofitable. This was what had been troubling his spirit all these weeks.

Bill got up. He was glowing now with that fervour which comes upon men in their hour of clear vision. He felt in his pocket for his pipe—the situation was distinctly one that demanded a series of thoughtfully smoked pipes—and found that he had left it in the flat. It being obviously impossible to think coherently without it, he returned home.

Judson, that model of tact and delicacy, was still out, and Bill was glad of it. He wanted solitude. He found his pipe where he had left it in the dining-room, beside that scarcely begun letter to Alice Coker, and proceeded to the sitting-room.

A marconigram was lying on the table. Bill opened it, hoping faintly that it might be from Flick, and experienced disappointment on discovering that it was from his Uncle Cooley. Uncle Cooley, said the marconigram, was due to dock at Southampton on the following morning. He hoped that Bill would meet him at the Antiquarians Club in Pall Mall at three in the afternoon.

It was news to Bill that Mr. Paradene was on the ocean at all, and his immediate feeling was a regret that he had not more stimulating news to give him of his activities in connexion with Mr. Wilfrid Slingsby. Yes, on the whole, it was a nuisance that Uncle Cooley had chosen just this time to come over.

However, being here, he could not be ignored. Bill came to the conclusion that it would be more respectful and would make a better impression if, instead of waiting till three o'clock, he went to Waterloo Station on the morrow and met the boat-train. Having made this decision, he sat down and plunged into pleasant, roseate dreams about Flick.

CHAPTER FOURTEEN

UNFORESEEN ENCHANTMENT AT WATERLOO STATION

§ 1

IT was with a light and jaunty step that Bill strode over Chelsea Bridge next morning on his way to Waterloo. There had been a time in the silent watches of the night when, lying in bed reviewing the position of affairs, he had had certain uncomfortable doubts as to the stability of his character. Was not a man, he asked himself, who could so swiftly rebound from one love to another incapable of love in its deepest sense ? Was not such a man incurably shallow and trivial and worthy of nothing but contempt ? From twelve-thirty till a quarter to two he had been inclined to answer these questions in the affirmative : but at one-forty-five precisely there had slid into his fevered mind the consoling recollection of Romeo.

Now, there was a chap. Generations of lovers had taken him as the archetype of their kind : and yet on Shakespeare's own showing the fellow had been a perfect byword among his friends up till—say—nine-thirty p.m. one night for his hopeless adoration of Rosaline, and it couldn't have been much more than nine-forty-five the same night before he was worshipping Juliet. And certainly nobody had ever accused Romeo of shallowness and triviality.

No, everything was absolutely all right. All that had happened was that the scales had fallen from his eyes, if you liked to put it that way : and that was the sort of thing that might happen to any one. With each step

241

that took him nearer to his destination Bill became more
whole-heartedly convinced that Flick was the only girl
in the world for him.   What he had felt for Alice Coker
had been the mere immature infatuation of a lad with
no knowledge of life.   He looked back to himself as he
had been two months ago and seemed to be contemplating another being.

In addition to having settled this soul-problem, he
had also got the practical side of the thing straight.
As soon as there was a boat he must go over to America,
find Flick and pour out his heart.   Every moment that
he spent three thousand miles away from her was a
moment irreparably wasted.

And somehow the thought of pouring out his heart to
Flick affected him with none of that nervous paralysis
which had come upon him on the occasion when he had
—mistakenly—revealed his emotions to Alice Coker.
Flick was different.   Flick was—well, she was Flick.
She was a pal.   By the time Bill reached Westminster
Bridge he was smiling at passers-by and telling policemen it was a nice morning, and in York Road he went
so far as to give a hawker half a crown for a penny box
of matches, thereby converting one who had always been
a stubborn sceptic to a belief in miracles.   He entered
the bustling precincts of Waterloo at a sort of joyous
trot, which increased to a gallop when a porter informed
him that the boat-train was even now discharging its
passengers at platform thirteen.

Bill had no difficulty in finding platform thirteen.
The march of progress has robbed Waterloo Station of
its mysteries.   Once it used to be a quaint, dim Wonderland in which bewildered Alices and their male counter-
parts wandered helplessly, seeking information of officials
as naïvely at sea as themselves.   But now it is orderly
and efficient.   Bill, not having known it in the days of
its picturesqueness, had no sense of romantic loss.   Yield-
ing up a penny for a platform ticket, he charged past
the barrier into the swirl of the crowd.

The platform was full of travellers and their friends
and relatives.   His native shrewdness telling him that

Uncle Cooley would probably be at the far end of the train looking after his baggage, Bill wasted no time. It was his intention to show zeal, to save his uncle trouble and annoyance by attending to the baggage himself, and incidentally to reveal himself in the light of the capable young man of affairs. He brushed aside a boy who was trying to sell him oranges and chocolates and sped upon his way : and was rewarded by the spectacle of Mr. Paradene hovering on the outskirts of the crowd like an undersized sportsman trying to get a glimpse of a dog-fight.

'Hullo, Uncle Cooley? How are you? Have a good voyage? Shall I get you a porter?' said Bill efficiently.

'Why, William,' said Mr. Paradene, turning, and speaking with an agreeable cordiality, 'I never expected to see you. Nice of you to come and meet me.'

'Thought I might save you trouble with your trunks.'

'Very good of you. But I'll look after them myself. I've got some valuable books I want to keep an eye on. I'll meet you down the platform. You'll find Horace there.'

The prospect of a chat with Horace did not cause Bill any noticeable elation : but Mr. Paradene, who had now intercepted a passing porter and was pointing out trunks to him in the manner of a connoisseur exhibiting the gems of his collection to a sympathetic fellow-enthusiast, seemed anxious to be alone.

'Go along and talk to him,' he said. 'That big one, that little one, and there are five more,' he added to the porter. 'You'll find another friend of yours with him. At least, she said she knew you.'

'She?'

'Girl named Sheridan. Felicia Sheridan. Niece of Sinclair Hammond, the man I've come to stay with.'

Waterloo Station is always in a seething and effervescent condition when a boat-train comes in, but to Bill as he heard these words it seemed to boil and bubble like a cauldron. Travellers, travellers' friends, travellers' relations, porters, paper-boys, station-masters and the persevering lad who was still trying to sell him oranges

and chocolates danced before his eyes in a weird sara-
band. The solid platform seemed to heave beneath his
feet. The whistle of an engine sounded like a scream of joy.

' Flick ! ' he gasped. ' Is Flick here ? '

But Mr. Paradene was too busy to reply. Accompanied by the porter, he was now in the centre of the
maelstrom, burrowing after trunks like a terrier in a
rabbit-warren. Bill, though he would have liked to ask
a number of questions, respected his uncle's preoccupa-
tion and, drawing a deep breath, plunged down the platform with as much direct forcefulness as if he had been
in sight of the enemy's goal-line with a football under
his arm. Indignant humanity scattered like smoke-
wreaths before him. And presently, after causing more
hard feelings among his fellow-creatures than a judge
at a baby-contest, he came to a space that was com-
paratively open. And there, her hand in the uncouth
paw of the boy Horace, stood Flick.

§ 2

In a world full of people who, happening upon Horace,
immediately wished him elsewhere, nobody had ever
wished him so far elsewhere as did Bill at that moment.
Not even Mr. Sherman Bastable in his least affectionate
mood could have found the boy's society more distasteful.
His mere presence was bad enough, but far worse was
that look of sardonic scorn on his freckled face—a look
that seemed to ridicule all romance and wither it with
a chilling blast. For an instant Bill had a sense of
defeat. There was something hideously immobile about
the boy's attitude that seemed to suggest that nothing
could shift him. ' Come one, come all, this platform
shall fly from its firm base as soon as I,' his demeanour
said, and Bill was at a loss to know what to do about
it, till suddenly an inspiration came to him. Few boys
are averse from a quiet snack at any hour, and Horace
was probably no exception to the rule.

' Hullo, Horace,' he said. ' You're looking tired and
thin. Take this. You'll find the refreshment-room down
there through those gates.'

The words acted like some magic spell. Horace's stomach had that quality which optimists try to persuade us belongs to the ladder of Fortune—there was always plenty of room at the top. Without a word— or, indeed, any acknowledgement, unless a sharp grunt was intended for a speech of thanks—he seized the money which Bill was thrusting upon him and hurried off. Bill turned to Flick, who during this brief business interview had been drinking him in with round and astonished eyes.

'Flick!' said Bill.

'Bill!' said Flick.

'You darling,' said Bill; 'I love you, I love you, I . . .'

'Oranges and chawklits,' said a dispassionate voice at his elbow. 'Oranges, sengwidges *and* chawklits.'

With prismatic dreams of murder filling his mind, Bill turned. Apart from the fact that any interruption at such a moment would have affected him like a blow behind the ear from a sand-bag, he had supposed that in his previous conversations with this lad he had disposed once and for all of this matter of oranges and chocolates. It was a perfectly straight issue, to settle which both sides had only to show a little reasonableness and intelligence. The boy thought Bill wanted oranges and chocolates. Bill did not want oranges and chocolates. And he had said so perfectly plainly. Yet it seemed now that they had been shouting at one another across seas of misunderstanding.

'I don't want any oranges,' he said tensely.

'Chawklits?' suggested the boy. 'Chawklits for the lidy?'

'The lady doesn't want chocolates . . .'

'Sengwidges?'

'Nor sengwidges.'

'Buns, sweets of all descriptions, chawklit, nut chawklit, sengwidges, oranges, apples, Banbury cikes and bananas!' chanted the lad lyrically. He had a clear, tuneful young voice and he chirruped like a thrush in Maytime. The thing only needed music by Jerome Kern to be a song-hit.

Bill grasped Flick's arm and hurried her along the
platform.   It is supposed to be a universal illusion on
the part of the young, when in love, that they are entirely
alone in the world, but Bill, great though his passion
was, could not achieve this state of mind.   Waterloo
Station seemed to him absolutely congested.   How there
were enough people in London, large city though it was,
to fill it up to such an extent amazed him.   The entire
population of the British Isles, together with visitors
from every part of America, seemed to have banded
together to prevent him getting a quiet word with Flick.

'Ever since you went away', he resumed, coming to
a halt behind a luggage-laden truck, 'I . . .'

The truck became suddenly endowed with movement.
It thrust itself between them like a Juggernaut.   And
when it had passed and he was about to speak again a
finger tapped him energetically upon the shoulder.

'Pardon *me*, sir,' asked a voice in rich Minnesotan,
'but could you di-rect me to the telegraph-office ? '

Adversity makes strategists of us all.   Bill grasped
the other's arm and whirled him round.

'I don't know myself,' he said, 'but that boy over
there could tell you.   The one with the orange-and-
chocolate tray.'

'Thank you, sir.   Thank you.'

'Don't mention it.   Flick, darling,' said Bill, 'ever
since you went away I've been perfectly miserable.   I
couldn't make out at first what was the matter with
me.   Then I suddenly realized.   I've got to talk quick,
so get this.   I love you.   I . . . I beg your pardon ? '
he broke off icily, turning as he received a sharp prod
in the ribs from what felt like the ferrule of an umbrella.

The stout woman with the brown veil flying from her
hat repeated her question.

'Where can you get a porter ? '   Bill spoke in an overwrought voice.   What there was about him that made
all these people flock to him as to some human Information Bureau he was at a loss to understand.   Goodness
knew, he had been trying to make his face look forbidding
enough, and yet they kept surging up to him in their

thousands as if he were their guardian angel. He began
to feel like one of those ' Ask Mr. Halleran ! ' men whose
cheery advertisements dot the road-sides throughout
Long Island. ' Anywhere round here. They are popping
about all over the place. There's one over there, standing by that boy with the chocolate-and-orange tray.'

' I don't see him.'

' He was there a moment ago.'

The stout woman wandered away discontentedly, her
veil flying behind her. Bill turned to Flick again.

' By your leave, sir.'

A porter this time, with a truck. The irony of the
situation afflicted Bill. Here was a porter interrupting
him, doubtless in search of stout women with baggage,
and a moment before the stout woman had interrupted
him in search of a porter. It would have been a kindly
act on his part to bring these kindred spirits together,
but he was otherwise occupied.

' I know what you're saying,' he resumed. ' You're
saying " What about Alice Coker ? " Never mind about
Alice Coker. That was a mere infatuation. Simply an
infatuation. I love you and only you and I believe—I
honestly believe—I've loved you from the very first
moment we met.' Amazing how easy it was to talk to
her like this. The mere sight of her encouraged him to
eloquence. She radiated confidence and comfort. It was
as simple as telling an old friend that you were glad to
see him. No trace now he felt of that fluttering self-
consciousness which had set him stammering under the
queenly gaze of Alice Coker. Silly nonsense that had
been, imagining for a single moment that he could be
in love with a girl who made him self-conscious. The
whole essence of love—and Bill now considered himself
an expert on this subject—was that it made you feel at
home with a girl, happy with her, at your ease with
her, just as if she were a part of you. ' Flick, darling,'
he said. ' Let's go off and get married—quick ! '

Her eyes were smiling up into his, the brightest, bluest
eyes that had ever danced in human face : and Waterloo
Station seemed to blaze with a brilliant and unearthly

light. It soothed every nerve in his body, that smile of hers. It set him aglow with a happiness beyond all dreaming. It was like a lighted window welcoming a weary traveller home across the snow. And, taking advantage of the fact that this delightful station was full of people who were kissing one another, he bent over with no more words and kissed Flick. And the kiss seemed like nothing so much as the formal affixing of a signature to a document whose pleasant terms had long since been agreed upon and settled. It was so entirely simple, so perfectly natural and in order. And somehow it seemed to put matters on such a sound and satisfactory footing that for the first time since she had come to him out of this whirl of restless humanity he found himself able to talk coherently and conversationally.

' What are you doing over here ? ' he asked. ' I was just coming over to America to find you.'

' I ran short of money and I had to cable home, and they cabled back that I was to go to your uncle. He has brought me over.'

' But didn't Alice Coker look after you ? '

' I never went near her.'

' Why not ? Why, of course you wouldn't,' said Bill with a flash of belated intelligence. ' What a consummate fool I was ever to think you would. The more I look back at myself, the more it seems to me that of all the hopeless fools in the world I was the worst.'

' You weren't.'

' I was. Taking all that time to realize that I loved you. Do you really love me, Flickie ? '

' Of course I do. I always have.'

' I'm hanged if I can see why,' said Bill candidly. ' I know you do. I can feel it in my bones. But why ? '

' Because you're the most wonderful man on earth.'

' By Jove ! I believe I am. Anyway, I feel I am when you look at me like that.'

Flick squeezed his arm.

' Bill, darling, what are we going to do ? '

Bill looked at her in astonishment.

' Why, get married. As soon as ever we can. That

reminds me. I shall have to be looking for work. Can't
live on nothing. But that will be all right. I have a
hunch that Uncle Cooley will come out strong. All I
need is a start.'

'It's going to be very difficult.'

'Not a bit. Watch me!'

'I mean, about me. I'm supposed to have come back
to marry Roderick.'

'What! You don't mean to say', demanded Bill with
honest amazement, 'that that silly business is still on?
Do you mean to tell me that in this twentieth century
people still think they can force a girl to marry some one
she doesn't want to?'

'When you get a man like Uncle George and a woman
like Aunt Francie making up their minds, it doesn't
matter what century it is,' said Flick simply.

'You wouldn't do it?' said Bill with a sudden swift
spasm of fear.

'Of course I wouldn't,' said Flick stoutly. 'But oh,
Bill, darling, we've got to hurry up and do something.
After what has happened I know as well as I know any-
thing that I shall be a sort of prisoner at Holly House.
I'm in disgrace. I'm like a convict that has tried to escape.
I daren't risk running away again until everything is
quite settled. You must let me know the moment you're
ready for me.'

'I'll write to you.'

'No, don't. They might see your letters, and then it
would be more difficult than ever.'

She broke off. Bill, whose eyes had never left her face,
saw her start.

'What is it?' he asked.

'Bill,' said Flick quickly in a low voice, 'don't do a
thing. Just stand where you are and try to look as if
you were perfectly ordinary. Aunt Francie is coming.
I might have guessed that she would be here to meet
me.'

The woman advancing up the platform was so exactly
what Bill would have imagined any sister of Flick's Uncle
George that he had a feeling almost as if they were old

acquaintances. Nevertheless, he was far from being at his ease. Aunt Francie was finding some difficulty in manœuvring round a truck, and Flick seized the opportunity for further counsel.

'Stay where you are. She'll think you're somebody I met on board.'

'How am I going to let you know?' said Bill hurriedly, as the enemy appeared round the truck. 'I've got it. What paper do you take in the morning?'

'The *Daily Record*. It's Uncle George's paper.'

'Watch the Agony Column,' whispered Bill.

Flick nodded briefly and turned to greet her formidable aunt.

'Aunt Francie!' she exclaimed.

There was a noticeable chill in the bearing of Mrs. Sinclair Hammond as she pecked at the cheek of her erring niece. Mrs. Hammond had much to say to her of a nature that could not well be said in front of strangers. The lecture of a lifetime hung on her firm lips, only waiting for Bill's departure to be released.

Flick turned to Bill.

'Good-bye, Mr. Rawlinson,' she said brightly, extending her hand. 'Thank you so much for looking after me.'

Bill took his cue. With a courteous bow in the direction of the more formidable than ever Aunt Francie he moved off down the platform. He had, as he went, something of the emotions of a knight of old compelled by other engagements to ride off and leave a maiden at the mercy of a dragon.

CHAPTER FIFTEEN

JUDSON FINDS AN OLD FRIEND

THE waiter, having brought coffee and cigars, retired, and Bill, leaning across the table, spoke in a low and confidential voice.

'Juddy,' he said, 'I've got something I want to tell you, old man.'

Several times during the meal which had just come to a conclusion he had been meaning to speak, but on each occasion the orchestra of the Regent Grill-Room, which has a nasty habit of bursting at unexpected moments into La Bohéme and even louder classics, had been seized with a spasm which had rendered low-voiced confidences impossible. This had caused Bill a good deal of annoyance, for the necessity of confiding his affairs to a sympathetic ear had become imperative. A week had elapsed since his momentous meeting with Flick at Waterloo Station, and all through that week he had been going about laden down with a secret which it had grown more and more irksome to keep to himself. The time had arrived when he simply had to talk about it to some one, and in all this great city there was no one except Judson whom he could elect to the position of confidant.

Judson puffed comfortably at his cigar.

'Spill it,' he said amiably.

He looked at his companion with friendly eyes. Apart from the fact that, having a pleasant secret of his own tucked away in his bosom, he was feeling well-disposed towards all humanity, he felt particularly genial towards Bill. During this past week all his old affection and esteem had returned. Bill, for so long a blighted flower, had suddenly revived as if some one had poured water

251

on him. He had gone whistling about the flat, and
to-night had reached such heights of jovial *camaraderie*
as actually to suggest a dinner at the Regent followed
by a visit to the Alhambra revue. Judson thoroughly
approved of the change.

Bill looked about him cautiously. The waiter had disappeared. The nearest diners were out of earshot. The
orchestra, its fever passed, was convalescing limply and
seemed incapable of further noise for quite a time. He
felt justified in continuing.

' I wonder ', he said, ' if you've noticed that I have
seemed somehow different these last few days ? '

' I should say so ! ' assented Judson cordially. ' Much
more the little ray of sunshine.'

' Well, I'll tell you why. Juddy old man, I've discovered what love really means.'

' What, again ! ' said Judson.

Bill frowned. Confidants ought to be more tactful.

' If you're thinking of Alice,' he said, ' that was just
infatuation.'

' I see.'

' This time it's the real thing.'

' Ah ! '

' What do you mean, ah ? ' demanded Bill. He was
sensitive.

' Nothing, o' man, nothing. Just " Ah ! " Surely ',
said Judson, who came of a free race, ' a fellow can say
" Ah ! " ? '

' You said it as if you thought I wasn't serious.'

' Not a bit of it, not a bit of it. I was only thinking. . . .'

' Thinking what ? '

' Well, isn't it a bit rapid ? I mean to say, a week
ago you were raving about Alice, and it seems to have
taken you just seven days to forget her and tack on to
some one else. Not that I'm blaming you, mind,' said
Judson handsomely. ' I admire a quick worker.'

Bill knocked his cigar-ash against his coffee-cup. He
was wishing that he had not been so peculiarly situated
as to be compelled to waste his finest thoughts on a

fellow like Judson. No soul. There you had Judson
Coker in two words. All right within his limitations,
and a pleasant chap to exchange trivialities with—but
no soul.

'I don't know what you mean by a quick worker,'
he said.

'Perhaps it doesn't seem quick to you,' said Judson
pacifically.

'I've known Flick for years.'

'Ah, Flick,' said Judson with enthusiasm. 'Now,
there's a girl in a million. If you'd been in love with
Flick . . .'

'I am in love with Flick.'

'Now, let's get this thing straight,' said Judson. He
drank coffee to clear his mind. The entertainment had
been on a strictly teetotal basis, but nevertheless he was
feeling slightly foggy. 'A week ago you were crazy
about my sister Alice. Then you switched to this other
girl you're telling me about. And now you say you're
in love with Flick. I don't get it, Bill o' man, I don't
get it. Sounds to me as if you were headed straight
for bigamy. Not ', he added broad-mindedly, ' that I've
anything personally against bigamy. Must be nice to
have two homes to go to.'

Bill groaned in spirit. Better to have poured out his
heart into a dictaphone than to be squandering words
on this poor worm.

'If you had twice as much sense, you'd be half-witted,'
he said sourly. 'Can't you understand that I've been
talking about Flick all the time ? '

'You mean Flick's the girl you're in love with ? '
groped Judson. 'The second girl, I mean, not the third
girl ? '

'There isn't any third girl,' said Bill between his teeth.

'But you said there was.'

'I didn't. I should have thought that any one with
one ounce more brains than a billiard-ball could have
understood. I've suddenly realized that Flick is the only
girl I have ever loved.'

'Ah! Now I see! Flick is the only girl you have

ever loved ? Well, it's a pity you didn't find it out before you let her go off to America.'

'If she hadn't gone to America, I might never have known what I felt.'

'Well, what are you going to do ? Send her a cable ? '

'She's back.'

'No, really ? '

'Yes. I found her at Waterloo last Saturday when I went to meet my uncle.' Bill's voice shook. 'I told her I loved her, Juddy, and she said she loved me.'

''At-a-boy ! '

'What she can see in me,' said Bill, 'I can't imagine.'

'No,' assented Judson heartily. 'No.'

'But there's a difficulty. You see, she has come back to marry that man Pyke.'

Judson started.

'Not the fellow who said it was Toddy van Riter who founded the Silks ? Good Lord, Bill, you must stop that. That would never do. I've nothing against Toddy— Toddy, I may as well tell you, has come out of the business extremely well : I had a letter from him this morning—but this bird Pyke is one of the worst. On no account must you permit a corker like Flick to marry him.'

'I won't,' said Bill firmly. 'But you see the position. She got broke in New York, and was scared, and cabled her people that she wanted to come home. They fixed it up for her to come home, but naturally it was on the understanding that she went ahead and married the fellow Pyke. . . .'

'The world's worst,' said Judson. 'The world's very punkest. It must not be.'

'It isn't going to be,' said Bill impatiently. 'But you see the difficulty. Obviously she can't run away from home again until she is quite certain that I can look after her. And just at present it's difficult to see how I am going to be able to look after her unless I get in really strong with my uncle.'

'You want to expose that crook Slingsby, and then he would eat out of your hand.'

' But how do we know he is a crook ? '

' He is, Bill o' man, he is,' said Judson earnestly. ' I didn't tell you before, but I went to get a drink out of him one night, and he palmed off a cup of cocoa on me, saying that it contained nourishing fats.'

' And now Flick writes and tells me that they are trying to rush this wedding through,' said Bill. ' I've been putting messages in the Agony Column of the *Record* every day, so we've kept in touch, and this morning I get a letter from her saying that they want to have the wedding come off next week. I seem to see myself letting them do it ! ' growled Bill. ' If they try to start anything like that I'll take Flick away and marry her and get a job of some kind. Any sort of job. Just something that will carry us along till I make good.'

' H'm, yes,' said Judson doubtfully. ' The only trouble is, Bill o' man, when it comes to getting jobs I should imagine that you're a sort of Half-way Henry.'

' A Half-way Henry ? '

' A fellow with not enough brains to own streets and too much to sweep them,' explained Judson.

' I'll sweep 'em, if it comes to that ! You don't know what love is, or you would realize that a man will do anything for the girl he wants to marry.'

The butterfly existence of a bachelor suited Judson so perfectly that this sort of thing was rather above his head.

' Can't say I've ever wanted to marry myself,' he mused. ' Still, I suppose there's something to be said for it. Must make a fellow feel pretty good, I imagine, to get up and say " No more, boys ! Not any more for me ! Got to be going now. Little woman waiting for me at home ! " '

' Exactly,' agreed Bill, pleasantly surprised at this evidence of sentiment in one whom he had supposed incapable of the finer emotions.

' But then ', proceeded Judson thoughtfully, ' there's the other side of the picture—when you sneak home at three in the morning and tiptoe up the steps and shove the key quietly into the keyhole which you carefully oiled the day before and turn the lock without a sound —only to discover that she has put the chain on the door. You've got to look at it from every angle, Bill o' man.'

Bill beckoned to the waiter, who had reappeared and was hovering in a meaning manner about the table. He was too revolted for speech. Once more he was regretting that necessity had compelled him ever to make a confidant of such a man. He paid the bill in silence, and rose from the table.

'One thing I've thought of,' said Judson, trotting in his wake down the aisle. 'You'll have to get a licence. Suppose you have to make a quick job of it, you'll need a licence. Can't get action without a licence.'

'I've got a licence,' said Bill coldly, and spoke no more till they were in their seats at the Alhambra. And then it was only to say 'Shut up!' to his companion, whose researches in the programme had caused him to start babbling excitedly.

'But it must be the same,' Judson was arguing with animation, thrusting his programme into Bill's face and indicating the name of one of the personnel of the ensemble with an eager finger. 'Prudence Stryker—such an unusual name. Must be the same girl I used to know in the Follies back in New York. I'll tell you in a second directly the chorus come on. . . . Yes! there she is! Second girl from that end. Well, I'm darned. Fancy her being over here.'

He relapsed into a momentary silence, only to emerge once more with a long and rambling story, told in a hissing undertone, about the night when he and Jimmy Boole and Freddy Osgood and Miss Stryker and a pal of Miss Stryker's, whose name was on the tip of his tongue, and a pal of Miss Stryker's pal, whose name had sounded like Biscuit, only it could hardly be that—anyway, something that had sounded very like Biscuit— had gone to celebrate Jimmy's birthday down at that place in Greenwich Village, and Freddy had got so plastered and tried to play the trap-drums, though in his calmer moments, mark you Freddy would have been the first to admit that he knew about as much about playing trap-drums as . . .

'Shut up!' said Bill.

'Oh, all right,' said Judson, aggrieved. 'Anyway, it's the same girl.'

There is a brisk delirium about a modern revue which, while entertaining to the care-free mind, has the unfortunate effect of irritating the man on whose soul anything in the nature of a deep problem is weighing. It was not long before Bill, rendered distrait by thoughts of that letter from Flick, began to regret that he had been foolish enough to suggest this expedition. The blare of the music and the restlessness of the chorus afflicted his nerves. By the time the curtain fell at the end of the first portion of the entertainment he was convinced that he could endure no more. What he wanted was a long walk.

'I'm going home,' he announced.

'Going home!' gasped Judson. 'But, look here . . .!'

'You needn't come, if you want to sit out the rest of it. I want to get away and think.'

'Oh, think? All right, then. See you later.'

Bill left the Alhambra, and, crossing Leicester Square, wandered aimlessly in the direction of Piccadilly. After the heat and turmoil of the theatre the cool night air was like a caress. The sky was a deep and mysterious blue, picked out with little stars that winked down at him as he walked as if they knew how he felt and would have liked to do something to help. It was a night for lovers to stand beneath their lady's window and . . .

Bill stopped so abruptly that he was nearly run down by a taxi-cab. He wondered he had not thought of that before. Obviously there was but one place for him on such a night. He hailed the taxi, which, after some slight eloquence on the part of its driver, was about to move on.

'Wimbledon Common,' he said.

CHAPTER SIXTEEN

A DINNER ENGAGEMENT FOR BILL

LONDON was a dead and empty city when Bill turned the corner into the Prince of Wales Road, Battersea. Even the coffee-stall at the end of the road was silent and deserted. Just how late it was he did not know, for his watch, like Time itself, seemed to have stopped. He was dimly aware of a not unpleasant fatigue, for, like Judson on a previous occasion, he had walked all the way back from Wimbledon—not, as had been the case with Judson, because he had to, but because his uplifted mood made any other form of locomotion impossible.

Lovers are a curious and unpractical race. If Bill had been asked what he imagined himself to have gained by his journey to Holly House and those hours of silent sentinel-duty in the shadows of its garden, he would not have been able to say: yet he was not conscious of having wasted his time. The fact, too, that it had been quite impossible for one with his slight knowledge of the topography of the house to guess which of those windows, whose lights had gone out one by one as he watched, belonged to Flick, did not in any way take the edge off his fervour. For all he knew, he might have been expending his emotional energy on the window of his Uncle Cooley or even on that of Mrs. Hammond ; but he did not care. He had done the only thing possible on such a night, and now he was ready to drop into bed and dream of quickly made fortunes and a life lived happily ever after.

He climbed the five flights of stairs that led to Number 9, Marmont Mansions : and, stepping delicately to avoid waking Judson, reached his room. Ten minutes later he was asleep.

Exactly when it was that he was woken by a noise that sounded like the sudden collapse of the roof, he could not have said. The evidence of his window, which had been an oblong of black and was now an oblong of dingy grey, seemed to point to the fact of several hours having passed. He was on the point of dismissing the noise as part of a dream, when the sound of a hearty chuckle outside his door came to convince him of its reality. There was somebody in the passage, and, however unpleasant it might be to get out of bed, it behoved him to go and look into the matter. Only an idiot burglar would burgle a place like this and laugh while doing so, but even idiot burglars must be thrown out by the conscientious householder. Bill put on a pair of slippers, grasped a chair as the handiest weapon, and charged forth.

The noise had evidently been caused by the falling of the hat-stand, and what had caused the hat-stand to fall had just as evidently been the efforts of Judson Coker to hang his hat on it. He was now leaning placidly against the front door, and he turned a happy face in Bill's direction as the latter came out of his room. He was still in full evening dress with the exception of the white tie conventionally worn with that costume. This he had apparently lost or given away : and in place of this he was decorated with a ribbon of light blue of the kind used to adorn the female hair, hanging diagonally athwart his shirt-front and giving him a vaguely ambassa- dorial look. His hair was disordered, and he beamed at Bill with an almost overpowering friendliness. Battersea at that moment contained no sunnier man than Judson Coker.

' Hallo, Bill o' man,' he cried jubilantly. ' Say, I can't get this darned thing to stand up, Bill o' man. Every time I try to make it stand up it falls down, and every time it falls down it makes the most awful noise, and every time it makes the most awful noise I try to stand it up, and every time I try to stand it up it falls down, and every time . . . Where was I ? ' he asked, puzzled.

Bill lowered his chair and regarded him sternly : then stooped and restored the hat-stand to an upright position. Judson, who had watched the process with a tense interest which would have been almost excessive if his friend had been trying to walk a tight rope across Niagara Falls, uttered an excited cry.

' You did it ! ' There was nothing petty or envious, no hidden note of jealousy about his admiration. ' You did it ! First shot ! You're a better man than I am, Gunga Din ! '

' Don't make such an infernal noise.'

' You're quite right, Bill o' man. Noise, yes. But not infernal noise. Well, Bill,' proceeded Judson genially, ' it's great seeing you again after all this long time. Yessir, that's what it is—great ! What have you been doing with yourself ? Sit down and tell me all about it.'

' What have you been doing, that's what I would like to know.'

Judson nodded owlishly.

' You're absolutely right, Bill, absolutely right. You're always absolutely right. And a great gift it is, too. Nothing to beat it. Well, Bill o' man, I've been out to supper. You remember my pointing out a girl to you at the Al-al . . . Al-hal . . . Wait ! ' said Judson with dignity, raising a compelling hand. ' Lots of fellows think I can't say the word. Oh yes, they do ! It's all over London that I cannot pronounce the word Al-hamber-er, but I can, I can, I can, and I'm glad ! glad ! ! glad ! ! ! Where was I ? '

Bill, somewhat recovered now from the moroseness which comes to those abruptly awakened in the small hours, was growing interested.

' Did you meet some one who took you to supper ? ' he asked.

' No, sir ! ' replied Judson with a touch of hauteur. ' I was the one that took some one to supper. Yes, I know what you're going to say. You're going to say, Where did I get the money to take some one to supper ?

And very frank and honest of you, too, to say so. Manly, that's what I call it, manly. I got that money, Bill o' man, because I've got a head.'

' You'll have one to-morrow all right,' said Bill unkindly.

' A smart business head,' resumed Judson. ' Lots of fellows haven't got smart business heads, and where are they ? Streeping the sweets. You know what I did ? Well, listen then, because you're a young man trying to get along, and this'll be useful to you. Alhambra ! I've said it once and I can say it again. You remember that piece there was in all the London papers about Toddy van Riter founding the Silks ? Well, I clipped that out and mailed it to Toddy and told him I'd had it put in all the London papers because he was a young man trying to get along and I wanted to do him a good turn. At the same time—and mark this, Bill, always bearing in mind the word Alhambra—at the same time I asked him to lend me a hundred smackers. And what ensued ? He sent 'em. They arrived this morning. And that's what I say to you—and I want to lay stress on this, Bill—that any one who thinks that just because I've been having a bite of supper, I can't say the word Alhambra, lies ! Lies ', said Judson, waving his hand spaciously and restoring his balance by a swift snatch at the hat-stand, ' in his teeth. And you know as well as I do, Bill, that it's the worst possible thing to lie in your teeth, because four in every five will get pyorrhoea.'

' You'd better go to bed,' said Bill.

' I will,' agreed Judson with a sage nod of his smart business head. ' That's just one little thing that I will do. I'd like ', he went on, eyeing the hat-stand with sudden truculence, ' to see the man who will stop me going to bed. That's me. Blunt and straightforward, and if people don't like it they can do the other thing. I'm going to bed. Just like that ! '

' This way,' said Bill. ' Watch your step.'

' Funny you should have said that, Bill o' man,' chuckled Judson. ' It's just what that girl said. The girl I met at the Al-hal.' He halted. ' Bill, there's something at the back of my mind that I want to tell you. Something important. But what is it? Ah! There you have me. But it'll come back. Oh yes, it'll come back. Never forget that, Bill. However black the sky, however dark the outlook, it'll come. Well, good night, Bill o' man. Mustn't keep me up,' said Judson, and with a brief ' Alhambra! ' vanished into his room.

Daylight was now streaming pinkly in through the window and the bird population of Battersea Park had begun to greet it with a vociferous chirping. The light and the noise combined prevented Bill from dropping off to sleep : which was just as well, for an hour later his door opened and Judson made his appearance, clad now in a suit of blue pyjamas.

' Just looked in to tell you that thing I forgot,' said Judson. ' It came to me in a flash only half a minute ago.'

' Well? '

Judson plunged into thoughtful silence for a moment. ' Sorry,' he said. ' Forgotten it again. Good night, o' man.'

He retired. Bill closed his eyes, and after what seemed the lapse of a few minutes, awoke to find that the morning was well advanced—so well advanced that he could hear down the passage as he opened his door the pleasing sound of one who prepared breakfast. He made his way to the bathroom, to the accompaniment of a musical snoring from behind Judson's closed door.

It was only after Bill had finished breakfast and was reading the Sunday papers that the heir of the Cokers presented himself. A trifle pale, he seemed nevertheless in far better condition than one meeting him some hours back would have supposed possible. His mental equilibrium also seemed to have re-established itself. He bade Bill a subdued but friendly good morning, and drank four cups of coffee in rapid succession.

' Did I dream it,' he said, ' or did I make a certain amount of noise coming in last night ? Seem to remember crashing into something.'

' That was when you upset the hat-stand.'

'The hat-stand!' said Judson, pleased. 'That was the clue I wanted. Now it all comes back to me. How much did I tell you, o' man, when I came in? Or didn't I? I seem to remember having a chat with you.'

'You told me Toddy van Riter had sent you a hundred dollars.'

'That's right.' Judson helped himself to more coffee, but declined with a gentle shake of the head and the soft, sad smile of a suffering saint Bill's offer of scrambled eggs. 'In fact,' he confessed, with reference to these wholesome food-stuffs, 'I don't believe I can even stand the sight of them. You might put a paper up in front of your plate, Bill. Thanks. It's funny about eggs on the morning after. They sort of look at you.' He drank deeply from his coffee-cup. 'Well, now, let's see. Did I tell you about taking Prudence Stryker to supper?'

'You told me you took some one to supper.'

'That's right. Prudence Stryker. The girl I pointed out to you. A dear old pal of mine back in New York. Remind me some time to tell you about the night she and I and Jimmy Boole and Freddy Osgood . . .'

'Thanks,' said Bill. 'You told me about that at the Alhambra.'

'Did I? Oh? Well, there she was, prancing about on the stage last night, and after the show I popped round and took her out for a bite of supper. We had quite a good time.'

'So I gathered.'

'Got in with a bunch of hearty mixers and went on to a fellow's apartment. Just a nice home-evening. It wasn't till about half-past three in the morning that the people in the apartment below sent for the police. Well, what I'm trying to tell you, Bill, is that Prudence handed me a bit of information that's going to send you singing up and down Battersea Park Road. I meant to tell you last night, only it slipped my memory.'

'You're sure you remember it now?'

'I certainly do. It was about that mutt Slingsby.'

'Slingsby!' Bill laid down his knife and fork, the better to attend. For the first time he permitted himself to hope that this news of Judson's might really be of importance. 'How does Slingsby come into it?'

Judson shook his head sadly, as one mourning over the wickedness of the world.

'Slingsby treated that poor girl darned badly, Bill o' man. I didn't get an absolute strangle-hold on the facts of the case, because, between ourselves, I wasn't feeling as bright as I could have wished at the moment: but I did get on to this, that Prudence and this fellow Slingsby were extremely matey for quite a time, and then he sneaked off and started going around with a girl from the Gaiety: and, one thing leading to another, Prudence did the square straightforward thing by blacking his eye and passing out of his life for ever.'

'She blacked his eye? Then that was . . .'

'Exactly. It happened the night before Flick went to work in his office. But that's neither here nor there, o' man. I'm coming to the really important part. We somehow or other got talking about you, and I mentioned that you were old Paradene's nephew and had come over to London to try to find out why the profits on the old boy's business had fallen off: and then she said that you were just the fellow she wanted to meet —because she could put you wise to where the dirty work was.'

Bill sat up excitedly.

'There really has been dirty work?'

'As far as I could gather from Prudence, it has been running on all six cylinders for years. And here's the point. I was verging on a state which you might call pie-eyed when she told me, but I gathered this much —that one night Slingsby, who must have been pretty well tanked himself to do such a bone-head thing, confided the whole business to her. Told her everything, o' man! Where the body was buried and all about it. The way fellows you would ordinarily think darned shrewd, level-headed birds make goofs of themselves with women beats me. Look at Samson! Or Marc Antony, for the matter of that. The bigger they are,' sighed Judson, 'the harder they fall.'

'But what was it? What has Slingsby been up to?'

'Ah! Now that', said Judson, 'she didn't tell me, because she's saving it up for you. She wants to give you the low-down in person, so that you can hand it on to the old man, thereby doing Slingsby dirt and putting him where he belongs. I've arranged everything. You're to give her dinner to-night.'

'To-night?'

'This very night. I'll come too, if you like.

'No, thanks.'

'Sure? No trouble, you know.'

'Quite sure, thanks.'

'Very well,' said Judson resignedly. 'Maybe you're right, at that,' he went on after a moment's meditation. 'The idea of a quiet evening and an early bed doesn't look so bad to me, I'm bound to admit. For some reason or other I've got an odd sort of headachy feeling to-day. I guess it's the weather. Well, she will meet you at Mario's at eight-fifteen. You can't miss her. Tall, dark, handsome girl, built rather on the lines of a motor-truck.'

'Mario's?' said Bill. 'No, hang it all, not Mario's.'

'Eh? Why not?'

'Mario's is sacred. It was there that I dined with Flick the last time we had dinner together before she went off to America.'

'You'll go to Mario's—and like it!' said Judson firmly. 'Good heavens, you can't expect the girl to start chopping and changing just to humour your whims. It's darned decent of her to take the trouble to meet you at all.'

'Yes,' admitted Bill, 'I suppose it is.'

'Eight-fifteen sharp in the lobby, then. You won't have any difficulty spotting her. She'll be wearing a red dress. She's rather Spanish in appearance, with great gleaming eyes and a good lot of teeth. . . .'

'Ugh!'

'Eh?' said Judson sharply.

'Nothing!'

'She's a thoroughly nice girl. Full of pep. You'll like her.'

'I will, if she really tells me something important about Slingsby. Gosh, Juddy, do you realize that this may mean the straightening out of everything? If she can tell me as much as you think she can, I shall be in the strongest possible position with Uncle Cooley.'

'Aces and eights,' agreed Judson.

'And then I shall be able to take Flick away from those confounded people of hers and marry her without any more delay. My God! Juddy, you don't know how I feel about Flick. She's like a wonderful inspiration. Sometimes, when I'm sitting all alone, I can see her face with those dear blue eyes of hers. . . .'

Judson reached for the *Referee* and hoisted it defensively in front of him. There are limits to the obligations of friendship.

'Some other time, o' man,' he said.

CHAPTER SEVENTEEN

SUNDAY NIGHT AT MARIO'S

§ 1

THE spirit of optimism and joviality which has just been shown sweetening the daily round of Number 9, Marmont Mansions, Battersea, had found during the week which had passed since Flick's arrival no counterpart at Holly House, Wimbledon. In spite of the fact that the return of prodigals is almost proverbially associated with joyful revellings and effervescent gaiety on the part of the whole strength of the company, with the possible exception of the fatted calf, Flick had found little to cheer her in the atmosphere of her revisited home ; and day by day, in every way, she had had need to fill her mind with thoughts of Bill in order to prevent depression claiming her for its own.

The lecture which her Aunt Frances had begun on the platform of Waterloo Station had continued intermittently throughout the week : and at seven o'clock on Sunday evening it gushed up into such a freshet of eloquence that Mr. Sinclair Hammond, bursting the bonds of years, put his foot down and asserted himself with a mild man's impressive ferocity.

'Flick,' said Mr. Hammond, interrupting his wife's remarks, in an odd, strained voice.

'Yes, Uncle Sinclair ? '

Just run away for a moment, will you ? '

Mrs. Hammond directed at him the gaze which had so often sent him cowering back among his books. But to-night it had no effect. Hell hath no fury like a mild and peace-loving man who has at last decided to give battle, and Mr. Hammond was strong with the strength of one who has been simmering for a week in a fury of suppressed animosity. Just as Bill West, another mild man, could be roused by a blow on the head with a stick, so could Sinclair Hammond be stirred to action by the spectacle of Flick, whom he loved, being talked to and talked at, and nagged and harried and generally rendered miserable.

' I am speaking to Felicia,' said Mrs. Hammond frostily.

' Get out, Flickie,' said Mr. Hammond, with a twisted half-smile. And Flick left the room.

Mrs. Hammond turned majestically on her husband. Unlike the king of France, she had no one to warn her that this was no mere revolt but a revolution, which was to destroy her supremacy in the home for ever : and she endeavoured to crush him in the old familiar way.

' Be quiet,' said Mr. Hammond.

And Mrs. Hammond was quiet.

' You've got to stop it, Francie,' said Mr. Hammond mildly, but holding her with a glittering eye. ' You've had plenty of time to say all there was any need to say on the subject of Flick's leaving home, and now you've finished. Do you understand ? Definitely and completely finished. I won't have the poor kid worried any more. And, to remove temptation from your path, I am now going to take her out to dinner somewhere. I am going to transport her to where there are lights and music and good, dyspepsia-promoting food. The band will play, the lights will gleam. Who knows, I may even dance with her. And when we come home—probably at about six in the morning—you will welcome her with your famous smile, you will dig up a motherly embrace, and your pleasant chatter will deal exclusively with the brighter side of life. Do I make myself clear ? '

' But, Sinclair,' protested Mrs. Hammond, and there was an awestruck note of appeal in her voice. ' You can't take Felicia out to dinner. George is coming to dinner ! '

' Your brother George ', said Mr. Hammond, ' is a man whom in many ways I respect and admire. But as a dinner-table companion for Flick at this particular moment he fails to qualify. He would lecture Flick, and I do not intend to have her lectured.'

' But he will think it so odd if Felicia is not here to meet him ! ' wailed Mrs. Hammond.

Mr. Hammond kissed her affectionately on the forehead. He was very fond of Francie.

' He may be able ', said Mr. Hammond frivolously, ' to get an article for *Pyke's Weekly* out of it. " Famous Nieces Who Have Behaved Oddly To Famous Uncles." Well, I must be going up to dress. I suppose it means a white waistcoat.' He sighed. ' Ah well, we must all make sacrifices in this world.'

He kissed Mrs. Hammond again, and left the room, humming.

' Flick,' he called.

Flick came out of the morning-room.

' Flickie,' said Mr. Hammond, ' we're a couple of reckless young fellows out for a good time. How would you like to come and have dinner somewhere ? Somewhere low and vulgar. Let's go to one of those Night-Clubs Which Are Living Hells, that *Society Spice* writes about.'

Flick gazed at him for a moment with an incredulous awe. Dearly as she loved her Uncle Sinclair, she had always recognized his limitations. And this was open rebellion. This was hoisting the skull and cross-bones.

' Wouldn't it be lovely ! ' she said wistfully.

' It will be lovely,' Mr. Hammond corrected.

' But Uncle George is coming to dinner,' Flick reminded him.

' I know. Think how jolly it will be to revel in some gay café and feel that Uncle George is sitting snugly all the while in yonder dining-room. It'll be like turning on the cold shower and standing over by the bathroom door, watching it.'

Flick hugged him.

' You are a darling, Uncle Sinclair ! '

' Well, I got a kind of idea that a little change would do you no harm to-night. Where shall we go ? Do you know a good Hell ? '

' Let's go to Mario's.'

' Mario's ? A new name to me. Considering that I am one of the wild and depraved Younger Generation they're

always writing about nowadays I know very little of
London's West End. Will it be devilish enough for me?
I want a place where I can throw bread at people. How
is the bread-throwing at Mario's?'

'Splendid! All the best shots go there. Mario's was
the place where young Lord Trevelyan picked off six
waiters with six consecutive rolls.'

'Six?' said Mr. Hammond musingly. 'Ah well, we
must see what we can do. But how do you come to know
of this low resort?'

'I went there once.' Flick hesitated. 'With somebody.'

'H'm! Oh? Ah!' said Mr. Hammond. He scruti-
nized her a little closely, and his manner took on a certain
gravity. 'Who took you to Mario's, Flickie?'

'Bill West. Mr. Paradene's nephew. You remember
my telling you about him in the garden that day?'

'I remember. So he is over in this country, and you
have met him again?'

'Yes.'

'Flickie,' said Mr. Hammond, 'I know you will think
me an awful old bore, but I'm afraid I shall have to begin
dinner by talking what you might call shop. You won't
mind?'

'I don't mind anything you do, Uncle Sinclair.'

'Right!' said Mr. Hammond cheerfully. 'I ought to
get finished by about the fish course. And after that we'll
start throwing bread. Were these waiters that Lord
Trevelyan bagged sitting or on the wing?'

'Rocketing.'

'Indeed?' said Mr. Hammond. 'Well, well, we can
only do our best. Hurry up and get some clothes on,
Flickie. I'm off to dig my white waistcoat out of the
moth-balls.'

§ 2

'Flag that waiter, old love,' said Miss Prudence Stryker,
indicating a sprinting martyr who was whizzing about
among the crowded tables in his efforts to do the work of
two ordinary men, 'and remind him that when he was a
little boy he promised to bring us a bottle of Lanson.'

Bill beamed politely, and turned to do her behest.
' Waiter ! '

' Louder,' recommended Miss Stryker. ' Less of the
Pekingese and a bit more of the bloodhound.'

' Waiter ! '

' That's better. You've got a nice voice. If you
studied and had it developed, you'd make a good train-
announcer.'

Bill beamed again.   It seemed to him that he had been
beaming through a dreadful eternity.

If it is true that a man may smile and smile, and be a
villain, it is equally the case that he may beam and beam
and yet be in an extremely acute state of discomfort.
Bill was not enjoying his evening out at Mario's celebrated
night club.

Even in the remote days when he had been wont to
add his presence to those parties in New York of which
Judson Coker had been the life and soul, Bill had never
really derived much pleasure from this type of entertainment.   Indeed, even before his mistaken infatuation for
Alice Coker had turned his thoughts to deeper things, he
had come quite definitely to the conclusion that parties
bored him to extinction.   To be at home at these Bohemian revels, a man has to have a nimble wit.   He must
be a strong kidder, a good scout, and a great old josher,
and must possess in addition an interior of cast steel and
asbestos.   Bill was deficient in all these qualities.   His
interior put up practically no resistance after the second
or third cocktail, and no one was more keenly alive than
he to the fact that he was a poor josher, an indifferent
scout, and hardly to be reckoned a kidder at all by an
impartial critic.

The present occasion was proving even more exacting
than those other orgies.   Then he had been one of a
crowd, while now he was in the position of having to
shoulder the whole weight of the entertainment himself.
And it had proved a considerable weight.   Apart from the
fact that the holy associations of the place made it distasteful for him to dine there with anybody but Flick,
there was a flamboyant exuberance about Miss Prudence

Stryker which had oppressed him from the very moment
when she had sailed forward to meet him in the lobby.
The accuracy of Judson's description of her had come
home to him right from the start.

Judson had said that she was built on the lines of a
motor-truck. She was. Judson had said that she would
be wearing a red dress. She was, though the adjective
was almost feeble. Judson had said that she was full of
pep. This also was true. The only point on which Judson had gone astray was in his prediction that Bill would
like Miss Stryker. He did not. He would have been hard
put to it to name any other living person whom he disliked more. He disliked her large and gleaming eyes. He
disliked her impressive physique. He disliked the tendency which she had developed as early as the soup course
to address him as ' old love '. And most of all he disliked
the way she bent forward and laughed merrily in his face
and her habit of pointing her witticisms by slapping him
on the arm. As Mr. Wilfrid Slingsby had discovered at
an earlier date, Prudence Stryker was a girl of muscle,
and her slaps were like the kicks of a playful horse.

Nevertheless, he persevered. Miss Stryker, whatever
her surface faults, had one outstanding merit that eclipsed
them all. She was the girl who knew where Mr. Slingsby
had buried the body : and, as such, must be conciliated.
So Bill, though speculating wanly as to what she would be
like if the waiter ever brought that Lanson, brought the
old bull-dog courage of the Wests to bear and set himself
grimly to see the thing through.

The exact nature of the body which Mr. Slingsby had
buried refused to reveal itself. All through the age-long
meal, Miss Stryker stoutly declined to talk what she
described as ' business ', confining herself to snappy anec-
dote and mirthful jest. All that Bill had gleaned by the
time the coffee arrived was that Mr. Slingsby's secret was
a pippin, well worth waiting for : and in the interval of
waiting he managed to achieve such a creditable imitation
of a vivacious host that Miss Stryker formally stamped
him with the seal of her approval as ' a good kid '. And,
as everybody knows, it is but a step from being a good kid

to eing a good scout, and from there a mere amble to
the giddy eminence of a great old josher. Shortly after
Bill had reached the good scout stage Miss Stryker expressed a desire to dance.

Bill rose politely. The idea of dancing with his fair
guest was one that filled him with loathing, but in pursuance of his policy of conciliation he forced himself to do
it. It was at the moment when they were circling round
the room for the second time that Flick entered the restaurant with her Uncle Sinclair and mounted the stairs that
led to the balcony. As a vague concession to old-fashioned
propriety Mr. Hammond had decided on a table in the
balcony in preference to one on the main floor. The main
floor, a glance told him, was infested to no little extent by
brilliant creatures who, while doubtless good-hearted and
kind to their mothers, seemed to him better seen at a
distance. The balcony, to which are banished those who
visit Mario's without dressing, had the appearance of being
ninety-nine per cent pure. His white waistcoat would be
wasted there, but that could not be helped.

How long Bill danced he could not have said. The process seemed interminable. From time to time the music
would stop and they would return for a brief instant to
their table, only to spring up once more at the bidding of
the saxophones. Eventually, however, just as he was
beginning to feel that Miss Stryker's powerful form must
be constructed of india-rubber, she confessed to a desire
for temporary repose. They sat down, and Bill, feeling
that if he missed this opportunity, another would not
occur until he was too weary to understand what she
said, leaned forward.

' I wish you would tell me about Slingsby,' he pleaded.

' Want to know about that ? ' said Miss Stryker
amiably.

' I do indeed.'

' Well then, listen, kid,' said Miss Stryker. ' Here it
comes ! '

Bill hitched his chair a few inches nearer, and beamed
devotedly into her face. Miss Stryker, with a preliminary
slap at his throbbing arm, began to speak.

§ 3

Mr. Hammond tugged at his waistcoat, which had grown mysteriously tight since its last public appearance, and looked down interestedly over the rail at the throng below.

' Nothing in this modern life of ours, Flickie,' he said, ' is more significant than the attitude of the good and respectable towards Sunday evening. Places like this are the outward and visible signs of the inward and spiritual change that has taken place in the life of the English family. Twenty years ago, a man of my decent stodginess and unblemished reputation would never have dreamed of moving out of his home on Sunday night. Twenty years ago, I would have spent the concluding hours of the Sabbath surrounded by my loved ones beneath my own roof-tree. There would have been supper, consisting of rather red cold beef, rather wet salad, cold clammy apple-pie, blancmange, and a very big, very yellow cheese. This would have been followed by hymns in the drawing-room —or possibly, if our views were a little lax, by some round-game played with pencils and pieces of paper. The fact that I am here and strongly tempted to drop a sardine on the head of that bald gentleman down below is due to what they call the March of Progress.' Mr. Hammond helped himself to *hors d'œuvres*. ' Having relieved myself of which prosy reflections,' he said, ' I will now turn the conversation to the subject of your previous visit to this place. How did you happen to come here ? '

' Bill brought me. He had been here once before with Mr. Slingsby, Mr. Paradene's manager in London.'

' And now about William,' said Mr. Hammond. ' Tell me all.'

Flick's kitten eyes searched his face gravely. She was wondering what would be the result if she really did tell him all ; if she confided in him the twin facts that she loved Bill and that Bill loved her, and the additional fact that, as soon as ever he gave the word, she proposed to elope with him. Consideration for her Uncle Sinclair's feelings caused her to decide against this course. It would have been comforting to herself to pour out her secret, and she knew that she could have relied on him to keep it—but it would be at the expense of his peace of mind. Poor darling, how he would worry !

' I happened to meet Bill the day I left home,' she said. ' And so, you see, when I was by myself in London, I naturally saw quite a lot of him.'

' I see,' said Mr. Hammond doubtfully.

' I used to dine with him a good deal.'

' I see.'

' And one of the times he brought me here.'

Mr. Hammond crumbled his bread.

' I seem to recollect your telling me in the garden that day that this William had been the ideal of your girlish dreams. Did he still exercise a spell when you met him again ? '

' He's very nice,' said Flick, guardedly.

' You didn't tell him, I suppose, that you had once worshipped the ground he trod on ? '

' Bill was in love with somebody else when I met him again in London.'

Mr. Hammond looked relieved.

' Ah ! ' he said.

' Madly and desperately,' said Flick, bubbling. ' He had twelve photographs of her in his sitting-room.'

Mr. Hammond's relief was now complete. He attacked his roast chicken with gusto.

' I'm bound to admit, Flickie,' he said, ' that you've taken a weight off my mind. You may have suspected occasionally during the past few years that I am mildly fond of you. I am a battered old hulk, with but little to live for. . . .'

' I thought you said you were one of the younger generation.'

' Never mind. For purposes of my big speech, I am a battered old hulk, with but little to live for except the. happiness of my golden-haired child. . . .'

' I wish I had been your child,' said Flick wistfully. ' How simple everything would have been then, wouldn't it ? '

'If you mean that you would have twisted me round your finger even more easily than you do at present, you are probably right. I've been a good deal worried about you, my Flickie. I want to see you doing the right thing, and I've come to the conclusion that your marrying young Roderick will be the right thing. The mere fact that he will eventually inherit several million pounds gives him a great glamour in my eyes.'

'I never knew you were so sordid! If I loved a man, I wouldn't mind how poor he was.'

'Brave words, child! But, never forget, poverty is the banana-skin on the doorstep of romance. . . . What are you gazing at so intensely? You have a spell-bound look.'

Flick had been watching the gyrating couples on the floor below. She withdrew her gaze with a start as he spoke, and turned to him once more. Had Mr. Hammond been an observant man, he would have noticed that her eyes had widened into a curiously fixed stare, and that about the corners of her mouth there was an oddly pinched look. But he was not an observant man. Moreover, he was smoking now, and the cigar, which he had purchased in a somewhat doubting spirit, was proving of such rare excellence that his mood had become dreamy and introspective.

'I was looking at those people down there dancing,' said Flick. She seemed to speak with difficulty.

'Weird creatures,' said Mr. Hammond, puffing comfortably.

Flick scrawled hieroglyphics on the tablecloth with nervous digs of her coffee-spoon.

'Uncle Sinclair,' she said at last, I suppose men are always falling in love with girls.'

'It has been known to occur,' admitted Mr. Hammond.

'I mean, thinking they are in love with girls and really not being in love with any particular girl but . . . oh, I don't know how to put it. I mean, there is a sort of man who might pretend he was in love with a girl and—and really seem to mean it, and make her think he meant it, while all the time he was perfectly happy with other girls and forgot all about her after they had been separated for a day or two.'

'I should imagine a great many young men were like that, unless they have changed a lot since my day. Constancy is a shy plant that blossoms only in the sunshine of middle age. Except, of course,' added Mr. Hammond hastily, 'in the case of a young fellow like Roderick. You wouldn't find him doing that sort of thing.'

'I wasn't thinking of Roderick,' said Flick. She traced another intricate pattern on the tablecloth, the little muscles working about her mouth. 'I suppose you're right, Uncle Sinclair.'

'In what respect?'

'I mean, about being sensible. I suppose—well—what you'd call Romance is rather silly, isn't it, and the only thing to do is to be sensible.'

'That is my opinion, given for what it is worth. Though mind you, I don't think that you would have any cause to complain of lack of romance where Roderick was concerned. The boy drips with it. Look at that tie he wears!'

'If you were a girl, Uncle Sinclair, would you marry a man if you found out you couldn't trust him?'

'What do you mean?'

'Well, suppose some one had pretended that he was in love with you, and then you suddenly found out that all the time he was going about with other girls—dining with them and dancing, and——' Flick shot a swift glance over the balcony rail—'and beaming up into their beastly faces as if he thought them the most wonderful thing in the world,' she went on viciously. 'Wouldn't that make you feel you had made a mistake?'

Mr. Hammond patted her hand paternally.

'Don't you worry, Flickie,' he said. 'Roderick isn't that sort of chap. Not that sort of chap at all. If he was, I would be the first to advise you to have nothing whatever to do with him. A fellow you can't trust isn't any good to anybody.'

CHAPTER EIGHTEEN

BLACK MONDAY

TO many people in this age of rush and hurry, indeed one might say to most people, the early hours of Monday morning are the worst of the week. For it is then that the soul, enfeebled by the soft ease of Saturday afternoon and Sunday, winces painfully from the thought of resuming the white man's burden and going to work again.

Mr. Wilfrid Slingsby, as he sat at breakfast in his house in Bruton Street on the morning after Bill's dinner with Miss Stryker, experienced nothing of this Monday feeling. Everything seemed to him for the best in the best of all possible worlds. His eye was bright and his mind at peace as he ate his kidneys on toast and read the pile of morning papers heaped beside his plate.

Most men are content with a single newspaper to help them through breakfast. Certain sybarites read two. Mr. Slingsby's pile contained every journal published in London. Not a single sheet, however humble, was unrepresented in that mountain of literature.

But his reading was that of a specialist. A glance at each periodical was enough for him before he threw it on the floor. Only one section of these papers interested him—that devoted to theatrical reviews. The previous Saturday night had seen the opening of a new and sprightly farce, Tell It To Papa, at the Bijou Theatre ; and this had the distinction of being the first theatrical venture for which Mr. Slingsby had assumed sole financial responsibility. And it seemed from the papers to-day, as it had seemed from the Sunday papers yesterday, that he had stumbled upon a gold-mine.

Mr. Slingsby finished the last review, and leaned back in his chair, a happy man. It is the dream of all those alchemists who dabble in theatrical ventures to discover one day the Philosopher's Stone, to produce a historic farce—one of those farces which flare over the horizon about once in every twenty years, and after a record-breaking career in London go on running for ever in the provinces. And this dream, judging from the criticisms of the Press taken in conjunction with the enthusiasm of the first-night audience, Mr. Slingsby seemed to have achieved. He finished his breakfast, smoked a leisurely cigar, and rang for his car to take him down to the City.

Complete happiness was Mr. Slingsby's. No thought of any Damocles sword suspended above his head came to mar his joy. From this day forward he was on velvet. He could abandon his commercial career and live the life of a leisured gentleman, confining his activities to smoking big cigars and telling dramatists that their second acts needed a lot of work done on them. As the car stopped outside his office building his heart was leaping high. Larks did not actually sing in the sky above St. Mary Axe, but to Mr. Slingsby they seemed to be singing. So exalted was his mood that he beamed upon Henry, the office boy, like a father, and was in two minds about giving him half a crown.

'Gentleman waiting to see you, sir,' said Henry.

'Gentleman, eh?' said Mr. Slingsby, almost adding 'Tra-la-la!' 'Where is he?'

'I showed him into your office, sir.'

'Quite right,' chanted Mr. Slingsby, just managing to check his right foot from executing a dance-step. 'Any name?'

'Mr. West, sir.'

'Mr. West, eh? Ah, Mr. West? Yes, yes!'

He curveted into the private office.

'Ah, West,' said Mr. Slingsby jovially, while the air seemed to echo with the clash of cymbals and the note of flutes. 'Hope I haven't kept you waiting.'

He had kept him waiting, but Bill did not mind that. Bill had come early and intended to stay late.

' Good morning,' he said frigidly. He wanted no
friendly overtures from this blue-chinned man. He was
about to execute the spiritual equivalent of hitting Mr.
Slingsby over the head with a hatchet, and he resented
the other's ebullient chumminess.

' Sit down. Make yourself comfortable. Have a cigar,'
said Mr. Slingsby.

Bill sat down, but waved away the proffered corona.
He waved it away with much the same cold aloofness
which an executioner might have exhibited towards a
cigar-case extended by a prisoner at the block. He was
feeling like an executioner. The conversation which he
had had at Mario's with Miss Stryker had made it plain
to him that Mr. Slingsby had indeed revealed to that
lady the location of the body's interment : and the body
was one of such magnitude that he marvelled at any
man, even when ' a good bit tanked ' and under the
weakening influence of love, confiding such a secret to
anybody.

' I came here this morning . . .' he began.

' You weren't by any chance at the opening of Tell
It To Papa at the Bijou on Saturday, were you ? ' interrupted Mr. Slingsby.

' No,' said Bill. ' I . . .'

' A riot, my dear fellow ! ' cried Mr. Slingsby. ' A
positive knock-out ! Not a single paper either yesterday
or this morning that doesn't rave its head off. It's the
first show I have ever owned outright, and it's the biggest
winner since Charley's Aunt. In fact, between ourselves,
I shouldn't be surprised if it doesn't make even more
money. Costs nothing to run—three acts with only one
set, an ordinary interior—and looks like playing to
capacity for a couple of years. It's a funny thing the
way people let these gold-mines slip away from them.
I know for a certain fact that at least six managers
turned it down cold. It was quite by accident that it
came my way. But I know a good play when I see
one, and the moment I read the first act——'

' I may as well tell you right away——' said Bill.

' —I knew I was on to a winner. Even then, of course,

I didn't know how big it really was. But I knew it couldn't fail. There's one scene where the fellow loses his trousers——'

The mere accident of Mr. Slingsby pausing at this moment to relight his cigar enabled Bill to escape hearing the entire plot of Tell It To Papa, and to jerk the conversation back on to a business plane. He had an uncomfortable sense of being bustled and hurried as he began to speak, and this made it difficult for him to be as impressive as he could have wished. But he relied on the subject-matter of his discourse to grip his audience.

'I dined last night with Miss Prudence Stryker,' he said, feeling that that was a statement which, if anything could, would divert Mr. Slingsby's mind from the humours of Tell It To Papa.

His confidence was justified. Mr. Slingsby let his cigar go out again, and stared fixedly across the desk. Mr. Slingsby did not actually say ' Proceed ! Your narrative interests me strangely ! ' but the mere fact of his silence was enough to convince Bill that his attention was arrested.

'And I may as well tell you ', proceeded Bill severely, ' that I know exactly what you've been up to.'

There was a weakness about the phrase which he did not like, but he had only just stopped himself saying ' I know all ! '

' Ah ! ' said Mr. Slingsby. There was nothing tremulous about the hand that struck the match that lighted his cigar for the third time, nor did his voice express undue emotion. But his dark eyes were gleaming. ' What do you know ? '

' I know that you are Higgins & Bennett ! '

' Higgins & Bennett ? ' murmured Mr. Slingsby, bewildered. ' Higgins & Bennett ? '

Bill had no patience with this childish attempt to evade the issue.

' Yes, Higgins & Bennett,' he repeated. ' The mysterious firm that has been buying up all Uncle Cooley's wood-pulp at the smallest possible prices. It was a nice, simple, ingenious trick, wasn't it ! You get the job of London manager to Uncle Cooley, and then you start a firm under another name and sell all the stuff to yourself and sell it again to other firms at a handsome profit. I don't wonder you can afford to put on your Tell Father's!'

'Not, Tell Father. Tell It To Papa. Much better title,' corrected Mr. Slingsby.

'Never mind that!' said Bill sternly.

'But it makes a difference,' urged Mr. Slingsby. 'You'd be surprised how many good shows have been killed by bad titles. You can see it for yourself if you think a minute. "Tell It To Papa." It rolls off the tongue. It looks well on the billing. It——'

'I didn't come here to discuss the titles of plays,' said Bill. 'What I want to know is what you intend to do about it.'

Mr. Slingsby's black eyebrows rose.

'Do about it?' he said. 'My dear fellow, what is there to do about it? There was always the chance of the thing coming out one of these days, and now apparently it has happened. You haven't got anything remotely resembling evidence as yet, of course, but unfortunately that doesn't matter. Now that you are on the track, you won't have any difficulty in getting evidence. I must clear out. That's plain enough. No argument about that.'

Bill was oppressed with a feeling that the scene was going all wrong. Even in this moment of his triumph the other's personality was too strong for him. Hardly in a less degree than on that other occasion when the blue-chinned one had trampled all over him at the luncheon-table, he felt himself a weak-kneed, diffident inferior. With an effort he forced himself to a spurt of truculence, sadly aware the while that it was not going to amount to anything. The second mate of a tramp steamer or one of Miss Ethel M. Dell's more virile heroes might have attempted truculence with Mr. Slingsby and got away with it, but Bill, even as he spoke, knew that he was not the man to do it. He did not even bother to bang the desk.

'Clear out?' he said, in what he tried to make a hard and intimidating voice. It sounded to him like an apologetic bleat. 'Suppose I have you arrested?'

Mr. Slingsby looked at him with a pained incredulity. This, Mr. Slingsby seemed to think, judging from his expression, was simply asinine—mere babble from the sick-bed.

'Have me arrested!' he said. 'Talk sense! You don't suppose your uncle is going to thank you for making a public exposure of this business and getting him laughed at by everybody? He will be only too glad to have the whole thing hushed up.'

He eyed Bill as if he expected him to apologize. And such was his magnetism that Bill very nearly did.

Mr. Slingsby summed up.

'Never', he said severely, 'go into a thing of this sort unless you are prepared to have it slip up on you at a moment's notice.' Bill just contrived to check himself from saying he wouldn't. 'I had the sense to make all my preparations long ago. My money is invested in South American securities, and I shall take the next boat to Buenos Aires.' He paused. 'No,' he went on, 'I shall go to New York first and arrange for the production of Tell It To Papa. Tell me,' he said, shelving the more trivial matter of his criminality, 'you have lived in New York for a number of years—who would you say was the best manager to go in with on the production of a nice clean farce with only one interior set for the three acts? It doesn't need money spent on it. The thing takes care of itself. All I need is an honest man.'

Bill, routed and discomfited, rallied for a brief counter-attack.

'What do you want with an honest man?' he said bitterly.

Mr. Slingsby was not to be jarred out of his geniality.

'There is no need to be personal,' he chided gently. 'No need for any hard feelings. I'm the one who ought to be grumbling. You've spoiled as nice a little income for me as ever a man had. Fortunately I can get on

without it. Tell It To Papa is all I shall want for the
rest of my life. You have no cause to be nasty. You
have done pretty well for yourself. Old Paradene ought
to come down handsome when you tell him. Besides,
you've learned a very valuable lesson—one that ought
to be a great help to you in your future life. Never,'
said Mr. Slingsby, and would have laid his hand on
Bill's shoulder if the latter had not drawn coldly back,
' never tell your business secrets to anybody. Anybody,
mind ! And, above all, never give yourself away in an
effort to impress a girl with your smartness. It doesn't
pay. In fact, better keep away from girls altogether.
They're tricky propositions. No sense of honesty.
Nothing fair and square about them. . . . How was
Prudence ? ' asked Mr. Slingsby chattily.

Bill found himself saying that Miss Stryker had seemed
pretty well.

' Quite a nice girl in her way,' said Mr. Slingsby toler-
antly. ' Beast of a temper and inclined to be deceitful,
but quite a good sort on the whole. I think I shall be
able to give her the part of the maid in one of the tour-
ing companies of Tell It To Papa. And now, my dear
fellow,' he said, making a little rustle of dismissal among
the papers on his desk, ' I'm afraid I shall have to ask
you to be going. I have a lot of cleaning up to do before
I leave. By the way, it would be most kind of you if
you didn't say anything about this little matter to your
uncle before I sail. I shall be able to get Wednesday's
boat. I should appreciate it extremely if you would
postpone telling him till I've gone. There's just an outside chance that, if I were actually ready to hand, so
to speak, he might take it into his head to be vindictive.
Better not tell him till I've gone. Eh ? What do you
think ? '

' All right,' said Bill.

He had no notion why he said it, except that it was
the only thing that he felt he could possibly say.

' Capital ! ' said Mr. Slingsby, his excellent teeth gleaming in a delightful smile. ' Well, good-bye, my dear
fellow. I hope we shall meet again one of these days.

Oh, before you go.' He scribbled on a card. 'Take this,' he said. 'Give it to the house-manager at the Bijou and he'll fix you up with a couple of seats any night you want. Better, perhaps, not make it a Saturday. I know you'll like the show. Best second act that's ever been put on the stage.'

It was not till late in the afternoon that Bill returned to Marmont Mansions. The necessity of stopping dazedly at intervals rendered his progress westward slow; and by the time the lunch-hour arrived he had not got beyond the Strand. He turned into a quiet restaurant, and the effect of the meal was so curative that he emerged again in a state of cheerfulness almost rivalling that of Mr. Slingsby.

He perceived that the impact of the other's powerful personality had led him to ignore the really vital fact. Whether Wilfrid Slingsby was crushed or defiant was immaterial: whether he stayed in or out of jail made no difference whatever. Crushed, defiant, free or in broad arrows, Mr. Slingsby had played his part. Whatever his demerits as a man, Wilfrid Slingsby had made it possible for him to do Mr. Paradene a momentous service. He had made it possible for him to achieve what he had come to London to do.

Yes, Uncle Cooley could hardly overlook a service like this. Now, surely, he must, as Mr. Slingsby had suggested, come down handsome. And, if he did, why then the last obstacle between himself and Flick was removed.

Through a world ringing with joy-bells Bill made his way to Marmont Mansions and floated airily up the stairs into his sitting-room.

There was a letter lying on the table: and the joy-bells seemed to ring louder than ever as he recognized Flick's handwriting.

He tore it open.

The joy-bells stopped as if they had been turned off with a switch. He collapsed on to the settee. There was a strange buzzing in his ears; the opposite wall seemed far away and obscured by a mist : at the pit of his stomach was a dull, aching feeling, as though some unseen hand had smitten him with violence.

He re-read the letter. . . . There must be some mistake. . . .

Mistake ! . . . That was what the letter said. ' . . . feel we have made a mistake . . . sure we should only be unhappy . . . marry Roderick on Wednesday . . . only thing to do. . . .' And for this extraordinary, this ghastly, this unbelievable change of heart she gave no reason. No reason whatever.

Bill stared before him, and the room grew darker and darker.

CHAPTER NINETEEN

BILL TRESPASSES

THE garden of Holly House slumbered in the moon-light. Trees threw dark shadows across the lawn, and in the bushes little breezes went whispering to and fro. To any man strolling there with his mind at rest, the place would have seemed a magic haven of peace : but on Bill, lurking warily in the shelter of the shrubbery, its romantic appeal was wasted. His mind was far from being at rest.

It was with no vague intention of hanging about in the darkness and keeping a sentimental watch on lighted windows that Bill had come to the garden this time. He was here to-night as the man of action. Hours of concentrated brooding over Flick's letter had brought him to the conclusion that it was an inspired letter, probably dictated word for word, with all the commas and full-stops complete, by that repellent woman who had forced them asunder in Waterloo Station. Yes, the more Bill thought about it the more definitely he seemed to see in that letter the hand of the demon aunt.

No man of action embarks on any enterprise without a settled plan. Bill had a settled plan. It involved the co-operation of one of the minor domestics of the Hammond household, and it was in quest of such a domestic that he had taken up his present position in the middle of a laurel bush facing the side of the house. He had reasoned the thing out. It would be useless to attempt to communicate with Flick through the ordinary medium of the post. A woman like that Water-loo Station woman, brimming over—as that brief glimpse of her had told him—with the lowest and most criminal

287

cunning, would undoubtedly be exercising supervision over Flick's correspondence. She would be watching for the postman like a bird-dog, all ready to intercept letters. As for district messenger boys, it would be sheer waste of money to employ them. No, the only thing to do was to lurk about here until one of the servants came out for a breath of air and then collar him or her and bribe her (or him) with untold gold to convey secretly to Flick the note which even now was burning holes in his left breast-pocket.

It was a good letter. The writing of it had occupied an hour and a half, but the results had justified the toil. In six closely filled sheets, it told all that there was to tell about his undying love, explained the roseate aspect of the situation as regarded the future when Uncle Cooley should have been informed of the Slingsby matter, and sketched out in detail a scheme for Flick to leave home privily next day, meet him under the clock at Charing Cross, and proceed with him to the registry office where he had made all arrangements for their immediate marriage. In the whole annals of love-correspondence there had probably never been a letter which so nicely combined the fervent and the practical ; and all that was needed now was a messenger to take it to her.

But the charms of the moonlit garden, obvious though they should have been, appeared to have no appeal for the domestic staff of Holly House. The breezes chuckled in the bushes, the moonbeams danced on the lawn, invisible flowers filled the air with a languorous scent, but not even a knife-and-boot boy was lured out of that back door. Little by little, as he kept shifting his position to avoid cramp, Bill began to be filled with sneering and contemptuous thoughts towards the British domestic. He seemed to picture these degraded creatures huddled together on this divine night in a stuffy kitchen, with all the windows shut and the fire going full blast, talking about the movies or reading Forget-Me-Not Novelettes.

And finally, after a distant clock had twice struck the hour, the strain of this waiting became too much for him. He burst from the bushes and marched up to the front door.

A long interval followed his ringing of the bell. Then a parlourmaid appeared. Bill, who had anticipated a butler and had been wondering if the latter would remember having seen him before, experienced a momentary relief: and had even got so far as feeling that here was the minor domestic for whom he had been waiting all these weary hours, when he caught sight of the girl's face and immediately withdrew the fingers that were fumbling in his pocket for the note. She wore spectacles, and through these her eyes seemed to glitter with so austere a light, that he suspected her instantly of being a minion, probably the demon aunt's right-hand woman.

Nevertheless, it being necessary to render some explanation of his presence, he plunged boldly ahead.

'I want to see Miss Sheridan,' he said.

The spectacles raked him with what seemed a shocked incredulity. The parlourmaid had the air of one who has been reading books of etiquette and is cognisant of the fact that calls upon young ladies at such an hour of the night are among the things that are not done. She made Bill feel like the villain of a 'What Is Wrong With This Picture?' advertisement.

'Miss Sheridan is nottertome, sir,' she replied in a voice of ice.

'Can I see Mr. Paradene?'

'Mr. Paradene is nottertome, sir.' She eyed Bill with critical spectacles, and went through the first stages of closing the door. Nor can we in justice blame her. Bill's vigil in the bushes had left him a good deal dishevelled and far from the sort of person one likes to find on one's front-door step after dark. 'They've all gone to the theatre.'

This was true. It had occurred to the amiable Mr. Hammond that Flick was looking pensive and depressed, and he had continued his good ministrations on her behalf by suggesting a dinner in town, and a visit to the theatre. And it was part of the irony which so marks mundane affairs that the manager enriched by the expedition was Mr. Wilfrid Slingsby, for it was at the Bijou Theatre that they had taken a box.

To Bill, however, there seemed no truth whatever in the statement. Its obvious falsity confirmed him in his opinion that this woman was a mere instrument of Flick's Aunt Frances. He withdrew sullenly as the door closed; and, after pausing for several moments in deep thought on the drive, sneaked round the corner of the house and hid himself once more in the bushes. There was no need to be discouraged by a single parlourmaid. A big house like this would have all sorts of servants, and at any moment one of a more benevolent disposition might pop out. He snuggled into his laurel bush and waited.

He had been waiting some ten minutes, when there suddenly came to him something that was practically an inspiration. On the night when he had taken refuge on top of that outhouse roof, Flick, he now recollected, had come climbing down her knotted sheet from a window immediately above it—presumably that of her bedroom. Silly of him not to think of that before. All he had to do was to locate that outhouse, climb on to its roof, and there he would be. If there was a light in the window, he could whistle softly till she appeared: and if the darkness showed that she was not there he could put the letter with a good-sized stone in his handkerchief and hurl the whole package in for her to find when she went to bed. He wasted no more time. Extricating himself from the bush, he made his way round the house.

There was his roof, just as he had left it. So far, good. But the window above it was dark. He groped about for a stone, found one, and was wrapping up his parcel when from somewhere above his head there came the sound of a window opening, followed by a soft but penetrating ' Hey ! '

A man who has been subjected to the amount of nervous strain which Bill had had to undergo that day is in no mood to have ' Hey ! ' said to him out of upper windows when he is trespassing in hostile gardens. Bill bit his tongue, dropped the stone and the note, and leaped side-

ways into the shadow of the outhouse. There he waited,
holding his breath, for the drama to develop.

It now became apparent that only his guilty conscience
had led him to suppose that he was the person whom
the mysterious voice had addressed ; for at this moment
there sounded from the darkness to his left a sharp
whistle and he perceived that he was not the only tres-
passer in this garden. The breeze, which for some time
had been freshening, now began to blow strongly, shred-
ding away the bank of clouds which had covered the
moon and illuminating the scene as if a spot-light had
been turned on. He, himself, was in the shadow of the
outhouse, but beyond this little pool of gloom the garden
was bright : and he saw all things clearly. Out of the
window, easily recognizable in the silver glow, protruded
the head and shoulders of his uncle's adopted son Horace :
while below, his large feet ruthlessly trampling some
choice begonias, stood a squat, burly figure—the figure
of a man whom Bill did not know : and with whom,
if he had had his choice, he would have been loath ever
to become acquainted. For, as plainly as if he had
carried a sign, this man wore the word ' plug-ugly '
written all over him. We, who have met Joe the Dip
at close quarters in the light of the sun, know that he
was not one of Nature's beauty-prize winners. Seen at
night, he was a human gargoyle.

The boy Horace was leaning farther out of the window.
' I've got 'em,' he said.

The wind was now blowing so strongly as to render
whispering impossible : and Horace's chest-notes came
plainly to Bill's ears, as did the plug-ugly's response.

' Good enough ! ' said the plug-ugly. ' Drop 'em down.'

For the first time, on hearing these words, Bill, though
still at a loss to know what all this was about, became
convinced that dark deeds were in progress. Possibly
the interview with Mr. Slingsby had blunted his genial
trust in human honesty. At any rate, he needed no
further words to tell him that sinister things were toward.
And this was fortunate, for there were no further words.
Horace reached back into the room, leaned forward again

balancing in his hands some solid object that looked like a bag, and dropped this into the depths, where it was neatly caught by the plug-ugly. The boy then retired and closed the window, and the plug-ugly, hereinafter to be called Joe the Dip, trampled down a few more begonias and began to steal down the path that led past Bill's hiding-place. He had arrived abreast of him when the latter spoke.

'Stop!' said Bill. 'What have you got there?'

In the normal round of his everyday life Joe the Dip was a man of phlegmatic habit. It took a good deal to stir him to any exhibition of mental distress more marked than the quiver of a raised eyebrow. But this was something special. It got right into his emotions and churned them up. With a single startled yelp of dismay he looked once over his shoulder and then began to pound off across the lawn as fast as his ample feet would take him.

It was a futile move. Even under ordinary conditions Bill could have given him fifty yards in a hundred and won comfortably: and now the welcome prospect of action coming after his long tedious wait in the bushes made him a super-sprinter. Joe, moreover, was hampered by a heavy bag. The race ended half-way across the lawn, where Joe, feeling the hot breath of the pursuer on his neck, turned at bay. He dropped the bag and flung himself on Bill.

Nothing could have been more admirably suited to the latter's frame of mind. Joe, standing beneath the window in the moonlight, had looked an ugly customer, but that did not damp his ardour. Bill had had a trying day, and what he felt at that moment was that they could not come too ugly for him. At the precise moment when Joe's clutching fingers closed upon his throat he induced him to relax them with a short, sharp upper-cut, which, from the click which followed its delivery, appeared to have landed squarely on the spot where it was calculated to do most good. There ensued a scrambling flurry of blows at close quarters, and then Joe, securing a grip, swung Bill off his feet, and they fell together. And for

some moments matters became confused, with Joe in
the ascendant.

But every fighter has his weak spot. With some it is
a too fragile jaw: while others have a finicky distaste
for being hit on the nose. Achilles, it will be remembered, could stand little punishment on the heel. None
of these weaknesses impaired the efficiency as a fighting-
machine of Joe the Dip. Strong men with hammers
could hit him on the nose and accomplish nothing; nor
was it easy to discourage him by buffets on the jaw-
bone. Nevertheless, he was but human. He had his
danger-spot, and it was one which had frequently undone
him in the rough-and-tumbles of his colourful past. He
was extraordinarily ticklish. You had but to prod Joe
with a sharp finger, and he became a spent force.

And this was what Bill did now—purely by chance as
he strove to overcome him in the wrestle. His wandering fingers suddenly roamed searchingly over his adver-
sary's ribs, and on the instant Joe wrenched himself free
with a stifled howl and staggered to his feet.

Bill also rose. There was nothing in his acquaintance
with Joe that led him to suppose that it was safe to remain
on the ground while the latter was standing. He jumped
up, and from that instant the tide of battle began to
turn. Joe was a massive rather than a nimble fighter.
When it came to long-range exchanges he was at a dis-
advantage. The wind had dropped now as suddenly as
it had risen, and clouds once more covered the moon:
but there still remained enough light for Bill's purposes.
He slid in and jabbed Joe in the eye. He swung forcefully and felt Joe's cauliflower ear yield squashily under
his fist. He slid in once more and smote Joe on the
other eye. And it was this last blow, delivered with all
the violence of one who had had a morning with Wilfrid
Slingsby, an afternoon with Flick's letter, and a night
in the Bushes of Holly House, that decided the issue.
It seemed to lend the final touch to Joe's discouragement.
Staggering back, he prolonged his stagger till it became a
run: then, making for the shrubbery, he cast himself
into it. And, working his way round till he came out

into the open, took to his heels and passed out of Bill's
life for ever.

Bill stood panting. This little turn-up had done him
a world of good. He felt happy and invigorated. Dismissing his late opponent from the scheme of things, he
picked up the bag and went back to the outhouse to find
the letter he had dropped. And it was here that he
received the final shock of this disturbing day.

The letter was not there. Nor was his handkerchief.
Both had been swept away into the darkness by that
unfriendly wind.

Bill searched well and thoroughly, but he could not
search the whole garden : and gradually there stole upon
him a sense of discouragement as poignant as that which
he had caused Joe the Dip to feel in the concluding
stages of their little disagreement. He was beaten. Fate
was against him, and there was no use struggling.

He slouched brokenly through the garden out into the
road, slouched half a mile down the road till he met a
taxi-cab, and, climbing wearily in, drove back to Marmont Mansions, where Judson greeted him with frank
amazement.

' What on earth ', Judson exclaimed, ' have you been
doing to your face, Bill o' man ? '

Bill had not been conscious of anything amiss with his
face. A glance at the mirror now revealed surprising
wounds. Judging from the evidence, at least one of Joe's
wandering wallops must have got home on his nose. He
placed the bag on the table and went off to the bathroom.

When he returned, cleansed and refreshed, he found
that Judson's simple curiosity had led him to open the
bag.

' What are you doing with all these old books, Bill ? '

' Books ? ' Bill began to understand. He told his
story briefly. ' That kid must be one of a gang of crooks,'
he said. ' He certainly dropped that bag out of window
to the fellow I had the scrap with.'

Joyous excitement lit up Judson's speaking countenance.

'Why, good gosh, Bill o' man,' he cried, 'this is the most amazing bit of luck that ever happened. Old Paradene can't in common decency do less than slip you half his fortune now. He's a nut about books. Many a time has my old father bored me stiff with stories about his library. If ever there was a blue-eyed boy, you will be it, once he hears about this. Make your terms stiff, Bill o' man! Slip it into his ribs! Don't weaken. He ought to give you half a million a year for this.'

'And a lot of good that will be,' grunted Bill moodily. 'Flick's marrying Roderick Pyke the day after tomorrow!'

'What! But I thought she was going to marry you.

'Well, she isn't. They've been getting at her, I suppose. I had a letter from her. That's why I went to Holly House. I thought I might be able to see her or at any rate get word to her.'

Judson's jaw had fallen. This calamity was affecting him deeply.

'Flick!' he cried. 'Marry that bird who said Toddy van Riter found the Silks? Not while I have my strength!'

'What are you going to do about it?' said Bill wearily.

'Do about it?' boomed Judson. 'Do about it? Why . . .' He paused reflectively. 'Well, I'm darned if I know!'

CHAPTER TWENTY

SIXPENNYWORTH OF RICE

§ 1

WEDNESDAY morning, eleven of the clock, and a fair, fresh day with a cheerful little breeze nipping along from the south-east. Placid, stolid, wrapped up in its own affairs and titanically indifferent to all else, London went about its daily business. From Putney to Sloane Square, from Cricklewood to Regent Street, from Sydenham Hill to the Strand, from everywhere to everywhere, red, yellow and maroon omnibuses clattered without ceasing. Policemen guarded the peace, stock-brokers dealt in stocks, beggars begged, hatters sold hats, loafers loafed, spatters sold spats, motors rolled in the Park, paper-boys hawked the three-o'clock editions of the evening papers, and retired colonels sat spaciously in the club-windows fronting on Piccadilly and Pall Mall, dreaming of lunch. The only things in all the great metropolis that even hinted that this was not just one of London's ordinary days were the striped awning stretched over the pavement in front of St. Peter's, Eaton Square, and the strip of red carpet which the awning shadowed—portents which indicated clearly to the *cognoscenti* that a marriage had been arranged and would shortly take place beneath that church's famous roof.

In addition to Bill, who was dressed in quiet grey picked out with a twill of invisible red and accompanied by Bob the Sealyham wearing a tan-coloured leash and a splash of mud on the tip of his nose, the *cognoscenti* already assembled on each side of the awning consisted of the usual group of old women, discussing other weddings they had seen in their time ; the usual seedy men, chat-

ting in undertones about snips and winners ; and the
usual baby, asleep in a perambulator, without whom
this kind of gathering never seems complete. These
would stand round, gaping until the bride and bridegroom emerged, when they would potter off, to reassemble
at the next wedding that happened along.

Of all those present, Bill alone had come to this spot
with a motive other than that of mere idle sight-seeing.
But what that motive was, he would have found it difficult to explain. He certainly expected to derive no
pleasure from watching Flick go into that church and
come out again on the arm of her husband—not even
the mild and vacuous pleasure which the old women
and the seedy men would experience. No, it would be
sheer torture to witness this ghastly thing : and yet he
knew that strong men with ropes would not have kept
him away. There is a deep-seated instinct in all human
beings that prompts them to twist the knife in the wound
and make things as unpleasant for themselves as possible :
and it was this instinct that Bill was obeying.

And even now, before any of the wedding-party had
appeared, he was not in the loosest sense of the word
enjoying himself. The struggles of Bob the Sealyham
alone would have prevented that. Bob was taking this
business of waiting hardly. His dog-soul was seething
in rebellion, for he considered that he had been cheated
and imposed upon. Observing Bill leaving the flat, he
had slipped adroitly through the door at the last moment
and asked quite civilly to be taken for a walk. To this
proposition Bill had apparently agreed, and they had
started out perfectly normally and all quite in order,
and now here he had been for twenty minutes marooned
in the middle of this beastly pavement, unable to move
more than a couple of yards in any direction. And he
was beginning to feel that this was going on for ever.
He expressed his resentment, accordingly, by a series of
determined efforts to strangle himself on the end of his
leash, weaving the leash about Bill's leg in order to get
a better purchase : and it was during the last of these
attempts at suicide that the cheerful little breeze, whip-

ping round the corner of the street, removed the latter's
hat and sent it trundling across the square.

To Bill's deeper sorrows, therefore, there was now
added the misery of being conspicuous and an object of
derision in the eyes of the *hoi polloi*. Of all spectacles
that enchant a simple-minded London audience, that of
a man chasing his hat on a windy day is the most exhilar-
ating. And when, in addition to chasing his hat, the
man is in imminent danger of being tripped up by a
frolicking dog, their enjoyment becomes complete. Bill's
little entertainment went with a roar; and when he
returned, hatted once more and full of hard feelings
towards his species, his chagrin was deepened by the
discovery that in the interval of his occupation elsewhere
Flick had arrived and gone into the church. The *cognoscenti*, when he rejoined their ranks, were already
engaged in discussing her and comparing her with other
brides of their distant acquaintance.

The notices on the whole were favourable. One lady
in a cloth cap and a cavalry moustache said she liked
'em plumper, but with this exception Flick had a good
Press. Adverse criticisms were reserved for the appearance of her ' Pa '. Bill, knowing that Flick possessed
no Pa, took this gentleman to be her Uncle Sinclair, to
whom doubtless would have been assigned the task of
giving away the bride. He had not gone very well with
the critics. Indeed, there was one man in a sweater and
a dented bowler hat who grew almost caustic on the
subject of Mr. Hammond's trouser-crease.

' Where's the groom ? ' inquired the lady whom Flick's
figure had displeased. ' 'E's late.'

' Of course 'e's late,' rejoined one who knew about
these things. ' Only natural 'e'd let her get there first,'
he explained, apparently with some recollection in his
mind of the habits of boxers.

' Looked a bit pale, I thought she did,' ventured a
rather diffident voice. The speaker seemed to be a com-
parative novice at these affairs and a little conscious of
the weakness of his position in the midst of these experts.

' They always look pale,' said the man who knew,

coldly.   Besides, I reckon you'd look pale if you was
properly up against it like 'er.   I seen a picture of 'im
in the *Record* this morning.   Nasty-lookin' bloke.'
  ' Yus ? '
  ' Yus ! '   The man of knowledge was not one of your
broad-minded fellows who are able to make allowances
for the alterations which reproduction in a cheap morning paper can effect in the human countenance.   The
fact that nobody could possibly really look as villainous
as Roderick had done in the *Record* did not occur to him.
' A nasty, mean-lookin' bloke with a smudge across his
face.   If you ask me, I think 'e'll beat 'er ! '
  Bill could endure no more.   Three courses suggested
themselves to him—to go away, to knock the speaker
down and trample upon his remains, and to go into the
church and sit there.   And because it was the unpleasant-
est and would make his torments the most complete, he
chose the last.   He made his way through the square,
found a handy tobacconist's, purchased an ounce of
tobacco in a forbidding wrapper, and on the strength of
this business deal left Bob in charge of the man behind
the counter ;   then walked out of the shop, threw away
the tobacco, and, returning to the church, strode boldly
in and sank into the nearest pew.
  It was dim and cool and rustling in here : and quite
against his wishes a feeling of peace was beginning to
steal over Bill, when he was roused to wrath once more
by a voice breathing delicately in his ear.
  ' Ticket ? ' whispered the voice.
  It was a pink youth, who looked hot and uncomfortable.   The scowl which Bill bestowed upon him was
so fierce and so packed with hatred, malice and unchari-
tableness that his heat and discomfort seemed to grow
even greater ;   and after backing a pace and blinking he
finally decided to withdraw from the affair.   The idea
of a man in a grey suit and minus a ticket being at a
wedding of any importance offended all his finest feelings,
but, even had the edifice he was in been of a less sacred
character, Bill had not the appearance of one with whom
it would be agreeable to wrangle.   Grey suits always

make a big man look bigger, and Bill's suit was very grey.

Bill sat on. After one startled glance at his suit the congregation appeared to have come to the conclusion that he was just one of the myriad sights of a great city and gave him no further attention. He plunged into mournful meditation.

Whispering had begun. The atmosphere had become suddenly disturbed and restless. It was a long time before Bill, deep in his thoughts, roused himself to observe this ; but, once it had come to his notice, it was unmistakable. People were murmuring with their heads together. People were shuffling. Plainly something was wrong.

An important-looking man with a badge pinned to his coat came down the aisle. He stopped and whispered sibilantly in the ear of an ornate woman in the pew in front of Bill's. The woman uttered an astonished squeak.

' Postponed ? '

The man with the badge nodded solemnly. There was more whispering.

' Then it's no use waiting ? ' said the woman.

' None,' said the man with the badge.

Others had apparently received the same information. The church was beginning to empty itself. Bill added himself to the stream, and was presently outside in the square, where disappointed and perplexed *cognoscenti* gaped in amazement at this strange anti-climax. They had been to many weddings in their time, but they had never yet been to one where nobody got married.

Bill sought his hospitable tobacconist, retrieved Bob, and began to walk aimlessly back. He was passing under the awning when a hand touched his arm, and, turning, he perceived Judson. Judson was looking intensely serious. His face was pasty and his eyes heavy. And it suddenly came to Bill that he had not seen the heir of the Cokers since they had dined together at eight o'clock on the previous night. A man in Bill's position cannot think of everything, and one of the things to which he had not given a thought was Judson. He remembered

now that the other had slipped out soon after dinner
for what he described as a quiet stroll. That stroll had
apparently lasted all night.

' Wedding off ? ' said Judson.

' There seems to have been a hitch of some sort,' said
Bill.

Judson smiled. It was a smile that seemed to cause
him some difficulty and even pain, but there was triumph
in it.

' You bet there's been a hitch,' he said. ' I popped
round last night and kidnapped the bridegroom ! '

§ 2

Judson stooped and began to tickle the Sealyham, who
was wiping his front feet affectionately on the leg of his
trousers.

' Kidnapped him ! ' cried Bill. His companion's statement had been plain and straightforward, and yet he
found himself puzzling dizzily over it as over some strange
cryptogram. ' Kidnapped him ! '

Judson removed his attention from Bob.

' Well, not exactly kidnapped him,' he said. ' It wasn't
necessary. When I got to his apartment and put the
thing to him as man to man I found he wanted to kid-
nap himself. That made everything jolly and simple.'

' I don't understand ! '

' What don't you understand, Bill o' man ? ' said Judson patiently. He blinked in a pained way at a passing
lorry, which was rattling by in a noisy and uncouth
manner, trying to a man who had had a disturbed night.

' You went to Pyke's apartment ? '

' Yes.' The lorry was out of earshot now, and Judson
felt more composed. ' After what you told me about
Flick going to marry him, I instantly saw that it was
necessary to take a strong line. I decided to slip round
and threaten him with horrible penalties if he did not
at once disappear. And it shows how you can misjudge
a fellow—he turned out to be a capital bird, perfectly
matey and an excellent host. But I didn't discover that
till later, of course. He was out when I got there, but

I managed to induce his valet to let me in, so I took a seat and waited. The valet, a most able man, asked me if I would like a drink. I said I would. I was having my third when the bimbo Pyke arrived.' He paused, and again that look of pain passed over his face. This time it was caused by Bob, who barked suddenly and gratingly at a cat. 'Pyke was considerably rattled at seeing me, but he calmed down after a while, and I got to business. I put it to him squarely. I said nobody was less fond of unpleasantness than I was, but, if he didn't disappear, the worst would inevitably ensue. And bit by bit, Bill o' man, it came out that he was only too anxious to disappear. Nothing he wanted less than to marry Flick. It seems there's another girl—she used to be a stenographer or something in the *Pyke's Weekly* office—whom he has long loved in a manner—well, he described his feelings to me, and, believe me, he had got it bad.'

'That must have been the girl I met him with in Battersea Park,' said Bill.

'Very probably. If you met him with a girl in Battersea Park, this would be the girl you met him in Battersea Park with, because he told me he had been meeting her on the sly for weeks past. He would have bolted with her like a shot months ago, only he was scared stiff of his father. His father would be the bozo who pursued you in the car, I take it ? '

'Yes. Sir George Pyke. Flick's uncle.'

'Well, the old dad had apparently got him hypnotized. I reasoned with the man. More drinks were produced, and we began to do ourselves pretty well. And with each snifter he took he seemed to come more and more round to my way of thinking. I've given up all that sort of thing now, but there's no doubt that, bad as it is for the constitution, there's nothing like a drop of drink for putting heart into a fellow. Round about one in the morning good old Pyke had begun to walk up and down the room and was talking about calling the old man up on the telephone and telling him just where he got off. "No need to do that," I said. "Just dis-

appear." " I will," he said. " That's right," I said.
" You really think so ? " he said. " I certainly do," I
said. " I ought to have done it before," he said. " Better
late than never," I said. . . . It turned out that, as far
as the money end of it was concerned, he was sitting
very pretty. Some time ago, in order to do down the
income-tax people, old Pyke had transferred a large mass
of wealth to this bird's account, the understanding being
that Roddy—I was calling him Roddy by this time—
was to return it in due season. " Be a man," I said.
" Collar the cash, send a few wires of farewell and leg
it for foreign parts." He burst into tears, clasped my
hand and said that I was one of the master-minds of the
age. In which, mark you, Bill o' man, he wasn't so
darned far wrong, for if ever one fellow had given another
fellow a bit of good advice I had. He said that it was
the dream of his life to go off to Italy and write poetry.
How would it be, he said, to tool off to Florence or Naples
or one of those wop spots ? Then he could write to the
girl to follow him out there and they could get married
and write poetry and eat spaghetti and live happily for
the rest of their lives. I said it was the peppiest scheme
of the age, a lallapaloosa. And the long and the short
of it is, that he left on the nine-o'clock train to catch
the boat at Dover. So that's that, Bill o' man.'

Bill was beyond speech. He pressed Judson's hand
silently. His faith in a great coherent, purposeful plan
governing this sometimes seemingly chaotic world of ours
was completely restored. It was a splendid, beautifully
managed world—a world in which even Judson had his
uses.

' And now ', proceeded Judson, ' I come to the really
important part. As I told you, we made a very fair
night of it, and I left Roddy's apartment, after sleeping
on the sofa, at about nine this morning. I had a couple
of hours to fill in before I came to find you here, and I
was thinking of going and sitting down in the Park.
Well, I was going along the Brompton Road, headed
for the Park, when I happened to pass a building into
which a good many people were popping, and I thought I

might just as well sit down in there. It was becoming pretty necessary for me to sit down somewhere right away.'

A large car had rolled up to the kerb. Bill moved away a step to frustrate Bob's apparent intention of casting himself beneath the wheels.

'And I'm darned, Bill o' man,' proceeded Judson earnestly, 'if I didn't find myself right plumb spang in the middle of a temperance lecture. A nasty shock, but it was simply too much effort to get up and leave, so I stayed where I was. Bill, it was the luckiest thing I ever did in my life. Made me a different man. Absolutely and entirely a changed man. No more alcohol for me. I'm off the stuff for life. Give you my word I hadn't the remotest conception till that moment what it did to a fellow. Makes your inside like a crumpled oak-leaf, that's what it does. I always had the idea that it was a valuable stimulant and carminative Medicinal, if you know what I mean. But when this bird shot a coloured slide on the screen showing the liver of the hard drinker——'

Bill was looking past him with bulging eyes. A morning-suited man of middle age and amiable aspect had come out of the church, and on this middle-aged man's arm walked a girl in bridal white. They crossed the pavement and entered the car.

' —And after that', said Judson, ' he took some worms and slipped them a stiff bracer, and, believe me or believe me not, Bill o' man, what it did to them was plenty. All bright and chirpy those worms had been at the start . . . jolly good fellows having one on the house. . . . But the minute they had got that stuff well over the larynx . . .'

He broke off. His audience had deserted him. Bill, coming out of his trance, had become a thing of action. The car had begun to move off, when he darted forward, flung open the door and without a word hurled himself in. Bob the Sealyham, trailing through the air on his leash like a kite, uttered a short, strangled yelp of disapproval.

§ 3

' Flick ! ' said Bill.

And for a space no more words were spoken. This was due principally to the behaviour of the Sealyham. It had taken Bob a moment or two to get the hang of things. At first sniff that wedding-dress of Flick's had had a strange and misleading smell. But now recognition had come, and he was giving a spirited imitation of six Sealyhams enclosed in a single limousine. To leap up, lick Flick's face, leap back, kick Bill in the eye, leap up again, knock Mr. Hammond's hat off, and plunge, panting stertorously, towards Flick once more was with him the work of a moment. He looked like one of those old-fashioned shimmering motion-pictures, and, with this emotional exhibition coming on top of the natural surprise consequent upon Bill's intrusion, conversation was for some few moments at a standstill.

Eventually Mr. Hammond, calm even in this crisis, retrieved his hat from the corner into which Bob had rolled it, and spoke, gazing mildly at Bill.

' If you are looking for a cab, sir,' he said pleasantly, ' you will probably find one along the street.'

' Flick,' said Bill, winding the leash round his fingers and pulling strongly, ' I got your letter. But I understood. I understood exactly what had happened. I know that it must have been dictated by that infernal fat-headed aunt of yours. . . .'

' My wife,' observed Mr. Hammond in pleased recognition. ' And, if it is not a rude question, who in the name of goodness are you ? '

A small voice spoke from the corner.

' This is Bill West, Uncle Sinclair.'

There was a pause. ' Flick,' resumed Bill, ' I was talking about that letter. I understood just why you had written it.'

' Did you see me ? ' said Flick, round-eyed.

' See you ? '

' At Mario's.'

A dizzy feeling began to grip Bill.

'See you at Mario's? What do you mean?'

'But you said you understood.'

'I . . .'

Flick held her hands out to him with a little cry.

'I don't care. I saw you with that girl, but I just don't care. Take me away, Bill. I want you to take me away.'

Bill took her hands mechanically.

'You saw me . . . Good heavens!' he exclaimed, enlightened. 'You don't mean you saw me dining with that girl at Mario's on Sunday night!'

'Yes, but I don't care. I want you to take me away.'

Bill slipped the leash into Mr. Hammond's hand.

Would you mind holding this animal for a moment,' he said. He gripped Flick's hands and drew her closer, oblivious of the keenly interested gaze of Mr. Hammond, who had just replaced the glasses which Bob had knocked off and was scrutinizing him as though he were some rare first edition. 'Flickie, my darling Flickie,' he cried, 'I can explain everything. I had to dine with that infernal girl. I hated it, but I had to go through with it. She knew all about Slingsby, and Judson met her and arranged this dinner so that she could tell me. And she told me! My gosh! she told me everything. I saw Slingsby next day and told him that I knew he had been swindling Uncle Cooley for years, and he has cleared out and directly I tell Uncle Cooley everything will be all right. He's sure to fix me up so that we can get married right away.'

Mr. Hammond coughed gently.

'Is it your intention to marry my niece?' he asked interestedly.

'Yes, it is!' said Bill. He turned to Flick again. 'Let's go right off now, Flickie! Roderick's run off and is going to marry some girl who used to be a stenographer or something.'

'Well, well!' said Mr. Hammond. 'Tell me,' he went on, turning to Bill, 'you look extraordinarily like a young man who dropped in one night at Holly House some months ago and chased my nephew Roderick sixteen

times or so round the garden.   Are you by any chance
the same ? '

' That was me,' said Bill.

' Then it was you who were responsible for my brother-
in-law, the eminent Sir George Pyke, falling into the
pond ? '

' I was.'

Mr. Hammond shook him warmly by the hand.   ' Take
him, Flickie ! ' he said.   ' I could wish you no better
husband !   Why, good heavens, a man who saved you
from drowning . . . whose image you cherished in your
heart through all those long, weary years . . . ! '   He
took up the speaking-tube.   ' Yates,' he said to the chauffeur, ' do you know a good registry office ? '   He turned
to Flick and Bill.   ' He says he does not.'

' There's one at 11, Beaumont Street, Pimlico,' cried
Bill enthusiastically.

' Yates,' said Mr. Hammond, speaking into the tube,
' drive to Number 11, Beaumont Street, Pimlico.'

He hung up the tube and leaned back.

' Oh, Uncle Sinclair ! ' said Flick breathlessly.

' After the ceremony ', said Mr. Hammond, ' I think
it would be judicious if you were to return home, Flick,
if only for a day or so.   It would be a little difficult
for me to explain your absence this morning.   Later on,
the atmosphere may grow a trifle less tense.'   He took
up the speaking-tube again.   ' Yates,' he said, ' stop at
the next grocer's you come to.   I wish to buy sixpenny-
worth of rice.'

CHAPTER TWENTY-ONE

ASTONISHING HUMILITY OF AN UNCLE

THE sun of a fair summer afternoon shone upon St. Mary Axe. Mr. Cooley Paradene, alighting from his taxi-cab at the door of the building that housed the London branch of his pulp and paper business, climbed listlessly up the three flights of stairs. Niobe, mourning for the loss of her children, was no more pathetic figure than Mr. Paradene, grieving over the mysterious disappearance of the most prized gems of his collection of old books. The mystery of the affair weighed on him sorely. When the theatre party had returned from its revels, which had included a late supper at a gay restaurant, there was no sign that any burglars had entered Holly House—no sign whatever. And yet the books were gone. Mr. Paradene had brooded over this astonishing affair ever since without ceasing : and the minor mystery of why his nephew Bill had telegraphed to him in such an urgent vein, bidding him come without fail to the office this afternoon, paled in comparison.

' Mr. West here ? ' he said gruffly.

Henry, the office boy, stepped forward, a model of smiling efficiency. Courteous and prompt in the presence of the boss. That was how young fellows got on in the business world.

' This way, sir.'

Bill looked up as the door of the private office opened. He had been seated in Mr. Slingsby's chair, but he rose and came forward with a promptness and courtesy which not even Henry had exceeded.

' Hallo, Uncle Cooley.'

Mr. Paradene glared about the room. He was in the

mood when a man feels that he can find a faint relief in quarrelling with some one, and he had decided that he was going to quarrel with Bill. Not that quarrel was the right word. It suggested a conflict. He proposed to squelch Bill. On what grounds he should squelch him he did not at present know. But doubtless time would provide an excuse.

'Where's Slingsby?' he grunted, as Henry, his duty done, stepped delicately out and closed the door.

'Slingsby's gone,' said Bill.

'Gone! At this hour of the afternoon? Where?'

'America.'

'America!'

Bill bent forward and tapped his uncle impressively on the arm.

'Don't paw me!' snapped Mr. Paradene. 'What are you pawing me for?'

'Slingsby', said Bill, uncowed by his forbidding manner, 'was a swindler and a crook. I was on to him from the very start, but you would insist that he was perfect.'

'Slingsby a swindler? What the devil are you talking about?'

A marked change crept over Mr. Paradene's demeanour as he listened to the story crisply unfolded by his nephew. Ferocity ebbed from him like some gas with which he had been inflated. For several long minutes after Bill had concluded, he was silent. Then he drew a deep breath.

'What I want is a nurse,' he said dejectedly. 'That's what I want, a nurse. I'm not fit to be trusted alone.'

Bill beamed upon him with jovial encouragement.

'What you want, Uncle Cooley,' he said, 'is a good live fellow like me looking after your business.'

Mr. Paradene eyed him with a strange humility.

'Would you like to come into my business, Bill?' he asked pathetically.

'I'm ready to start learning now.'

'Then you shall. And name your own salary.'

'Anything you say, uncle. Only make it large enough for two. I've got a wife to support.'

Mr. Paradene blinked.

' A wife ! '

' Yes. I think you know her. Your friend Sinclair Hammond's niece.'

' What ! When did this happen ? '

' It's a secret at present, but perhaps you could break it gently to my aunt-in-law. It happened yesterday.'

' Yesterday ! '

' Yes.'

' But she was going to marry some one else yesterday.'

' She was. But I met her and we talked it over and she went off and married me. We young business-men move fast nowadays, Uncle Cooley. Time is money with us.' He reached under the desk. ' Oh, by the way, uncle, I think these books belong to you.'

Often as Mr. Paradene had gazed upon the contents of the bag which Bill had pushed across the desk, he had never gazed so fixedly as now. And stunned though the look was which he had bestowed upon them, it was as nothing to that which he now directed at Bill.

' Where—where—where did you get these ? '

' Oh, I just happened to run across your adopted son Horace as he was handing them down from a window at Holly House to a pal of his in the garden. Here, there and everywhere—that's me ! I hate to have to tell you, Uncle Cooley, but that boy is a member in good standing of a gang of crooks. They seem to have planted him on you with the idea of having him pass out the swag.'

Mr. Paradene sighed deeply.

' A nurse ! ' he muttered. ' A nurse ! '

There was a silence.

' Bill,' said Mr. Paradene brokenly, ' I take back everything I may have said in the heat of the moment about my relatives. They are a ghastly crew, but, by George ! you restore the average. From now on ', he said as he rose, ' I don't move a step without you.'

' I'm afraid you'll have to, if you intend leaving now. I promised my wife I'd meet her here. I'm expecting her any moment. Why don't you stay and have a chat ? '

Mr. Paradene shook his head.

' Some other day, Bill,' he said. ' Give her my love, but I can't stop now. I'm going back to Wimbledon.' He swished his stick militantly through the air. ' I'm going to have a talk with that boy Horace. Bill,' said Mr. Paradene, ' I seem to have made a fool of myself in practically every direction, but this is one job I'm going to carry through. I started it and I'm going to finish it. I'm going to make that boy Horace a credit to Society if I have to wallop him every day for the rest of my life. I'll send him to a good school, by gad, and I'll employ ten tutors with sawn-off shot-guns to look after him during the holidays. By the time he's grown up I'll have him making the hero of a Sunday-school story look like Jesse James. Good-bye, Bill, my boy. Come and lunch with me at the Antiquarians one of these days. You're a great fellow ! '

' You're forgetting your books, Uncle Cooley.'

Mr. Paradene, who had reached the door, returned. ' So I am,' he said humbly. ' So I am. Yes, I certainly do need a nurse. If you see any good nurses, Bill, reserve one for me.'

Flick, arriving a few minutes later, found her husband smiling glassily at the opposite wall. The recent interview had affected Bill rather like a strong application of ether. It needed Flick's womanly presence to restore him to a sense of belonging to the world of solid things.

' Well ? ' said Flick eagerly.

Bill smiled another glassy smile.

' Everything's all right, darling,' he replied. ' As right as it can possibly be. Uncle Cooley has gone away promising me vast fortunes and thinking me the most wonderful fellow in the world.'

' So you are,' said Flick.

Bill frowned thoughtfully.

' I wonder,' he mused. ' I'm the luckiest, I know,' he said. ' I've only got to look at you to realize that. But . . . Look here, you know, I've been thinking over things, and from start to finish I can't see a single thing in the whole business that I've actually done myself.

It was you who first got on Slingsby's track. It was Judson who introduced me to Prudence Stryker. It was Prudence Stryker who told me where Slingsby had buried the body. It was Horace who obligingly chose the moment when I was standing under the window to shove his head out and drop that bag of books. It was Judson who got Roderick out of the way in time to prevent . . .'

Flick ruffled his hair lovingly.

'I shouldn't worry, precious,' she said. 'Don't you know it's the one sure sign that a man is really great when he has all sorts of people working for him? Look at Pierpont Morgan and Henry Ford and Selfridge and all of them—they don't do the work themselves. They just sit and let other people do it for them. That's what shows they are such great men.'

'Something in that,' said Bill gratefully. 'Yes, there's certainly something in that.'

He drew her to him. Henry, the office boy, who was standing on a stool and looking in through the transom, sighed quietly. He was a lad of sentiment.